STONE AND SCALE
BOOK ONE

RED SUMMER

ANA LEE

Cover design by Beautiful Covers by Ivy

Original design by Yulia at Miblart

First edition 2025

Element Ventures Publishing

Library of Congress Control Number:

2025909240

Praise for Red Summer

Three-time recipient of Readers' Favorite Five-Star Rating

"Reminiscent of author Cassandra Clare, Red Summer is engaging and highly readable with a strong emotional core. The pacing rises and falls in rhythm with the characters' emotional journeys, and thoughtful use of vocabulary helps each character feel fully realized. The novel tackles weighty themes, grounding fantasy elements in emotional reality. Power struggles between light and dark, good and evil, and the hunger for vengeance are central, and the world-building is creative and immersive. The writing is fluid and believable, and while it begins with a familiar "boy who feels different" trope, this story quickly proves itself to be far more nuanced. Red Summer is a thoughtful, well-crafted novel that stands confidently on its own within the genre." — Readers' Favorite Editorial Review

—

"Ana Lee delivers a brilliant urban fantasy in Red Summer, an amazing world any reader can happily get lost in. Characters are described with a depth that surpasses the norm. Descriptions are vivid, filled with sensory stimulation that will have you reeling from one page to the next. Red Summer ticks all the boxes for plot, action, and adventure. I now have another favorite author and eagerly look forward to the next book." — Readers' Favorite Editorial Review

—

RED SUMMER

"An enthralling novel. In this epic tale of hope, pride, self-discovery, friendship, and vengeance, the author brings together fascinating world-building, magic, and action, along with well-developed and intriguing characters, all combined with fantasy elements and emotional depth. This urban fantasy, with a Southern Gothic and New Orleans flair, should be at the top of the must-read list for those interested in ancient dark magic, forbidden love, high stakes, and whispers of lost dragons. Red Summer is a brilliant and immersive story." — Readers' Favorite Editorial Review

Soli Deo Gloria

CONTENTS

PART ONE

CHAPTER ONE

Wilder still had no idea how the fire had started.

Sitting alone in the Child Protective Services office, Wilder wrung his hands, his foot beating an unsteady, anxious rhythm into the ground. The door opened, and a short woman garbed in a red suit entered, her heels tapping across the floor as she moved to her desk. Susannah's brown eyes remained fixed on the pages within a thick green file in her hands, the name 'Wilder Ansley' printed in sharp, black lettering across the front.

"Would you like to explain what happened?" Susannah asked, sweeping her dark hair behind her shoulder. Her matter-of-fact tone did little to hide her annoyance, her brows rising over bronzed cheeks and a pretty oval face. Taking a seat in the chair across from him, Susannah dropped the folder with a muffled thump onto the desk.

She was the seventh social worker that had been assigned to Wilder over the last seventeen years of his life. Or was it the eighth? He had lost track a long time ago. Out of all of them, though, he had liked her the most. She actually seemed to care.

"What story should I tell you this time, Susannah?" Wilder reclined in his seat, the cold leather biting the skin on his arms as he shoved his soot-stained hands into his jacket, hiding the evidence of the last few hours. Silk met his fingertips, its touch his only consolation. "The truth or the same story Bernard and Emily told you?"

Susannah leaned back in her own chair, crossing her arms over her suit jacket and scowling. "Unfortunately, Wilder, I have no reason to believe the two aren't the same."

"Of course you don't." Wilder's hands clenched around the fabric in his pocket. But Wilder knew she was right. Nothing he could say, not even the truth, could adequately explain away what had happened. Not this time.

And the truth was—well, Wilder wasn't sure *what* the truth was.

He had just gotten home from a tough day at school when he found his foster brother, Kyle, rifling through his bag. The bag had held what little Wilder owned, including the red and gold swaddling blanket Wilder had been found in as a baby—his only connection to a family he knew in his gut had once wanted him.

"What're you doing?" Wilder had asked Kyle, panic setting in as he rushed forward and snatched the bag out of his hands.

"Nothing." Kyle leered at him. He stuffed something under his pillow before running his fingers through his too long, mousy brown hair. Only a year younger than Wilder, though a head taller, Kyle had a rap sheet a mile long, and theft was top of that list.

Wilder's blood began to boil.

He knew he could probably take him, but he also knew better than to try. Wilder usually had a handle on his reactions to most things. He had learned a long time ago to shove them down—to muffle them until he couldn't feel them at all. It was the only way to avoid situations like this. Situations he knew would lead to unexplainable problems and unanswerable questions.

But this time, Wilder wasn't quick enough.

"Give it back," he seethed, each word a threatening promise Wilder, and Kyle, knew he'd never keep. Another rush of rage surged through his veins. His eyes narrowed on Kyle's obnoxious grin.

"And if I don't?"

Wilder tried to tamp down his roiling anger, to douse it with the numbness he knew so well. But when he blinked, the corner of the room was on fire. Hot orange flames engulfed Kyle's fourposter bed and smoke billowed in dark gray plumes through the open windows. All Wilder could hear were Kyle's shrieks as he tried to escape the blaze, and his own voice screaming "No!" as he tried to make sense of what was happening.

Everything was a chaotic blur.

Rage flipped to panic. Sprinting forward, Wilder seized Kyle from the fire, the red silk still clutched in his hand. Without a moment's hesitation, Wilder hurled him from the burning bed. But then a loud crack echoed through the space, and Wilder's heart stopped. Kyle's head had smacked the wall more forcibly than should have been possible, and he crumpled to the ground, his still body a barely visible heap in the smoky room.

Shit. Shit…

Wilder's whole body trembled as he struggled to comprehend what had just happened.

It was just adrenaline. That's all it could have been…

As the flames spread, Wilder careened out of the room, returning a heartbeat later with the fire extinguisher from down the hall. He sprayed the flames until they quieted, a white dust settling over the charred sheets like fresh snow, the muted sizzle and scent of burning fabric clinging to the air. Somehow, he had contained the bulk of the damage to just the bed. But Kyle was another matter entirely.

Dropping the extinguisher, Wilder didn't take a moment to consider whether his own hands had been burned as he knelt beside Kyle's unmoving body, pressing his fingers to his neck.

Please don't be dead. Please.

A steady thrum pulsed at Wilder's blackened fingertips, the subtle lift and fall of life moving across Kyle's chest. Wilder heaved a sigh when he heard Kyle grumble. As his foster brother stirred, Wilder ripped the red cloth from his hand, stuffing it into his pocket.

The insistent click of nails across a keyboard shook Wilder from the memory.

"Listen, I swear Susannah, it was an accident," Wilder said. "The police searched me. I didn't have any matches or lighters. There's no way I could have done this. You *know* I never…" Wilder swallowed, his voice caught on the lump in his throat. He looked at her, pleading. She knew him better than this. "I promise. It was an electrical fire or something. It had to have been. Just let me talk to Bernard and Emily. I'll clear it all up—"

"They won't have you back, Wil," Susannah said, her voice firm. She folded her hands on her desk. Letting out a sigh, her gaze on him softened. "Kyle's in the hospital with a broken collarbone and a serious concussion. You're lucky they're not pressing charges for arson or assault. But you're being moved to a new placement, and a temporary one at that."

Wilder's mouth fell open, the blood draining from his face. *This can't be happening.* He was so close. He only had a year left before he was out from under the thumb of the state, and it couldn't happen quickly enough.

Before Susannah could see his reaction, he closed his mouth, gritting his teeth. "What do you mean, temporary?"

Susannah sighed again. "You're wait-listed for a live-in correctional school on the north side of town. There's a spot opening up there at the end of next month. Until then, you'll be with a new family. They have experience with situations like this." Pausing, she studied him. "I really think you'll like them, Wil."

Wilder scowled. She was always sugarcoating things. *'Live-in correctional school'.* It didn't matter what they wanted to call it. They were sending him to boot camp. Locking him away.

"Hardly matters what I think about them, doesn't it?" He stood from his seat, slinging his backpack over his shoulder. "I'll be saying goodbye soon enough."

CHAPTER TWO

Three days later, Wilder slinked through the wide halls of Prescott High, keeping his eyes on his boots. He shouldered past the press of bodies, his classmates bustling to row after row of bright blue lockers.

Over the weekend, he had been unceremoniously removed from one placement to yet another, his belongings gathered into trash bags and delivered to him at his new residence. At least he'd be staying in New Orleans. There were rules about that within the agency; about the importance of keeping the kids as close to 'home' as possible. But Wilder always worried one day he'd mess up so unforgivably, they'd make him leave the city altogether.

Wilder braved a glance up. He used to make it through most days without drawing much attention to himself. He could *usually* fade into the circus that was senior year, invisible in the sea of perpetual noise and motion. But word about Kyle had gotten around, and suddenly, it felt like everyone knew who he was. And what he had done. Pulling his black cap down over his unruly mane of red hair, Wilder fixed his gaze back on the ground, avoiding the curious stares following him.

A shoulder bumped into his. "Never pinned you for an arsonist, Ansley," said a familiar voice, and relief flooded him.

Wilder peered over to find Evan, his closest, and really only friend, striding next to him. His mousy face was pulled into a huge grin, lighting his powder blue eyes.

"Me neither," Wilder grumbled, not sharing in his amusement. Evan never took anything too seriously, but that's what Wilder liked most about him. "Guess there's a first time for everything."

Evan's usual lazy smile faltered, and he looked at him with a level of understanding few people in Wilder's life ever gave him. He'd miss that.

"You didn't mean for it to happen, did you?" Evan asked.

"What do you think?" Wilder returned, his voice bitter as he pulled his locker door open.

Nodding, Evan glanced at the ground, inspecting his sneakers. "What's the damage this time, then?" he asked, his stringy blond hair falling over his forehead.

"New placement," Wilder said, looking for his homework in the mess of paper he had shoved into his backpack earlier that morning. He paused, considering. "And they're sending me to a correctional school next month."

Evan peered back at him and sighed. "Final straw, huh?"

"Guess so." Wilder trained his voice to sound bored, but he could feel his throat tightening.

Putting his hands in his pockets, Evan rested against the lockers. "Well, now's as good a time as any to tell you the news."

Wilder stopped shuffling through his backpack and turned to look at his friend. "Don't be shy. Get it out."

"Sounds like we're both out of here," Evan said, smirking, but Wilder could tell his heart wasn't in it. "Dad got new orders overseas. Somewhere near Greece. We're leaving next month."

Wilder's stomach dropped. It shouldn't have mattered where Evan ended up, especially since Wilder was leaving, too. But for some reason, it did.

Before Wilder could respond, a petite girl with chestnut hair sidled up to the locker next to them. Wilder glanced over long enough to realize she was new, and from the way she struggled with the latch, apparently new to lockers as well. The two watched her for a moment, suppressing their laughter before Wilder finally took pity on her.

"Press the door in and shove up," Wilder told her, his voice gruff as he dropped the last book into his backpack.

The girl turned to glare at him, the look on her tawny face suggesting she didn't need his help. "I know how to use—". But as her bright green eyes, striking over a set of high cheekbones, caught his, they widened in surprise. She sucked in a breath.

Wilder's stomach dropped again, but this time for a completely different reason he couldn't figure out. He ignored it. Lifting a single eyebrow, he waited for her to finish whatever she meant to say, but she turned away without another word. Instead, she shoved up hard on her locker and the door swung open.

"Thanks," he heard the girl say, her voice muffled by the thin steel between them. She grabbed a single book from her backpack, dropped it in the locker and pressed it shut again. Turning back to him, she scanned his features for a moment too long, studying his red hair and stormy gray eyes, as if searching for something. Wilder recoiled at the inspection.

The girl cleared her throat. "Sorry. I'm Terra," she finally said, smiling and holding out a small hand. "I just moved here."

Wilder wondered if this girl had any idea who she was talking to. She probably hadn't been here long enough to figure it out.

"Clearly," Wilder said, disregarding her hand and smirking. He had meant for the response to sound more sarcastic, but her genuine friendliness had caught him off-guard. As he turned away, her stare continued to search him, narrowing on his hair and eyes.

A bell clanged through the loudspeakers, and all three of them started as the sound reverberated through the hall.

Wilder snapped his locker shut without a second look back at the girl. "Good luck finding your classes." He turned to Evan, who was still draped against his locker, watching the interaction with an amused expression, a single blond eyebrow raised as his gaze flashed between Wilder and the girl.

Wilder gave him his usual '*Don't even think about it*' look. "We'll chat later," he told him.

Shrugging, Evan threw him a wink. Wilder ignored it, turning on his heel and stalking away.

He hated being dismissive, but Wilder figured he was doing the girl a favor. Being friends with Evan was one thing. The guy had basically forced his friendship on him when Evan had moved here two years ago. Since then, Evan had proven he could handle the weirdness that came along with Wilder's friendship, even if Evan could never understand it.

But this girl. She clearly hadn't gotten the memo that the arsonist foster kid was bad news—and best avoided.

Most of the day passed without incident—other than the continued stares that followed Wilder from class to class. After lunch, Evan left school for an appointment, leaving Wilder on his own.

He shuffled into the art room, angling for the two-seated table furthest from the front. Dropping his backpack on the floor, he stooped to grab his art supplies as the rest of the class meandered into the room. To his left, Wilder heard the unexpected sound of another bag dropping onto his table.

He peered up. Yet again, a blindsiding set of emerald green irises met his.

Damn it.

The way this girl looked at him—seemed to watch him—was unnerving. As she sat down, Wilder tensed, his blood pricking at her proximity, the tiny hairs on his arms standing on end. Cracking his neck and readjusting his shoulders, Wilder tried to shake off whatever reaction he was having to her. Maybe he was coming down with something.

Wilder finished fishing his supplies from his bag, straightened in his seat, and stared forward. The girl did the same. But out of the corner of his eye, he could tell she was watching him out of hers. Like she was waiting for something.

The way the animals that had followed him his entire life always seemed to be waiting for something. The ones he knew no one else could see.

Wilder blinked, fixing his attention toward the whiteboard and pretended she wasn't there — all while bitterly priding himself at how good he had gotten at pretending such things. No one knew about the hallucinations; the animals, or the people in the trees. Not anymore.

"Morning, class," Mrs. Tumnus said from the front of the room, beginning their lesson.

As one of his classmates raised their hand, Wilder flipped through his sketchbook to find the next blank page.

"Interesting drawings," Terra said, her voice so low only he could hear. Her gaze flashed across Wilder's charcoal depictions of dragons, wolves, and trees with faces.

"What's it to you?" he whispered, snapping the book to an untouched page.

The girl's eyes narrowed in confusion, a light blush rising to her cheeks. "I'm just making conversation."

But Wilder couldn't shake the feeling her curiosity went beyond a general, friendly interest. "Well, don't. I won't be here long enough for it to matter."

Terra cocked her head, the sun from the window behind Wilder highlighting the bronze undertones of her skin. Her stare was intense—calculating. "What do you mean, you won't be here long enough?" If Wilder hadn't known better, he could have sworn there was a pointed searching to her question. Geez, couldn't this girl catch a hint?

"Listen," Wilder said. "I get it. You're new. You're trying to make friends. But don't waste that energy on me. I'm getting shipped off to boarding school next month. Why don't you join the French club or something? You seem nice enough. I'm sure you'll find plenty of friends somewhere else."

"Well, with that attitude, sounds like you won't have any trouble finding many either." Crossing her arms, she reclined in her chair, her attention settling on the slideshow Mrs. Tumnus was flipping through.

Taken aback, the corners of Wilder's mouth lifted into a slight smile. His gaze trailed the lines of the girl's heart-shaped face and the annoyance marking her features, and he almost felt sorry he'd be leaving. With her candor, charm, and quick wit, this girl would have no trouble collecting friends as quickly as he repelled them. If she hadn't been so damn insistent…Nope. No. He wouldn't go there.

Terra didn't say another word to him as they moved into their lesson. But Wilder continued to watch her. Now entirely consumed with their project, the whole of her attention remained focused on the precise shading of her drawing of a library. In the corner of the piece, a giant stone geode stood among the bookshelves. There was something mesmerizing about the intensity with which she worked to get the play of lights and shadows just right.

It felt like time had barely passed when the bell rang for the end of the school day. Without another word or a second glance back, Wilder shoved from his chair. After depositing his books in his locker, he rushed out the front door. To his dismay, Terra had somehow beaten him outside. She sat on the concrete steps, her head bent over a textbook Wilder was fairly certain they weren't using in any of their classes. He forced his attention to the path in front of him, but not quickly enough.

Out of nowhere, an oddly large mouse scampered across his feet. Wilder tripped, stumbling backward. Righting himself, his gaze trailed the path of the culprit. On the mouse's back, a tiny knight with translucent gold wings, outfitted in full body armor, sat holding a set of reins. Every centimeter of the armor's brushed metal appeared detailed with alarming precision in fine silver filigree.

Wilder's eyes shot up, scanning the crowd milling about the lawn. No one else had seen what he had. Of course they hadn't. They never did. Wilder spun in the opposite direction of wherever his hallucinations had wandered off to. He knew better than to acknowledge them. It only ever led to uncomfortable questions he didn't want to answer, and assumptions he didn't want to deal with.

Thank goodness *these* didn't stick around long enough to follow him home. Wilder often saw them together, the animals and the tiny people in the trees, like they were partnering to rattle him. But rattled felt like an understatement. On days like today, he wondered if 'unhinged' was more accurate.

As Wilder turned to leave, set on pushing the whole ordeal out of his mind, he locked eyes with the last person he wanted to see at that moment. The shock on Wilder's face must have been plain enough, because Terra had forgotten all about the history book laying open in her lap, and was once again focusing on *him*. Wilder figured she was wondering what on earth could possibly be wrong with him. He didn't blame her. He wondered that about himself every damn day.

Glowering at her, Wilder stalked away, ignoring her gaze as she watched him go.

Who reads history books for fun, anyway?

CHAPTER THREE

The late February sun shone high above the Carrollton district, warming Wilder as he strode along another row of historic New Orleans homes after school. Pausing at an intersection, he waited for a car to pass, trying to put the past few hours, and the past few days, behind him.

Getting lost in this multifaceted city, with its high-spirited and eclectic vivacity, was his favorite distraction. This city was the only part of his life he could wholly rely on. It couldn't move away or choose to leave him. It was home—whatever that might be worth.

Wilder usually spent these walks imagining a life on the other side of the ivy-covered columns, wrought-iron fencing, and heavy oak doors, surrounded by a family of his own. A family that bickered and ate chocolate-chip cookies on Tuesdays after school. A mother that made him chamomile tea when the kids at school made fun of him. An understanding father that, despite the crazy situations Wilder got himself into, would reassure him all would turn out fine, reminiscing about that one time when he was his own age.

He imagined what it would be like to have a sister—one that would annoy him to the ends of the earth and refuse to leave him alone, but he'd adore her anyway. Though no, she still couldn't go in his room.

He imagined a family that would never give up on him.

The distant improbability of all of it was something Wilder had come to terms with, just like the truth about life in general. People left. That's just the way things were. Evan leaving, Wilder leaving—it was all a stark reminder of that truth. No one sticks around forever. Wilder had grown used to it, though the thought didn't blunt his disappointment. It was his seventeenth birthday, after all.

Picking up a fallen leaf from the sidewalk, crisped by the cold, he held it by its stem. "Happy birthday," Wilder said to himself. Blowing the leaf from his fingertips like a candle on a cake, it garnered passage on a fleeting breeze. As he watched it go, Wilder caught sight of a snowy white barn owl sitting atop a fountain in the courtyard next to him. The yard's countless magnolias flaunted their creamy whites and pale pinks in the new spring sun. As the owl stared at Wilder, Wilder scrutinized *it*. He could always tell the difference between normal animals and the ones that turned out to be hallucinations—the latter always acted weirder. More *aware*.

The bird cocked its head and hooted, the sound piercing the silence between them, as if intrigued by their interaction. Its beady black eyes never left Wilder. Stiffening, he took a measured step back and crept away. As the bird watched him leave, he wondered once again if he *was* just a little bit crazy.

Twenty minutes later, Wilder ambled up the grassy knolls of City Park, a steaming paper cup of black Cafe Du Monde coffee warming his palms. Ahead, he noticed a tiny old woman sitting alone at a stone table inlaid with a chessboard, moving the black and white marble pieces from square to square, playing both sides of the game.

Whenever Wilder came by the park after school, which was more often than not, he would join the various old-timers playing chess or checkers among the swooping oaks. Listening to their stories, he'd find himself grateful for the moments they gave him, treating him like a fellow human being. He had his favorites. There was Mark, who grew African violets on every windowsill in his home. Rebecca, who ran a bookstore two blocks away. Whenever he went in, the whole place teemed with every breed of dog and cat—each ready to curl up into the lap of whichever unsuspecting reader took a seat in the plush chairs littering the store. And there was Michael, who never shared much about his own life, but always seemed interested in Wilder's. This woman, however, wasn't one of the regulars.

Wilder glanced around, but nobody was joining the old woman. Striding into the chess plaza, he took a seat at her table, putting his paper cup on the edge.

"Oh good. You've made it," the woman said, collecting the pieces into lines along the sides as she finished her game. Her wiry gray hair flared in wild curls around her head like a massive halo, and the thinnest of wrinkles collected at her eyes and lips.

Wilder lifted his brow and smirked, dropping his bag onto the ground. Nothing about this woman was familiar, but he played along. "Um, yeah, sorry I'm late. I'm Wilder. Nice to meet you…" He left the words open for her to introduce herself.

"Who you think you are is trivial, boy. As is your timing," the woman said, her tone abrupt. She never met his gaze. "It'll all happen as it's meant to. Now, what'll it be? Light or dark?"

"What?" he asked, before realizing she meant the chess pieces. "Oh, white is fine."

The woman smiled, still moving the pieces, seeming pleased by his answer. She gave him a quick nod, and he helped her reposition the pieces onto the board. The woman didn't say another word as they played, the silence between them interrupted only by marble tapping across tile and the gentle rush of a fountain in the center of the lake beside them. Now and then, Wilder caught the woman smirking whenever he struggled to make a move, though she always seemed to know her next one. Her tenacity never faltered, and Wilder's eyes grew wider and wider as, piece by piece, his army fell to hers.

Just as she took another of his bishops, putting his king into check, Wilder noticed a fox and a squirrel at the edge of the wood, watching their game. Wilder blinked, hoping his eyes were playing tricks on him, hoping they were just normal animals that would scurry away the moment they were noticed.

The fox and the squirrel met his stare, but didn't move.

Pausing her assault to follow his perturbed gaze, the woman huffed. "Never minding their own business," the woman said, pursing her lips. "Bunch of busybodies, if you ask me."

Wilder's stare flashed to her. "You can see them?" he asked, heat flushing his cheeks. His whole head felt warm, and a loud buzzing filled his ears. No one had ever been able to see them before, and Wilder had learned the hard way to never bring it up.

"Of course I can. I'm not blind like the rest of these fools," the woman said, waving her arm toward a couple pushing a stroller down the path. They remained entirely unaware of the creatures standing just feet away.

Jaw dropping, Wilder's mouth suddenly felt dry. The woman lifted her knight and knocked down his king. "Checkmate, deary. I say, they said you'd be better at this."

"I'm sorry, who said what?" Wilder shook his head. It was starting to spin uncomfortably. He took another drink of his now-cold coffee, but knew it wouldn't do much to calm his racing heart. "I don't understand. How can you see them? Who are they? What—"

"Never you mind," the woman said, swatting away his questions with a gnarled hand. She never met his gaze. "Like I said, it'll happen as it's meant to." She stood from their game, turning to leave without a second glance at Wilder or the animals watching them.

"Wait!" Wilder shouted after her, struggling to stand. But his legs had fallen dead asleep and wouldn't let him move. His head grew woozy, his eyesight blurred. He felt like he was in one of those dreams where he'd try to run, but his feet remained rooted to the ground. Had there been something in his coffee?

"Wait," he said again, his voice straining as he forced himself to remain standing, fighting against whatever was holding him captive. "How can you see them?" he kept trying to ask her, but his voice in his own ears sounded muffled. "Just tell me what's happening. You can't leave. Not yet."

The woman turned, finally meeting his stare. Her gaze was a piercing ocean blue, and he felt like she could shred apart his soul if she wanted to. Wilder's heart stopped and he finally gave up, collapsing into his seat.

"Will you be here tomorrow?" he asked her, struggling for breath. "I'll come back. I just need answers. You're the only one I've ever met who—"

"I may be," the woman said, raising a single knobbly finger and cutting him off, but she didn't seem at all annoyed by his questions. "But I'm not so sure about you." Her gaze softened, and he could almost feel her sympathy washing over him like ocean waves. Turning away, she strolled down the concrete path, leaving a dazed Wilder powerless to go after her.

Breathing hard, he scrunched his eyes closed, trying to blink away the buzzing muddling his mind. After a minute, the feeling in his legs returned, but when Wilder peered up, finally able to see straight, he knew in his gut he wouldn't see the woman there. She had disappeared along with the animals.

Releasing a heavy sigh, Wilder resolved to come back tomorrow, and the day after that, and the day after that, until he saw the woman again. She knew something. Knew him—somehow. Maybe she'd know where he had come from. Why he was the way he was. He at least had to try.

His heart plummeted, realizing once again he was being sent away at the end of the month. What if he couldn't find her again before then? How often would he be able to make it back here?

Grabbing his empty cup, the chill of the coming evening pricked his skin. Wilder pulled the collar of his jacket up around his neck. He didn't understand what was happening. He'd never had so many episodes occur in such a short span of time. Hallucinations. All hell breaking loose. Things had never gotten this bad before. Sure, now and again, something crazy would happen. An animal would follow him, a flowery face would peer down at him from a tree above, whispering and giggling to get his attention. On rare occasions, he'd lose control, and something might blow up. A microwave might short circuit, or a door would rip off its hinges. All things he could come up with some excuse for. All things everyone else could explain away by an aggressive temper and a dumb kid's troubled past.

But a person? A real-life person that could see the animals too? And what had she done to keep him from going after her? He couldn't explain *that* away. He didn't hallucinate people. At least he didn't think he did.

Lost in his thoughts, Wilder rose to leave, but a sharp glint caught his eye from between the trees. He turned to see another woman leaning against an aged trunk at the edge of the wood, hidden amongst the dark pine needles. She looked far younger, with pin straight hair the precise color of hematite, and dark almond-shaped eyes that never left him. A silver blade played between her fingers, glimmering in the weak late-day sun.

The hair on the back of Wilder's neck stood at attention, but it had nothing to do with the cold. Drawing his eyes away, he tried to ignore her, starting down the path out of the park. But out of the corner of his eye, he noticed the woman step toward him.

Something in Wilder's gut told him to run—fast.

Just then, a familiar white owl swooped down from the canopy, its talons readying to claw and snatch. Wilder sucked in a breath. The bird's squawk sliced through the dusk as it shot for the woman, and she stumbled back, glaring up and lifting her arm just in time to block its descent. The bird's talons seemed to strike against something solid, but invisible, before the owl bounced back up with another loud squawk, leaving the woman untouched.

Turning back to Wilder, the woman's gaze narrowed, as if angered by the interruption. But a moment later, she had disappeared, absorbed into the darkness. The last thing Wilder saw of the two were the soft beating of white wings disappearing into the pines.

CHAPTER FOUR

Two hours later, Wilder struggled to catch his breath as he arrived back at his new placement.

Wilder had been there for three days now, since the evening following the fire, but from what he had gathered, his new foster parents, Maris and Steven, weren't all that different from the other ten placements over the last seventeen years. At least they didn't padlock the fridge or beat him with a belt.

Susannah had said Maris and Steven had experience with kids like him; kids who couldn't make it work anywhere else. Being so close to eighteen, Wilder had scoffed, but she had refused to hear any argument that he was hardly a 'kid' anymore.

Maris dropped a plate of food on the table as Wilder took a seat for dinner. The plate clattered onto the glass surface. Wilder peered up just long enough to notice the fury on Maris's face, and figured it best not to say anything. He knew better than to cross any foster parent when they got like this.

"You're late," Maris said in a low hiss.

"Sorry, Maris," Wilder muttered, staring down at the plate. "I missed the bus leaving the park today. I had to run a mile to catch the next one."

"There's always some excuse with all of you. We have rules," Maris told him, an unattractive vein pulsing along her forehead. "We've been over this. If you cannot respect the rules of this house, rules that have been set in place for your benefit, you're more than welcome to leave."

Heat rose to Wilder's cheeks, but he didn't respond, instead trailing Steven's stare to the television screen in the corner of the room. The news flashed photographs of several missing men and women who had disappeared from the city within the last few months.

"Authorities remain perplexed by the increasing number of disappearances, and now believe this might be the work of a serial killer. If you or anyone you know has information leading to the recovery of these individuals, please dial—"

"Are you even listening?" Maris asked, her voice rising over the broadcaster's as she slammed her fist against the table, making the cups rattle. "You know, this is probably why your parents didn't want you. Between your insolence and your arrogance, you clearly have no respect for anyone but yourself. I'm not surprised. You're all the same. Why should I expect *you* to be any different?"

"Now Maris, that might be a little uncalled for," Steven said from his seat across the table. His tone stayed flat, his attention never leaving the screen as he munched on a leaf of garden salad, vaguely reminding Wilder of a bored turtle.

But Steven had a point. Maris didn't know Wilder's story. She hadn't cared enough to enlighten herself. A bitter bile rose from his gut, burning his throat. Of course she'd believe Wilder was no different than any of the other fosters she claimed to home out of the goodness of her heart. Wilder was sure her altruism had *nothing* to do with the sizeable paycheck she received every month that, coincidentally, Wilder never saw one red cent of.

Wilder stared down at his plate and forked at his food, his jaw clenching. Maris didn't know nor care that Wilder had been left alone on the edge of some wooded city park at a mere three months old, only to be found by a little old lady walking her dogs.

"It's no matter," Maris said, her tone evening as she took a seat. "Susannah called today. Spend the evening getting your things together. You're leaving tomorrow."

Wilder's fork clattered against the porcelain plate. "Tomorrow?" His chest tightened. "But I'm not supposed to leave 'til next month…"

"The New Orleans spot got filled before Susannah could get your name in. She found another school near Caddo Lake that said they'd take you. You're leaving tomorrow morning." Maris's words dripped with a smug haughtiness.

"Caddo Lake? But that's five hours away." Wilder argued, his voice shaky, his blood pounding in his ears as realization hit.

Maris just shrugged, taking a sip of her wine and turning her attention to the television.

Leave. New Orleans. He'd be leaving New Orleans.

Sucking in a breath, Wilder tried to push down a familiar rush of boiling panic. But that control was quickly unraveling. Maris's insistence to paint him a delinquent, the decisions being made without his consent, and the fact that this was all happening on his birthday, was more than he could handle.

Wilder shoved from the table, the feet of his chair scraping across the linoleum floor. Steven still didn't look up as Wilder left the room and stormed upstairs. Maris moved to follow, yelling something about being respectful at the dinner table. He ignored her, making it to his room and slamming the locked door behind him. Outside, he could see raging storm clouds gathering; coalescing with unsettling precision over the house—mirroring his fury. Lightning streamed through the night and thunder clapped so near overhead it shook the walls, rumbling through to the foundations of the house.

Looking around his cramped room, he ignored Maris's shrieks from the hallway. The end of his bed jutted so close to the narrow closet, barely any space remained for him to squeeze through. Rain pummeled the windows and harrowing winds howled through the eaves. In a frenzy, Wilder snatched up his threadbare backpack, the thin fabric falling apart at the seams. He packed it with the handful of things he had held onto throughout the years: his drawing pad and pencils, his phone, the silk blanket, a week's worth of clothes, and a tattered book of dragon lore an old friend had given him years ago.

Donning an oversized rain jacket, Wilder shoved his feet into his sneakers, opened the window, and slid down the wet rooftop shingles. He landed on all fours onto the unforgiving soaked turf below, muddying his hands and the knees of his holey jeans. Getting to his feet, Wilder wiped his hands on the wet grass and readjusted his backpack, ignoring the storm as it continued to rage around him.

***

Wilder hadn't realized the storm had gotten so ferocious until he was standing in it. Trudging through the violent wind, he squinted through the darkness. Already robed in muck and mud, Wilder concentrated on where he put his feet in the thick dark, heading for a grove of trees at the end of the street. His current lack of visibility, and the unfortunate realization that he didn't know when his next shower might be, made him far more cautious than he would be otherwise.

A puddle of ankle deep mud squished beneath his feet as he wandered into a dense thicket, the canopy above blocking the onslaught of rain.

Where would he go? In his anger, in the revelation that they were going to take him from New Orleans, he hadn't been thinking straight. He hadn't thought that far ahead. But as the cool chill of rain met his cheeks, the crushing weight of reality set in. Maybe he could go to Evan's, but he knew Evan's dad would likely bring him right back.

All he knew was he had to find that woman again. Had to know if she somehow knew who he was, where he might have come from, and how she could see the animals, too. Had to know if she could somehow help him control what kept happening to him. Suddenly, brilliant white lit the surrounding night, jolting him from his thoughts. But it didn't fade with the lightning.

Wheeling around, Wilder stared at the entrance to the grove, at where a pillar of light now shone, extinguishing the darkness. The pillar stood nearly seven feet tall, the dim shape of a man within its center. But when Wilder blinked, it was gone. He squinted into the dark again, trying to readjust to the change in light. He scanned the branches, but couldn't find a single explanation for what he'd seen.

It was only lightning, he told himself. But the light had been too contained—too *solid.* Too unnatural.

A soft *who* sounded above his head, and Wilder whipped his gaze upward. The same white barn owl who had been staring at him earlier—that had scared off the woman in the woods—sat perched on a tangle of wet branches. Its feathers ruffled as it shook beads of rain from its wings. Cocking its head, the bird considered him, as if Wilder were today's featured sideshow.

"What do you want?" Wilder snapped, glowering at the bird. "Why are you following me?"

Great. Now he wasn't just seeing things, he was talking to them too. Wilder rubbed at his eyes and tried to ground himself. In the past, he had taught himself to ignore the things he had learned, through trial and bitter error, weren't real. The animals that followed him. The people in the trees—those curious little faces that'd peer down at him from the branches above, the flowers that'd turn to look at him as he passed. But after today, after his interaction with both of the women at the park, Wilder questioned whether he knew what 'real' even was.

Hooting again, the owl shook another mist of water from its feathers. Wilder put his hands on his hips and scowled up at it, grateful at least the owl didn't talk back. Lowering himself onto a lush clump of moss, Wilder heaved another sigh and waited for the remnants of the storm to pass. The owl fluttered down from its perch and hopped over to Wilder.

It turned its head back and forth, studying his face, his damp red hair, and his belongings. With one last look up at him, it hopped away and distracted itself with a few attempts to unearth a mouse from under the roots of an oak tree—either out of genuine hunger or mere boredom. After a few minutes, it gave up, returning to study Wilder some more.

Outside the grove, the storm eased, the hammering thunder retreating farther and farther away. As the rain calmed to a light drizzle, Wilder collected himself and his belongings. Taking out his phone to text Evan, he found the screen cracked in half, the entire thing refusing to turn on.

Just my luck.

"Peace out, weird bird," Wilder said. Throwing the broken phone into his bag, he waved a tired hand at the animal before venturing to the main road—no real direction in mind. Maybe he'd try to talk to Susannah in the morning, get her to see reason, beg her to give him another chance, place him with another family, at least until he was eighteen and could fend for himself.

But the owl apparently had other ideas. Landing at his feet, it halted his procession, peering up at him with an almost human audacity. *Who,* it echoed, skipping forward a few steps, making it quite clear which direction Wilder would be going. His suspicion of the creature mounted. No way in hell was he following some screwball bird—and a hallucination, at that—into the night. But the owl just stared at him, flapping its wings in agitation as if to say, 'Must I repeat myself?'

"Fine," Wilder said, throwing up his hands in defeat, "but only because I have nothing better to do." Trying, and failing, to convince himself he hadn't completely lost his mind, Wilder followed the hopping owl as it led him through the city—down dark, empty streets and through glowing stop lights. Greens, golds, and royal purples colored the city, every establishment strewn with banners, streamers, and cheap plastic carnival masks—preparations for the city's upcoming riotous activities. At the owl's cue, they hopped on a late bus-circuit traveling two districts over. The owl rode on his shoulder, its weight heavy as it swayed back and forth in sync with the rhythm of the road.

The bus wasn't crowded, but those aboard didn't look twice at the strange boy and his bird, making Wilder feel, once again, like he was losing his grip. After passing through the Warehouse District, they finally came to a stop at the far end of the French Quarter, the owl pecking at Wilder's cheek to signal their exit. This part of town was as familiar as the rest of the city: rundown properties, streets scattered with the revelries of the evening, and a few wayward souls wandering home. Nothing out of the ordinary.

The owl hopped off his shoulder, guiding him to the entrance of a towering but dilapidated building. Shattered and boarded windows circled the structure, the trimmings weather beaten and laden with years of grime. The doors hung halfway off their hinges, the warped wood split, its paint chipped and discolored. Wilder wouldn't have been surprised if the property had been condemned and largely forgotten by the rest of the city. But the owl—this weird, annoying owl that was getting on the last of Wilder's frayed nerves—remained unbothered by the building's concerning condition.

"Are you sure about this?" Wilder asked. Though if he was asking the owl, or himself, he wasn't sure.

Fluttering off his shoulder, the bird landed with a soft thump onto the ground and hopped up the darkened steps ahead, each one caked with dirt and dead leaves. Jumping into the air, the owl wrapped its talons around a twisted rope hidden behind rotting metal work. Wilder grimaced.

That cannot be sanitary.

The rope pulled down under the owl's weight, and bells—deafening church bells—rang glorious through the night, their tolling piercing the silent breeze and Wilder's now stunned eardrums.

Oh, crap.

Whipping his head around, Wilder scanned the empty avenue. The last thing he needed was to be arrested for trespassing, and he doubted the police would believe some wild tale about an owl making him do it. Just as he decided it was in his best interest to vacate the premises, leaving the deranged little owl and their outlandish adventure at the doorstep, a shimmer caught his eye, as if a translucent veil lay hung between him and the condemned structure. Wilder reached out to touch the air, his fingers seeming to sink into the folds of time itself. A heartbeat later, the veil disappeared, falling away in streams of dimly twinkling stars.

Where the rundown building had been only moments before, a Gothic-style cathedral now stood, complete with artisan stained glass and wide abutting towers along the perimeter. The front doors opened with a wide groan, and Wilder blinked up at the light now streaming from the doorway as the silhouette of a well-kept older gentleman stepped out of the church to meet them.

The dark-skinned man stood a head taller than Wilder, and wore an unassuming pair of gray and white plaid pajamas, tufts of snowy gray sprinkling his dark hair. A pair of fluffy white slippers warmed his feet, and he greeted Wilder with an enormous Cheshire grin. "Evening, young man. Don't you look a little lost…"

"Uhhh…" Wilder gathered his thoughts, still unsure of what was happening, how he had found his way there, or how to explain his association with the jumped-up owl—all while appearing sane.

"Ahh, yes, hello Hennie." Reaching into the air, the man grinned as the bird flapped and floated around his head. So the man knew the owl? Could see it too? A moment later, Hennie landed on his wrist and gave the man a nip to his finger. "Welcome home. I'll go get Terra."

The hair along Wilder's arms pricked up at the name. *Terra?*

As he turned to leave, the man looked Wilder over. Wilder assumed his drenched and muddied clothing would do nothing to encourage an invite into this man's home, but to Wilder's surprise, the man added,

"Please come in. You are most welcome." Waving his arm through the open doors, he stepped aside to allow Wilder to pass.

Disoriented, and not too keen on being arrested, Wilder wandered into the foyer. As the man retreated down the hall, Wilder surveyed his surroundings. Wood floors stretched through the downstairs, meeting a wide staircase leading upward, and hints of cedar wood and sage lingered in the airy hallway, the scent easing at least some of Wilder's trepidation. Victorian wall sconces lit the forest-green papered walls, their every inch lined from head height to ceiling with artwork.

Scanning the frames, Wilder found each piece to be as beautiful a depiction as the last: a woman rising from a lake to hand a sword to a young man on the shore; a little girl playing a harp under the shade of an elm, surrounded by woodland creatures; a trio of witches dancing around a large boiling cauldron; a sinister and pale fanged creature seducing a spellbound young woman; two glowing hands playing marbles with nine multicolored orbs; and a human bodied man with the face of a wolf, its sharp fangs held in a malicious sneer. The most prominent of the paintings was a large, glossy rendering of an angel astride a shining golden dragon, his glowing sword set ablaze with heavenly fire.

"Well, hey there," a familiar voice echoed from somewhere down the hall. Wilder stiffened, the hair on the back of his neck standing on end. He turned toward the voice, only to see a white barn owl nuzzled into the collar of a girl, her messy chestnut hair pulled into a bun atop her head. She wore a set of navy pajamas speckled with stars, her wavy flyaway wisps framing a delicate amused face he knew all too well. Cautious emerald eyes stared back at him.

Wilder stared. And stared. *Her* presence in this hallway, however unfamiliar this place was, rendered it impossible for any of this to not be real; for the owl to have been a hallucination. Unless he had also been imagining Terra the whole time.

But no. Evan had seen her too…

There's no way. Wilder shook his head, clearing the dust gathering between his ears as his carefully maintained lines between real and not-real began to blur.

CHAPTER FIVE

"Did you need to borrow some notes for Chemistry? I hate to break it to you, but that test's going to suck no matter how hard you study for it," Terra said, crossing her arms. She searched his features, as if trying to read his reaction.

Wilder thought he heard a *thunk* somewhere in the recesses of his brain. His mouth had fallen open at some point, but at the present he didn't have the wherewithal to close it.

"Earth to Wilder." Terra snapped her fingers at him. "Not one for jokes, I take it?"

"Why am I here?" Wilder blurted out, closing his mouth with a snap. "Why are *you* here?" The muscles along his neck tensed and he tried to keep his cool, but he felt miles from it. "And where the hell is *here?*" he added, motioning to the art-filled foyer they still stood in. The man with the Cheshire grin had left without so much as a goodnight.

"Like, existentially speaking? Or were you hoping for a more time-bound response?" A puckish smirk played on Terra's lips.

"Don't be cute," Wilder growled, his nostrils flaring. "I was rather hoping for the latter, if you don't mind."

Terra huffed an easy sigh, as if disappointed but otherwise unfazed by his reaction. "Well, since you asked so nicely. You're here because my owl, who you've already had the pleasure of meeting earlier today, decided you were lost and needed to be found."

Wilder's eyes snapped to the owl still huddled on her shoulder. "I wasn't lost," he said slowly, on his last leg of patience for the day. "I knew exactly where I was."

"Existentially speaking, or…?" Terra shot him a charming grin. But at the pinch of aggravation on Wilder's face, her lips thinned.

"Never mind. Look, I'll try to explain, but you may want to sit down for this." The girl gestured to the plush seats in a parlor off the main foyer. "Care to join me for some tea, at least?"

Wilder hesitated, half of him wanting to tell the girl to screw off. But his curiosity was piqued, and he reminded himself he had nowhere else to go. He had followed what he thought was a hallucination across town, and it had turned out to be real. What would it hurt to gather his thoughts and dry off for a while? Wilder took off his shoes, careful to not spread mud across the flooring, and followed Terra into the next room.

The parlor had been styled in a rustic air and warm, dark hues. Finished walnut shelving laden with expensive brass trinkets and leather-bound tomes adorned the walls. A brushed-copper telescope stood undisturbed beside a window through which Wilder could see the faint glow of the waning quarter moon. Crackling against the wall, a broad stone-worked fireplace imbued the space with heat and life. A number of midnight blue antique couches and armchairs, offset by chenille silver throws and beaded pillows, littered the room's center.

The girl settled on a loveseat facing a long settee. A coffee table scattered with candles and an entire tea service sat between them. Leaving as much space as possible between himself and the girl, Wilder chose the far end of the settee.

Terra took a deep breath, as if steeling herself. "This evening, the New Orleans Council was informed of an unanticipated thunderstorm manifesting directly above your home. They sent Hennie to investigate, and when they realized the storm's origins…*you,*" Terra pointed at him, "Hennie was told to bring you here. It's time you were informed about some things. Things that might be a little hard to hear, or believe." Folding her hands in her lap, her back pin straight, Terra studied his reaction again. She spoke as if this conversation were merely a part of some job.

"What things?" Wilder asked, scoffing. "And what do you mean, the storm came from me? That's ridiculous." Wilder felt his stomach churn.

"We'll get there," Terra said, giving him a warm smile despite the acidity in his tone. "Based on what we know about most unfound Céad, such as yourself, we can assume there might be some things in your past you can't explain. At least not without feeling a little unhinged. Am I right? You might have done something you didn't intend? Or saw something no one else could? Had something completely out of your control happen when your emotions got the better of you?"

Wilder gaped at her, grappling with what she was asking him. "Wait, how do you know where I live? Are you stalking me? And what the hell is a Céad?" Indignation began to mount in his gut. *Does this girl know about the fire too? The people in the trees?* Wilder thought back to the woman in the park—how she could see the animals when no one else could. And now Terra was here, one of those strange animals now half-asleep on the couch next to her.

"Stalking?" Terra answered. "No…Well, yes. But no. I'm sorry." Stumbling through her words, a light flush painted her cheeks as she wrung her hands between her knees. "I knew this wouldn't go well." Terra paused, collecting herself. "A Céad is someone that isn't quite *human*. They're different species who have been concealed from the humans because of what they are, and the magic they're capable of. We can get more into that later. I know this all probably sounds absurd, but we're rarely wrong about these kinds of things. The Council, that is. The ones that assigned me to check you out and bring you here." She added this as if that clarity might absolve her of some guilt; might make this whole situation somehow more palatable.

"Magic? Not *human*? Assigned you to *check me out*? Like at school? You were there because of *me?*" Wilder was sputtering each question now.

I can't believe this. This girl is crazy.

"Yes, Wilder," Terra said, her tone steady, her emerald eyes blazing. "You're here because you aren't the same as those around you. Not the same as the humans, at least. Just like I'm not the same, either."

Discomfort crept through Wilder's bones, his skin flushing cold and clammy, but he let her continue.

"You and I might live among them, but we're worlds apart. We exist—truly exist—behind a veil; our true selves hidden from the humans. And, in your case, likely hidden from yourself as well."

She was nuts. He knew it. Wilder was in the last place, with the last person, he should be associating with. The last thing he needed was Child Protective Services thinking he wasn't just some runaway delinquent, but mentally disturbed to boot. Scanning the parlor, he tried to calculate the best way to make an immediate escape, eyeing every block of furniture between him and the door.

Terra continued, seemingly unaware of his brewing intentions. "Plenty of Céad are born into families that know exactly what's happening. But a lot of us don't until things get out of hand. That's where we come in. It's our job, the Council, all of us here, to bring in Céad just discovering their abilities and may need help."

She had struck a nerve. "I don't need help," Wilder snapped, his temper flaring. "I'm not some charity case."

While so much of what she said resonated with him—a small, wistful part he had tucked away, along with the little boy that waited for a family and answers that had never come—the more realistic side knew where talk like this would lead. Straight into an institution, where he'd be forced to endure agonizing hours of a drugged up mental void for the rest of his life. It was a possibility he had worked tirelessly to avoid since he had first realized no one else could see what he could.

"Is that why you kept talking to me at school?" Wilder asked, his tone scathing. "Helping me looks like convincing me of some ludicrous world that no one else can see? Is this your idea of some sick joke?" He needed to leave. Now. Shoving into the couch cushions so hard he felt the frame beneath his knuckles, he stood up. "And keep your bat-shit owl away from me."

"Sit down." Terra's firm tenor thundered through every crevice in the room, reverberating off of the walls and vibrating the brass trinkets on the shelves. The entry to the foyer slammed shut, and the candles and flames in the fireplace shot up an extra five inches.

Wilder froze before inching down into his seat. He eyed everything, including the girl, warily. "How…did you…*do that?*"

"Sorry for the theatrics," she said. Her tone returning to an apologetic calm, she acted as if whatever power she had just displayed was an entirely normal reaction to his response. "Sometimes it's necessary."

Wilder gawked at her.

Pausing for another moment, she studied him, as if deliberating whether he too had finished with his own theatrics. "You," she finally said, her voice steady and careful, "are what we call 'fae'. The Fae are the oldest of the Céad, all of whom were cast into the Eadar—behind the Shroud—thousands of years ago, according to our legends."

Wilder felt sure he was having an aneurysm.

"Each fae has power, abilities intrinsically linked to their blood. Our assumption is that you were kidnapped from your parents as a baby, then left for dead among the humans. It's happened to a lot of fae newborns over the last couple of decades." Her tone had gone hard and exacting, her bright green eyes never leaving his. Silence filled the space between them.

"So, no rainbows and unicorns, then?" Wilder finally asked, his tone snide.

"'Fraid not."

He paused, his gray eyes boring into hers. He didn't know if he could believe her. But he also couldn't walk away now, not when she had just displayed the same kind of power he had so many times before. This was his only chance at an explanation.

"Why are you only telling me this now? You were at school with me earlier. Why not then?" As his breathing evened, genuine curiosity bloomed at the edges of his questions.

The corners of Terra's lips rose into a crestfallen smile. "Given your reaction to me tonight, how do you think that conversation would have gone? '*Oh by the way, new guy I just met. You're not human, neither am I, and there's a whole world out there you know nothing about. Please don't tell all your friends I'm a nut job.*' Could you honestly tell me you would've believed me? Would have given me the time of day? And in my defense, I didn't know yet, and I couldn't risk it until I knew for sure. Until the Council was sure. If we had been mistaken, if you *had* been human…we just couldn't take that risk. And you were a particularly tough case to crack."

Wilder fidgeted in his seat, staring down at his hands. The girl had a point. He likely would have lost it on her.

"Look," he said, "I'm not saying I believe you, but if I did, what ended up giving me away? What made you think I'm…well, whatever it is you think I am? And why did you come looking in the first place?"

Terra leaned forward, lacing her fingers together. "First, we heard about the fire. How you claimed you had nothing on you that could've started it. It made the papers."

A flush rose to Wilder's cheeks.

"I got sent to Prescott to check you out. And then, when I finally met you, I don't know. It was just a feeling. It was weird. I've never had it with other lost Céad before, but it's not unheard of. I just knew something about you was different—wasn't human, I mean. After we met at the lockers, I got the office to let me into your art class. And then I saw your drawings. Dragons, wolves, trees with faces. Either you had a pretty wild imagination—which could have been an explanation—or you were one of us. But it wasn't enough for me to be sure."

Terra paused and peered at him, sympathy in her eyes as they locked on his. "Then, right after school, I thought I saw you react when one of the Natuine passed by. The small creature you saw on the mouse's back? They're a type of Céad. Another of the Fae, like you. Why they were there, and why they targeted you like that, I have no clue. But your reaction to them, how easily you brushed it off… I couldn't be sure you had seen them at all. I couldn't risk saying anything until we saw your powers actually manifest."

Terra bit at her bottom lip, and Wilder found himself leaning forward in his own seat. "It wasn't until tonight," she continued, "with the storm, that the full Council was finally convinced. Hennie came and told us what happened, and as soon as we knew, we sent her back to get you."

Wilder's brow furrowed. "Why do you keep mentioning the storm?" he asked. "Are you trying to suggest I started it?"

"I think you've done far more than just that, Wilder," Terra said. Pausing again, her eyes never left his. "Listen. I know it's hard to hear. But your abilities, the things you've done, there's no getting around it—you can manipulate elements, like many fae can. Chances are you've been covering it up. Or at least trying to. Something in your past likely taught you that displaying it put you at risk of discovery. That's why these incidents have been so…*explosive.* Every Céad should be able to use their power at their own will, should have complete control over it. But you. If you've spent your whole life shoving it down, keeping it masked—it's bound to leak out in unexpected and *inconvenient* ways."

Terra looked at him with such sympathy it made Wilder recoil at the intensity. He didn't want or need her pity, but the callousness prodding at him was short-lived. Everything she was saying made complete sense. Staring down at his hands again, Wilder waded through all that had happened throughout his life. All the things he had seen but couldn't explain, all the things he had done that had never made sense. How whenever he lost his temper, lost control of the roiling in his blood, bad things always happened. He thought about the times he had wished someone had been on his side, or had an explanation for him that didn't make him feel unhinged.

He remembered one of his first sets of foster parents—how he had told them about the people he saw in the trees when he played outside, and the way they had looked at him afterward. He had been moved to a new placement the next week.

As if she could hear Wilder's thoughts, Terra's voice reached across the space between them, the sound a gentle assurance. "You're not crazy, Wilder. You were just in the wrong place. It's time you got to come home."

Exhaling, Wilder lifted his gaze to meet hers and pushed down the pressure building behind his eyes. "So…" Wilder said, clearing his throat. "Why are these babies you mentioned being kidnapped?"

Terra beamed, her gaze lighting with a good-humored twinkle. The tension she held in her shoulders eased. Even the flames around the room, which had burned hot and sporadic since her show of magic, tempered to a steady, tranquil glow. Guilt colored Wilder's cheeks as he realized his recent lack of control, and his general lack of friendliness, had unsettled her.

"It's a long story," she said, smiling at him. "But in a nutshell, our people are at war. And we have been for nearly eighteen years. Fae, like yourself, are being kidnapped and killed even now. And the rest of the Céad have been no less affected."

"Okay…" Wilder said slowly. Absurdity aside, nothing spelled trouble like getting involved in some hidden world war, but he shoved that thought down. He was closer now than he had ever been to answers—actual answers. "And who are you, and who is this 'Council', in all of this?"

The girl grinned. "I'm Terra, as you know. Nice to officially meet you, Wilder." She held her hand out across the tea tray. Giving her a skeptical look, he wrapped his fingers around hers, trying to ignore the way his skin tingled at her touch. She didn't seem to notice anything.

"I live here with my parents and the rest of the Council," she said, her hand returning to her lap. "They help run this Council House and handle all other Céad matters within the region, including finding lost fae, like yourself. There are a few different Council Houses across the states, and scattered throughout the world."

"And *what* are you? Aside from a stalker of lost boys." Wilder offered her a slim smirk in apology for his previous behavior. "Are you one of these 'fae', too?"

A blush rose to Terra's cheeks. "No, actually. I'm a wyte," she said. "I come from a line called the Magem. We're different from the Fae, but we still have access to magic."

Inclining on the couch, Wilder surveyed the room, allowing his mind to open to what she was suggesting. *Magic.* It was the only thing that made sense. The only thing that could explain every question he had, every strange thing he had ever done.

A gorgeous canvas watercolor portraying a young man beguiling a spellbound girl captured Wilder's attention. Every aspect of the man's appearance had been drawn sharp and angular. The wings protruding from his back could have been mistaken for the blade of the finest silver sword, and his single visible ear, coming to a razored point above his hairline, was rendered in acute contrast to the curves of the foliage encircling the couple. His cheekbones and mandible were set in such severity, they could have pierced the canvas itself. He was the epitome of how every fairytale Wilder had ever heard would have described the mythological beings.

"If I'm a fae," Wilder asked, gesturing to the depiction. "Why don't I look like that?"

"Well, you've gotta give the artist some creative license," Terra said, chuckling under her breath. Wilder raised a single eyebrow at her. "But really, you don't look like that because you made yourself change. Some fae are natural shapeshifters. They can change appearance at will, sometimes just for kicks, and sometimes for their own protection. Humans aren't supposed to be able to tell the difference, aren't supposed to see the Céad as anything but human…but accidents happen. Some fae babies left in the human world, if they realize the humans can see their true forms, shift to reflect what the humans want to see. They become humans themselves in all but actuality."

"But I've never changed how I look," Wilder said. He had always been him; scrawny, with a mess of red hair, smoky gray eyes, and definitely no wings.

Though, was that actually true?

A half-remembered story of the old lady who had found him rose in a jumbled haze from the depths of his mind. The police had said the woman was senile. They had told Child Protective Services she had made strange claims about the little boy; that he had wings and elf ears. That he couldn't be natural. But no one else could corroborate her tale, so they discounted it as the ravings of a batty old woman.

"Well, you wouldn't remember it, would you?" Terra said, shaking him from his thoughts. "It likely happened when you were still a baby. Chances are your ears were more pointed than they are now, and you likely had wings. Who's to say what other changes you made? As you get adjusted to being fae, to accessing your magic—and as you're trained up—you'll figure out how to release the shift you've been holding onto."

Terra glanced at the nearby grandfather clock as it chimed two in the morning. Her eyes had grown heavy, and she yawned. "But for now, it's probably time to get some sleep." Rising, she started blowing out the candles Wilder was sure she could have extinguished with the same magic she had displayed earlier.

"Trained up? As I get *adjusted*?" Wilder asked, his breathing quickening at the nonchalant dissolution of their conversation. "Terra, I still have no clue what's going on. I still have so many questions…"

She continued to ready the parlor for their exit. "All for tomorrow, I think. And some questions, unfortunately, are not for me to answer. The Council is much better at explaining all of this than I am." Her voice had fallen to a whisper as she scooped up her dozing owl. Hennie nuzzled into Terra's arms and released a serene sigh, ruffling her feathers and sinking deeper into her embrace.

Between the inundating warmth of the fire, the steady, hypnotic ticking of the clock, and the lateness of the hour, Wilder felt more than a little drowsy. "How do you even know I'll stay?" he asked. His exhaustion, and the vulnerability she had forced him into, had triggered his defensiveness. He knew he was being ridiculous, but he pushed anyway. "How do you know I won't just take off?"

"Forgive me if I'm wrong, Wilder, but I was under the impression you had nowhere else to go." Her snide tone seemed playful, smirking as she rubbed the feathered crown of the slumbering bird's head. "Plus, I bet you the bed is better than anything you've ever slept on. I'll even ask James to whip up some of his famous shrimp and grits in the morning. You're welcome to leave whenever you'd like. You're not a prisoner here. But I hope it won't be anytime soon." She raised a single eyebrow in challenge before walking out of the room without a second glance back.

He nodded to himself, too depleted to continue the runaway ruse. Quickly rising from his seat, he padded after her, rushing to catch up. Terra led him from the parlor, up the set of stairs he saw earlier, and down enough hallways he lost count. They arrived at a heavy wooden door flanked by several identical ones stretching the length of the hall. It opened to a modest dormitory darkened by the hour, and Wilder could make out the silhouettes of a full sized bed, a desk, a dresser, a bookshelf, and two doors at the far end of the room. He had never had a space like this to call his own, but he knew not to get too comfortable.

"Goodnight, Wilder," she said, patting his shoulder and turning down the hall. Loose waves bounced around the nape of her neck as she trotted away.

"'Night, Terra," he said in a sleepy daze. As he reconciled the implausibility of the last twenty-four hours, he remembered to call after her. "Oh, and it's Wil! You can call me Wil."

"I figured I would anyway," she called back, her voice floating over from the end of the hallway. As he prepared to step into the room, she peered around the corner. "By the way, happy birthday, Wil!"

She left him with a smile as she rounded the corner from view.

CHAPTER SIX

Wilder woke the next morning to the sound of chatter in the hallway outside his door. The cadences of a bright and cheery female voice greeted the morning as she passed. Although he *was* curled up in the most comfortable bed he had ever laid in, it had taken two more hours of tossing and turning before sleep had finally settled his senses. Even then, his mind had raced well into the night. As the morning sunlight yawned through his windows, stretching across the walls, his mind returned to that same uncomfortable velocity.

Wilder rose from the bed and took his time getting acquainted with his surroundings. Despite the frankly life-changing revelations Terra had shared last night, he was far from convinced he wanted to stay here. But he might as well figure out where *here* was.

Padding barefoot to one of the large, tracery windows streaming with daylight, his eyes fell on a vast garden below. Fountains splashed and rippled as finches sang and darted through the cascading water, bathing their ruffled feathers. Bushes and brambles displaying blooms of every conceivable color lined a swaying cobbled path as it wandered through neatly trimmed hedges. Scattered groves of fruit trees and ivy covered pergolas shielded sets of benches from the elements. The entire garden appeared contained within the soaring walls of the Council House, its turrets and towers rising high above the building, casting their shadows across the foliage.

Movement within the garden caught his eye, and Wilder noticed a thin girl in a yellow sundress and strappy gold sandals skipping along the garden path. Her brown skin shone bronze in the new spring sun, while a pale boy with sweeping black hair walked alongside her, his hands in the pockets of his shorts. As they talked, his attention never left her. They looked to be around Wilder's age, but were too far away for him to be sure.

Removing her sandals, the girl skipped off the path, through the bushes, and into a grove of fruit trees. Wilder's eyes widened as the girl jumped high into the trees, captured a branch with one hand, plucked an orange with the other, and dropped with unearthly grace back onto the dirt. Unruffled by the display, the boy shot her an amused smirk before she rejoined him and offered him the fruit. Removing the peel, he handed half back, and they resumed their stroll.

Wilder blinked. If he did stay, this place might take some getting used to.

Wilder turned to investigate the room. Opening one of the doors on the far side, he found a closet large enough to hold four times the clothes he actually owned. A peek beyond the second door revealed a cavernous bathroom—the marble surfaces aglow with sunlight streaming from a skylight overhead.

Wandering over to the dresser, Wilder noticed its crafter had taken extreme care with the woodwork. He ran a calloused finger over one of the palm-sized knobs, which displayed the clever face of a fox. The ridges had been carved with such unreal accuracy he could have sworn the creature peered back at him. Wilder shuddered, remembering the fox in the park.

After pulling a set of clean clothes from his bag, Wilder padded to the bathroom, where he stood under the steaming hot spray of the shower for the next twenty-five minutes. Lathering himself with every ounce of soap and lotion he could get his hands on, any leftover mud melted from his skin. The steam suffused the room with the scent of lavender and chamomile, relaxing his mind and muscles. He had never been allowed to shower with such abandon, as an irate someone surely would have been knocking at the door by now, shouting about him taking too long. Finishing, he mussed his hair, dried with a towel, and dressed quickly. He stowed the rest of his belongings in the dresser and left the room, letting the door shut behind him with a click.

Eyeing the stretch of hall, realization dawned that he had no idea where to go. He tried retracing his steps from the night before and ended up staring through the open double doors of an octagonal room built into one of the cathedral's turrets. Padded sparring mats covered the floors, and the walls were lined with a shocking array of non-lethal and very lethal weaponry. Steel swords glinted silver in the sunlight streaming from another skylight, the rays breaking across thick wooden rafters running the length of the ceiling. A wicked collection of crossbows hung unloaded in one corner, their silver-tipped arrows resting in black leather quivers on a table beneath them.

A young boy—with sharp-angled ears, white blond locks, flawless porcelain skin, and languid, flowing movements—stood in front of a punching bag descending from the rafters. With each pummel and punch, the bag arced with astonishing force, as if the boy had far more power in his still developing body than his slight frame let on. He couldn't have been older than twelve. Hearing footsteps behind him, the boy pivoted to find Wilder watching. Wilder was sure his jaw was hanging on the floor.

"Hey, how ya doin'?" the boy asked, a welcoming grin spreading across his face as he removed the padded gloves and cloth wrappings twisted around his small hands. He had a casual, unbothered air, as if he hadn't just been in the middle of an entirely inhuman display of strength. The boy sauntered over. "You just get in?"

Wilder shut his mouth and cleared his throat. "Um, yeah…I guess so. Uh, do you know where Terra is? Or how to get down to the kitchen?"

Wilder's stomach did an aggressive somersault, reminding him he hadn't eaten since lunch the day before.

"Sure!" The boy's sunny temperament was disarming, especially after the vigorous display he had just witnessed. As Wilder followed him from the room, the boy added with another grin, "I'm Barrett, by the way."

"Wil," Wilder said, comforted by the boy's friendliness, but continuing to eye his unearthly appearance. Was he supposed to look like him?

"So, when'd you get here?" Barrett asked as they strode along another hallway of blank wooden doors, though some of these had thin golden placards engraved with titles like 'R. Hemming Office' and 'Magical Artifacts'.

"Last night, around midnight, I guess. I don't really know for sure." Wilder rubbed at his neck. "I'm still a little out of it."

"Yeah, sounds about right." Barrett threw Wilder a smirk. "That's how it usually is. Don't worry too much about it. The first night is always the hardest. Or at least that's what I've been told."

"By who?" Wilder asked.

The boy shrugged as they strode down a familiar set of stairs. "The other Céad we find. Wolf, vamp, magem, fae; we've seen them all. They come here after, or sometimes before," Barrett gestured to Wilder, "learning what they are. They'll stay here a bit, figuring out their next move. Usually, they find a place with whatever Céad they belong to. Though sometimes not."

Wilder was relieved to hear someone else corroborating Terra's claims. "What about you? What do you do here?" Wilder asked.

"Me? I live here with my parents and my brother. And the Council. Sometimes I go to the schools to check if any kids are showing signs of magic. A lot of us younger ones do that, while we still look the part. Sometimes I have training of my own. But I also get to help train the newcomers like you, if they decide to hang around." Barrett beamed and puffed out his chest. "It's a pretty fun gig."

Wilder smirked at the thought of being 'trained' in whatever combat he had witnessed earlier by a kid half his size. But then he remembered just how hard that kid could throw a punch.

They crossed into an enormous kitchen, complete with state-of-the-art appliances Wilder had only ever seen in cooking shows. A large stainless steel fridge, big enough to hold enough food for an entire army, stood at one end—thankfully void of padlocks. Fresh fruits, savory breads, and bags of groceries covered a long island stretching the length of the room. Barrett settled at one of the brushed metal barstools.

The skinny man with the Cheshire smile stood by a window looking into the garden, humming along to an oldies tune playing from an antique radio on the windowsill. Swaying to the music, he stirred something mouthwatering over the stovetop. Distracted by the glorious scent wafting in his direction, Wilder almost didn't notice Terra join them.

"Welcome to the land of the living," she said, nudging his arm.

"That's a stretch." Wilder let out a yawn, but he noted her warm tone and relaxed, relieved she didn't seem to be holding his hostility the night before against him. Hunger ate at his stomach and it let out an audible rumble.

"Well, that's no way to start your day," the Cheshire man said. "Orders up. Dig in." He dished out four bowls of buttery shrimp and grits, sliding one to Barrett.

"Thanks, James," Barrett said, cradling his bowl. Leaning over, he answered Wilder's unasked question. "James is half master of the house, half chef extraordinaire. He's been here since before any of us and will probably be here long after. Technically, the entire Council House is his. He just lets us stay here."

"And you're lucky I still do!" James said, pressing his knuckles into his hips as disapproval arched his brow. "Was it not *you* that tracked mud up and down my hallway last night?"

Wilder swallowed, shrinking in his skin, but Barrett threw him a wink.

"Ah. Sorry, James. I must have been in a rush." Barrett gazed into his grits, his features drawn as faux guilt colored his cheeks.

"Those grits ain't gonna save you from the moppin' you'll be doin' for the next two hours, boy. No magic allowed. And you're lucky that's all it is."

"Yessir," Barrett answered, his sunny warmth tempered as he forked at his bowl. But Wilder saw the corner of his mouth tilt into an imperceptible smirk. Terra smiled at Barrett, her green eyes twinkling as she mussed his white blond hair. He swatted at her, grinning, as James handed her two bowls of grits.

"Terra, darlin', be a dear and spell those. It's got a bit more salt than I think our new friend can handle."

"Of course." She took the bowls, deposited one on the island, and cradled the other in her palm before handing it to Wilder.

"Uh, how do you know I don't like salty food?" Wilder asked James, surprised at the man's assumption.

Barrett answered instead, "All fae hate salt," as if anyone would know that.

"Then how come you ate it?" Wilder furrowed his brow as a shrimp disappeared into Barrett's mouth with a slurp.

Terra answered for him, as Barrett was now otherwise preoccupied with a mouthful of breakfast. "He can unsalt it himself. You'll learn how, too. Eventually."

As Terra spoke, the girl from the gardens strode into the kitchen, her yellow sun-dress swaying along the tops of her knees. Her dark hair fell in tight curls down to her chin, her button nose scrunching as she sniffed at the scent of breakfast. She smiled brightly, and directly at Wilder, appraising him.

"Good morning, everyone!" she announced to the room. "And good morning, new friend. It's a pleasure to meet you. I'm Olivia—honorary house lycan. But you can call me Liv." She gave Wilder a curtsy and offered her hand. Hers was unmistakably the voice that had awoken him that morning.

Her hand felt tiny in his as he shook it, though with not nearly as much enthusiasm as she had. He didn't know if he could even contain that level of exuberance in his body. "Hey. I'm Wil. Nice to meet you."

Liv edged a step closer, the girl's wide smile never faltering. "I was just telling Harry how exciting it is to have a new face around here. Don't you think, James?"

James continued to lean against the sink, munching on a shrimp and seemingly absorbed with a spot on the blank wall across from him. "Mmm, yes, Miss Olivia. Quite."

Olivia's caramel gaze shifted to Wilder, her large eyes peering up at him through thick, dark lashes. She stood about two heads shorter than him. "Have you met the Magi yet?" she asked, looking between him and Terra.

"Um…" Wilder glanced at Terra, unsure of what to say, or who 'the Magi' was.

Terra thankfully responded for him. "Not yet, but I think we're ready to head over. You done?" Before Wilder could answer, she seized his still half-full bowl and loaded it next to her empty one in the sink.

"Thank you for breakfast, James," Terra said, throwing him a charming smile as she strode to the doorway.

"Oh good! I'll go with you!" Olivia skipped after her, interlocking Terra's arm with her own as she peered back at Wilder. Cocking her head, she waited for him to join. Terra raised an eyebrow, but otherwise shrugged. "Alright then."

Eyeing his now discarded breakfast, its contents submerged under a thin layer of soapy water, he admitted he still felt rather hungry, but figured he now had somewhere else to be. Terra and Olivia strode arm-in-arm and out of sight, Olivia chattering away, while Wilder hastened to follow. As he left the kitchen, he glanced back at Barrett waving goodbye, a miserable expression painting his no longer sunny features. James glared down at him—mop extended. Wilder made a note to thank him later.

CHAPTER SEVEN

The Magi's office was on the second floor of the Council House, the chamber decorated in mahogany and gold—regal damask foiled wallpaper lining the room. A fire crackled in the hearth of the wrought gold fireplace; each inch worked in gold filigree. Wilder noticed that despite the large blaze, the fire itself didn't give off any heat.

A neat man in a smart, charcoal gray three-piece suit, his crisp white hair the color of fresh snow, busied himself behind a desk. Sunlight streamed through three bay windows, opened to the scents of the blooming garden below. On the far right of the desk, a gold-rimmed glass tank lay open wide, as if the man had little concern about its resident—a lime green chameleon—getting loose. The chameleon, currently basking in the rays of the sun, swiveled a turreted eye toward the trio as they approached.

"Good morning. Good morning," the man said without looking up. Bent over the desk, he scribbled something on a piece of parchment, his glasses slipping down the bridge of his nose. He pushed them back up with the tip of his finger. "Or is it afternoon?" The man abandoned the letter, spinning around to inspect the day outside. "Yes. I do believe afternoon. Indeed." With a final nod, as if his assertion had decided the matter, he cleared his throat and spun again to face the trio. "Quite the evening I hear you had, Mr. Ansley."

Wilder gulped, stopping himself from taking a step back. The man appeared otherwise ordinary. Except for his eyes. Behind a thin set of spectacles, the man caught his gaze with one piercing blue iris, as blue as the ocean's depths, through which he now seemed to stare into Wilder's soul. But his other—blank and snowy white, without a hint of color or pupil—seemed just as capable of disarming anyone it gazed upon. Wilder had no clue how old the man might be. Despite his stark white hair, he appeared rather young. Wilder wouldn't guess any older than forty. But he effused an aged wisdom that made Wilder believe he could be far older.

If the man was at all aware of Wilder's reaction, he did him the courtesy of ignoring it. "Welcome to the New Orleans Council House. I'm Magi Maynestream, Head Magister for the Council. We're happy to have you." He shuffled from behind the desk. "I hope your stay so far has been agreeable?"

"Yes, sir." Wilder nodded, trying not to let his stare fall too long on the man's white eye. "It's been fine." An onslaught of fresh questions brewed anew in his mind.

"Quite good to hear, Mr. Ansley. I'm glad my charges are taking good care of you." He beamed at Terra and Olivia before peering again at Wilder, his blue eye scanning his features with an intensity that made Wilder's blood run cold. The Magi lifted his attention to Terra. "I understand our Terra has already explained a little to you? About why you were brought here?"

"Some." Wilder nodded again. He wracked his brain, trying to work out which of the Céad Barrett had mentioned this man might possibly be.

"Wonderful!" The Magi clapped his hands. "Ladies, you may leave us." He nodded once at Terra and Olivia, gesturing to the door. As they left the room, Terra gave Wilder an encouraging smile. Returning to his desk, the Magi began pouring a pot of tea into two glass teacups sitting atop a gold breakfast tray, which hadn't been there a moment ago. A plate of scrumptious cranberry scones sat steaming alongside it. "Scone?" the Magi offered.

The man's eyes were actually quite kind once Wilder got over the initial shock of them. Loosing a breath, his shoulders relaxed a fraction. "Yes, please. Thank you." Wilder accepted the scone and took a bite, ignoring the slight burn on his tongue. Half a bowl of grits had not been enough, and the scone was warm, sweet, and filling.

"Have a seat, Mr. Ansley." The Magi gestured to two leather armchairs near the fire. "Let us chat. I'm sure you have quite a bit on your mind."

Wilder nodded and padded to the hearth. He didn't know where to start. After placing his cup on a mahogany side-table, he settled into a cushioned armchair. The leather hugged every fold of his back, soft against the skin of his arms, and Wilder wondered how it could be so impossibly cozy, just as the bed had been the night before.

"Is the furniture here made with magic?" He shut his mouth with a snap, realizing how stupid the question sounded. Of all the questions he could have started with…

If the Magi had thought his question ridiculous, he didn't show it. He only beamed, as if delighted by Wilder's bewilderment. "In a way," the Magi answered. "Most things here were crafted by fae, like yourself, who possess incredible abilities. Often, through the process of creating, fae can imbue the things they make with elements of their own power. These things can be quite beautiful, unbelievably comfortable, or even rather dark and dangerous. It is, in the end, all about the heart. Creation is one of the many ways the Fae still contribute to this world we share with the humans. It's their only way left to be adored by them, since humans can no longer appreciate the Fae's more inherent allure."

"Wait, do you mean to say the humans once knew about the fae?" Wilder asked. He had obviously read stories about the mythical, mystical creatures growing up. Every little kid had. But they had always been just that—stories. No more truth to them than that of the Loch Ness Monster or Santa Claus.

"Indeed," the Magi said, his blue eye settling on him. "They knew about all the Céad. The Lycan, the Vampyrs, and the Magem as well. The stories I'm sure you're familiar with came from somewhere, after all." The gentleman winked. "We once lived in peace among them, without the need to hide our true selves. We once served as their protectors, even."

"What happened then?" Wilder asked. The fire popped, making him startle.

"Pride." The Magi shrugged, taking a sip of his steaming tea. "The ultimate downfall of all mankind, I'm afraid. The Céad included."

Staring down at his hands, Wilder felt unsure of which direction to take his questioning. "Okay, if it's not all just a story, and I am what you say I am, how come I didn't know about this—about any of you—before now? Why can't other people see what I can?" Wilder thought of the woman in the park, and stopped short. Had she been Céad, too?

"Because you, my friend, are not like other people," the Magi said. "You are not human. Regardless of how hard you've tried to appear so. When you reflect upon your life, can you honestly tell me you never knew? Never wondered if something was different about you? Whether you might have been in the wrong place?"

Wilder shifted in his seat. "No offense, sir, but I've been in 'wrong place' after 'wrong place' my entire life." He cleared his throat. "Aside from that, then, why can't *the humans* see any of it? Terra explained a little last night. But if they knew about us before, why don't they now?"

The Magi reached for his cup and took a sip of tea. The flickering fire made the gold edging of his spectacles glow. "It's been thousands of years since the humans have known of us. You see, the Eadar, our realm, exists behind a veil—a Shroud. The Shroud was created to protect the humans from the knowledge of us. And in a way, it protects us as well."

"Created? By who? And why is it so bad for them to know about us?" Wilder asked. "It definitely would have been a lot easier for me if I hadn't thought I was a lunatic half my life."

"I'm sure of it." The Magi gave Wilder a sad smile. "It's a rather long story, I'm afraid. It all happened with the Fall. You see, some time after our creation, the first Céad proved themselves incapable of protecting the humans the way the Magíck, our creator, had intended us to. In the power they had been given, there were those who grew foolish, believing themselves little less than the Creator himself. And unfortunately, there are those among us who still believe we are." The Magi lifted his chin, staring into the happily crackling fire.

"Tribe turned against tribe, and humans against the Céad. Death and disorder followed. Great wars. Bloody battles. The near extinction of so many species. Our legends say the Magíck would not stand for the chaos that ensued—for its own creation to be so destructively at odds with one another. So the Magíck and the gods that serve it placed a Shroud across the land. The Shroud keeps the humans from the knowledge of us so they might live in peace. That they might go about their days believing the things that go bump in the night don't exist at all, and are no longer out to get them. Those of us who still live according to an eternal covenant of service and protection to them, continue to do so. Even though we've become nothing more than a mere bedtime story."

"I guess that makes sense," Wilder said, trying to keep his mind open. "What I don't understand is what happened to me. Terra told me I was kidnapped as a baby. *That* I get. But if humans aren't supposed to know about us, how could they see me? How could I have lived my whole life thinking I was one of them?"

"The Shroud does not keep us from interacting with them. There are plenty of Céad that choose to live among the humans—alongside them. The Shroud only keeps them from *the knowledge* of us. In theory, where we might see a vampyr, they would find only a human. Where we might see magic, their minds would make sense of it in some other way, protecting them from that knowledge."

Wilder thought about the woman who had found him in the woods as a baby—the claims she had made. "But that doesn't make sense," Wilder told the Magi. "The woman who first found me said she saw wings. Pointy ears. How could she have seen that as a human?"

The Magi grew uncomfortable, shifting in his seat as he readjusted his gray coat. "A question for the masses. Evidence over the past few decades has suggested the Shroud might be…*thinning*. Instances where humans have seen things they, by our understanding, should not have."

"Not very convenient if you're trying to stay hidden," Wilder said, letting out a sardonic laugh.

"Right you are." The Magi didn't return his smile, but tipped his cup at him before taking another drink.

"Alright, so she saw wings on me. Pointy ears. But I clearly don't have any now. And I can't remember ever having them either. So what happened? If I see things nobody else can, why can't I see my own wings? Why couldn't Terra see them when she met me? Or why can't you right now? Terra mentioned something about me *shifting?*"

Magi Maynestream nodded. "A fair observation. Yes. Even as a baby, you learned to change yourself to protect those around you from seeing the truth. It was instinctual. The Shroud failed, but you did not. Each Céad, when among the humans, will often do the same. Your shift was the Magíck working through you, through your lifeblood, to obey the covenant, since you were too young to make the choice for yourself. You likely opted to protect the humans that found you, and just as much, to protect yourself from them. It is the same with your magic, or lack thereof. You may have chosen, whether consciously or not, to hide that as well. Tell me, what did others think of you whenever you accidentally displayed your power? Or whenever the Eadar showed itself to you?"

Wilder thought back over his life. How he had always thought he was crazy, because *others* thought he was crazy. "They thought I was nuts.

And understandably. I was seeing things that weren't there. Doing things that made no sense," Wilder added, remembering Kyle and the fire.

The Magi nodded. "A troubling side-effect of the Shroud, I'm afraid. The instinct to see you as delusional, troubled, is another way the Shroud protects them. Humans will always reject what they cannot see—cannot understand—just as they will reject those who claim otherwise, or those who act against their beliefs of what is real. It keeps them from knowing about us. But unfortunately, it also keeps them from truly knowing the Magíck that created them."

Wilder's stare drifted into the roaring fire as the Magi settled farther into his seat. After a moment, Wilder said, "I'm not entirely sure I understand what you mean by 'the Magíck'. A great creator? You talk as if there's some being with a hand in it all. I don't mean to be rude, but it sounds like a load of crock to me—a story kids are spun to make sense of things. To keep them in line. How can you know this 'Magíck' exists? Has anyone seen it? Interacted with it?"

The Magi smiled at him, as if he had heard this line of questioning before. "My dear boy, whether you believe will make no difference to its existence. The difference it *will* make is within you." The Magi studied him through a pair of horn-rimmed glasses. "I will not say there aren't those who agree with you—who also do not believe the Magíck plays a pivotal role in each of our lives. Each species maintains its inherent magic regardless of their beliefs. As do you, though given your lack of use, it may lie dormant in you right now. In the end, your decision is ultimately up to you. The Magíck grants each of its creation freewill, and you are free to do what you want with it." He released a sigh. "And though the 'Magíck' may appear to be mere conjecture, I suppose—a story to make sense of this world, as one might say…" He winked at Wilder. "It could, by all means, prove true." He took another sip of his tea.

Wilder realized he hadn't touched his own. Bringing the cup to his lips, he swallowed a gulp, mulling over the Magi's words. "Alright, existence aside, what does this have to do with me? How does any of this help me figure out the last seventeen years of my life? Why I was kidnapped? Why it took so long for you all to find me?" The words spilled out of Wilder before he could stop himself.

"Ah." Magi Maynestream placed his teacup back on the table. "I'd say that has everything to do with existence." The gentleman's mouth tugged into a knowing smile. "The answers to many of your questions have yet to be determined, and can really only be determined by you. My belief, though you may not share it, is that you were found right when you were supposed to be, and for such a time as this. You have a choice to make, Wilder," the Magi said.

Wilder's attention flashed to him from where he stared into the fire, summoned by the gravity in the Magi's tone.

"There is a role for you to play in all of this, should you choose to accept it. Or you can carry on with your life—eking an existence out of running from place to place, counting the days until something changes. You can escape once more into the human world, like you always have. Or you can rise into your birthright as the son of a realm, of a people, that could use you. You don't have to decide right now. But, believe in it or not, there will come a time when the Magíck will ask you to make a decision, and likely when you least expect it."

Wilder stared into the Magi's piercing blue eye that never broke from his gaze, and found himself deeply unsettled. He couldn't shake the feeling there was more to the story, and Wilder's involvement in it, than what the man with the curious eye let on.

***

After leaving the Magi's office, Wilder found himself shirtless in front of his bathroom mirror—a practice he didn't usually make a habit of. He studied his ears, willing them to change with such gusto he thought he felt a distinct *plunk* in the recesses of his brain. Twisting around, he struggled to inspect his back, surveying it for any scars or imperfections he might not have noticed before—any sign he might have once had wings. But his skin remained as unblemished as ever.

His palms flat on the marble, Wilder leaned against the counter to steady himself. The unbearable weight of expectation clung to him, sinking into the muscles of his shoulders. He knew the Magi wanted him to stay; he had all but said so. But staying meant Wilder would have to perform—to become something he wasn't convinced he could. Wilder knew the feeling well. Every foster had been the same, always with their unrealistic expectations, always readying him to leave as soon as they realized he wouldn't measure up.

Everyone, it seemed—Terra, the Magi, probably the others as well—expected him to flip a switch and go full fae. To turn on some dormant magic like it was no big deal. But he didn't have anything close to Olivia's grace or Barrett's strength. Aside from his unwilling hand in a few unfortunate catastrophes, Wilder was sure there wasn't a single ounce of this so called 'Magick' in his body.

A muffled knock at his bedroom door jerked him from his reverie. Wilder threw his shirt back on, but in the rush, stuck his arm through the neck hole. "Be there in a sec!" Pulling his shirt off, he tried again. Finally righting himself, he bounded for the door as a second knock sounded. He opened it to find a shock of bright green staring at him, Terra's knuckles raised to go for a third rattle.

She wore a long gray sweatshirt, its neckline running across her shoulders, exposing the length of her tawny neck. The hem hung over a simple pair of black leggings clinging to her shape, her wavy hair braided and slung over her shoulder. "We were thinking about heading to dinner," she said, cocking her head as he steadied himself at the door. Her lips lifted into a smirk. "You need a minute?"

"Uh, no. I'm good," Wilder said, a blush rushing to his cheeks as he pulled the hem of his shirt down from where it had gotten caught against his torso. "Dinner?" Wilder twisted around, peering out through the window behind him. The sun was beginning to set over the eaves of the abbey. More time had passed with the Magi than he had realized. "Sure. Yeah. Dinner sounds great." The grits, scone, and no lunch had done little to appease the hunger he had woken with.

Terra led him downstairs and into a living room off the foyer. Scenes from the nightly news flashed across a flatscreen TV, displaying the faces of seven young men and women, all missing from the area over the last few weeks. A grave voice announced through the speakers—*"Authorities are requesting any information to aid in the search for these missing individuals…"*

"It's so sad." Olivia sat on a powder blue sofa, her chin in her hands, her expression sullen. The boy with the black hair sat on the armrest next to her, his hand resting on the sofa near her shoulder.

A taller boy—though he easily passed for a fully grown man—shouldered a wall across the room as he watched the news story, his arms crossed over a broad chest. He had the same white blond hair as Barrett, but lengthier and messier, as if he had been putting off a haircut for weeks. He wore a long-sleeved black shirt, rolled up to expose his forearms. The black markings of a set of tattoos peeked out from the cuffs around his elbows, their inky dark tendrils in notable contrast to his pale, porcelain skin. Where Wilder was all red and gold, from his hair to the brush of freckles painting his cheekbones, this boy seemed crafted of pure white ice. Glacial blue eyes flashed from the news story to Wilder and Terra, scanning the space between them. The boy's features grew taut and severe, his stare lingering on Terra before returning to the screen.

But as Terra drummed up a conversation with Olivia, the boy continued to follow her movements out of the corner of his eye. Olivia and the dark-haired boy, however, welcomed Wilder with far more enthusiasm, standing from their seats.

"Hello again, Wil!" Olivia said, her lilt its usual bright cadence.

The boy with the black hair stepped forward, his hand outstretched. He wore a dark green graphic tee that brought out the jungle-green of his eyes, and his easy smile reached from ear to ear. "Hey. I'm Harry." Wilder shook his hand. He reminded Wilder of Evan, and instantly liked him. Harry's grip was firm and warm, and Wilder wondered what kind of Céad this boy was. Aside from his rather pale skin, he easily passed as human. But maybe he had shifted too?

"I heard you got attacked by an owl last night." Harry's mouth quirked into a mischievous smirk.

"Eh, yeah. You could say that." Wilder scratched his head. "But in my defense, it was an annoyingly insistent owl." Wilder grinned down at Terra, and she rolled her eyes, but smiled. The blond boy silently watched their interaction.

"I believe that." Harry said, chuckling. "Remind me to tell you about the time I got in a fight with Terra, and Hennie decided I wasn't allowed in the west wing of the House anymore. I still have the scars…" He frowned, playfully wincing for effect. "Either way, glad you're here. It was getting boring without some fresh blood."

"Oh, funny joke…" Olivia scoffed, punching his shoulder.

"I'm here all week." Harry winked at her, his dark lashes fluttering against a pale, dimpled cheek. He glanced back at his icy-eyed friend, who hadn't moved an inch but continued to study the group with the blankest of expressions. He radiated either confidence or arrogance.

"Don't mind him," Harry told Wilder, loud enough for the blond boy to hear. "He thinks he's intimidating."

Arrogance, then.

Clearing his throat, the blond boy moved from the wall, sauntering over in one fluid motion. The white strands of his hair swept back, exposing the tip of a sharp, angled ear beneath. He was at least a few inches taller than Wilder, far more built—and by Wilder's guess—unmistakably fae.

"Tristian." The icy boy offered Wilder a wired hand, his air of command freezing the space between them. Every inch of him appeared crafted of muscle, evidence of spending a significant amount of time in heavy physical training. The guy could pummel him into dust if he wanted to, and Wilder made a mental note not to get on his bad side. But from the way Tristian's gaze narrowed on him, Wilder wondered if it might be too late for that. Tristian either didn't like Wilder, or hadn't yet decided whether he should bother.

Accepting his hand, Wilder stifled a wince. Peering up in surprise, he noticed a small smirk play on the edges of the tall boy's perfect features, and Wilder wondered if the guy had *intended* to crack every bone in his now sore and throbbing right hand.

CHAPTER EIGHT

Wilder should have expected Pablo's Pizza wouldn't be like anything he had ever experienced. As they stood on the sidewalk of Frenchman Street, he squinted up at the flashy red and white restaurant front. The building was nestled unobtrusively between two businesses he had frequently passed in his travels around the Quarter, as if it had always been there. But until that moment, he hadn't been aware of anything existing between the two.

The diner itself was styled in 50s retro candor, complete with bold checkerboard tiling, bright turquoise booths, and a cherry red counter running around the central kitchen. A handful of patrons on leather cushioned barstools were draped over the counter, enjoying opalescent milkshakes or steaming plates of foods Wilder had no name for.

Surveying the room, his eyes widened. A multi-hued fae girl in fluffy white roller skates buzzed a pizza to a table of seemingly ordinary, though slightly pale, gentlemen. The fae's wings grew from her back in four sharp leaves, wiry venules spreading through the thin material. The leaves fluttered as her lavender hair floated on an absent breeze, as if suspended in water. She placed the gentlemen's order on the table and Wilder did a double-take. He couldn't be sure if the deep red sauce she drizzled from a squeeze bottle was marinara or something else entirely.

As she left the gentlemen, Terra waved down the waitress. Gliding to the group, her wings flared as she slid to a graceful stop in front of them. "How many?" she asked, her voice simpering. Lifting her gaze from a readied notepad, she eyed Tristian through long lavender lashes.

He threw her a knowing smirk, his hands digging into the pockets of his jeans, but said nothing.

They settled into a circular booth and Wilder studied the menu. The options were all normal, if not somewhat creative, styles of pizza. After taking their orders, the waitress's fingers ghosted along Tristian's wrist before she drifted away, and the group eased into a discussion of the day's events. To Wilder's discomfort, that particular discussion revolved wholly around him.

"So you don't remember anything?" Liv asked as he gnawed on a slice of pizza. "Nothing about what you looked like before you made yourself human?"

Wilder swallowed. "Not a bit. As far as I know, you're all just as crazy for thinking I'm supposed to look different as everyone else thinks *I am* for seeing things. I can't remember a time when I didn't look exactly like this."

"Well, with any luck," Terra said between bites of a massive slice of supreme pizza called 'Winona's Wonder'. "You'll be able to shift back in no time."

Wilder stilled. He wasn't sure he *wanted* to change.

"How was your afternoon with the Magi?" Olivia cut in, leaning forward, her eyes locked on him. Harry peered at her but didn't say a word.

"Intense," Wilder said. "But informative." Clearing his throat, he stared at his pizza. "Um, what—what *is* he?"

Harry finished chewing his fourth slice. "He's a Myx. A Céad hybrid, so to speak. A combination of two different species. In his case, Fae and Magem."

"Are there many of those?" Wilder asked. "Myxes, I mean."

"No." Tristian's voice was gruff. He hadn't spoken since they had first arrived. He inspected Wilder now, his icy blue eyes calculating. "Most Myx die in the womb, or at birth. It's a mutilation of the blood. The blending of two incompatible brands of magic. The ones that don't die are neither one nor the other, but may have abilities of either. In Maynestream's case, he's adept at both fae and mage magic, and he can see into time, though he says it's rarely clear."

"And he has a familiar," Terra pointed out.

"What's a familiar?" Wilder asked.

Terra explained how each magem, either mage or wyte, is found by their familiar when they first become aware of their magic. No one really knows where the familiars come from, just that it always happens. Hennie came to her when she was six. Familiars connect deeply with their magem, and magem, with training, can learn to channel through their familiars. Some more advanced magem have been able to use magic through their familiars, even if they're miles apart.

"Well, that's convenient." Wilder wondered whether the Magi might send his chameleon to keep tabs on him, and figured he wouldn't put it past him. "What about all of you?" he asked. "Are you all part of this 'Council' too?"

"Nope," Harry said, adding red pepper flakes to a meat-covered slice of pizza. "Some of us are training for it though, just in case we decide to join the Magistrie." He gestured to Tristian and Terra, and Terra glowed with pride at the addition, but Tristian wasn't paying attention to the conversation at all.

"What's the Magistrie?" Wilder asked.

"The Council is a subset of the Magistrie, our government. The Council is its seat in this region," Terra said.

"We might not be officially sworn, but we do what we can to help," Harry added. "Most of us visit schools. Like how Terra found you."

"Are there more than just fae hiding out in the human world?" Wilder asked, thinking of the old woman from the park. "Barrett mentioned other types of Céad. 'Wolves and vamps'? And Terra, you said you're a 'wyte'? Are there other types still out there with the humans, like I was?"

"Absolutely," Harry said. "Some choose to live among them, for their own reasons. Lycans like Liv are born, but sometimes to humans who don't know what their kid is." Wilder noticed Olivia still. "It's the same for some magem, too. Vampyrs, like myself, are made—but their creators don't often stick around to help the transition, so new ones can become displaced too."

"Fair enough." Wilder took a bite from his third slice, aptly called 'Hook's Revenge', positive his stomach would be taking revenge on him later. "And as a vampyr, or a lycan, what can you guys *do*?"

"Well, I'm a wolf. As you know," Olivia said, her bright smile returning. She threw him a wink. "Lycan, like all your old werewolf legends say, change at the full moon. But, with training, we learn to change at will. And we can bring out parts of our wolf form while we're in our human form."

Harry leaned in, his shoulder brushing Olivia's. "Vampyrs don't shift at all. Except for the occasional descent of scary teeth." He lifted his lips to show off his white fangs, snapping teasingly at Liv, who giggled and swatted him away.

"Most fae," Tristian said, finally joining the conversation, "are shapeshifters too. But unlike the Lycan, we're not animals." Tristian threw Olivia a smug grin and looked back at Wilder before he could see her roll her eyes. "Some of us can change our appearance to look more human, as you have." He gestured to Wilder. "We can change our hair, our eyes, our skin color. But mostly we enjoy staying the way we're born. The Magíck made us attractive enough. No need to improve upon perfection." He popped the neckline of his shirt in mock pride and smirked at Terra. She punched him in the arm, but seemed to regret it instantly, mouthing a silent but exaggerated 'ow' as she nursed her injured knuckles.

"Don't hurt yourself, darling," Tristian crooned in a patronizing tone. Grabbing her hand, he began massaging it along her knuckles. She let him, watching him warily. Within a few moments, her muscles seemed to loosen, and she opened and closed her fingers, testing their dexterity.

Terra gave Tristian an annoyed but grateful expression. "Thanks," she said in a hiss. Whipping her hand out of his, she turned back to Wilder. Her cheeks darkened, and Wilder wondered if something was going on between them.

"All that to say," Terra added, straightening in her seat and rubbing her hand. "Since it's clear you shifted, there are only two types of fae you might be: a Watern or a Fairn. But the Watern tend to avoid humans, and the rest of the Céad too. They're rarely accessible enough to be kidnapped. And their powers are different than the Fairn. Each fae is gifted by the Magíck with a unique set of skills. The Fairn are more externalizing. They have more of an influence over the elements, like fires and storms." She gave him a knowing look. "Though each one can only manipulate specific elements to varying degrees. It seems like storms and fires are the ones you're strongest in."

"What about the other fae? The Watern you mentioned," Wilder asked.

Terra nodded. "Watern are much more internal. They can compel humans better than any vampyr can, can sense a Céad miles away, and can read and influence minds and emotions. And they're hands down the most *alluring* of the Fae." She shot Tristian a thorny glance, but he pretended not to notice, turning to track the movements of the waitress gliding from table to table. Though Wilder was sure he heard him huff.

"So I'm definitely a Fairn, then?" Wilder asked, lifting a single eyebrow. He hoped each new discovery might lead him closer and closer to where he had first come from. Where his parents might be.

"After that little storm display last night?" Harry asked, chuckling. "Yeah, bud. No doubts there."

"It's for the best," Tristian interjected, rejoining the conversation. "The Watern are obnoxious and an absolute pain to deal with. They loathe the

Magistrie and dislike the rest of the Eadar. Lazy lot. But they somehow always find their own conniving ways to influence things." He ripped a chunk from his pizza, seeming to collect his thoughts as he chewed.

Harry smiled at him. "Geez, Tristian. Tell us how you really feel."

Tristian rolled his eyes before continuing. "The Fairn, though, are fairly involved with the Magistrie. The Queen herself sits on the High Council."

"The Fae have a queen?" Wilder asked, trying to tie together all the strings of information being thrown at him.

"*Most* of the Fae have a queen," Tristian said, correcting him. "And a King. The Fae, aside from the Watern, who refuse to bow to anyone, have always maintained a royal line through the Fairn." Tristian's features grew cold. "It's too much to get into now, but the line of succession is partly the reason our war started. Right now, the throne belongs to Summer. But historically its belonged to each of the Seasons at some point."

"Seasons?" Wilder felt so lost.

"The Fairn are made up of four Seasons of fae," Terra explained, giving him a reassuring smile. "Each with a unique look to them. Tristian and Barrett are Winters, and our *lovely* waitress," Terra threw a thorny glance at the lavender haired fae, "is a Spring." Tristian cocked an eyebrow at her and smirked, but she ignored him.

"You," Terra continued, gesturing to his mess of red hair, "are definitely a Summer, unless you changed your hair color for some reason, which I doubt." She inspected his face. "Your eyes do confuse me, though. Summers usually have amber eyes."

After considering him for a moment, Terra continued. "Tristian and Barrett are Winters, and are part of the Seasuír Court and royal line. Their parents are prominent members of the Seasuír, as well as within the Magistrie." Wilder expected Tristian to look smug at this information, but he, once again, no longer seemed to be paying attention.

"So, there are other fae, then? That look like me?" Wilder asked. A small hope cautiously peeked from its dormant hiding place.

Terra gave him an apologetic smile. "Unfortunately, even knowing your Season, there's no way to tell exactly where, or who, you came from. But the Magi is putting some feelers out. Just to see."

Wilder's shoulders slumped. He peered at the remnants of his pizza, doing his best to hide his disappointment. The hope building since the night before—the prospect of finding his parents through all of this—now lay crushed among the vestiges of half eaten crust, black olives, and parmesan cheese.

Olivia, in her now familiar style of lightening the mood, clapped her hands on the table and announced, "Enough with the heavy! Let's get out of here. Explore the city or something."

Terra looked at her uneasily, biting her bottom lip. "I don't know, Liv. Maybe we should head back..."

"Oh, come on, Terra," Olivia begged. "Live a little. We'll be *fine*."

Wilder looked up to see nearly empty plates in front of everyone, and vaguely realized he had made it through half an extra-large pizza by himself.

"Yeah, give me a minute," Tristian said, nudging past Terra from the booth. Making a striding beeline for the waitress, he caught her elbow as she fluttered past him. He swung her to where he stood at the diner's counter, and she laughed as she narrowly avoided colliding with him.

"Incorrigible, that one," Liv said, pursing her lips as they watched the interaction. Terra stared but made no comment, her features impressively blank.

As Tristian and the waitress flirted, the rest of them trudged outside. The evening had bloomed into full night, and a cool, humid breeze wafted across the pot-marked cobblestoned streets. Terra pulled the collar of her jacket up around her neck. After a moment, Tristian sauntered through the door, clasping a cardboard cupholder with four milk-shakes. He sipped at his own through an oversized straw.

"Your treat?" Harry asked, raising an eyebrow as he snagged a strawberry shake.

"Mm. No," Tristian mumbled through a mouthful of vanilla. Swallowing, he said, "Kallie's treat. *And* I finally got her number." He nudged Harry's arm, a broad smirk reaching across his face as he flicked a small scrap of paper in front of Harry's.

Terra and Liv crossed their arms, glaring at him, but Harry didn't look the least bit annoyed. He returned his grin. "Right. Well, let's see if you even remember her name tomorrow."

***

The walk back was entertaining, to say the least. Olivia, Harry, and Tristian raced each other down the vacant streets, competing to see who could swing the farthest from balcony to balcony. Terra and Wilder served as the judges.

"How're you feeling?" Terra asked, her voice low as they watched the three bound from building to building, their laughter filling the night. Terra's hand hung close to his as they walked a little behind, and he tried to ignore the way her proximity made his blood pulse. Terra was cute, gorgeous even, if he'd let himself think about it. But life was already getting confusing enough, and if she was involved with Tristian, he'd rather not piss off a guy that could kill him with barely a flick of his wrist.

"I know tonight's probably been a lot," she continued, her gaze drawn toward the trio hopping from rooftop to rooftop.

"I don't know," Wilder said, fighting the urge to both step away and step closer. "It *has* been a lot, and somehow still not enough. I feel like I still don't know even half of what I should."

"I get that." Terra looked at him, her emerald eyes glowing gold in the light of the streetlamps.

A loud *whoop* passed overhead, and they raised their heads to see Olivia vault clear across the avenue before jumping to the ground. The other two followed. Wilder took the moment to step away as the three gathered back on the street. Tristian came to stand next to Terra, and the three lined up, readying to run again.

Terra counted them off, and the trio bolted. Harry outmatched them both, though just barely outrunning Tristian. Olivia easily leapt higher than Harry, somersaulting over him in an impressive arc solely for their amusement. Tristian maintained a close second, but was by far the victor in maneuvering across the trellises, each fluid motion silent and deadly.

They returned to the street, but as Harry and Tristian argued about who would claim the victory in a one-handed wrestling match, Harry stopped. His features shifted to steady and severe, and he tensed, angling to search the empty road behind them. The line of his jaw tightened as he strained to monitor the sounds of the night. The rest of the group quieted—waiting. All Wilder could hear were the echoes of the crowds out on nearby Bourbon Street clamoring from bar to bar in a raucous haze.

"Something's happening," Harry said, his tone decided. "We need to go back." He spun and lurched toward the diner, the others trailing him. Harry slowed just enough for them to keep up.

"What do you hear?" Tristian asked at Harry's side. His voice held all the authority of a military general.

"Two men. A vampyr and a lycan, from what I can tell," Harry said. They rushed down the road. "Possibly rogues. I'm not sure. I overheard them getting ready to compel a girl nearby." Wilder gasped for breath as he struggled to follow.

As they rounded a corner, Wilder saw two men coaxing a young woman, likely in her early twenties, into an alleyway off the main

Bourbon street drag fifty yards away. A peculiar glimmer shone over their eyes, as if they gazed straight into the moon itself. Around them, a massive block party had blossomed to life. The loud lights and cacophonous rumble of Bourbon Street roared into the awakening night. Through the crowd, Wilder saw one of the men bare a set of sharp, white incisors at his colleague before staring into the depths of the woman's eyes. He said something to her, caressing her face and throat with his pale fingers, encouraging her away from the throng of partiers. Wilder's stomach dropped.

"Liv," Harry said, his voice firm as he reached for her hand, his stare steadying. "Stay with Wil."

She huffed, taken aback. "Harry, no. I can help," she said, looking annoyed at being kept from the fight.

"Liv, don't leave him." Harry's jungle green eyes bore into hers, and she nodded in assent. With one last squeeze of her hand, Harry joined Terra and Tristian as they careened toward the alleyway, shoving through the growing crowd.

Street vendors shouted their wares and revelers stumbled across the sidewalks, nursing brightly colored frozen drinks. From their hideaway across the street, Olivia and Wilder peered through the meandering crowd.

"Who are they?" Wilder asked Olivia as the woman and the moon-eyed men disappeared from view.

"Markus's rogues. His minions. They've been kidnapping the humans around here for the last few months."

Before Wilder could ask who Markus was, their friends were gone, swallowed up by the dark depths of the alley.

"Shit," Liv cursed under her breath, craning her neck to see above the mob of blissfully ignorant carousers. Her fists tightened, her knuckles lightening beneath her dark skin. "We can't stay here," she told Wilder. "Let's go." Seizing his hand, she dragged him through the crowd. At the alley's entrance, they hid themselves among the horde of drunk celebrators, who remained unaware of the goings-on thirty feet away. From where they stood, Wilder could make out a dark, shimmery mass thrumming along the back wall of the alley.

And the moon-eyed rogues were guiding the woman toward it.

Harry got there first, sprinting behind one of the rogues. Whipping him around, he delivered a sprawling roundhouse kick to his torso. It sent the unsuspecting lycan crashing into the brick wall. The vampyr, his fingers still clenched around the woman's upper arm, wheeled at the disturbance. Finding his colleague feebly righting himself, the vampyr sliced a piercing glare at the oncoming trio. He rushed the woman closer to the throbbing portal.

Extending her arms, Terra shouted something Wilder couldn't hear. The planted vines inching up the neighboring buildings separated themselves from the terraces and jetted for the rogue vampyr, wrapping his wrists in their thorns and bristles. The vines cut deep welts into his skin. He released the woman, who dropped like a rag-doll.

Tristian's attention snapped to the dazed, fallen woman on the cobblestones. He rushed forward, but the rogue lycan had made a full recovery, lunging to intercept him. Pivoting, Tristian bounced off the alley wall, narrowly avoiding the outstretched arms of the rogue. The woman whipped her head back and forth, as if awaking from a dream. Her eyes darted around at the unfolding scene. She lay just feet from the back wall, the shimmering mass's tendrils probing the night air, as if sensing her proximity.

Harry bounded after the lycan, leaping onto his back and locking his arms around the rogue's shoulders. Snarling, the man jerked like a rabid dog chomping at an annoying flea. The muscles along the lycan's arms rippled and swelled, and his moonlit eyes shifted yellow. Tristian's eyes widened as he tried to guard the woman. Breaking through Harry's hold, the rogue dislodged him, flinging him into the wall. Harry's head cracked against the brick before he toppled to the ground and lay motionless.

"Harry…" Wilder heard Liv whimper, anxiety plastered across her features. Every inch of her tense frame fought not to run to him.

The rogue wolf stalked toward Tristian, foaming at the mouth. Edging closer to the unprotected woman, Tristian tried to keep a close watch on both the lycan and on Terra, who continued to fight to restrain the vampyr. But beads of sweat were forming along Terra's brow and temples, the muscles along her forearms straining to hold the magic. Strands of the vines loosened and split as the vampyr fought against them. Tristian noticed too. He surveyed the situation for a moment too long, distracted by Terra, and the lycan lunged, throwing the entire weight of his hulking body against Tristian's. The two smashed into the ground.

The woman's eyes had cleared, and she now seemed partially aware of the events. She screamed in terror. But Wilder couldn't hear it, and he was sure no one else could either—the sound drowned out by the raging festivities along the main road. In a haze, Wilder wondered why no one could see everything happening right in front of them. Why no one was coming to help.

Tristian and the lycan rolled across the cobblestones, vying for control. Taking on significant injuries, Tristian's flawless countenance grew masked in pain. The wolfman extended his claws and broad, silver soaked slashes drug across Tristian's chest. But Tristian remained unbendable, maneuvering atop the lycan and pinning the wolf beneath him. Wrapping his hands around the rogue's throat, his palms glowed red, shots of flame licking Tristian's fingers. As Wilder watched, arcing swaths of flame bloomed from Tristian's back, lighting the darkened alley, and Wilder's mouth fell open at the display. The rogue's body writhed beneath the burning, his mouth opening in a silent scream.

Across the way, Terra's arms shuddered, and the vampyr rogue ripped free of her snare. Bounding with inhuman speed toward the screaming woman, he dodged the small balls of flame Terra shot his way. But then she faltered, and Wilder saw the panic on Terra's face as she glanced toward the woman, worry rising she might hit her. Taking advantage of her hesitation, the vampyr yanked the woman into his clutches. He unsheathed a shining blade from his belt and held it across her throat.

Terra's breath caught and she lifted her hands in surrender, stopping her advances completely. Tristian remained in the alleyway beyond, his wings still spread behind him as he kept the struggling lycan at bay. But his expression grew drained as the battle tore on, the light from his flaming wings flickering as he lost more and more blood. He glanced up, his eyes full of worry as he remained powerless to intervene with the vampyr.

Wilder's own panic had grown to an uncomfortable boil, rippling and crackling through his bones.

Olivia champed at the bit. "I have to go in. There's no other way."

"No," Wilder said. He grabbed a hold of Liv's arm, but he had no idea where the words were coming from. "You're no good to them if you're hurt, too."

A look of torn agreement and disbelief crossed her features. A moment later, Tristian collapsed into a small pool of thick, metallic silver, the flames extinguished, the motionless body of the rogue lying next to him. The vampyr said something to Terra, his moonlit eyes glinting. Blood drained from her face as she seemed to realize how hopeless the situation had become. He continued to hold the gleaming blade along the woman's skin, and a small trickle of blood pooled at the base of her neck, soaking the collar of her shirt.

A familiar thrum coursed through Wilder as something from deep within took complete control. A presence altogether separate, but altogether a part of him. Fierce protection for his new friends, and for the defenseless human woman, swelled in his chest. Before he knew what was happening, a jolt careened through his blood, and the sky above the fray cracked open. A single, perfect lightning bolt hit the vampyr head on, scorching the rogue's body to a burnt cinder, but leaving the woman untouched.

The blade at her neck clattered to the floor as a rumbling crash of thunder followed. The charred body of the vampyr crumpled to the ground. Releasing a gasp, Wilder wobbled on his feet, his vision going blurry, before he collapsed to his knees with exhaustion. Through the buzzing in his ears, Wilder heard the crowds on the main street scream at the sound of the thunder, the shattering glass from the restaurant windows, and the breaking storm. A whisper echoed through him, almost inaudible under the mounting chaos.

Prepare. He's coming.

Wilder shook his head, unsure if he had heard the voice, or if it was just his bleary confusion. Within moments, the streets emptied; the crowd taking shelter in the bars, eateries, and shops. The surge in Wilder's blood quelled to a low hum. The voice didn't return. Olivia stared at him, her eyes widening in something like awe.

"Are you okay?" she asked, worry marking her tone as she inspected his face.

A cold sweat had broken out across his forehead and cheeks, and he swerved on his knees, placing his palms on the cobblestones for balance. "I think so," Wilder said, the buzzing in his ears lessening as the world came into focus. After another moment to catch his breath, Wilder rose to his feet, nodded at her once, and they dashed into the alleyway.

Terra had bolted toward the woman when the vampyr had collapsed, and Wilder heard her whispering, assuring her everything would be alright. Reaching Harry, Liv knelt down, pulling his head into her lap and smoothing his hair. As he woke, she helped him rise and steady himself. He rubbed at his head, his face contorting with pain. Tristian, his destroyed shirt soaked in drying silver, rolled his quivering body onto all fours and groaned. Peering up to make sure the fight had subsided, he forced himself to kneel and inspected his injuries. The gashes along his body no longer oozed blood, and were shining instead with raw skin in the streetlight.

Harry hobbled over to the woman. She cried out in a whispered, pleading panic, tears streaming down her face. "Please don't hurt me," she begged. "I have money. I promise, you can take whatever you want."

But Harry only knelt down and stared into the depths of her brimming hazel eyes. "You won't remember a thing. Go into the restaurant next door, call a friend, and have them take you home." The sound of his voice was gentle as he smiled at her like an old friend. "And don't go out partying by yourself ever again."

The woman calmed—her gasping breaths evening and her tears fading to a subtle sniffle. She nodded, her eyes once again shadowed in a daze. Harry bit his wrist and dropped a bead of his blood into her mouth. The cut on her neck stitched together. After guiding her to the main street, he and Liv watched her as she toddled into the nearest restaurant.

At the back of the alley, Tristian and Terra dragged the fallen rogues bodies toward the still pulsing portal. Tristian paused and looked into the dark deep gateway, his hands balling into fists, as if contemplating running inside. Seeming to resolve against it, he booted the bodies into the shimmering dark. The shimmer faded, and they watched as a blank, concrete wall took its place.

CHAPTER NINE

"Good job, kid." Tristian clapped Wilder's back as they limped toward the Council House. Wilder stumbled but regained his balance. Olivia had told them what had happened while Tristian and Harry were knocked out before she and Terra had retreated a few paces behind them. Wilder could have sworn Tristian now looked at him with some semblance of pride, a subtle grin inching across his indifferent features.

The storm had dissipated, the crowds in the bars and restaurants carrying on with their evenings.

"I don't understand," Wilder said. "Why did I collapse like that after what I did?" Wilder was still piecing together *how* he had made that lightning hit the rogue, but he knew in his gut it hadn't had anything to do with him.

"You used too much power at once," Tristian explained. "And you don't have enough practice with how to use it. Though I have no idea how you accessed that much to begin with."

"But it didn't feel like me. It felt like something, someone, else," Wilder said, his brow knitting.

Tristian peered at him, skepticism marking his own features. "Be careful with that. With what you let in. When you reach your end, when you overuse your magic, there's always something else waiting to fill the gap."

Wilder nodded. His whole body felt ripped to shreds by the power that had burned through him. "Why did that even happen in the first place? Who were those guys?"

"Markus's rogues," Tristian said, rubbing at his still healing chest. "They've been pretty active in the city lately. All those kidnappings you've seen on the news—that's all him. And it's not just here that it's happening. But we don't think the humans have realized how widespread this is. The ones around here still think it's some serial killer."

"But why?" Wilder asked. "Who's Markus, and why's he doing it?"

"Remember when I mentioned the war starting because of the royal line?" Tristian said. "Markus is why. He's pissed his father didn't name him as heir. Now he's taking it out on the Eadar, and on the humans."

"But why the humans?" Wilder asked. "It's not like they were involved in the decision. They don't even know about you all."

"It's all about revenge," Harry added while Tristian eyed each dark corner along their path. "Markus blames them for a lot of what's happened to our people. It's a hatred that goes back farther than just this war. This is his retribution."

A chill ran down Wilder's spine. He knew Markus had been kidnapping fae. But humans too? "What's he doing with them?"

Glancing at each other, uncomfortable expressions shadowed Tristian and Harry's features. Wilder heard a sniffle behind him. Olivia had been much more troubled by the evening than the others. After ensuring everyone was okay, she had withdrawn from the conversation, lost in thought, a glisten collecting along her lashes. Terra strode next to her in silence, her arm wrapped around her friend.

"He's murdering them," Harry finally said, his voice so low only Wilder and Tristian could hear. "And he isn't quick about it. He makes them suffer." He glanced at Terra and Olivia. "I won't go into detail, not right now, but it's not pretty."

"How do you know?" Wilder asked. "Is there a way to get to them? To help them?"

"No. There's no way in. Not to where he's keeping them," Tristian said, a savage darkness to his words. "And we know because the rogues have dumped some of the bodies. Not all of them. Just enough to remind us what he's capable of. Each one comes back drained of blood and so disfigured they're unrecognizable. It's sickening."

Wilder shuddered. He couldn't imagine what their grieving families were going through. They'd never see their loved ones again, always seeking a closure that would never come.

Thinking through everything that had just happened, Wilder felt woefully unprepared for the world he now found himself in. It was one thing to know a war was going on. It was another thing to witness it coming to life right in front of him. But something gnawed at him. Something the Magi had said earlier.

"There will come a time when the Magick will ask you to make a decision, and likely when you are least expecting it."

Was tonight that moment? Was the Magíck, or whatever these people claimed existed, asking him to join some great cosmic fight? Was this what he wanted for himself—probable death at the hands of some murderous maniac and his cronies?

Wilder remembered the woman, her eyes pleading, unaware of how close she had come to a long suffering and brutal death. He didn't want to imagine what would have happened if they hadn't intervened.

★★★

They arrived at the Council House to find Magi Maynestream and another tall, skinny man Wilder didn't recognize waiting in the parlor. The man's pale skin, similar to Harry's, was offset by pinkened cheeks under thin cheekbones. His pointed face framed a high, discerning brow, and deep-set russet eyes that reminded Wilder of a dark forest.

A distressed squawk announced their entrance, and a white bird swooped from atop a bookshelf, its frantic wings flapping in Terra's face.

"Hennie! Calm down! It's okay!" Terra tried to grab her owl's manic body. Landing with all her strength on to Terra's wrist, Hennie's talons wrapped around it, narrowly avoiding slicing her skin. Her beak clamped onto her finger, hard enough to look like it hurt, but not enough to draw blood.

"I'm so sorry," Terra said as the bird continued to glare, its beady eyes glinting. "I'm okay, I promise." Hennie must have decided the slight worth forgiving, because she released her taloned grip, hopped onto Terra's shoulder, and nuzzled into her neck. Resting her cheek on Hennie's ruffled head, Terra rubbed her stomach.

The man Wilder didn't recognize rushed to Harry and Olivia before gripping Harry's shoulders. "Are you two alright?" he asked, concern cracking his even tone. They nodded, but Olivia's eyes brimmed.

As Terra and Olivia settled on a couch, Hennie hopped onto its back. Tristian, the most collected of the group, recounted the night's events to the two men, including Wilder's unexpected contribution.

The expression on the new man's face shifted from attentive to concerned, two lines appearing between his brows. "This is the second kidnapping this week," he said, rubbing his chin. "They're escalating. And quickly. We're seeing the same patterns in other regions as well."

"What're you thinking, Rickard?" the Magi asked him.

Rickard's lips thinned. "We've been under the impression these kidnappings are Markus's revenge on the humans for what happened during the Dirge."

"Of course they are," Tristian argued. "Now he's got the army he needs to retaliate. And to fight us for trying to stop him. He's already taken the throne. Why wouldn't he take the humans too? It's as simple as that."

"The Dirge?" Wilder asked, peering between the two of them.

"It was a mass plague that crippled the Céad years ago. Markus is convinced the humans caused it." Rickard turned back to Tristian. "But I'm not so sure it's that simple anymore," Rickard said. "Given the circumstances, the intensity of the killings, I wonder if there's something darker at hand. Something more than just retribution."

"What do you mean?" Terra asked, lifting her brow at the suggestion.

"I don't know yet," Rickard said. "But something feels off. Something I can't quite put my finger on. Something perhaps connected to the stones…"

The stones? What're the stones?

Shaking his head, as if to clear it, Rickard returned to the group. "Thoughts for another night, I think. Either way, we're happy you're all alright. We've already sent word to Teír. Your parents," he added, looking to Tristian and Terra, "should be on their way home within the week."

Terra nodded, but Tristian's whole body tensed.

"I'm not a child, Rickard. I'm nineteen. More than old enough to handle myself. They don't need to come back early. They're of much better use at Court than here."

Rickard studied him, his expression kind but stern. "Unfortunately, I have to disagree with you, Tristian. Instead of alerting us immediately to the situation, you *all* deliberately put yourselves, and those with no battle experience," he glanced at Wilder, "in harm's way."

Harry stared at the ground, but Tristian met Rickard's even gaze with his own fire. Clenching his fists, his knuckles turned white, and he looked ready to leap back into battle.

"There wasn't any time—"

"A decision," Rickard said, shutting down Tristian's defense, "that is not the mark of a young man claiming to be old enough to *handle himself*. Any of you could have died. Or could have been taken into Lus Halla to a fate far worse. And you should know, better than anyone, we couldn't have gone after you." Tristian flinched at his assessment.

Rickard continued. "If you truly want to serve in the Fae Army, Snow, you'll need to start considering the larger picture. You'll need to make decisions for the good of the entire battalion. You cannot allow yourself to be taken in by the rush of battle. I want to be *very* clear just how lucky you are to be alive right now."

Tristian glowered, fury lighting behind the icy blue of his glare. Without another word, he stalked from the room. Rickard freed a heavy sigh as he watched him leave, then fixed his attention on the rest of the group.

"The same goes for all of you," Rickard said in the same unwavering resolve, his hands clasped behind him. "You're lucky to be alive. From here on out, you'll need to be more careful leaving the Council House. There's no telling why the kidnappings are picking up this close, but we can't take any chances. No more leaving without the protection of irids, and no more chasing down rogues. Regardless of what you see."

They each nodded, their heads hung in shame. Wilder inspected the dark whirls within the floorboards.

"As for you, Mr. Ansley," Rickard turned to him. "I believe we have more to discuss. Forgive me for not introducing myself sooner. My name is Rickard Hemming; New Orleans Ambassador for the Magistrie."

Wilder nodded in greeting, but was taken aback. Had he done something wrong? Well, other than what they had already been reprimanded for?

"It's clear your powers are presenting themselves, and have been for some time," Rickard said. "I had planned to have this conversation to-morrow morning, but after this evening's *adventures*—now seems as good a time as any." He cleared his throat. "You have some options. There are several schools across the Eadar you could attend that would help you hone your skills. Alternatively, you may opt to live with your kind. You could learn more about them. Perhaps become an apprentice in a trade, or work with a tutor. Or, if you'd prefer, you may return to your life among the humans." He said all of this with frank propriety, as if he shared this same spiel regularly. "It's been an eventful evening, so the Council understands if you're unable to decide right now. But it is something you should think over in the coming days."

Wilder glanced at the others, deliberating. Terra made a good show of appearing unattached to his response, drawing her lips into a tight line. But a hint of curiosity betrayed her as she studied his expression. Twelve hours ago, Wilder would have opted for the latter of the options. No part of him had wanted anything to do with this increasingly dangerous place. But after this evening, he felt a stirring in him he couldn't still. A new school could be interesting; somewhere he didn't feel like the weird one. Where he could learn to control whatever was happening to him. But after tonight, the idea of leaving them—these unbelievable strangers becoming friends, these people that didn't treat him like something to just tolerate—felt *off*.

"Can I stay?" Wilder asked in a rush. "Here? Can I learn whatever I need to learn with you all?" Wilder glanced at Terra, her withdrawn features shifting to surprise.

Rickard's eyes widened, but he remained otherwise congenial. "Well, of course." Rickard turned to Magi Maynestream in as much surprise. "We had thought you had little interest in staying, but we'd be happy to work with you here, if that's what you'd prefer."

Olivia and Terra beamed, and Harry let out a *whoop*, coming to pat Wilder's back. Wilder peered at Magi Maynestream. The man's off-kilter stare inspected Wilder before lighting with a grandfatherly warmth, an approving smile dimpling his cheeks.

"Yes, very good," Rickard agreed, exhaustion weighing his eyelids. "Well, the hour is late, and as of a moment ago, you will all have a busy day of training ahead of you. I advise you to get a good night's sleep."

He gave them a wane smile, clapped Harry on the shoulder, and left the room with Magi Maynestream.

"Looks like we're keeping the Summer!" Harry threw his arm around Wilder's shoulder. "Don't worry, kid. I'll take it easy on you." A mischievous glint sharpened his wide-set gaze. "Alright. G'night, guys. And see *you* in the morning." Giving Wilder a lighthearted shove, he winked at Olivia and exited the room.

Exhaustion hit Wilder like a freight train, and the remaining trio padded upstairs. With a brief wave at Wilder and Olivia, her stare flashing between the two of them, Terra turned down her own hallway without another word.

"You doing okay?" Wilder asked Olivia as they walked further down the hall.

"Yeah," she said, her voice low and steady. She still seemed pretty shaken up. "It was just a lot to handle tonight. But I'm glad you were there with us. And I'm glad you're staying." Her thick voice sounded so unlike her usual cheery lilt. As they reached her door, she peered up at him, her eyes twinkling a golden caramel in the lamplight.

Wilder ruffled an errant hand through his hair. "Um, thanks. Yeah, I'm excited, actually." He was finally letting himself wonder what might happen over the next few days, months, or even years. Finally allowing himself to consider the possibility of staying in one place long enough to call it home.

"Well, I'm right here." Olivia gestured to the door, as if expecting him to say something more. When he didn't, she added, "I'll see you tomorrow?" The words sounded laced with a deeper expectation than the question let on.

"Um, sure." Wilder said, shrugging. "Goodnight then."

Wilder ambled down the hall toward his own suite. Yawning, he jammed his hands into his jacket pockets, his eyes fixed ahead. His mind altogether elsewhere, he barely registered Olivia watching him walk away.

CHAPTER TEN
Terra

A muffled knock sounded at Terra's door, as if the person on the other side hesitated—either at waking her, or at choosing to be there altogether. Rolling over, Terra checked her clock. The dim red analog glow showed almost two in the morning. It didn't matter much. She hadn't been able to fall asleep anyway. Adrenaline still coursed through her from the fight, and her mind had been wavering between waking and dreaming for the last four hours.

Terra whipped her covers from her bare legs and padded across the room. Grabbing the doorknob, she paused, resting her forehead against the cold wood, preparing herself for what lay on the other side. Opening the door, she winced at the light streaming in from the hallway, its stinging broken only by Tristian's towering frame.

Terra groaned, groggy with half-sleep. "What?" she asked, not caring to suppress her snap as she opened the door just wide enough for him to come inside.

"Good morning to you too, sunshine." Raising his eyebrows, Tristian shouldered past. She closed the door behind him—mostly to block out the offensive light. "Why so charming?" he asked.

Terra glared at him, but she couldn't be sure he saw it. They stood in a dim darkness, the only light the faint glow from the streetlamps outside her window. She didn't have the energy for his teasing or games tonight. "You would be too if you had just gotten woken up well before dawn for no good reason."

Striding further into the room, familiar with the space, Tristian reclined against her far wall, keeping his distance. She could give him some credit for that, at least. He tucked his hands behind him, as if to show her he meant no harm. His glacial eyes, pinpricks of starlight in the dark, searched what he could make out of her features.

"You weren't sleeping," he finally said, his tone too self-assured for her to argue with, though she'd be damned if she didn't try. Before she could, he added, "I just came to check on you." His gaze shifted to a warm fire, as comforting as sitting at the foot of a blazing hearth while snow blankets the world outside. "Are you okay?"

A better woman would have melted, but Terra would have none of it. "You couldn't check on me at a normal hour like everyone else?" she asked, ignoring his question and refusing to let go of her challenging tone despite his uncharacteristic warmth. Returning to the edge of her bed, she sat down and wished Liv could see him like this. Just so she'd believe her—believe this side of him *did exist*, even if it was fleeting and rare.

But Terra knew why Tristian waited until now, until everyone else was asleep, to check on her. Even if he'd never admit to it. He didn't want anyone knowing, didn't want to make his concern for her obvious. Terra knew a part of him didn't want that information getting back to his father, didn't want to deal with the mess that would cause—within the Council, within his family. Within hers. But the other part of him—she knew that's why he was really here in the first place. Tristian had a heart of rebellion, and she was his.

Tristian ignored her question, taking a step closer to her before repeating himself. "Terr. Are you okay? It looked like that spell took a lot out of you." He paused, as if realizing it might be better to keep his distance.

Terra sighed, too tired to fight him. "Yeah, I'm okay." She rubbed her eyes, the lids sore from the bone-deep exhaustion permeating her every inch. Even her voice sounded hollow. "I had a few irids on me, but I depleted them. I was running on fumes near the end. I saw you collapse and knew I couldn't. But I got close, Tristian. We got really lucky with Wilder stepping in when he did."

A look crossed Tristan's features, but before Terra could place it, it had disappeared.

"Yeah, lucky…" he grumbled, shoving his hands into his pockets, his jaw clenching at the mention of Wilder's name.

"Oh, don't start, Tristian. He's seems like a perfectly okay guy. He can't help his Season. And it's not like he was raised by them. You can't seriously hold that against him."

Tristian's eyes narrowed, his body stock-still. "I see no reason why I shouldn't. Summers are all the same. It's in their blood. I'll believe he's different, decent, when he proves it." His clipped tone marked the end of his input on the subject.

"He can't prove it if you don't give him a chance," Terra challenged again.

Tristian didn't respond. Instead, he paced to the front door, needing to do something with his body. The gesture was familiar. Terra had seen him do it a thousand times, always when his anxiety ramped up.

"I just can't believe he called our parents back—like they're going to help at all," Tristian said. "What was Rickard thinking?"

Terra swallowed, her gaze trailing Tristian as he paced back to the wall. "Probably that we got attacked, and haven't been in a long time. It's getting worse Tristian. You have to see that."

As much as Terra also wished her parents would stay in Teír, she agreed with Rickard's decision. What had happened tonight—there was no getting around it. Things in New Orleans were intensifying. Fast. The rogues had never attacked so brashly before, right in plain sight. And with the Shroud thinning, there was no telling who saw what. "He hardly had a choice. They *should* come back. Reconvene. Maybe they'll know something we don't."

Pacing to the door, Tristian's steps were a measured beat, almost lulling Terra to sleep. Gods, she was so tired.

"I doubt that," Tristian scoffed. "It's just unnecessary. It's not like the rogues attacked the Council House. They're not doing anything new. We just happened to catch them in the act. We handled it. The last thing I need is for my dad to come in questioning everything."

And there it was.

Tristian's strides between the door and wall had reached a frantic pace. Terra's face warmed, beginning to get annoyed by his continued presence, and beginning to lock in on his real intention for being there so late. "Listen Tristian. As much as I love talking about your dear old dad, shouldn't you be off talking to Kallie or whatever her name is?"

Tristian stopped short, halfway between the door and the wall. "What does Kallie have to do with anything?" Looking at Terra, the warmth in his eyes faded to a cold glower.

"What do *I*?" Lifting her hands in exasperation, Terra's voice cracked with exhaustion. At least she hoped that's what it was. "Why are you *here*, Tristian?"

Tristian took a measured step closer, just enough for the outside lamps to cast their glow over his worn features. The deep circles beneath his eyes rivaled her own, evidence he hadn't gotten a minute of sleep that night either. He looked too old for nineteen. Life had already begun to steal his youth, and Terra's heart did melt then. Just a little.

"Don't be like that, Terra," he said, his voice slowing, lowering. His tone grew as weary as hers, as if this topic was the last thing he wanted to talk about. "This isn't about any of that. She's not you. You've always been more than whatever goes on with those girls."

"What does that even mean, Tristian?" Terra's voice rose an octave, and Tristian threw a fleeting glance at the door, as if someone were listening on the other side. Terra huffed in disbelief. "See, this is what I'm talking about. At the end of the day, you're only here because it'll piss off your dad if he knew, and you're only here *now,* in the middle of the night, because you're scared he'll find out. It's emotional whiplash. As much as you try to hide it, I was just a rebellious phase for you. And on nights like tonight, I still am. I'm so tired, Tristian. I can't do the back and forth anymore. You care, and then you don't, and only when it's most convenient for you."

Tristian's mouth fell open, his eyes hardening to silver steel. "Of course I care. I never stopped caring." His voice rose from a whisper to his usual firm tone. As if her calling him out had suddenly made him less wary about who might hear them. As if trying to prove her wrong. "How can you believe that, Terra?"

"It shocks me that you don't." Terra shrugged, her own voice, barely a whisper, cracking once again. Pressure built behind her steady stare, and she wasn't sure if she was just tired or about to fall completely apart. If she'd had the brain power to accept it, she'd probably admit it was a little of both. "*You* ended things, Tristian. Can you please just let it stay that way? You can't keep coming here like this."

Tristian swallowed, the hard lines of his face going slack, his icy blues softening to a temperance she rarely saw. Stepping forward a few more steps, he knelt right in front of her, bringing his gaze to her own.

"Terra, I just…" he paused, as if *she* were the one tearing *his* heart out. "You're my *friend.* Before anything else. And you know me better than anyone. Despite everything, in spite of what happened with us—I don't know. Sometimes you're just… the only place I know I can go." He pulled her hand into his, his jaw gripped iron-tight once again, as if preparing for the worst.

Terra's mouth popped open, shocked at his display of vulnerability. Silence as wide as the night filled the space between them until she finally cleared her throat.

"Okay," Terra said, heaving a breath. His eyes widened a fraction, a childlike hope in his gaze, as if she had offered him the moon. "You've got an hour. Then I really do need to sleep."

Part Two

CHAPTER ELEVEN

A crash sounded through Wilder's room, and he woke with a start. Shooting upright, Wilder glimpsed Harry standing in his doorway, his silhouette framed by the hallway light.

Bounding in, Harry looked far more eager than Wilder felt. "It's training day! Get up, buttercup! We're getting breakfast, then I'm putting you to work."

Blurry eyed and not at all ready for the day, Wilder collapsed back down and groaned into his pillow. His sheets were still damp from the cold sweat coating his skin. Wilder didn't usually dream, but last night had been an unfortunate exception.

He remembered red. Lots of red.

Tortured human faces danced around a blazing fire as other, more menacing faces, marked by their moonlit eyes and array of elongated teeth or ears, jeered at the performers. Women and men alike were flung over shoulders and carried—screaming and fighting pitifully for their lives—into the darkened recesses of his mind.

A lean man with cruel, amber eyes watched it all from a throne draped in dead flowers, sneering in delight at the scene.

Wilder tried to clear the images from his mind. The events of the night before must have gotten to him. Peering outside, he saw the sun peeking above the abbey's roofline. He untangled himself from the bedding and glanced up to find Harry inspecting him, his nose scrunched.

"Yeah. Maybe shower first. You look rough."

★★★

Twenty minutes later, they strode into what Harry called the sun-room. The enclosure stood next to the garden, its white aluminum frame encased entirely in transparent glass panels, exposing Wilder and Harry to a clear view of the world outside. The March sun reached above the eastern horizon, lighting the start of another flawless day as it bore down from beyond the ramparts in all its glory.

The room's roof appeared constructed of various stained glass scenes, displaying what Wilder assumed must be the Fae at the height of their reign, before whatever Fall the Magi had mentioned. At the center of the ceiling, a large yellow dragon engraved with veins of metallic gold filled the panel, his wings outstretched in front of a colossal, snow-capped mountain. Mounted on the dragon's back was a small fae warrior. He gripped the winged pommel of an elongated sword, raising it above his head in a war cry.

"Wait. Are there dragons in the Eadar?" Wilder asked Harry, his eyes widening as he stared at the image. He figured nothing would surprise him at this point.

Harry joined him. "No," he said, his gaze trailing upward. "*If* they existed at all, they don't anymore. The few that believe they existed say the Magíck took them away as punishment for the Fae's pride. For believing that because only they could ride the dragons, they were somehow gods. The dragons are just a metaphor, though. Just a representation of a greater power the Fae once had, but don't have anymore. And a symbol of the peace the Earth knew before the Shroud." Harry studied the dragon for a moment longer before strolling away.

"Interesting analogy," Wilder said, still eyeing the depiction. "The people that believe they existed; where do they think the dragons all went?" He tore his stare from the golden dragon and followed Harry to a white wicker patio table ladened with breakfast.

"They don't really say." Harry shrugged, piling a plate high with food. "But they do believe we still have some of their eggs."

Wilder perked up, his brow lifting.

"It's nothing like that," Harry said, chuckling and waving his hand to stop Wilder's line of thinking. "They're made of stone. They're not eggs at all. They're just old rocks kept in a vault somewhere over in Teír. Talismans made by some old mage. Our legends say one day the Magíck will forgive the Céad for the folly that caused the Fall. That they might let 'the dragons' return." He lifted his fingers in air quotes. "They keep the 'eggs' as some kind of homage to that hope. That the Magíck will restore the peace and power it took from us. But it's just an old-wives' tale. Given the current state of things, I kind of doubt the Magíck has any intention of forgiving us anytime soon." Harry smiled, attempting to make a joke of it, but it didn't reach his eyes.

For breakfast, James had prepared soft-boiled eggs, toast, and bacon, kindly leaving the salt off of Wilder's plate.

"Bad dream last night?" Harry asked Wilder, lifting his low brow as he buttered his toast. "You looked rough this morning."

"Definitely not great," Wilder said, the screams still echoing in his ears. "Is that normal? When Céad start figuring out who they are? Vivid dreams? I've never really dreamt before. At least, not that I can remember. Not 'til coming here."

"Can't say I've heard anything about it," Harry offered. "But my guess is Terra might know. She's good at that kind of stuff."

"What kind of stuff?" Wilder asked. He rubbed at his neck, flattening the hair standing on end at the mention of her. Yet another thing he couldn't understand, but he needed to keep himself in check. Things were getting complicated enough without *that* distraction.

"Just knowing things. She's smart. Quick as a whip. She gets it from her dad. I'm sure she'd know all about dreaming."

"Gotcha," Wilder mumbled, ignoring the image of green eyes flashing across his mind. He watched Harry shovel some eggs into his mouth. "Sorry if this is a weird question. But, how can you eat that?"

"What do you mean?" Harry asked between mouthfuls of eggs and bacon. "The same way you do." He gestured to Wilder's plate. "And because I'm hungry. What? Are you a vegetarian or something? I'll take your bacon if you don't want it."

"No, I mean, aren't you a 'vampyr'? Aren't you just supposed to drink blood or something?" Wilder asked, remembering the old mythologies he had read as a kid.

"Oh!" Harry laughed, his expression lighting as he brushed the crumbs from his hands. "Well, yeah. We do drink blood, but that satisfies a different hunger than this." He held up his toast, and an emerald ring on his right hand glinted handsomely in the sunlight, creating green refractions across the table. Wilder could have sworn he saw something move within it.

"It's hard to explain. I crave blood just as much as human food. Sometimes even more. But they do different things for me. It's like, the food runs the more human side of my body, and the blood runs the magic. But the two are linked. If I don't drink blood, after a while my whole body shuts down, and no amount of regular food helps that."

"I see," Wilder said, munching on his toast.

"You'll realize a lot of what you've heard in your human stories have a *little* truth to them, but are also more than a little off. They're loose interpretations of the Eadar from people who usually have no idea what they're talking about. Plus, the Magistrie has a way of redirecting anyone spouting-off more than the humans should know. Humans can easily be made to forget. And if Céad get caught sharing…" Harry 'tsk'ed under his breath.

"So, what's true, then?" Wilder asked. "And what's not? Do vampyrs attack humans? Are you repelled by garlic? Do you have a reflection?" Wilder checked if there was a mirror nearby.

Harry chuckled. "The bit about vampyrs attacking humans is complicated. We were created to, yeah. But I don't. I was taught not to. I do drink human blood. Most vampyrs outside of Teír, the Céad's homeland, do. But Rickard taught me to control myself. How to do it without hurting people. Besides a few mistakes when I was younger, I stick to blood bags we've nicked from local clinics or hospitals. I could technically drink animal blood, but it's not as effective. I'd lose the full scope of my magic. But there are a lot of vamps that choose that life. As for garlic, I hate it. Kind of like your thing about salt. But I can eat it just fine. And yes, I've got a completely normal reflection. The only thing I have to watch out for is the sun. But that's been taken care of." He held up the wrought-iron emerald ring.

"What's that?" Wilder asked, noting the intricate patterns along the band.

"Just a ring," Harry explained. "But Terra's mom Sofia spelled it to protect me so I can walk in the sun like anyone else."

Wilder took a breath, slouching in his chair. How much of what he had grown up thinking were just stories, were actually real?

"Don't worry," Harry reassured him. "You'll get the hang of it. It just takes time."

Chapter Twelve

After breakfast, Wilder followed Harry through a side door into the garden. The air felt alive with the scent of rich magnolias and jasmine touched with morning dew.

"This morning we'll be working on the ins and outs of compelling," Harry said, bringing them to the shaded center of the garden. "You witnessed the method in action last night between the rogue and the woman. But it was used with ill intent. What I did with her afterwards was also compelling, but to render aid rather than harm. Every ability a Céad has, in itself, is never harmful or hurtful. It's the heart behind its use that makes them dangerous. But," he countered, a wariness settling over his pale features, "you'd be surprised how quickly someone can justify crossing the line. So be careful with all of this. It's easy to get carried away." He gave Wilder a half smile before continuing.

"Only vampyrs and some fae can compel, and typically, only humans can be compelled. With some exceptions." He gave Wilder a look that made him wonder what he meant by that. "*Most* Céad have enough magic to naturally protect themselves from another Céad's compellation. But given how new you are to this, and how inconsistent your magic is, I suspect that's not the case for you." Harry gave him an apologetic look, and uneasiness mounted in Wilder's gut.

"I hate to break it to you, but today isn't about you learning how to compel. You're Fairn, and they just can't do it. It's the Watern that have the true skill, even better than vampyrs. Right now, our biggest concern is your lack of access to magic, which makes you susceptible to *being* compelled. Lucky for us, it's a great way to teach you what it feels like."

But Wilder didn't feel lucky at all. "So, what? You're just going to strip my free will, and I'm supposed to just *let* you?"

"Oh, by all means, do try to defend yourself," Harry said, laughing. His genuine grin put Wilder slightly at ease, despite the deteriorating situation. "After all, that's what you're here to learn. In the long run, any inability to protect yourself will become a liability. Especially if you're sticking around here. So until you show enough progress, we'll work on it."

Harry noticed Wilder's resignation and added, "The good thing is, every type of magic you practice brings you closer to your natural access, so I'm sure it won't take long at all."

"Yeah, I get it," Wilder said. Last night had been an obvious lesson in how unprepared he was—every new encounter a roaring reminder of how little he understood. If letting Harry control his mind would bring him closer to whatever powers he supposedly had, he figured it was worth a shot.

"I'm down for anything that keeps me alive, I guess." Wilder watched a finch flit along the cracked path, pecking at the earth for bugs, and he felt rather like one of those beetles, about to get eaten alive.

"That's the spirit." Harry grinned and punched his shoulder, but it didn't do much to ease the rest of Wilder's nerves. "Now stand still. I'm going to show you how it's done."

Harry locked eyes with Wilder. They were a raging green—a rain forest teeming with animalistic life—and Wilder found himself lost in them, his body melting into the rush of canopied trees. Harry was speaking again, but he couldn't hear him through the sheaths of light washing over him. It felt like floating on liquid diamonds, and Wilder forgot to care about anything but the pulsing joy now surging through him. But something Harry was saying seemed really important. Life or death important. And he knew it was absolutely vital he pay rapt attention, or else the light might go out. And he couldn't let that happen.

In his bones, Wilder felt Harry instruct him to jump onto the concrete bench next to them. Yes. He really needed to do that, and the liquid flow of the diamond light guided him there. Heeding its call, Wilder jumped, settling into the comfort of the radiant flow once more.

For a moment, though, he felt oddly disconnected from his body. The diamond light flickered, and a whisper of gold hummed against his blood, calling out to him. Wilder remembered he had forgotten something, like he needed to do something important, something other than what Harry wanted. But he just couldn't bring himself to care what it might be.

All of a sudden, the light snapped, and Wilder jarringly reentered reality. The flow trickled away, leaving him drained and dizzy. Standing awkwardly on the bench, he had only a vague inkling of how he had gotten there. Within seconds, the dream of jungles and diamonds disappeared into his dazed mind. Staring down at Harry, Wilder struggled to recall what had happened.

"What the hell…" he whispered, inspecting the garden as if the flowers and bushes would help him make sense of the last few minutes. "What happened?"

"I compelled you." Harry said, his broad smile crinkling his eyes. Clasping his hands behind him, he peered up at Wilder on the bench. "And it took a lot to not make you dance around like a monkey, too. You're welcome."

"Yeah… Thanks for that," Wilder said, still grasping at reality. He stepped precariously off the bench and back onto the pathway, his head spinning at a nauseating pace. He realized with a tinge of annoyance that even if Harry *had* made him dance like a monkey, he wouldn't have remembered it, anyway.

"Now you know what it feels like," Harry said. "I won't push you much farther today. It's difficult to be continuously compelled. The longer it's in place, the harder it is to come back. And it'll drain me as well. But we'll keep working on it. At some point, you'll start recognizing what's happening and fight against it."

Wilder sat down again, his head in his hands, struggling to regain his bearings. Harry left the path and strode into the garden, returning to offer him an apple from a nearby grove.

"Food helps. It's grounding," Harry said.

Accepting it, Wilder took a bite. The sweet juices tasted more real than anything he had ever eaten. He heaved a sigh. The garden had finally stopped spinning and he no longer felt like throwing up whenever he opened his mouth. Wilder looked at Harry. "Hey, I had been meaning to ask. Who was that guy from last night? Rickard?"

"Ah, yeah. Rickard's my sire. He turned me when I was seven. But he's more like a dad than anything else. He's kind of the same with Liv, too. She came here around the same time, and he's watched over us ever since."

"You were turned when you were *seven*?" Wilder asked, confused. "Aren't you supposed to stay the same age? Immortal and unchanging and all that?"

Harry shook his head. "Another loose interpretation for you. Vampyrs aren't the undead we've been made out to be. We grow old and die just like anyone else, but at a pace more like the other Céad. We age roughly the same way: similar to humans for the first twenty-five years—until we reach maturity. Then our aging slows. Every Céad can easily live more than a hundred years. And most a lot longer than that. None of us are really immortal, but we live long enough for it to seem that way."

"So, what happened to you? You were human once?" Wilder studied Harry with a new understanding. Harry had once been more human than Wilder ever had. "Why did Rickard change you? How?"

Harry settled onto the bench while Wilder munched on his apple.

"Vampyrism is like a virus," he said. "It changes our genetic code. But magic is involved in the entire process. To really understand what happened to me, it's important to understand who we are as a species, and who Rickard is. Vampyrs were originally created solely for the purpose of taking human life. Because of that, vampyrs get a bit of a bad rap about being out-of-control, self-serving animals. But Rickard's always had a really good heart, and he wants to change that. He wants to prove the stereotype wrong; to show people that while we can't change how we're made, we can change who we are and what we do with it. He refuses to use his abilities for anything but good. That's why he joined the Council." Harry stared into the trees ahead.

"When I was just a kid, I was dying of a degenerative brain disorder. Rickard frequented hospitals in the area, particularly in the children's ward, where they kept the hopeless cases. He'd pose as a traveling physician, healing anyone he could with his blood. There were a few, though, myself included, that weren't so lucky. The doctors couldn't do anything more for me, and I was past the point vampyr blood could have healed me. I was just waiting to die. I could barely function, let alone understand what was happening.

"Rickard posed as a minister and came to see my parents, to perform my final rites. I remember them crying and holding each other. The minister asked them to leave so he could have a word with me. I was barely lucid. I hadn't been able to speak for months. But I was coherent enough to understand what he was saying. He offered me a second chance at living, but told me life would be different. I wouldn't see my parents again, or any of my friends. I'd have to leave everything behind. I agreed. Even then, I knew regardless of what I chose, I'd never see them again, anyway."

Wilder swallowed his bite of fruit, watching Harry's expression shift as he waded through the memories.

"He drained me of my blood until I was close to death, and everything went black. He told me later that he had used his own blood to heal the wound so the doctors wouldn't know. The monitors didn't show life, but the magic in my veins kept me just alive enough. The doctors believed I had finally succumbed to my illness. He compelled my parents to cremate the remains through his own services, which he offered free of charge, and provided them instead with wood ash. He brought me back here to turn. I died with his blood in my veins, and it was his blood that brought me back to life."

Wilder listened intently. The mechanics of the transition were so similar, and yet so different, from the stories of his childhood.

"I was vicious at first. I even broke out of the Council House one night during my first few months to attack a lady jogging nearby. Just the smell of her…" Harry groaned, remembering. His fists gripped the edge of the bench, his knuckles going white. "It was unbearable. Rickard caught me in time to spare her life. He healed her and compelled her to forget all of it. I still feel awful about that day. The guilt doesn't make it any easier to accept what I did, but it does help curb the craving on the harder days. I'll never forget her face.

"Rickard started training me to control my impulses. He taught me everything about being a vampyr, and the power I had to do good with it. There were definitely times at the beginning that I resented him for changing me. But the longer I've been here, and the more I've met vampyrs without the same upbringing, the more thankful I am to not only be alive, but that it was Rickard who changed me. He's the epitome of the goodness and humanity that still exists within a creature most believe knows nothing but blood-lust and savagery.

"So many Céad still think that way. And most vampyrs believe it about themselves. They weren't as lucky as me. Their sires deserted them, either not realizing they had sired them, or just not caring. Without support, new vampyrs resort to their baser instincts. Unchecked, they don't last very long. They're either killed by another Céad, by the Magistrie, or sent to Rhaenor Gaol, the Eadar's prison, to live out their days in the deep sleep. The Council tries to find them and help them before it gets to that point. Unfortunately, there aren't too many of us because of it. And most live in Teír, one of the only places we Céad can still claim as our own. Its distance from the rest of the world keeps the vampyrs there from the temptation that living beside humans can create."

Wilder considered everything Harry was saying, wondering idly where this 'Teír' was, and if he'd ever get the chance to see it. He wondered if his family, the people he knew in his gut were still out there, were perhaps in this hidden country, far from the prying eyes of the humans.

"Do you ever miss your parents?" Wilder asked. He never expected when he arrived here that he'd meet someone who had lost family like he had. Even though he'd never known his parents, he without a doubt missed them.

"Sometimes." Harry nodded. "I've gone to see them a few times—without them knowing. It took a while, but I think they found peace. And that's all I really wish for them. I miss them, but I'd be endangering them if I got too close. And I have a new family here."

"You mentioned Olivia coming here around the same time. Was she changed the same way?" Wilder asked.

A light flush rose to Harry's pale cheeks, something flashing in his eyes at Olivia's name, but just said, "No. Lycans are only conceived. And her story isn't as sunshine and rainbows as mine, but it's not really mine to share. She still struggles with a lot of it."

Wilder hardly thought of Harry's story as anything close to sunshine and rainbows, but he didn't protest. "You guys are together a lot," he said, letting his unasked question hang in the air.

Harry laughed, but the sound was hollow. "We are, but it's not what you're thinking. Though I can't say I'd mind if it was. Olivia's the most positive person I know. And one of the strongest. She's a breath of fresh air in all of this mess, honestly. But she'd never see me that way. I'm only like a brother to her."

It wasn't lost on Wilder that Harry didn't compare Olivia to like a sister for him. While Wilder didn't have nearly enough experience with females to empathize with the situation, he knew what it felt like to want something that didn't want him back. "I genuinely hope that's not the case," Wilder said, gripping Harry's shoulder.

"Yeah, thanks." Harry ran his fingers through his dark hair. "Anyway, great job today. I thought I actually saw you fight it for a second. We'll work on it more later. Liv's probably waiting for you by now. For your next session."

Standing, they trekked back to the Council House along the cracked garden path, and Wilder hoped whatever came next wouldn't be as exhausting.

Chapter Thirteen

Any illusions Wilder had had for an easy, or at least productive, rest of the morning were dashed when Olivia announced they'd be working on shapeshifting. Barrett came to join them, and the two tag-teamed helping Wilder understand the mechanics of it all.

"Try not to be so hard on yourself," Liv told him, an exasperated sigh escaping him after another failed attempt to change the hue of his skin. "It'll happen, eventually. And I really do think you look slightly more green!"

Wilder wondered if that had less to do with magic and more to do with how nauseous he felt.

"You just have to feel the Magick move through you, and then push it into the places you want to change," Barrett said. Sitting on a bench nearby, he munched on a roll of fresh-baked bread from the kitchen.

"I'll be honest. All I feel is aggravation," Wilder said. Twenty minutes in, their beaming smiles were beginning to infuriate him, regardless of how appreciative he was for their tutelage. This had been the one part of training he'd been dreading, knowing full well he had zero ability to change a damn thing about himself. And it turned out he was right.

Olivia spent the next few minutes explaining the differences between shapeshifting in fae and lycan, and how in Wilder's case, he has an internal self he was born displaying, and an outer self he's become. But for both, the power they display can sometimes be reliant on their shift.

"I've learned I can jump really high and run really fast in my human form," Liv clarified. "But I can't jump *as* high, or run *as* fast as when

I'm full wolf. The more wolf I let myself display, the more powerful I become. Does that make sense?"

"Um. Sure," Wilder said. Though he felt certain he wasn't sure about anything.

"Let me show you," Olivia said. Before Wilder was ready, two long ears grew straight through the dark curls haloing her head. Her caramel eyes shifted to a glowing yellow, made brighter by the sunlight, and her nails—previously cut short and squared off—grew a full inch, sharpening into razors. Wilder's mouth dropped open, and he took a step away, unsure if he was even breathing anymore. Olivia drew her lips, baring her teeth. But where there had once been a beaming smile, a set of pointed white incisors had taken their place.

Wilder trembled, the blood draining from his face. "Whoa."

"Now watch," she said, her bright voice coming out in a snarl. A moment later, she was gone. All Wilder saw was the flash of her sequined blue dress glittering from across the garden before she barreled towards them. She ran far faster than he had seen her run the night before.

Barrett looked on, unfazed, but the corners of his mouth tilted into a slight smile, as if mildly impressed by her antics. Olivia shifted back before she returned; her snarl easing into her familiar wide grin. She strode up to Wilder, her hands on her hips.

"My power is linked to my shift, and that's how it is for fae too," she said. "Fae can use their magic without shifting, sure. But their greatest access comes during their full shift." Wilder thought back to the night before, how Tristian had shifted, displaying his wings, while he had fought the rogue.

"Now you; I think you've gone and covered up *a lot* of your fae side," Olivia continued.

"Hey, what's that supposed to mean?" Wilder asked, vaguely affronted. He turned to study himself in the elongated mirror Olivia had brought out to assist with the midday activities.

"Not *necessarily* looks wise!" she backtracked. "You've definitely got some fae going on." She eyed his broad cheekbones and hard jawline thoughtfully, a playful smirk playing on her lips. "But you're obviously lacking in the ears and wings department. That could be why you're struggling so much with your abilities."

"Right," Barrett said, the young boy standing to join them from the bench. "Think about it this way. As a fae, I can change my appearance whenever I want, but regardless of how I look, I'm going to be stronger and more agile than your typical human. At least I hope. But my magic is at its strongest when I'm fully myself, exactly how I was born, wings and all. When I push to the full extent of my power, my full presentation comes out. What Liv is saying is that in covering up your physical features, you've also covered up your abilities."

"Why would I have done that?" Wilder asked, trying to ignore the not-so-subtle way Olivia was watching him. Wilder didn't doubt that what they said about his abilities was true. He had always hated how clumsy he was, and he couldn't throw a punch to save his life.

"Fear, probably," Barrett explained. "Anything to keep the humans from suspecting anything *inhuman* about you. Honestly, you did a really good job. You must have been really scared. A lot of unfound fae get discovered because they're way too good at track-and-field or something."

Wilder wondered if that's what Terra had meant when she said he had been a tough case to crack.

"I don't know. Maybe we're going about this the wrong way." Olivia looked at Barrett, finally sounding as exasperated as Wilder felt. "Maybe we should backtrack and work on tapping into your core self. Yeah?"

Needless to say, that didn't go well either. Barrett showed Wilder how to concentrate, feeling around for the aspects he wanted to draw out. "The key is finding the Magíck in your blood first. Some of us get by without that step, but I've never seen the point. It makes the whole process a lot easier," Barrett told him.

Closing his eyes, the boy went silent. When he opened them, his irises, still the crystalline blue of the sky above, had a more airy quality to them, as if filled with the wind itself. At Barrett's back, Wilder noticed tendrils and wisps of cloudy air coalescing into four distinct sections, bringing with them floating petals and leaves from the surrounding garden. Each section came together to form the shape of wings. A sharp wind blew through the trees, sending the nesting birds fluttering away.

A moment later, the breeze stopped, and the wind left Barrett's gaze. Silence reigned between them.

"It's going to take you a while to get to that point," Barrett said. "Or maybe not. You seem capable enough from time to time. We just have to figure out what's blocking you up the rest of it."

Wilder nodded and tried to find whatever 'Magíck' was apparently supposed to be hiding somewhere in his blood. But the whole time, he felt like he was throwing himself headfirst against a stone wall of dread, any previous pulsing in his veins recoiling behind it. The longer he worked at it, the harder the throbbing in his head became. In the end, nothing happened, and the only thing he managed to locate were the pangs of oncoming hunger.

Barrett eventually had to leave for his own training. Olivia, still trying to be as encouraging as possible, started to look rightfully annoyed. Though if it was at herself, at Wilder, or at the situation, he couldn't tell. She did her best to mask her frustration, remaining endlessly positive and assuring him it would all happen when he was ready.

As they worked, Wilder studied Olivia with mild curiosity, marking how her bright and airy persona floated like ruffling feathers over a brewing chaos beneath—a star on fire about to go supernova. Her eyes, focused on him while tracking every situation developing in the world around her, carefully concealed an edge. It seemed—at the back of her renegade mind, only comfortable going a million miles an hour—she couldn't stop expecting something terrible to happen.

Wilder decided, whether out of trepidation or concern, it wasn't the time to ask her how she had first gotten there. Though he could tell, in so many ways, she was similar to him. She battled a past she wished she could forget, and was trying to create a life for herself here instead. It was what he wanted for himself, and he could respect that.

After a few more failed attempts, they finally padded, weary and exhausted, back to the abbey for lunch. Watching her, Wilder recalled Olivia's reaction to the woman's abduction, and how distressed Olivia had become. He couldn't begin to guess what had happened to her, but Wilder was starting to understand why Harry thought she was the strongest person he knew.

Chapter Fourteen

Jasmine rice and handcrafted steamed dumplings waited for them at lunch. While Wilder was too exhausted to admire the intricate tones of the dish, he appreciated the sustenance after that morning. Olivia, Harry, Tristian, and Rickard joined him. The group talked amongst themselves, while Wilder was content to think of nothing at all.

Unfortunately, his mental peace grew steadily interrupted by a stream of intruding anxieties. His worry and unease spiraled as he reflected on his training—and his utter lack of magic or ability. After this morning's endeavors, it was clear whatever magic he possessed was determined to stay hidden until *it* decided otherwise. No shifting, no strength, no magical protection. How much more standing around and wasting space would the Council tolerate before finally kicking him out? How long before they admitted they had made a mistake about who, or what, they believed he was? Any delusions Wilder had allowed himself at finally finding a place to belong—where he finally felt wanted—dissipated with the steam from his dumplings.

Two firm hands gripped his shoulders, jolting Wilder from his thoughts. "Alright, Summer," a brusque voice announced. "Combat training. Let's go." Closing his eyes and dropping his head in defeat, Wilder groaned into his core.

He had prayed today's training, which he had christened 'the series of unending humiliations', was over. He felt so ready to sleep off the current barrage of inadequacy clinging to him. But that now seemed wholly unlikely in the face of the towering blond fae breathing down his neck.

Apparently fate saw fit that he wouldn't be spared yet another debilitating blow to his pride—and likely the majority of his bones—by Tristian.

The sharp backwards jerk of Wilder's chair announced Tristian's insistence, and Wilder took one last glum look at his dumplings before standing. His body screamed in protest as Tristian led him up the main flight of stairs and down the hall. They entered the same expansive room where Wilder had first found Barrett sparring with a punching bag. The bag had been removed, likely shoved into an adjoining closet, but the floor remained covered with thick, cushioned pads.

Wilder resisted the urge to collapse onto them.

Tristian closed the door and Wilder let out a weary sigh. "How was your morning?" Tristian asked, ignoring Wilder as he readjusted the mats closer together. Wilder idly thought this must be his attempt at friendliness, or at least cordiality. But little in Tristian's tone indicated he cared in the least how Wilder's morning had been.

"Fine," Wilder lied. He wasn't too keen on sharing his complete lack of success, especially with some guy that clearly didn't like him and was readying to beat the daylights out of him.

"*Hmph*," Tristian rumbled. After finishing with the mats, he lifted his gaze, locking his intense icy stare on Wilder. Wilder gulped.

Straightening into the rigid carriage of a drill sergeant, Tristian clasped his tattooed arms behind his back. He strode over and circled Wilder, assessing his frame and build. Wilder could have sworn he heard him snicker.

"Welcome to combat training, Summer." Boredom colored Tristian's introduction. "As you probably know by now, we're in the midst of a war. And though you know little about it, that doesn't change your involvement in it. It's your responsibility to not only protect yourself, but at least make an attempt to protect others. Thankfully, your performance last night is a step in the right direction." A look of vague commendation briefly crossed Tristian's features before they returned to their usual, cool deportment. "But you still have work to do. Your best chance at survival is reliant on your ability to not only access your magic, but to become adept at using it."

Shame colored Wilder's cheeks.

"As a fae," Tristian continued, "you have inbuilt strength and agility. Or at least you should. *You,*" he added, indicating Wilder with a crisp nod, "clearly do not." Wilder glared at him, but Tristian didn't seem to notice nor care.

Stalking to a long wooden table running along one of the walls, Tristian picked up two thick cushioned pads from among a mess of equipment and strapped them onto his muscled forearms. "First things, first. Strength." Tristian latched the final strap. "You'll not only need to access it—which I expect you won't do much of today—but you'll need to build it. You're puny. Even for a human. And kind of a liability."

"Gee, thanks," Wilder shot back. But Wilder knew he had a point. For the second time that day, he was reminded just how useless he was.

Tristian lifted a single eyebrow, the corner of his mouth pulling into a half-grin. "Anytime." He sauntered to where Wilder stood, his countenance seeming to ease and enliven at the prospect of the upcoming skirmish. "Now punch me."

"What?" Wilder gasped, his eyes narrowing on Tristian in disbelief.

Tristian promptly smacked him on the head with one of the pads, sending Wilder reeling. The hit wasn't hard enough to hurt, but it proved his point.

"Your reaction time is deficient, at best," Tristian assessed. "Punch me. Or the cushions. But maybe leave the face out of it. I've got a date later." Tristian winked, his broad grin cocky and obnoxious. Wilder scowled. "Though I doubt you'd do much damage either way." Tristian shrugged, the tendrils of his dark tattoos furling along his shoulders with the movement.

Annoyance got the better of Wilder. He swung hard, more out of contempt for Tristian's arrogance than because Tristian had instructed him to. But Tristian didn't seem to care what Wilder's motive had been. Raising the padded white cushion with expert precision and timing, he blocked Wilder's right hook. The cushion released a muffled tuft as the white padding enveloped his fist. Peeking out from behind the pad, Tristian threw Wilder a cheeky grin that lifted his severe cheekbones even higher.

"Awesome. That almost felt like it had some *umph* to it." His eyes glowed with an animation Wilder hadn't seen on him before. "Maybe you're not a lost cause after all." Tristian repositioned himself. "Do it again."

Wilder spent the next ten minutes swinging at Tristian in every conceivable direction, but Tristian blocked each strike. Utilizing his now tried-and-true brand of instigation, Tristian goaded Wilder forward. After a few more rounds, Tristian began to side-step, avoiding the oncoming hurls before Wilder could even touch him or the cushion.

"Come on, Summer. Where're the sparks you showed last night?" Tristian asked between blows.

"I told you, that wasn't *me* doing that," Wilder answered breathlessly, not letting up.

"Give yourself some credit, kid." Tristian blocked a swing with a swift lift of his forearm. "There's just something blocking you. We'll have to knock it loose."

Wilder paused and took a breath, his blood boiling. He'd have to concentrate more on the direction of his blows than on the strength behind them. Advancing on Tristian again, Wilder readied for another strike, the electricity in his blood pooling in his fist. But a moment later, he found himself flat on his back; the air knocked clear out of his lungs. Tristian had swiped his foot behind Wilder's knees, kicking his legs out from beneath him.

Above, he noticed the lights flicker off before returning to their steady glow. A rush of shame, the same Wilder felt everytime magic left his body, gripped him. Wilder tamped it down, and the thrumming electricity in his blood went with it. Coughing breath into his lungs, Wilder looked up in confusion. Inspecting the lights, Tristian cocked an eyebrow and retreated a step, chuckling. Holding out a hand, he helped Wilder to his feet.

"That was great." Tristian gaged. Though the dull throbbing now running along Wilder's neck and back felt anything but. "I told you; you were just stopped up. Now do it again." He voiced his command as if asking Wilder to perform the most menial of tasks.

"I don't know if—" Wilder started, his head spinning.

"Don't tell me you're as weak as I think you are," Tristian heckled, but his boyish grin never left his face.

Wilder glared, but admitted to himself that he might actually be enjoying the brawl. Exploding with a bone-deep fervor, Wilder leapt forward, jabbing and swinging at Tristian again and again, but this time he forced himself to keep his cool. He wouldn't let Tristian's antagonizing get the better of him. He couldn't lose control. But over and over, Tristian either parried away his strikes or knocked Wilder off his feet. And each time Wilder fell, no other inkling of power rushed to the surface.

Wilder was certain his entire backside was now bruised from the falls. He felt like he was running on pure adrenaline, but the rush was waning. Tristian moved too fast for Wilder to sneak in. Concentrating harder, Wilder focused on both making contact with anything solid in Tristian's general direction, and checking his periphery for Tristian's errant kicks. His arms felt like limp noodles. Even if the cushions weren't in play, he knew he couldn't even touch Tristian.

But *there*. Noticing a slight stiffening and twitch in Tristian's left leg, Wilder leapt away, narrowly avoiding a swipe that would have buckled his knees for the thirtieth time that afternoon. Tristian stopped and took a step away, grinning at Wilder in what appeared to be an authentic beam of approval.

"Good," Tristian said, nodding as he unstrapped the cushions from his forearms. "Awareness is going to be your best friend. You don't need magic, strength, or agility to be aware of what's happening around you. Those things help with your reactions, and you clearly need to work on them. But they'll do nothing for you if you can't respond to what's going on right in front of you. And if you can't look out for yourself, you can't protect others. Whoever you're fighting with will have to worry about you instead of focusing on the real battle."

"I'll keep that in mind," Wilder groaned, rubbing his sore neck. "No offense, but you're kind of intense about this."

"Of course I am," Tristian said. His brows lifted in surprise, as if anyone even somewhat intelligent would have the exact same mindset. "I have to be. We all have to be. This war is escalating regardless of anyone's willingness, or *unwillingness*, to participate." He glared at Wilder, any trace of friendliness extinguished.

"Plus, I need to be this intense to have any chance of being chosen for the Fae Army. To have any chance of becoming consequential enough to take Markus out myself." His eyes lit with purpose, as if Markus's ultimate demise at his hand was the surest thing in the world. "And I want to," Tristian added, "more than anything. *I'm* going to be the one that kills that bastard. At least for what he's done to our people, if not for what he's done to my family." A darkness shadowed his stare, and fury flared his nostrils, painting a rise of red on his high cheekbones. "And I won't be quick about it either. Our people never should have been forced to live in such fear, especially by one of our own."

"I don't mean to be an idiot about this, but what exactly *has* he done to your people?" Wilder asked.

"They're your people too, dimwit," Tristian snapped, and he looked about ready to punch Wilder again. Wilder stood his ground.

"To clarify the severity of things for you," Tristian continued, "not only has he completely displaced us and stolen an *entire* ancient city, which he's now disgraced and transformed into some harbor for torture, but he's kidnapped or murdered so many of our people, we've lost count. It won't be long before we're extinct. What's left is stuck sheltering in Teír, exiled from Daoine and so many other of the fae cities, too scared to go home. Those of us in the Council House are even more at risk. Not only because of who we are and what we stand for, but because we don't have the same protections as Teír. And it's not just our people suffering. You saw just yesterday what he's been doing to the humans. No one like that should be allowed to walk this earth unchecked."

"I don't disagree," Wilder said. "But why hasn't he been? Checked, I mean. A lunatic as active as this guy—why hasn't anyone stopped him?"

Tristian paused, the blaze in his stare settling to an even glow. "No one can find him," he said. "No one can get to him. We don't even know where to begin." He strode away from Wilder, his gait defeated, and stooped to start picking up the mats.

"I thought you all said he's in this 'Lus Halla'? Whatever that is," Wilder asked, confused.

"He is," Tristian confirmed, stacking two mats in the corner. "But right now, we don't even know where Lus Halla *is*."

"Oh. Right. Yeah. Of course not," Wilder said, sarcasm biting his tone as he feigned having any real idea what Tristian was talking about.

"Lus Halla, and Daoine, *move,*" Tristian clarified, pausing his cleaning to explain the nuances of the Eadar. He sounded exasperated, as if explaining night and day to a four-year-old. "Lus Halla is the beating heart of the fae people, our throne. It's in Daoine, our homeland. The Tuatha, our gods, created it especially for us. But Markus stole it, exiling our people from it. Historically, it's only supposed to move when a new Season takes the throne, and only to one of four already known locations, depending on which Season ascends. But Markus has somehow moved it somewhere new. We don't know where. Or if he even stays in one place long enough for it to be worth us figuring it out. The Magistrie's done everything to find him. Locater spells, water watching, the works. They've even asked the Watern for help, which says a lot. But even they can't do much." Tristian paused, a shadow passing over his angled features. "The Magistrie's sent troops through the same portals you saw last night—*if* they ever caught one open. Which is still rare. But no one's ever returned. At least not alive. So they've stopped trying."

"Oh," Wilder said, and he felt incredibly stupid for both saying it, and for not saying more.

"Yeah. So now you can see why I'm so *intense* about this. This isn't some insignificant human war where little boys shoot each other with their big shiny weapons. Markus is gathering more strength than any one fae has ever possessed, and there is literally nothing we can do about it. It's going to affect all of humanity, not just the Céad. It already has. Maybe *that* will encourage you to take your training a bit more seriously."

"Hey, I am taking this seriously!" Wilder rebutted. Though he realized how much he sounded like a petulant child.

"Yeah. We'll see," Tristian scoffed, shoving past Wilder's shoulder. "Anyway, rest up tomorrow. You're training with me every other day from now on. We need to get you in better shape."

"Joy," Wilder muttered under his breath. He turned away from Tristian, trudging from the room. As Wilder moved to close the door, he glanced back. Tristian stood slouched against one of the wooden beams along the far wall, his eyes shut and his usual confidence utterly drained. Resting his head in his raised hands, Tristian massaged at his temples—any air of arrogance extinguished from the now worn and weary contours of his features.

★★★

Wilder laid in his bed and stared at the ceiling, listening to the gentle patter of a spring storm on his window. Alone in his room, he lifted his hands, willing some kind of magic to happen like it had with Tristian in the training room. But whatever power had livened during the fight had settled back to sleep, unwilling to be awoken by his prodding.

A knock on his door summoned him to get up. Groaning, and in very much pain, Wilder forced himself out of bed. Opening the door, he held himself up against the frame, relief sinking into his bones as Terra stared at him for the first time that day. She wore her sun-kissed brown hair in loose, cascading waves down her shoulders. The highlights brought out the gold flecks in her eyes.

"Hey," she said with far more enthusiasm than he had the energy to return. Looking him over, her gaze rested on his stiff muscles and the bruises covering his exposed arms. Her face fell. "You look rough."

"Wow. Thanks." Wilder's voice was strained as he returned to his bed, collapsing onto his stomach. Terra followed behind.

"I guess it really isn't necessary to ask how your day was?" She knelt next to him.

"Yeah, I wouldn't," Wilder said, his voice muted by his comforter as his face lay smashed firmly into its folds.

Terra sighed, and he felt her hand rest along his shoulder-blades. Instinct snarled at him to recoil at the closeness, to not let her see him like this, but at her touch, a roaring peace calmed every muscle in his body. He decided to ignore the snarling, just for today.

"I think I have something that could help," she said.

Peering at her from his pillow, she cocked her head to the side, a slight smile crinkling her nose.

"Okay," he said weakly, and she offered him a hand to help him up.

CHAPTER FIFTEEN

Wilder and Terra walked slowly down the hallway and the stairs—a harder task than he could have imagined—before heading east on the main floor and down an unassuming paneled corridor past the kitchen. Wilder hadn't explored this side of the abbey yet. As Terra opened a door to another passage, Wilder groaned at the sight of another staircase sinking into the dark.

She gave him an encouraging smile. "Almost there. Promise."

This staircase and the walls weren't like those in the rest of the building, the passage built entirely of bare stone. Wilder felt the temperature drop as they descended deep into the earth below.

"I take it you trained with Tristian today," Terra asked. They edged farther into the depths of the abbey, their steps solely lit by the dim dregs of light coming from individual antique bulbs hung at intervals from the stone ceiling.

"You betcha," Wilder answered, his tone scathing. "He's a treat."

"Yeah, he's not everyone's cup of tea," Terra agreed. "But he's not all bad. Once you get to know him. His heart's in the right place, even if he's not so great at showing it."

"That's the understatement of a century," Wilder rebutted, but looked at her curiously. She seemed to have a soft spot for him. Terra chuckled.

The staircase came to an unceremonious end, opening into a large stone chamber lit by flamed torches, candles, and electric lamp light. Wilder blinked as he surveyed the room, and his eyes widened. The walls were lined with shelves upon shelves, cut from the stone itself.

Some held collections of little glass bottles and jars of tinctures, salves, and herbs—all labeled with minute inked script. Others were stacked tightly with books, held at each end by the split halves of small crystalline geodes. The content of the books ranged from Alchemy, Astrology, and Astronomy to History, Prophecy, and Plant Identification. There wasn't a subject not included in the compendium.

"Well, this explains the history book," Wilder muttered.

"Huh?" Terra asked, two lines appearing between her brows. But Wilder only smirked down at her before walking further into the chamber.

Gorgeous imposing geodes stood in every corner, towering over the space. Flickering firelight danced across their jeweled surfaces, and Wilder realized this was the place he had first seen Terra drawing during art class. Despite the cold, Wilder felt a warmth to the room, as if the whole chamber crackled and hummed, afire with energy. As if the earth itself was alive and breathing around him.

"This is our Apotéca," Terra told him. "A magem's best magic is done deep in the earth, so magem and covens all over the world create spaces like this."

"It's incredible," Wilder murmured, still staring in awe at its immensity. He felt like he could actually touch the magic permeating through the stone walls of the chamber.

"Oh, this one is nothing compared to what most covens have, but thank you." Terra smiled and strode to a table against the right wall. After locating a bottle-green glass jar, she walked back to Wilder, screwing off the lid. "Here." She handed him the jar. "It'll help with the pain."

The salve smelled familiar, imbued with hints of eucalyptus and mint, though there were undertones to the rub Wilder couldn't place. Fingering the gel, he instantly felt it cooling his skin. Within seconds of massaging the salve onto his arms, some of the amassed tension and pain melted from his muscles. Wilder sighed. Reaching over his shoulder, he tried to rub the salve onto his back, but the pain kept him from getting very far.

"I could help if you'd like," Terra offered, her hesitant smile sympathetic. There wasn't any hint of expectation in her tone, but as Wilder met her steady gaze, he wondered if he would have minded if there had been. "I do have training as a healer," she clarified.

"I…Yeah, I guess that's fine," Wilder stuttered, shrugging. He regretted the motion immediately and handed her the jar.

Terra retrieved a barstool and motioned for him to take a seat. Settling onto the cold metal, he leaned forward, and she raised the hem of his shirt to rest along his neckline. Wilder swallowed hard, praying that wytes didn't have increased hearing like vampyrs, knowing for certain his heartbeat would betray his nerves if they did.

The moment her fingertips met his skin, he felt a jolt shoot through him. *Please let it be the salve doing that…*

Wilder told himself to keep it together. *She's just another girl trying to help me out. It's just Terra.* He shuddered, realizing *that* particular thought didn't help the situation. It was Terra. Behind his closed eyes, he saw the flash of green of hers—the memory of the first day they met—and the way his stomach had leapt at meeting her.

"Too cold?" Terra asked, her palm pausing at his shoulder.

"Oh, no, you're good. Just a sore spot," Wilder hastily said, chastising himself for his escalating heart rate. He sensed Terra nod behind him. If she noticed anything more, she generously ignored it.

I'm an idiot. Wilder rubbed at his temples. *Get it together, man.*

Terra massaged the salve into his shoulder blades and ribcage, somehow sensing where the sorest spots were and rubbing the salve into tight, concentric circles. As the tension released, Wilder became acutely aware of how soft her hands were, and of the steady thrum of electricity now passing between them.

Every centimeter of his body felt knotted, and he knew in his gut it wasn't just from combat training. The pads of her fingers pressed gently into his spine, working the salve into each muscle group. Wilder tried not to wince at the pressure. His muscles began to loosen, the tension replaced by a quiet numbness, and the absence of pain felt so alleviating, he had almost forgotten Terra stood right behind him. His breathing returned to a level pace.

"Any better?" Terra asked, and Wilder could have sworn he heard her voice crack.

His breath hitched and he cleared his throat. "Um, yeah! All better. For sure. That's great stuff." Straightening, Wilder fumbled the hem of his shirt back down and turned to face Terra. Fighting himself to look anywhere but at her, he stared instead at his shoelaces.

"Yeah, it is," he heard her say, her tone steady and unfazed. "It has essence of murtlap. It's supposed to draw any residual magic into your muscles for quicker healing."

He glanced up at her. She was still far more composed than he felt, graciously remaining unaffected by his weirdness. Or at least pretending to be. "You can take the rest with you," she added brightly, offering him the salve. "You'll probably need it tomorrow."

"If this afternoon was any indication, I probably will." Wilder chuckled dryly, letting himself ease at the calming confidence in her tone. Something about her made him feel so *in place.*

"So, the Apotéca," Wilder asked, surprising himself as he tried to extend his time with her. "What exactly do you guys do down here?"

"Glad you asked." Terra beamed and stepped away to show him around the room. "A lot, really. Spells, enchantments, charms. We make potions and tinctures, and salves like the one we just used." Wilder couldn't help but smile at the passion radiating from her.

"*This* Apotéca," she continued, "serves a dual purpose as protection for the Council House. This entire chamber extends underneath the perimeter of the abbey." She gestured down a darkened passage Wilder hadn't noticed before. "You see all these geodes? They can hold a ton of magic. Like enough to take down a hundred-story building. There are more placed all along the perimeter. They help keep random passerby away by making them see the abbey as something they'd typically avoid. And they keep anyone with ill intentions out by surrounding the entire place with wards."

"That's comforting." Wilder strode to a corner and stared into the heart of one of the geodes. It glinted in the firelight, but Wilder thought he saw movement within it, far deeper than the surface level shine.

"Do I get to come down here and learn how to cast spells and make potions like you, then?" Wilder asked. He couldn't help but stare at her smile—at the way she came alive when she talked about magic. And he couldn't stop himself from noticing how her eyes were somehow the brightest lights in the room.

Wilder swallowed hard and turned away again. *Not good, Wil,* he told himself, remembering how badly his body hurt from his last hour with Tristian. And he hadn't even been *trying* to hurt Wilder then.

Terra laughed. "Yes. And no. Our magic is different than the Fae's. Magem access Earth magic, but it's only a muted derivative of the kind fae use. Fae have more direct access to its truest form—the Magíck itself. And the Magem can't hold magic in our blood and bones the same way you do. Fae magic comes straight from the source. It's a part of you. Ours comes from the Earth, from all around us. We can feel it there, access it, manipulate it, but we don't hold it. Theoretically, though, yeah. Any fae should be able to do the same things we can. I guess we'll find out if that's the case with you."

"I don't get it. I keep hearing you guys talk about this Magíck like its magic, but also like its something else. Like its some kind of person," Wilder said. "The Magi called it your creator."

"It's a bit abstract, but yeah. Our legends say it was the Magíck that created us, the universe, and whatever else is out there. It made us and gave us our abilities. All of our power, in some way or another, comes from the Magíck."

"So you believe in this all-powerful being, then?" Wilder asked, fingering a notch in a wooden bookshelf next to him. "Doesn't it make more sense that you all just *have* magic? I mean, even the Magi said there are plenty of you that don't believe in that and are still powerful enough." Wilder didn't know if he could believe any of it. Not after everything that had happened to him. It all seemed like a crock. But then again, so did everything else that had happened in the last few days.

"Of course I do," Terra said. "I don't know about everyone else, but I just can't experience this life and not know there's something greater than ourselves out there. A mastermind behind all of this."

"But have any of you ever seen 'the Magíck?' Or these 'gods' the Magi mentioned? What if it's all just random chance?" Wilder rebutted. "A made-up bedtime story to keep your people in line?"

Terra smiled again, though it didn't reach her eyes. Her expression seemed tinged instead with a subtle sorrow. "Careful, Wil. You're starting to sound a lot like Markus." Wilder winced, but Terra added, "I don't know about the Magíck. But there *are* stories of people who have seen things they couldn't explain. People who claim they've seen the gods. And I don't know. Maybe it is just a story. You could be right. Or…" she shrugged, a playful glint returning to her features, "maybe you just haven't experienced the Magíck for yourself yet."

"I guess I'll just have to let you know if I do." But Wilder doubted it would ever happen.

Terra gave him a tour of the Apotéca. Apparently, most magem were avid researchers and often served the Magistrie that way, Terra's parents included. It explained the expansive library held within the chamber. They valued history and the mechanics of the world. They believed absolutely every aspect of the lived experience had worth, and was therefore worth knowing as much as possible about. From politics to gardening, nothing was too insignificant. While each magem might have a focus of more interest to them than another, they were all regularly well versed on most matters. Terra, Wilder was unsurprised to hear, loved history.

"The thing that makes history so compelling," Terra said, "is how all of creation—humans and Céad alike—never quite learn from their mistakes. A few generations pass, and we all end up doing the exact same things our ancestors did—like going to war without consideration for the consequences."

"What an encouraging way to see the world, Terra," Wilder joked. Terra blushed. "I mean, it's no surprise," he said. "Isn't it the same case in our own lives? It's gotta be human nature—or, well…whatever you'd call it."

"What do you mean?" Terra asked, leaning over a table to stare at him. He cowered a little under the intensity of her gaze.

"I mean, don't we all tend to fall into that same fallacy?" Wilder pondered aloud. "Knowing exactly what the outcome of a certain situation will likely be, but somehow thinking this next time, things will be different? That maybe our situation is special in some new way. But then we just end up repeating history, finding ourselves surprised when nothing changes at all." Wilder thought about all the times he believed moving to a new placement would make things different, make things better, for him. It never did.

Terra sat down on a barstool, folding her arms on a table. "Maybe," Terra ventured, "but I don't know. I think that also negates the possibility of hope. The idea that maybe things really *will* be different… That maybe we really *can* change things, especially for the people we care about."

Wilder thought there was a tinge of blind optimism in her words. He studied her for a moment, wondering what situation she might be thinking about, and if it had something to do with Tristian. "You don't strike me as naïve, Terra." He didn't intend for the statement to be insulting, but by the look on her face, he realized he could have been more tactful with his wording.

"I'm not being naïve, Wil," Terra shot back. "I just find your lack of hope bleak and unhelpful."

Wilder grinned, appreciating her candor. "Look," he offered, raising his hands in a careful surrender, "all I'm saying is, I spent my life *hoping* for something that never happened. Every day, I wished for whatever next set of parents I got to be *the ones.* The ones that would take me seriously, the ones that would stick it out through whatever I threw their way. But after a while, I stopped hoping. It always led to disappointment and more hurt than I care to admit." Wilder was surprised how vulnerable he was being with her. It was more than he had been with anyone for quite a long time.

"I get your need for hope, especially in the midst of a war," he said. "I do. And especially since you seem to care so much about others and want to believe the best of them. I like that about you." A slight heat rose beneath his freckles, and he was glad the room was so dim. "But sometimes hope is just more of a downfall than any kind of saving grace."

"Have you ever considered," Terra tried, her voice firm, "that maybe having *hope* wasn't your issue? Maybe it was the things you were hoping *for?*"

Wilder stood silent as he considered her words. *Why would hoping for a family be a bad thing?*

Before he could respond, she added, "If you had ended up finding those parents—ended up being adopted—you likely never would have found *us.* You likely never would have discovered who you are. Maybe there was a reason your hopes weren't answered in the way you wanted. Maybe there was something better waiting for you, something more important." Wilder shuffled on his feet, considering the truth in it.

"And," she continued, "for me, I just can't help but hope, Wil. I can't not believe that the people I care about are going to change for the better. I can't help but wonder if I just did something different, changed some part of me to better meet them where they're at—things might be okay. That it would help them enough for them to be okay."

The desperation he heard in her voice made him want to protect her from it—from whatever had hurt her. "Listen. You're preaching to the choir," he told her. "I get wanting to give up any possible part of yourself just to make a situation work. But a lot of times, it ultimately doesn't. And that's not on you. And it's not *good* for you to think it should be. It doesn't sound like hope is your issue either. It's that your hope is founded in *you* having to do something to change someone else. That's not hope, Terra. That's self-reliance. And that's how you burn out. That's how you lose yourself. All you're doing is forcing the situation when it might not be what the situation needs. Have you ever considered focusing a little less on everyone else and a little more on you? Maybe there's a way for you to hold onto your hope for someone without sacrificing yourself in the process."

Terra stilled, her eyes widening, evidently taken aback by what he'd said. "That seems a little selfish, don't you think?"

Wilder shrugged. "Maybe there's a balance. You're right—you should think of others and maybe be sacrificial *at times.* But there's gotta be a limit, Terra. Sometimes you have to put your own gas mask on first."

Terra considered him before nodding. Releasing a heavy sigh, she let her head fall back to stare at the ceiling. Her orange top brought out the bronze of her neck and shoulders, and Wilder couldn't help but trace the curve with his eyes. "Sorry for snapping," Terra finally said, lowering her head and pinching her nose. "I try not to get too weighty too often. It's just been a long day."

"No worries. It was…refreshing—to hear your perspective. You were right. All things I don't think I've ever considered." Wilder moved a barstool to sit in front of her, letting his knees lightly knock against hers. "Care to share what happened today?"

"Ah, it's no big deal." Terra let out another heavy sigh, her shoulders slumping, before she met Wilder's stare. "I just had a bit of a blowout with Tristian this morning and it's stuck with me most of the day. He can be a little overwhelming sometimes."

"You're telling me," Wilder said, chuckling. "Explains why he was so testy this afternoon. I hope you don't mind me asking, but are you two, uh, more than friends?" Wilder could feel the blood rising to his cheeks again.

Terra readjusted in her seat and laughed, though it sounded tinged with bitterness. "Gods, no. Not anymore, anyway. We dated briefly. It obviously didn't go well. He likes to think he still likes me. But he doesn't. Not really. He's too busy with other girls for me to take him seriously. And at the end of the day, he's far too proud to end up with anyone other than a fae, and I could really only end up with a mage. The whole thing was a waste of time on both our parts." She cut herself off and looked down at her hands, her brow furrowing as if realizing she had shared more than she should have. "Either way, none of it really matters."

"Oh." Wilder's heart dropped, and he did his best to conceal anything that might come across as disappointment. When had he suddenly started thinking about Terra that way, anyway? Why would it matter to him who she could or couldn't be with?

"Is that something all Céad do?" Wilder asked. "I mean, stick to their own kind?"

"Some do. Some don't." Terra shrugged, looking up at him. "It's really a matter of preference. Historically, it's looked down on. And it doesn't come without its complications. For me, it's always been a family thing. I have a lineage I need to pass down. Dad makes that *abundantly* clear. And I can really only do that with another of my own kind." She said this as if it easily settled the matter, but her stare had gone blank, as if there were something deeper she didn't care to acknowledge.

"Olivia doesn't have a preference though," Terra added, her expression still shadowed. But there was an inquisitiveness in the way she looked at him, as if trying to determine what his reaction might be to the information.

Wilder straightened and cleared his throat, his response dry and measured. "I guess that's good for Harry then."

Terra gave him a thin smile but didn't say anything else. Breaking from his gaze, she stood from her seat. "What about you? Are you leaving anyone behind on the human side?"

"Um, no, not at all. I've never really had time for any of that." Wilder feigned cavalier disinterest, drawing his mouth into a tight line and shrugging. Terra's stare narrowed on him, as if studying him again.

Wilder regrouped. "I mean—I had a best friend that was a girl—as a kid. But she moved away. And that was way before I even thought about any of that. Honestly, I think girls have just never really been interested."

"Maybe," Terra surmised, appearing to stifle a smirk. "Or maybe you've just never let them be."

Chapter Sixteen

The next day found Wilder in Rickard's office. Similar to the parlor downstairs, it brimmed with warm, elegant wood and aged, leather-bound books. Art from every movement and style adorned the walls, encased in gilded frames burnished by the ravages of time. Upon seeing the paintings, Wilder realized who must be responsible for the decor in the foyer. He and Rickard sat at a heavy rosewood table, its surface scattered with sheets of scrawled parchment, ink bottles, and sharpened feathered quills. Rickard clearly had a penchant for an era far before their current one. A plate of smoked turkey and brie sandwiches lay on a pine breakfast platter, as of yet untouched.

Rickard listened to Wilder's report on his first training sessions, though Wilder had conveniently left out the more personal bits. He did, however, express his concerns about his ability—or rather, inability—to willfully access any semblance of magic.

"I understand your frustrations. But I wouldn't put much weight on it just yet," Rickard reassured him. "There could be a number of reasons you're not able to do so, and you wouldn't be the first to struggle. I've been here for quite some time and have seen many a fae come through our doors with no idea of what they're doing. Some with the same concerns as yourself. As with all good things, your magic will come with time. And most importantly, with patience—especially with yourself."

Wilder slouched and crossed his arms, releasing a pained sigh that did nothing to relax the tension coiled around his shoulders and neck. His whole body hurt like hell, every muscle screaming in revolt at his every movement. The numbing relief of the salve he had put on that morning, in whatever places he could actually reach, was unfortunately waning.

Noting Wilder's discomfort, Rickard added, "though, for your own sake, I do hope your abilities reveal themselves sooner rather than later. It seems your body isn't a fan of combat training. I daresay it would be much easier for you if you healed as quickly as a fae should."

It had slipped Wilder's mind that fae healed quicker than humans, remembering Tristian's recovery after the fight in the alleyway. He slumped further in his seat and audibly groaned, defeated by the reminder of yet another inaccessible skill that could be helping him right now.

"Isn't there anything I can do?" Wilder asked, sitting up and baring his palms in desperation. "Anything that could help trigger these changes I'm supposed to be seeing?"

"Unfortunately, my friend, the only thing that will be of immediate help is identifying the reasons you decided to cover it all up in the first place. At this point, we can assume it's not subconsciously about keeping any humans safe. If it was, your magic would have little issue displaying itself here, in your day to day. It's far more likely this is about some decision you've made to hide it. Other than that, I'm afraid the only thing we can do is practice."

Wilder blew a heated breath of disappointment, tickling the mess of strands falling across his forehead. He thought about the brief moment with Tristian, how he had lost control, how the lights had flickered. And he thought about the shame that had followed immediately after.

Rickard had Wilder walk him through each time his powers had presented themselves, and any experience with the Eadar he could re-member. While Wilder didn't exactly feel all that fond of revisiting the memories, he knew it was the least he could do.

"It does seem like your powers manifest most commonly when you experience extreme emotions," Rickard said. "This makes sense. It's gen-erally believed the Magíck shows itself most often when we feel we need it the most. But it is also clear that you've done significant work to temper those extremes, have you not?"

"Well, yeah. It's not exactly like I enjoy being angry. It's never really gotten me anywhere helpful."

"Understandable, to be sure." Rickard nodded, his russet eyes fixed on Wilder. While Rickard looked nothing like Harry, there was something about the steady compassion—his ability to truly see someone—that Harry had definitely gotten from his sire.

Rickard continued. "But I theorize you've linked those extreme emotions so much so to your powers, and your more 'composed' self to your powerless self, that you could very well be sabotaging them. Or struggling to recognize them at all. Your ability to see the Eadar freely shows us that there is at least a semblance of your magic breaking through, but not quite enough. Since you're avoiding those extremes, have categorized them as negative, you're essentially avoiding any display of your powers until you're in dire straights. Until some survival instinct kicks in. It is not uncommon for a Céad's powers to be linked to their emotions, at times. But theoretically, you should have full control over your abilities, regardless of your emotional state. *That* is something we will have to work on."

"But I do want my powers," Wilder argued. "I'm tired of getting the crap beat out of me, in every sense of the word." Both his body and mind were drained and throbbing, and he dreaded the endless days ahead of the same beat downs.

"I believe it. But the mind, especially the subconscious mind, is stubborn. If there's a chance your mind has decided your powers—or your true fae appearance—puts you at some kind of risk, it may take some time to convince it otherwise. Your mind has to either decide accessing your powers is more important than avoiding that risk, more important than being safe, or it has to change its mind about how safe you actually are."

Wilder didn't know whether he knew what 'safe' meant. If the feeling was something he had ever experienced. "Lovely," Wilder scoffed.

"We'll get there," Rickard said, his hooked nose crinkling with an encouraging smile. "Until then, I suggest putting yourself in the very positions you might typically avoid. When you do so, allow yourself to lean into those stronger emotions as they arise—particularly anger. That seems to be where your magic is the most explosive. It'll help you recognize what your magic feels like, so you can begin controlling it. Can you think of anything or anyone that's made you mad recently?"

Just the entire last twenty-four hours, Wilder thought to himself. "Oh, I think I've got something in mind." He pictured the right hook he'd like to plant on Tristian's flawless jawline.

"Great. Whatever it is, as long as it's reasonably safe, do that," Rickard instructed, clapping his hands on his knees much more gleefully than Wilder felt. Wilder didn't know exactly how safe it would be to start a row with Tristian, though more due to the danger for Wilder himself than for the towering blond war machine on the receiving end. But at least he knew Tristian could handle it.

"Now," Rickard rose and moved away from the table, putting a hand on Wilder's shoulder, "come with me." He walked across the office to his desk and Wilder followed.

Through the large window behind Rickard, the sky hovered a bleak, non-conform gray—a stark contrast to the early spring sun that had welcomed Wilder when he had first arrived. More scrawled papers and worn books littered Rickard's desk: letters with the mien of staunch importance, heavy tomes covered in hieroglyphs, and sketched images on opened scrolls that appeared to be hundreds of years old, if not older.

"Excuse the mess," Rickard apologized. "I've been getting a touch lost in my research lately. Now, you'll have to remind me how much you know about the Red War. I'm sure the others have shared some information, but it's important for you to be aware exactly the kind of threat we're currently facing, especially after your own run-in with the rogues. I realized tonight you know little about any of this, through no fault of your own. I agreed to let you stay here without giving you any real idea what you had signed up for."

Wilder had never heard a formal name given for the war, and briefly wondered about it as he reiterated what he could recall. He told Rickard what he knew about Markus, Lus Halla, the bright-eyed rogues, and the human kidnappings. About Terra's suspicions Wilder had been kidnapped, and that other fae babies had gone through the same. He added what Tristian had said the day before—about no one being able to find Markus, and people disappearing whenever they tried.

"The war in a nutshell, yes. But there are a few more points that are pertinent for anyone to truly understand the situation. Have you perhaps wondered how Markus has become so powerful?" Rickard asked. "Powerful enough to evade every single Céad out looking for him? Powerful enough to move an entire ancient city into hiding? So powerful he could raise an entire army to fight beside him before anyone figured out it was happening?" Rickard hunched over his desk, his palms pressing into the wrinkled pages.

"I mean, yeah. I wondered," Wilder said, shrugging and crossing his arms. "But I figured it was just more magic stuff I didn't understand."

"Well, it is. But believe it or not, it's also a lot of 'magic stuff' many of us didn't understand either, or at least hadn't considered—not until recently. Not until we began to uncover more about the situation. For a long time after the war started, the Magistrie and the Councils, and the majority of the Eadar, were completely in the dark as to how any of this had happened. This war, these circumstances, they're unprecedented. The Magistrie has dealt with rebellious or disgruntled Céad before. It's what it was created to do. But no one, to our knowledge, has displayed this type of power in thousands of years. Not since before The Great Wars. Not since the dragonstones."

"The dragonstones?" Wilder asked. "Harry told me about the dragons, or at least your stories about them, but nothing about any stones, other than what are supposedly their eggs."

"Ah, no. These are quite a different matter entirely. And no. I imagine he wouldn't have mentioned them. Many find the possibility of their involvement in any of this hard to believe, as hard to believe in as the dragons themselves. Harry included. The likelihood of dragonstones being involved now goes completely against our legends, and against our beliefs about them."

"What do you mean?"

Rickard paced from behind his desk. "What did the Magi tell you about the Fall and the Great Wars?"

Wilder tried to dig up the memory. "Um, only that it was pride that caused it. That the Céad were supposed to protect the humans, but they didn't, so they got cursed with the Shroud."

Rickard nodded. "Yes, and yet there was so much more that happened before that. So much that we don't consider, thinking it irrelevant to now. But our history, however outdated, is rarely ever irrelevant." Rickard sat on the edge of his desk, the cuffs of his button-down rolled to his elbows.

"You see, according to our legends, before the Fall, the Magick granted the gods, the servants of the Magick, authority to gift the Fae special powers linking them to the spirit of the Magick itself. These powers were supposedly gifted through creatures called the dragons, and what we call the dragonstones.

"What's important to realize here is that until now, our interpretations have only ever indicated these special gifts, these 'dragonstones', as a closer connection with the Magick, and as higher levels of magic the Fae once had. Especially since the Fae still hold similar abilities, though far weaker. The 'dragons' pointed to none other than those powerful fae who held that closer connection, and who subsequently lost that connection in the folly of their people. The fae who had been granted these abilities were called the Dragoned, after all. It is even rumored some fae still possess far greater power than others, though these rumors remain just that—old wives' tales."

Rickard continued. "No proof had ever been found suggesting the existence of any actual stones bearing these abilities, nor any actual dragons, making our initial interpretations quite sound. And while there *are* magically protected stones many believe to be dragon eggs still safeguarded in Teír, we have little reason to believe they are anything more than talismans crafted by our forefathers to remind us of the much needed lesson that came out of the Great Wars. A lesson about the folly of pride."

Wilder stared at Rickard, his brow knitting. "You said no proof *had* been found…"

The corner of Rickard's lip pulled into an almost imperceptible smirk. "Yes. *Had.*" He returned behind his desk, shuffling through the pages there. "Some ancient texts have been recently uncovered. Old translations of some of our writings that suggest our current translations may not have been the most…*accurate.* And that our interpretations of those texts, therefore, were limited, at best. These new texts have pointed to the existence of stones, real stones, that granted the bearer enhanced abilities, and that acted as an elemental bridge between the Earth and the Heavens." Pulling out one of the pages, he laid it on top of the mess. It displayed a number of beautiful multicolor orbs, illegible script penned beside each image.

Eyes widening, Wilder asked, "This sounds like pretty groundbreaking stuff. How come Harry or Tristian didn't mention any of it?"

"The information is so new, so fresh; and the Eadar and its people so set in their ways. I know, for the two of them, and for many others, this is insignificant information. Too old for them to give any credit to. Too difficult for them to believe until they see some other kind of proof."

Wilder stared down at the images and remembered the stained glass dragon in the sunroom. "If these stones could supposedly be real, what about the dragons?"

"Your guess is as good as mine. While we are still working to decipher the information about the stones, we haven't found anything to suggest the actual existence of dragons, though the stories certainly point to the possibility of them."

"What happened in the rest of the story?" Wilder asked. "Why did the Fae lose their power?"

Rickard scratched at his chin, a rough stubble beginning to darken his jawline. "According to the legends, the dragons and their stones were meant to be a reminder to all the Céad, and to the humans, of the greatness of the Magíck they worshiped. But the Fae grew prideful in their power, as you know, perceiving it as a blessing from the Magíck, and themselves as little less than their Creator. The Fae pressed the humans, and the rest of the Céad, to revere them as the truest representation of the Magíck on Earth."

"Yeah, Harry mentioned something like that. I'm sure that didn't go well," Wilder remarked.

Rickard chuckled under his breath, his brown hair falling over his brow. "It did not. The dragons and the stones—which were intended to represent the authority of the Magíck—instead began to symbolize the Fae's rule. The Great Wars followed. Humans, the weakest of the creation, fell victim to the crossfires, no longer protected by those who had once been sworn to them. And in fear for their lives, the humans hunted down members of the Céad. It was turmoil, from what we understand. Creation was lucky to not have been annihilated." Rickard pushed his glasses up the bridge of his nose.

"To punish its creation for their arrogance, and to remedy what had befallen all of humanity, the Magíck created the Shroud, reclaimed the 'dragons', and scattered the 'dragonstones' across the Earth—to the unseen places where only the worthy could hope to recover them. The only way for either the stones or the dragons to come back, according to our legends, was through the forgiveness of the Magick. Only that could restore the dragonstones to their rightful people, and only then would the dragons return. We have, of course, come to understand this only as a valuable lesson about pride and folly, and how our connection to our creator is hindered by both."

"Harry said something about there being no way the Magick would forgive us anytime soon," Wilder said.

Rickard's thin lips tugged into a proud smile. "He's a smart boy, that one," he said. "I'd venture to agree with him. Sure, some may earn such a gift, but as an entire people, nothing in our histories point to such a thing ever happening."

"So what do the dragonstones, or this new information about them, have to do with what's going on now?" Wilder asked.

Rickard swallowed hard. "Like I said, most scholars didn't think they existed. But when Markus rose to power, there were many who questioned how on earth he could have gotten so powerful, so quickly. His rebellion is the very reason these new texts were uncovered. We unfortunately now have reason to believe Markus may actually be in possession of one of these stones. A physical stone. The War Stone in particular."

Wilder's mouth popped open. "What makes you think that?" he asked. "And what does it do?"

Rickard sighed deeply. "From what we've learned, the War Stone is supposedly one of the nine dragonstones," he explained. "It's thought to give the possessor the ability to control and manipulate the elements of battle. It is believed to encourage wisdom, discernment, and an understanding of winning strategic maneuvering in war. But, when used with ill intent, it is also believed to incite a drive for fight in those the possessor chooses to influence. We do know the Watern may hold powers similar to this, though we've rarely seen it used by them. In addition, according to our research, the longer someone is under the influence of any of the stones, the more he or she becomes in awe of its power, and of its keeper. They serve the stone and its master without question. It is also said that their eyes look as if they're staring into the heart of the stone itself."

Wilder thought of the distinct shine he had seen glimmering over the eyes of the rogues the other night, and looked up at Rickard in shock.

"Not only do many of the rogues we have captured fit the description of someone under the influence of a stone," Rickard went on, "but some of them, oddly enough, have a difficult time reasonably telling us what they are even fighting for. They only know they are supposed to be. These men and women are not in their right minds, and are convinced in their tenacity to not only serve Markus, but also of a desperate need for war. To further support our theories, many of these rogues have described, with astonishing detail, a stone Markus has in his possession that he is quite protective of. So much so that he does not allow any of his accomplices to touch it. A blood-red stone, they say, that 'shines from within'."

"Wait, so if this is true, every single person fighting for Markus has absolutely no idea what they're doing? They're just obsessed with this stone?" Wilder's mouth fell open. "That's ridiculous."

"Not necessarily. Unfortunately, we do know there are a number of Céad that fully agree with Markus's stand against the Magistrie and the humans. No magical compellation required. Though I'm not entirely convinced he did not manipulate a fair few into fighting a war quite different from the one he truly intended to start, or at least the one he is now fully in the trenches of," Rickard said.

"What do you mean?" Wilder asked.

Rickard scanned Wilder's features. "I often forget how little you know of our world." He cleared his throat. "When Markus first attacked the Céad, many of the Fae believed it to do with his father's choice to name his younger brother as the Fairn heir, rather than Markus. And he drew many to his cause, claiming the Magistrie had undue power over the decision, and over many of the decisions made by and for each independent tribe or species. But it was not the first time a fae had been unhappy about the outcome of a succession, nor will it be the last, to be sure. Despite the following he gathered, many across the Eadar believed the issue should be resolved within the Fae themselves, as it had been in the past. So most ignored the small uprisings that followed, thinking they'd resolve on their own.

"However, while Markus's discontent with the succession remains *one* of the reasons behind the start of his war, it is not the most substantial. Those who were closest to him then, but chose to remain loyal to the Magistrie, have since shared more about Markus than most of us knew. His true reasons for the war apparently involve a concerning perspective Markus has held for some time—regarding the humans and our role as their protectors. It was this stance that played a primary role in his father Samael's choice to opt against him when naming his heir."

Wilder figured he looked perplexed, so Rickard clarified.

"Markus has preached to his followers that the humans stole the Earth from the Céad during The Great Wars, and that the Magistrie is doing nothing to serve its people, forcing them to remain behind the Shroud while the humans destroy our world and take what is rightfully ours. Markus believes our entire history is nothing more than a farce to keep the Céad in line. That there are no gods and no Magíck. That our legends are nothing more than a nursery rhyme devised to keep the Céad from achieving their full potential. He believes protecting the humans is doing nothing but hurting us."

Wilder grimaced, recalling his conversation with Terra and the statements he had made about the existence of the Magíck.

"I, however, am skeptical of some of these claims," Rickard finished.

"Why?" Wilder asked. "Which claims?"

"Well, given Markus's clear possession of a dragonstone, I find it difficult to believe he could write off our entire history. In my opinion, though not shared by all, Markus not only believes in the whole of our origin story, but is actively working against the Magick and the gods that serve it. And most of the Council here has come to agree. To what end, I'm not yet sure. Undiluted power, perhaps. It seems farfetched, I know. We have little support within the Magistrie to my claims. And I don't blame them. Many of us are just now coming to terms with the believability of so much of the story. Most are still set on this being more about Markus's hatred for the Magistrie and the humans than anything else. But his affinity for such complete chaos, for such mass murder, that he has displayed these last eighteen years…" Rickard placed his hands on the desk and stared unseeing down at the papers beneath his palms. "There's something far greater at hand. I just can't quite put my finger on it."

"But you mentioned they captured some of the rogues, right? What happened to them? Couldn't they be used to get to Markus? To understand his true motives?" Wilder asked.

"That may be one of the most heartbreaking parts of all of this. Neither Magem nor Fae have been able to break through whatever dark magic has latched onto their psyches. Most attempts to do so have resulted in complete lunacy for the rogues in question, if not death—and often by their own hand." Rickard's voice sounded tinged with regret. "Year after year, each side of this war has faced innumerable losses, and there is no end in sight—besides the inevitable extinction of one people group or another."

Wilder crossed his arms again, the pain in his body all but forgotten as he rifled through the information. "But how did he get it?" he whispered, staring down at the papers.

"Pardon?" Rickard looked up from his desk.

"The stone," Wilder wondered. "How did he get the stone? Weren't they supposed to be 'scattered to where only the worthy could hope to find them' or something like that? He hardly strikes me as someone your 'Magíck' would deem worthy."

"Ah." Rickard paused, pulling his previously disregarded chair closer. He took a seat and leaned into the leather, taking a breath. His voice sounded tired. "A valid question, and one we would all love to know the answer to. What we do know is that since the beginning of the war, Markus has been in a constant partnership with a wyte we know only as Haman. No one knows much about her or from where she came. But what we do know is that she practices a very dangerous and very illegal form of blood magic called Maluum." Rickard placed a hand on the hieroglyphed book in front of him.

"Blood magic in itself is looked down upon. Forbidden from being taught in any of our sanctioned schools. It is a distortion of the Magíck that only brings harm to any who practice it. But Maluum—it's a brand of magic many of us had thought to be as lost as the stones themselves. Maluum taps into the heart of the Dahrk, the very antithesis of the Magíck, in ways that are irreversible. Given the inordinate level of power a Maluum practitioner can possess, we have no doubt that Markus's associations with Haman likely led, in some way, to his acquisition of the stone. We just aren't quite sure how," Rickard said.

"So what now? What can I do to help?" Wilder asked, champing at the bit to be useful.

Rickard peered at him with fatherly concern. "You can help," his tone amused, his eyes shining, "by allowing the adults in the Council to do what the Council does best: protect. Yourself included. And while we're doing that, it's of utmost importance you concentrate on your studies and work diligently to improve your abilities. I don't want to see or hear of anymore haphazard street fighting, whether it be with Markus's rogues or not."

Wilder made to counter the request, to assert that he was more than old enough to handle himself, but thought better of it. Tristian had made that very same argument, and it had gotten him nowhere. "Yes, sir," Wilder said, clasping his hands behind him, his mouth drawing into a tight line as he nodded in defeat. But while Wilder couldn't have stopped anything that had happened the other night, he didn't think he would've had he had the opportunity. He knew there was no chance that woman would be alive now if they hadn't intervened, and everything in him itched to return to the fight. Or at the very least, experience his powers again.

Wilder conceded to Rickard, assuring him he could rely on his promise of good behavior—minus a skirmish or two to incite his powers. But Wilder conveniently left that part out.

"Good," Rickard said, checking his watch. "We should head downstairs. I received word about an hour ago that we'll soon be welcoming an addition to our family party."

CHAPTER SEVENTEEN

As Wilder and Rickard arrived in the living room, Wilder noticed two couples he hadn't seen before deep in conversation with Terra, Tristian, and Barrett.

Terra spoke to a tall, dark-skinned man with closely trimmed black hair dusted with sprigs of wiry gray. He wore a pristine navy blue suit cut to his frame, and unconsciously pushed the thin metal setting of his rounded spectacles up the bridge of a familiarly refined nose. The man held the arm of an agelessly beautiful woman with emerald green eyes that Wilder assumed must be his wife. Her delicate hand resting along where their elbows met, their implicit interactions spoke of an unflinching devotion. These were Terra's parents by no mistake.

Tristian and Barrett, however, could only attribute their wintery, paled looks to their father—an even taller, stockier man with an instant authoritarian air to him. His eyes were the same icy glacial blue, and his hair the same white blond. He moved with a demanding brusqueness that seemed to make the air quiver around him. Tristian's mother, on the other hand, looked nothing like either of her sons, except for the same angled jawline and a slight build similar to Barrett's. She had a long face and a rush of auburn hair that Wilder thought looked like an autumn waterfall, and hazel eyes with prominent flecks of russet and gold. Though in her languid, graceful movements, Wilder could see both of her sons.

Wilder's attention returned to Terra and her parents.

"But you're alright then?" Terra's mother asked her, concern written across her features as she smoothed down the unruly chestnut waves Terra had clearly inherited from her.

"*Yes*, mom. Perfectly fine," Terra assured, lightly pushing her mother's hand away, her cheeks darkening. They must have been discussing the fight in the alleyway. "There's someone I'd like you to meet, though." Terra gestured to where Wilder stood at the door. Rickard had disappeared toward the kitchen, likely to check in about dinner. Terra signaled to Wilder, and he sheepishly entered the room. To his surprise, Terra's father held out his hand. Wilder accepted it.

"Tremaine Sampson," he introduced. Wilder thought he'd find him intimidating, but there wasn't anything other than a genuine friendliness to the gesture. "And this is my wife, Sofia."

She nodded at Wilder, her smile warm, though her astute gaze shone with an edge of curiosity. "It's a pleasure to meet you, Wil. I believe we owe you a debt of gratitude for your part in the escapades these deviants got themselves into the other night."

"Oh, it was nothing. Happy to be there," Wilder stuttered, instantly regretting his choice of words as they tumbled from his mouth. Swallowing hard, his cheeks warmed. Sofia gave him a gentle smile, her familiar eyes twinkling.

Wilder heard a gruff clearing of throat next to him, and found that Tristian's father had strode over, stopping uncomfortably close to Wilder. Stiffening, he found himself taken aback by the authority the man seemed to carry wherever he moved.

"Yes. How lucky we are that you found your way to us *just in time*," Tristian's father added, his tone mocking and drenched in suspicion. Wilder tried not to instantly dislike him. "Caolin Snow," he extended his hand. "I hear my son has the pleasure of training you in combat."

Wilder thought Tristian must have gotten a lot more than his looks from this cold and calculating man. Caolin's smile did not reach his eyes as Wilder shook his hand. Holding it fast, Caolin seemed to freeze Wilder in place, and he found himself unable to step away from the broad man's towering frame, and the icy chill emanating from him. While Tristian and Barrett were a display of the beauty of winter, this man was the personification of its harshness.

Caolin stared down at him, his hard eyes assessing every aspect of Wilder's appearance—starting with his stormy gray eyes and ending with a prolonged inspection of his freckled face and unruly red hair. Wilder felt Caolin's breath on him, and he thought he smelled distinctly like the frozen ground. "Forgive me," Caolin said, his timbre a whisper. "You remind me of someone I used to know." With another icy sweep over Wilder's features, he let go of his hand.

Wilder stumbled back and gulped for air. "Um, yeah. No problem," he gasped, regaining his composure.

Sofia threw Caolin an impressive scowl reminiscent of the many Terra had given Wilder. But before she could reprimand him, Olivia popped around the corner. Her bright features were an unexpectedly welcome sight, allowing Wilder a respite from the intense inspection as all eyes turned to her.

"Dinner's up!" she announced, and the party echoed a joint approval as they promenaded into the dining room. Wilder waited until most of the others had found a seat, not wanting to step on any toes in case there were places the newcomers were partial to. Anything to keep the peace.

From somewhere behind him, a small arm snuck past his elbow, interlocking with his own. Wilder glanced down to find Olivia leading him to a seat next to her, smiling vividly at the energy in the room. She was in her element—the more people, the better—and Wilder noted how different the two of them were. As they sat down, she began chatting idly at him about all the delicious foods, and how she had helped James with some of the pies. Nodding at her, Wilder stared down at his plate, not even sure what he was agreeing to.

"Not one for small talk, are you?" she asked him, leaning over the armrest of his chair so only he could hear her.

"Not if I can help it," Wilder told her, watching the interactions of everyone else at the table.

"That's okay," she said. He turned to meet her gaze, and she beamed up at him. "I can handle a challenge."

Heat rose to Wilder's cheeks, and he coughed to clear his throat, reaching to grab his water.

Wilder noticed he wasn't the only person considering Olivia's interest in making sure Wilder got a helping of everything at the table. As most of the room busied themselves, Wilder saw Harry watching them out of the corner of his eye, his expression a trained neutral. But the tight corners of his mouth, his absent dimples, and the tense set of his shoulders betrayed his otherwise unbothered features.

A few seats to Harry's left, Terra watched them as well. Though her reaction looked to be one of…hurt? Disappointment? Before Wilder could pinpoint the expression, it disappeared, replaced with a warm smile directed at Tristian's mother, who was inquiring about Terra's studies into fifteenth century magic.

Wilder bit out a thank you to Olivia and did his best to talk to just about anyone else for the rest of the evening, starting up a particularly boring conversation with Magi Maynestream about the shedding cycles of chameleons. He had no desire to cause a rift between him and Harry. Olivia really was cute, and friendly, and honestly a catch, but Wilder had little interest in her as more than a friend. Wilder didn't know a thing about girls, other than that they were a little more sensitive, and Wilder liked Olivia enough to not want to hurt her feelings. As he stared down at his plate, rolling his brussel sprouts from one side to the other, he found himself at a complete loss, and in a complete panic, about what to do.

★★★

After the longest thirty minutes of his life, Wilder choked down the rest of his food. As soon as Terra rose to help clean the table, he jumped up, excused himself, and grabbed whatever empty dishes were within arm's reach. He practically chased her into the kitchen, finding her unloading the mess into the sinks.

"Hey!" Wilder hung on the counter, breathless but making an impressive effort to appear casual.

"Hey?" Peering at him from over her shoulder, Terra stacked bowls into the soapy water. "You good?" Her eyes narrowed at the way he awkwardly held himself.

Taking a sharp breath, he dropped the act. "Um, do you think we…could we maybe…uh…that we could go for a walk or something?" Wilder stuttered, fumbling over his words as his nerves got the better of him.

"Like right now?" she asked, peering around him to check on the rest of the group still in the dining room. Olivia was in her prime, trying to convince the table to play a game of musical charades.

"Or whenever works," Wilder shrugged. "It's no big deal, just—" He lowered his head in his hands, rubbing at his temples. Now he couldn't even finish his sentences.

She's going to think I'm an idiot.

Wilder heard Terra sigh and looked up. She rested against the sink, her arms crossed, the soapy suds covering her hands dripping onto the tiles below. Her gaze flashed across his features, as if trying to figure out what could possibly be wrong with him. It wasn't a new look for her. Meeting his panicked gaze, she gave him a half smile, seemingly amused by his mounting discomfort. "Sure. We can go for a walk. Just let me finish up here." She gestured toward the sink.

"Alright. Great. Um. I'm going to head back to my room for a bit then…" he said, throwing a thumb over his shoulder as he started out of the room. "Get a bit of air."

Terra raised her eyebrows but nodded, assuring him she'd let the rest of them know he hadn't been feeling well.

In his room, Wilder stared at the ceiling with no real purpose other than to will himself to melt into his sheets. A knock on his door jostled him upright, and he silently prayed Olivia hadn't come to check on him. What would he even say?

'Sorry you made me nervous and not in a good way and I'd really like to stay friends with the only guy here my age that doesn't kind of hate me, and since he happens to be in love with you and all—'

Relief flooded him as he found Terra on the other side of the door, the tension he had been holding in his shoulders easing.

"Come on," she said, motioning for him to follow as she turned back toward the hallway. "I want to show you something."

CHAPTER EIGHTEEN

Terra led him to a large silver and blue tapestry hung draped from corner to corner at the end of one of the numerous hallways. Lifting the covering, she guided him into a narrow, unfinished wooden staircase. It looked as if it hadn't been touched in decades, if not longer.

Moonlight peeked through arched cutouts in the stone walls, lighting the passage as they descended the dusty steps. The stairs ended at an unmarked wall, and Terra placed a hand on its surface, closing her eyes. An arched block of the wall shifted beneath her fingers and the grinding of stone against stone filled the narrow passage. A moment later, a doorway appeared, its outline lit by the light shining from the other side of the barrier.

Terra pushed her palm against the stone, and it slid away. The door opened to what Wilder recognized as the covered patio on the far side of the gardens, far from the main living quarters. This section of the abbey, usually unvisited by everyone else, remained silent. Even the wind seemed hushed as it carried the scent of blooming magnolias past them. Along the covered patio, old Gothic-style windows looked in on darkened rooms. Wilder peered through one of the window frames, vaguely making out a fourposter bed, a small writing desk, and a plain wooden wardrobe.

Terra continued into the garden, and Wilder tore himself away from his exploring to follow. From where they were, Wilder could see silhouettes move across the lit windows on the other side of the courtyard, their owners preparing to settle in for the night. They strolled along the garden path, crossing underneath trellises and pergolas interlaced with the same wild ivy that snaked around the columns encircling the garden. This side of the Council House, Wilder thought, looked more like the abbey he had first believed the old building to be. Terra, as if reading his mind, confirmed his theory.

"Before this was a Council House—and it's been a Council House for a really long time—it was a monastery. It's rumored one of the friars that lived here, Fr. Henry Peckett, was actually a lycan, and his brothers in the church, instead of turning him in, protected him here. They brought in multiple young men with the same affliction, without the church's knowledge, and aided them when their families deserted them.

"When Peckett had been here for too long to be reasonably considered human by the diocese, he left the monastery. But the monastery continued to help lost lycan like him. Almost 50 years later, the church closed the abbey, displacing the last of the lycan who had sought refuge here. They eventually sold the building to a gentleman who called himself James Stillwater. Though, according to some lesser known history books, Stillwater bore an uncanny resemblance to Peckett himself." Terra smiled knowingly. "When the Magistrie sought to extend their reach into this region, Stillwater volunteered his newly acquired abbey to the cause. He installed a Council House here, but continued to reach out to each of the displaced lycan whom had once called this place home, inviting them to return. With Stillwater as its Head Magister, this Council House soon became the first to institute a structured method of reaching out to unfound Céad in need of help, though most other Council Houses eventually followed suit."

"You know your history," Wilder said, stuffing his hands into his pockets as he cocked an eyebrow at her.

"It's nice to know where we come from. To be reminded why we do what we do," Terra said.

They strode in a comfortable silence, the only sound the wind brushing the leaves of the trees and the distant gurgle of a fountain somewhere beyond their view. Wilder reveled in how much easier it was to breathe out here, to think straight.

"Liv seems to like you," Terra stated plainly, staring down at her feet as she walked. She seemed to be paying special attention to maintaining even steps. Despite the nonchalance in her tone, Wilder could make out the shadow of a rueful smile playing at her lips.

"I guess so," Wilder said, releasing a burst of heavy breath and running a hand through his hair. "I don't really know what to do about it, to be honest."

"Well, what do you *want* to do about it?" Fastening her gaze on the pathway ahead, not a single ounce of emotion betrayed her matter-of-fact tone.

Wilder inhaled through his nose and stopped walking. Wheeling to face Terra, he said, "I *want* her to not." He could hear the exasperation in his tone. "It's not that I don't like her. You know—*platonically*. She's cool. She really is. But she's just not my type."

Terra turned to look up at him, and he locked his eyes on hers, his stare fixed on how their green glittered emerald in unison with the starlight above. Swallowing, he tore his stare away and moved on. "Our personalities are too different, and I just don't think we'd mesh well. Her peppiness would wear on me. But besides all that, I really like Harry, and I don't feel like making an enemy here for no reason. I don't understand why she doesn't just go for *him*. He's great. And he's clearly in love with her. Why me? I literally just got here, and I'm not the least bit impressive."

Terra smirked, evidently amused by his rant, but didn't interrupt. When he had finished, she said, "Well, first of all, I'm not entirely sure you see yourself clearly. I'd hardly call you unimpressive. But, in case you haven't noticed yet, Olivia's a bit of a firecracker. And sometimes not the good kind. She's working through a lot of stuff—about herself, about her past. She likes to distract herself from that, and I'm entirely sure her infatuation with you is nothing more than that—a fun distraction. Give it time. It'll disappear within the month." Terra paused and bit at her lip, as if deciding what she wanted to say next. "All that aside, she truly is an amazing person, and if you did decide to give something there a chance, I doubt anyone—including Harry—would fault you."

Wilder stared at her, but her blank expression refused to belie any other true feeling she had about the situation. But something in his gut, something in the way Terra's even breaths and steps matched his own, assured him his mind wasn't playing tricks on him. There was something there, even if she didn't want to admit it yet. He didn't blame her. He wasn't sure he wanted to admit it, either. With everything else going on, he knew Terra wasn't a distraction he should allow himself.

But as he watched her now, at the way she spoke with such confidence, at the way she defended her friend with such loyalty—damn if he didn't want to.

"As for her and Harry," Terra continued, "he's always been a constant for her, and she knows that. But I think she's terrified of losing that. Liv worries that if she truly loves anyone—allows herself to depend on anyone—they'll leave. Or they won't want her anymore. Deep down, she knows she loves Harry. But admitting to that opens her up to the possibility of a loss she couldn't bear. So I wouldn't take her attentions too seriously. I also wouldn't be too concerned about Harry's perception of it, either. Maybe just let on that you're not interested. Harry knows Olivia. She's never been able to get serious with anyone. He's had to watch her flit around from one fling to another for years. If he can love her through all that, I'm sure he'll love her through whatever fixation she's going through right now."

Wilder rubbed at his neck and nodded, staring down at her. Glancing away, Terra continued walking, but the conversation seemed to have made Terra more lively. Despite his reservations, Wilder made a mental note of it. The subtle pull of his skin seemed to mark it too, as if encouraging him to get closer, to touch her own. To make it clear where *his* attentions had settled. But he shoved the feeling away.

They continued to stroll down the cracked pavement, taking in the evening's spring chill, talking about how Wilder's training and Terra's studies were going, their conversation easy. The hour had grown far later than they had anticipated when they finally wandered back across the garden. Keeping their steps and voices hushed, they snuck into the House near the kitchens. They had thought everyone would be in bed, but they were dismally wrong. As they tiptoed to the staircase, Wilder and Terra came across the bulk of the Council, all in their nightclothes, gathered in the foyer with strained looks on their faces.

"Goodness, Terra!" Sofia cried. A pitch black cat mewed peacefully in her arms. "What on earth are you doing out so late? It's nearly two in the morning!"

Tremaine said nothing, but his investigative stare never left Wilder.

"We were just talking, Mom," Terra said, brushing off her concern with a wave of her hand. "What's wrong? What's happened?" Terra eyed the gathered Council warily.

Rickard's normally calm, collected tone cracked in distress. "Did either of you see or hear anything out of the ordinary while you were outside?"

Caolin studied Wilder with an intense glare. His hands shoved into the pockets of his stark white pajama bottoms, he held himself straight as an arrow. The air around him seemed to cower in his presence, and Wilder did the same.

"No, I don't think so," Wilder answered, shaking his head as he tried to ignore Caolin's scrutiny.

Another man Wilder hadn't met before descended the staircase, nearly tripping over himself on the final step. Unlike the rest of the Council, he wore daytime clothing, but appeared rather disheveled. Wilder couldn't be sure if the dishevelment had more to do with the lateness of the evening, or a general propensity towards unkemptness.

"Master Lyre. Thank you for joining us. Did you find anything?" Rickard asked as the man scuttled toward the gathered Council.

"All seems to be in order. Nothing was taken as far as I can tell. Though the library windows and skylight will need to be repaired," Master Lyre announced. His glasses sat slightly askew on his round, mousy face.

"The wards held then?" Tristian's mother asked.

"Thankfully, yes. Though I'm sure the irids will need to be replenished before we all return to bed," Master Lyre noted.

"Raiya and I will take care of it," Sofia said, looking to Tristian's mother, who nodded at her. They left the foyer and headed toward the Apotéca. Caolin, Tremaine, and Magi Maynestream moved to exit through the front doors to do a thorough search of the grounds.

Terra strode over to the newcomer. "Master Lyre," Terra said with a familiarity suggesting she knew the librarian well. "What's happened?"

"Ah, quite an evening, dearest." The slight man pushed his rounded pewter spectacles up along the bridge of his hawkish nose. "We believe someone may have attempted to break into the library shortly after the rest of the house went to bed."

"They weren't able to get in, as far as we can tell," Rickard, who had stayed behind, quickly clarified.

"What did they want? Do you know?" Panic lit Terra's gaze as it flashed between Rickard and Master Lyre.

"We aren't sure—" Rickard started, but Master Lyre cut him off.

"Ah well, I have a theory." Master Lyre lifted an index finger to silence Rickard as he readjusted his glasses again.

"Gerald, I hardly think…" Rickard started again, but Master Lyre would hear none of it. He promptly dove into a retelling of his grand tale for anyone who cared to hear, which, at the moment, comprised solely of Terra and Wilder.

"Quite a good many years ago, there lived here a man named Gideon Allark. An eccentric, yes, but altogether genius man whom we have to thank for many a spell and charm, I might add. It is rumored..."

"Though not at all proven or probable..." Rickard added quickly in a defeated sigh, staring up at the ceiling in disbelief and crossing his arms in resignation.

"It is *rumored*..." Master Lyre repeated, his squeak of a voice rising slightly over Rickard's. Rickard rolled his eyes behind him. "...that Gideon hid, somewhere in the library, The Book of Scales—a compendium of invaluable knowledge and spell work collected by an ancient magem who had worked closely with the dragons, their riders, and the dragonstones, all before the Fall. After the Fall, it remained well protected for quite some time before it was stolen from one of the most well-guarded vaults in Teír. From thence it was again stolen, and then bartered, and then traded, traveling from hand to hand and land to land, knowledge of its importance waning each time it was exchanged. Finally, it found homage with Gideon, who immediately recognized its irreplaceable worth and hid it *here*. It is hearsay, to be sure. And many," Master Lyre sliced a glare at Rickard, his lips pursing and eyes narrowing, "believe the tale to be nonsense. The library has, of course, been searched, reconstructed, and searched again. No such tome, or even a whisper of it, has ever been located. I daresay had our rogue friends even managed to break in this evening, they too could not have found it."

"We don't even *know* that's what they were looking for, Gerald," Rickard said, exasperated.

"Ah, but we don't know that they weren't..." Master Lyre rebutted, wagging a finger at him. "I could scarcely think of anything else they could possibly be after." He puffed out his chest and gave the trio a quick nod, as if the matter had been settled entirely.

Rickard's shoulders slumped, a wave of exhaustion hitting him. "Well, you're likely right there," Rickard amended. But his eyes shifted momentarily to Wilder before looking away again.

Master Lyre, not noticing, nodded solemnly. "Indeed. Indeed."

"Alright," Rickard clapped his hands together, abruptly ending the conversation. "It's time you two were headed to bed." He gestured to Terra and Wilder. "We'll all be up bright and early cleaning up and repairing the library."

"But…But we can help now!" Terra argued, her eyes darting around the empty foyer. "I could—"

Rickard cut her off with a firm tone. "*You* will be of the most help by proceeding to exactly where we expected you two to be three hours ago—*your beds.*"

And with that, he grabbed them each by their shoulders and steered them toward the staircase, where they said their clipped goodbyes and went their separate ways to bed.

CHAPTER NINETEEN
Terra

Terra had always been a morning person, waking up hours before the rest of the house to read or enjoy the quiet of a new day. This morning should not have been any different. Except that the main reason she found herself awake well before dawn was because she had never gone to sleep at all. After leaving the unexpected excitement in the foyer the night before, Terra had tossed and turned in bed for another three hours before giving up on the venture entirely.

She had tried to read, but exhaustion made it impossible. She had tried to journal, but she could hardly string an intelligible sentence together. Her brain raced a mile a minute, and yet got nowhere fast. Between her parents return to New Orleans (which always came with a fresh wave of their anticipation of some glorious achievement, followed shortly by their eventual disappointment), Tristian's constant moodiness, Olivia's recent unpredictability, and now the break-in, Terra felt—in every sense of the word—on edge. But to top it all off, she was realizing she might now have another problem to worry about.

Wilder.

I need coffee. The thought plunked through her fried brain while she stared out her window, the rising sun lighting a cloudless sky. But she couldn't really see it at all. All she saw was gray.

For now, she'd have to settle with a cold shower.

Terra finished dressing in what she hoped was distracting enough attire to draw prying eyes away from the sunken purple half-moons atop her cheekbones. A moment later, an eager knock racked at her door. Brow furrowing, she glanced at her clock.

7:12am. Who else would possibly be up this early?

She opened the door to find exhausted but wired gray eyes staring back at her, and she sucked in a breath, her skin prickling. Their owner bore two steaming mugs of black dark roast coffee alongside a pair of lemon poppy seed muffins—all balanced precariously on top of each other.

Terra let out a small gasp. "Bless you…" she said, immediately grabbing one of the mugs and taking a large gulp.

"Careful! It's—" Wilder tried to warn her, but she was too far gone, the coffee already burning her throat. She ignored the discomfort, savoring the heat in hopes the caffeine would soon hit her bloodstream.

"Good morning to you too." Wilder smirked, evidently amused by her lack of usual decorum. He dropped the rest of their breakfast on a dresser near the door, crossed his freckled, muscled arms over his broad chest, and inclined against her doorframe, watching her.

"Mhm," she sounded through her mouthful of drink, giving him a dazed nod before looking away. She always felt like she was toeing the line between looking at him, and gawking. After downing another gulp, she felt life spark through her brain again. Closing her eyes, she savored the rush. "Praise the coffee gods," she mumbled aloud, and she heard Wilder chuckle. Opening her eyes, she noticed his stare had never left her. "Why are *you* up so early?" she finally asked, ignoring his intense inspection.

"I could ask you the same." Wilder's eyes flashed across her tired face and the mess of hair piled atop her head before retrieving his own mug from the dresser and taking a sip.

"I couldn't sleep," Terra answered, her tone unattached as she tried to keep her fatigue from betraying the emotional tumult she had been battling since the night before. Since he had made it crystal clear he had no interest in Olivia, and had seemed compelled to make that point to *her,* specifically. She didn't know what to do with that, or what she even *wanted* to do with that. Was she attracted to Wilder? Sure. She could admit that to herself, at least. Did she want to deal with the complications that would come from that? Unequivocally, no.

"Me neither," Wilder said, his eyes wide with an inexplicable excitement. Terra stared at him warily. "I wanted to talk to you about something."

Oh no, Terra thought. *I can't do this right now.*

"Wilder, I—"

"Terra. Is James Stillwater from the monastery the same James that still lives here?" His gray eyes on hers were alight with a curious fervor, and likely a generous dose of caffeine.

Terra breathed an internal sigh of relief. "Oh! Um. Yeah, actually. It's not common knowledge. I think he doesn't like people knowing how old he is. And not too many have bothered to ask. Most don't even know how this Council House got started. Why?"

Wilder bit at his bottom lip. "Do you think James could have known Gideon Allark while he was here?" he proposed.

Breath hitching, Terra's eyes widened. She stared at Wilder for a moment, processing what he had asked. "I… hadn't thought of that. I mean, I hadn't even heard of the book or of Gideon until last night." Terra grabbed a muffin and left Wilder at the door, beginning to pace around her room and chomping down on a bite of lemon. "It would stand to reason…" she said, her voice muffled as she chewed.

Wilder quirked an eyebrow at her, but smiled, trailing her movement. "Where do you think James is now?" he asked.

Closing her eyes, Terra forced her mind to clear. "If he's not still asleep, I'd assume he's helping in the library."

"Great, let's go." Wilder took a giant gulp of his coffee before setting his mug on the dresser. But then he stopped, cocking his head like he had belatedly realized something. His smoky stare flicked to hers, and the intensity in his gaze stopped her pacing. He took a few measured strides into the room, stopping directly in front of her, his eyes boring into hers, and waited. She barely reached his chin.

He didn't say anything at first, still searching her face for some kind of reaction, and Terra swallowed her bite of muffin whole. Was he baiting her? At this proximity, she could practically smell him, waves of coffee and burnt earth barreling off of him.

"Terra. Was there something else you *thought* I had wanted to talk about?" he asked, his words careful as he continued to search her expression.

"Oh!" Terra backpedaled. She couldn't do this. Not right now. Not like this. Not with him standing right in front of her, staring at her like he knew her heart had stopped beating. Her throat went dry. "It was nothing important. Probably just something about the library. Let's find James, yeah?" She broke from his stare. Side-stepping around him, she set down her cup and rushed him from her room.

★★★

Terra and Wilder found James assisting Master Lyre in the library, sweeping up the loose shards and fragments of colored glass littering the wood and carpeted floors. The morning sun lit the large circular room, located at the top of one of the abbey's turrets. Daybreak streamed through multiple broken windows and a smashed skylight above, the sun's rays scattering into colored shafts as it poured through the jagged edges of the shattered stained glass remaining in the window frames.

Terra stifled a cry as she surveyed the scene. Picking up a shard of indigo glass, her heart lurched. She couldn't bear to see the library like this. This place had always been her favorite part of the Council House. She had spent hours upon hours lurking the aisles and huddled in corners, escaping into old stories about fae pirates, sea monsters, or the long-lost dragons and the First Council. This was where she would hide away when she didn't want to think about whatever came next for her. It was the only place she could disappear.

Each window, now utterly destroyed, had once held timeless stained glass artwork from the first construction of the abbey, likely never to be recovered. Half of the windows were now boarded with rudimentary planks. The Council would have to contract someone to replace them, along with the skylight above. A crash sounded from behind her, and she turned to see Tristian and Harry stumble into the room carrying a massive amethyst geode, similar to the other irids under the foundations of the abbey, each heavily spelled to maintain the wards.

"Where do you want this, Lyre?" Tristian shouted toward a stack of bookshelves as they rested the geode on the ground. Tristian looked up, locking eyes with Terra before his gaze flashed to Wilder's presence next to her. His features darkened, and Terra realized how it must look that Wilder had arrived with her so early in the morning.

Great. Another thing I'll have to deal with later.

"One under each window, and at least four under the skylight, gentlemen," Master Lyre squeaked from beyond the shelves. He scuttled into the room a moment later. "We'll need to increase the protections here just in case we have a repeat of last night."

"You got it." Harry bent to lift the geode again. Tristian stared at Terra for a moment longer, a perceptible scowl inching across his face, before he rejoined him.

Master Lyre shuffled away to supervise Harry and Tristian. Now away from prying eyes, Terra and Wilder approached James, who had been whistling a playful tune since they had arrived.

"Good morning James," Terra said. "Have you been up here for a while?"

"Since sunrise, Miss Terra. A right shame they've gone and done this. That was some pretty glass they smashed up, whoever they were. And mighty old, too. I reckon I might just remember when it was first put in." Heaving a forlorn sigh, James stared down at the colored glass shards in his dustpan.

"James," Terra asked slowly, "would you happen to know *what* they were trying to take? Whoever broke in?"

James stilled, but let no other reaction escape him. Finally, he said, "Ah, well, it could've been anything, huh? Far be it for me to know. Can't read minds like those water fae, can I?" He chuckled, but the laugh was thin.

"Well no," Terra considered carefully, "only…I was wondering if you…maybe you knew about Gideon Allark. Or, I mean, had known him while he was here?"

James stopped sweeping and his dark eyes moved to Terra. Leaning on the handle of his broom, he hooked one ankle around the other. He gave Terra an amused and knowing smile. "Ah. You've always been too quick for your own good, Miss Terra." He shook a finger at her. "So you'll be thinking whoever broke in was after that book, then?" Righting himself, he looked down and resumed his sweeping. In a mumbled voice, almost too low to hear, he added, "Aye. I knew the boy."

Terra felt her heart pound in her chest. "Is it real? The book? Did he leave it here? I mean, that you know of?" she asked him in a low, fervent voice, barely leaving enough room for him to get an answer in between her questions. She could hear the voices of Master Lyre and the others coming closer. Wilder peered between the shelves next to her, ready to let her know if they got too close.

"Ack, that blasted book. Every few decades it gets someone else up in a hustle." He chuckled, but the sound was thin. "Aye. He might've left it, sure. A clever lad, that one. But if he did, there's no telling where it ended up. And you'd be better off not tryin' to find it, either."

"So he really did have the book?" Wilder whispered hurriedly, ignoring James's warnings. Wilder's eyes flashed towards the voices of the others approaching.

"Aye, he had the book," James said. "Saw it once, even. And I wouldn't doubt it's still here, just like they say. But like I said. *You'd be better off forgettin about it.* I can promise you that." James eyed them with uncharacteristic earnest, gravity shading his usually easy lilt.

"Here in the library?" Terra asked, her brow lifting in surprise.

James rolled his eyes at them, recognizing his warnings were falling on deaf ears. "Mmm. Library? That's what they've been sayin for years, huh? Only thing is, this ain't the only library." Tapping a finger at his temple, his Cheshire smile widened. He clearly took the story as seriously as Master Lyre, but Terra couldn't be sure if he was trying to help them or deter them.

"You mean to say they never searched any of the other libraries?" Terra asked curiously, trying to read his always unreadable expression. But the man had too many years on her, and was far more cunning than he let on.

"Not to my knowing, Miss Terra. But, like I said, Gideon was a clever one. A lot like you. Even if they had looked for it, they probably wouldn't have found anythin'."

Terra made a mental note to tear apart every other library in the House. How had the Council been so oblivious to something so obvious? Had they even bothered to look at all?

"Thank you James." Terra nodded to him.

"You're welcome Miss Terra." He chuckled again, the sound much more affectionate. "Listen, you two just try not to get yourselves into any real mischief, you hear? The Council's got quite enough to be worryin' about without you kids goin' on wild treasure hunts."

"Yes sir, Master James," Terra assured him, but with little intention to do any such thing. That book was a priceless piece of history, and she was determined to find it. James padded away, sweeping glass fragments from beneath another window.

"Do you think it might be somewhere else?" Wilder whispered as James moved out of earshot. "Maybe in the Apotéca?"

"Maybe. But we can't risk looking for it now." Terra's eyes flew to the rest of the group reentering the library's center. She continued hurriedly, "At best they'd stop us and tell us we're wasting time better spent training. At worst, we'd be interfering with an ongoing investigation. We should keep our heads down until things relax. We don't want to raise any suspicion."

"You've thought about this," Wilder said, pausing to look at her. She caught his searching gray stare, and the red-gold of his lashes made his eyes look like unfurling smoke. A cough sounded, and Wilder straightened, taking a step away just in time for Tristian and Harry to appear.

"Quit the flirting, Summer," Tristian commanded coolly, his icy gaze falling on Terra. Harry grabbed Wilder's arm, his face painted with a mischievous grin. Terra didn't miss the remnant of betrayal crossing Tristian's features before he trained them to his usual aloof expression.

Figures.

"Yeah, all hands on deck! Consider this strength training," Harry joked, dragging Wilder away.

"I guess I'm needed elsewhere." Wilder shrugged at Terra, though his sportive grin attested to the growing camaraderie between the three males.

Terra smirked, waving goodbye just as Olivia entered the room, side stepping their exit and throwing a curious glance back at the sight of Wilder being hauled away. Terra looked her over. Liv appeared as worn out as Terra had felt that morning. What on earth had she been up to?

"Hey!" Liv said, nothing about her bright lilt suggesting anything amiss. "I was looking for you! Wanna get some coffee?" Olivia tucked her arm through Terra's, resting her temple against her shoulder. The gesture felt familiar, a sure sign Olivia needed comfort.

"Absolutely," Terra said, her smile crinkling her eyes as she pressed her cheek atop Liv's curls. "A barrel of it, preferably."

CHAPTER TWENTY
Terra

The outside patio of Café Du Monde thrummed with the comings and goings of strangers. Terra knew Liv thrived on the hustle and bustle of the city, so this was the perfect place for her to recuperate from whatever had put her in a funk.

Taking a bite of her beignet, Terra wiped the powdered sugar from her top lip. The bread tasted soft and warm and reminded her of being a little girl. When she had been young, Terra and her father would come to City Park every Sunday. They'd stroll hand in hand around the lake, weaving through the towering oaks and talking about whatever Terra was learning. It had been her favorite day of the week. Her dad would let her climb the trees as high as she wanted, watching closely to make sure she didn't fall. Under his attentive gaze, she knew she never would.

Sometimes they would go to Storyland, a massive playground where larger-than-life storybook sculptures loomed over her as she meandered through the flowering gardens. Terra remembered feeling so insignificant among the giant characters, but dad had always been there whenever she felt too scared of the fire-breathing dragons. After a few hours, they'd end their day with beignets and chocolate milk. His whole body would shake with laughter at the sight of her little face masked in milk and powdered sugar, but he'd always get her one extra for the road.

Then Terra got older, and her father's responsibilities to the Council and the Coven increased. Their visits to the park grew less frequent. Soon they only went once a month, then a couple times a year, until the trips stopped entirely.

Taking a sip of her coffee to wash down the beignet, Terra let the memories slip away with the taste of cream and sugar. "Out late?" she asked Liv, eyeing the fatigue lining Liv's normally radiant skin.

"Not *too* late." Liv gave her a coy smile, but the deep half-moons beneath her lashes suggested otherwise.

Terra let out a disbelieving scoff. "I doubt that, Liv. You look like you never even saw your bed last night."

"Harsh, Terr!" Liv scrubbed at her face to bring some life to it. "Okay, okay. So maybe I was out a little late," she laughed, "but you're one to talk. Been on any romantic late night strolls with the House's newest attraction, lately?" Liv flashed her a gamesome grin, but Terra saw the subtle hurt she made a decent effort to conceal.

Terra paused and gave Liv a considering look. "Liv, I promise you, there's nothing going on there. And I don't know that Wil is interested in anything with anyone right now. And I don't blame him. He's got enough going on."

"Right," Liv said, smirking. "The same way Tristian isn't interested in anyone that isn't Seasuír, and you only go for magem? Please, Terr. Don't tell me you're that delusional."

Terra looked down at her coffee and didn't respond. She was right, of course, but Terra also could have called her out, could have told her she did the same with Harry… "Either way, Liv. What's got you so interested?" Terra reclined in her chair, resting her wrists along the iron armrests. "You don't know anything about him. None of us do. I'm not saying he's a bad option, but we don't know him well enough to know if he's a good one either…"

Liv tilted her head, her lips pulling up in a snide smile, her dark curls bobbing with the movement. "You're joking, right? Have you seen him? Plus, he seems nice enough. And we've both got the whole sad backstory kind of thing going on, you know? It could work," Liv bartered. But Terra could see the remnants of chaos lighting the backs of her eyes, like gunpowder set aflame. Something was eating at her.

"I can see what you're getting at," Terra said carefully, "but I don't know if those are necessarily the best reasons to go for someone."

"Oh? Then what *is* a good reason, Terr? *You* went for Tristian, and he's a jerk. Sorry," she shrugged again. Terra knew Liv hadn't intended to be mean, and she had a point. Terra telling Liv not to go for Wilder was like the pot calling the kettle black. Only worse. "Pretty face though," Liv cocked another grin and winked. "Good on you."

Heat flooded Terra's cheeks. "Yeah, and we both know how *that* turned out. Don't you see what I'm talking about? That wasn't my brightest moment. We both know that. And you saw the outcome first hand, so you should know better than anyone. Don't you want better than what I had to deal with? What I'm *still* dealing with? I'm not saying Wil would be anything like him, but you never know—he is a fae. Fae can be trouble, even when they don't know they are. And you deserve better. You know that."

Liv was her best friend. They had practically grown up together. They had struggled beside each other, seen each other at their worst, and had carried one another through heartache, guilt, and their constant fight for a place in their crumbling, war-torn world. And despite Liv's tendency to overlook an obviously bad idea for the sake of a good time, she could still be both incredibly strong and incredibly wise. When she decided it suited her.

Today, however, didn't seem to be one of those days.

"Of course I do!" Liv admitted.

Well, at least there's that.

"Whatever. It doesn't matter about Wilder," Liv said. She waved an errant hand and took another sip of her coffee. "He's clearly not interested. It sucks, but no big deal. We can all see he's too goo-goo for you, and I just can't compete with that level of perfection." Liv gave Terra a loving smile as she toyed with one of her flawless ringlets. "There's someone else I've been talking to, anyway." Her sweet smile turned mischievous.

"Oh?" Terra's eyes widened in surprise, before narrowing in on her. "That was quick."

"Don't be so judgey," Liv chastised. "Pieter and I have been hanging out since before Wilder came into the picture. He's just been a little busy with some shows, so I haven't seen him around as much, but—"

"Shows?" Terra interrupted, struggling to keep the word from sounding like a full-on snap.

"Oh. Right. I forgot to tell you. He's a drummer." Olivia's eyes glazed over in a dreamy stare, as if recalling some recent unforgettable rendezvous.

Goodie. Here we go again.

Terra remembered the last time Liv had gotten involved with some punk pretending to be a big shot music artist. A year ago it had been a DJ. He had taken her to a 21-and-up venue he'd been playing at, getting her in with a fake ID and some greased elbows. Before the night was over, he had ditched a drunk, sixteen-year-old Liv for some pole dancer, leaving her to find her own way home. Tristian had been so pissed when he had finally brought her back.

But no one in their right mind dared to tell Harry until a few days later. The moment he found out, he disappeared, only returning to the Council House days later. Rickard had been furious, grounding him for a month, but Harry hadn't cared. To this day, Terra still had no idea where Harry had gone, but when Liv had recklessly reached out to the DJ after that, she received a curt response telling her that under no uncertain terms should she ever contact him again.

Terra stared at Liv, her own face schooled into as blank of an expression as she could muster. "Okay. Drummer. That's…*great*, Liv." If Liv had caught on that Terra didn't really mean it, she didn't let on. "Is he a Céad?" Terra asked. "Human?"

"Wolf!" Liv squeaked, grabbing Terra's wrist in excitement. Her smile reached all the way to her sunlit chocolate eyes. "It's perfect, Terr! He's part of one of the local clans."

Terra's heart sunk. She knew the reputations *most* of the clans had, especially the ones around here, and they were anything but good, let alone *'perfect'*. And Council kids weren't exactly their preferred choice of company, lycan or not. Terra couldn't shake the feeling there might be some ill intentions involved in Pieter's interest with Liv.

"*Which* of the local clans, Liv? You're being careful? You know which wolves to hang with, right?" Terra pleaded.

"What's that supposed to mean, Terra?" Liv snarled, her features shifting from a blush to explosively combative in a split second.

Terra flinched. While Liv had always been a bit of an emotional rollercoaster, this aggressiveness—and honestly, borderline irrationality—caught Terra off-guard.

"What's the *right* kind of wolf, Terra? You remember I am one, right? We can't all be perfect little wytes like you, pampered and preened by mom and dad to take over the family business."

Wincing, Terra gaped at her, Liv's verbal blow a visceral punch to her gut. She fought back the tear pricking the corner of her eye. Steadying herself, she trained her face once again to a safe blank slate, reminding herself that something was up with her friend. That she'd never say something like that otherwise.

"Liv, you know that's not what I mean," Terra said, her tone more hushed, more defeated than before. "I just...I just want to make sure you're being safe."

Something seemed to settle within Liv. Her shoulders relaxed and the snarl lifting her cheeks fell away.

"Of course I am, Terr." Liv's haughty air was steeped with more adult authority than Terra felt comfortable with. Terra was only a year older than Liv, but sometimes it felt like decades when Liv acted like this. "Just chill, okay?" Taking the last sip of the mocha sludge settled at the bottom of her now empty coffee, Liv gave Terra her trademark charming smile. "He's good people. They all are. You have nothing to worry about."

But Terra saw a dark, chaotic ripple behind her eyes. And she didn't miss Olivia's clear avoidance of naming which clan Pieter hailed from. Terra wanted so desperately to believe her. That Liv had this whole thing handled. But she had a sneaking suspicion she would, in fact, soon have plenty to worry about.

CHAPTER TWENTY-ONE
Terra

Back in her room, Terra unloaded the few purchases she had made during her and Liv's spontaneous post-coffee shopping spree. Buzzed on far too much caffeine, Liv had boldly announced she was going to 'redefine' herself, which apparently meant buying as many rocker crop tops and thigh-high boots as she could find.

Terra's purchases were limited to a couple of new writing journals, a gold fountain pen, and a jade green summer dress Liv had convinced her to get—telling her that Terra was, quite frankly, far too good-looking to restrict herself to her usual jeans and plain tees all the time. Terra acquiesced, if only to keep Olivia from forcing a full-on makeover on her.

Through the crack Terra had left in her door, a slender black cat squeezed through, mewing up at her as it padded into the room. "Oh, shoot." Terra kicked herself for leaving the door open. "Hello, Bean."

The cat mewed again as Terra's mother, Sofia, followed shortly after. "There you are, Bean! I was looking *all* over for you. It looks like you found our little Terra!" She crooned to the mewling ball of fur.

Terra rolled her eyes. She knew full well her mom had sent Bean to scout the territory and see if Terra was around. And Sofia knew she knew.

"Hi, mom," Terra said stoically, pinching her nose. "What do you need?" She loved her mother terribly. But she had a vague suspicion she knew exactly why her mother had come here, and she had little interest in entertaining *that* conversation.

"Oh, don't be so petulant, Terra. I'm just here to see how my favorite daughter is doing." Sofia held Bean aloft in her arms, petting him between the ears. Her gaze scanning Terra's features, it finally came to rest on the dark circles beneath her eyes.

"I'm sure," Terra said wryly. She plopped down on her comforter and picked up one of her new journals, rifling through it to signal to her mother her disinterest in company at the moment.

Sofia sidled over to Terra's desk, where a set of framed pictures stood, showcasing Terra, her family, and her friends throughout the years. Her whole life condensed into a few colored sheets of thin paper, encased in glass and wood. How easily they could all burst into flame.

"It's only…I had heard from Madam Malia that the Coven hasn't seen you in a while. And with preparations for Summer Solstice coming up, they were wondering if you were planning on joining them anytime soon. There's quite a lot of work to do," Sofia explained, "and I can't imagine it will help your claim to the Priestess seat if you continue to forgo your responsibilities." There was an edge of calculation to her last line.

Ah, and the other shoe drops.

Terra shook her head in disbelief. The older she got, the harder it was to swallow how any of this could be important in light of the war raging around them. But Terra would never, could never, say that to her parents. Her place in the Coven meant far too much to them. "There's been a lot going on here too, mom," was all Terra could muster. "I have responsibilities to the Council just as I do to the Coven."

"You should be more careful, Terra." There was an ice to Sofia's soft warning as she continued to rub Bean's ears. "Some might *misunderstand* where your loyalties lie. Especially if you continue to prioritize your Council work, and your fraternizations with certain fae, over your more paramount obligations to the Coven."

Her meaning was not lost on Terra. Closing the journal in her hands with a snap, Terra felt her cheeks burn and her ears redden. Sofia must have decided her message was adequately received, because she added a hastened, "Your new friend does seem nice. We're glad to have him here," before she exited the room with Bean. The door closed behind her with a soft click.

Sucking in a rush of air as far into her lungs as she could, Terra held her breath for a measure of four, releasing in a measure of six, over and over, until she had quieted her seething. As much as Terra loved her parents, and was grateful to them for the opportunities their positions in the Coven and the Council provided her, their constant expectation of excellence was arduous—at best. Every step out of line was disastrous to her future, and every idea or notion she had that didn't completely align with their plans was out of the question.

Terra knew they wanted the best for her, but she wished that she could have more of a say in her own life. She wished they would stay in Teír long enough for her to make just one decision on her own. For her to prove to them she could—and still survive. Just getting them to let her stay and work with the Council, instead of sending her to Breakmoth for school, had been like pulling teeth. It had involved her guarantee she would stay fully engaged in her work with the Coven as well, which included the underhanded trainings meant to prepare her for the Priestess seat, the position all but promised to her since before she could even walk. Solely because of who she was. Who her parents were.

And while her parents hadn't gone as far as to limit her friendships and romantic interests, per se... they made their sentiments about interspecies mingling quite clear: she was a Sampson, a descendant of one of the most powerful magem lines. She would not, under any circumstances, muddy that line with the blood of 'an alternate species'. After her mom had found out about the full scope of Terra's *fraternizations with certain fae'*, she had made sure a discreet procurement of a monthly contraceptive potion always arrived at her doorstep. Just in case.

Terra didn't bother telling her mom the potion wasn't necessary anymore, and hadn't really been necessary at all but for the one, misguided instance.

A knock on her door called Terra away from her ruminations. Hennie, who had been sleeping in the corner of Terra's room this whole time, peeked through one squinted black eye and *'who'*ed. Unlatching the door, Terra found none other than Tristian himself standing outside, his white-blond hair sweeping over his darkened glacial gaze. Terra's eyes widened, shocked to find him there in the middle of the day, especially with his dad around. He wore a thin white button down hardly obscuring the tracing of pitch black markings snaking up his arms. They peeked through at his neck and elbow, where the sleeves were rolled into cuffs. The tattoos were a story, he had once told her—the story of his people. He said the next time he'd add another would be the day he finally killed Markus. The last would come when his people returned to Lus Halla.

Tristian stepped in, holding himself up against the door frame, his hands in his pockets and a marked scowl spread severe across his features. His eyes locked on hers as he towered over her. Terra shuddered. He always made her feel like he could tear her soul apart when he looked at her like that. Like he was about to call out everything she had ever tried to hide from anyone—including herself.

Sighing, Terra's shoulders slumped. She wondered how much more of this day she had the energy to handle tactfully. "Hi." She trained her tone into something far more flat and emotionless than she felt. "What's up?"

Tristian just stood there, as if trying to remember why he had bothered to come by. His gaze narrowed, tracking any emotion she let flash across her features. Something seemed to resolve within him, because he blurted out, "What's going on with you and the new kid?"

"Leave it to you to get right to the point." Rolling her eyes, Terra opened the door wider. She didn't feel like having this conversation in an exposed hallway, especially when she knew it would get heated. "The kid has a name, Tristian. And I already told you. Nothing."

"Then why are you always with him, Terr? I'm not stupid. Don't treat me like I am." He stalked into her room and she shut the door quietly behind him. "You might have everyone else fooled, maybe even yourself. But I know you."

"He's new here, Tristian," Terra said, but she didn't know if she was defending Wilder or herself. "You might have never had to experience what he's going through, but it's not exactly easy to be taken from the only life you've ever known and have to completely build a new one for yourself. Give him a break. And give me a break. I'm just being nice."

"I know exactly what that's like, Terra. Every Seasuír does." Tristian's icy blue eyes grew perceptibly colder, and Terra looked down at her shoes, feeling guilty for her choice of words.

Terra made to apologize. "I'm sorry, that's not what I—"

"And yeah, maybe I could cut the kid a break. He seems decent enough. For a Summer anyway. But *you*?" He scoffed. "Not going to happen."

Terra could tell he was suppressing something that had been burning in him for a while. She just couldn't tell what it was. Staring up at him, her brow knitting, she wondered once again why he was there—why he should care how she did or didn't feel about anyone else. Whatever they once had was never meant to be anything more than a fling. They had both been of the same mind: he had to marry a fae, and she would marry a mage. It was their duty to their families. Whatever relationship had been between them had been nothing more than a fun distraction at best. At least, that's what it should have been...But damn if she wasn't still putting herself back together because of it.

"Listen, I hate to bring this back up, but it needs to be said. You told me where you were at with us and I accepted that," Tristian said, beginning to pace between her wall and door. "You said you weren't interested in anything with anyone other than one of your own, so I let it be. Now *this*? What the hell, Terra." Tristian paused to glare at her, his eyes wild with anger, and hurt, and what Terra could only guess was panic. The kind of panicked he gets when he loses control of things.

Terra knew there must have been something else going on, some kind of pressure he was under from his parents. But Terra had little patience today, and she felt her control over her own life slowly dwindling. She didn't have it in her to hold everything together for him, too. Not this time.

"*You* were the one to end things, Tristian," Terra clarified for him. "Don't come at me like I'm the one that put us in this situation. We both agreed ahead of time that nothing was going to come from this. And we made the right choice; both of us. Convention doesn't allow for anything more than what we agreed to, and we're past the point where what we had before would even be an option now. It lasted too long, and we went too far. Even you said we're getting too old for this. That we *'need to take these kinds of decisions more seriously'*. That's what *you* said. So I am. And as there's no hope for anything between you and me, I have no idea why you're here. Again." Terra felt her nostrils flare, her heart a stifled war drum inside her chest.

Tristian crossed the room and sat on her bed, looking up to stare at her, or glare—really for him they were one and the same. His expression remained focused, locked on her, the setting sun from the windows behind her transforming the glacial blue of his irises to pure crystal.

She remembered him staring up at her with those same, exacting eyes only three months ago, when he had snuck into her room after the Council's annual winter solstice party and her joint eighteenth birthday. They had all been sneaking mouthfuls of drink from Caolin's personal stock of mulled mead the entire evening, but Terra and Liv had both drunk more than either of them had any business drinking. Tristian had too, but he had been far better at maintaining his composure.

By the time dinner had finished, Liv was falling asleep on her plate. Harry had to keep kicking her under the table to stop her from snoring. Joking about her being a lightweight, Tristian told Harry to take her to her room and let her sleep it off, and Tristian was left to deal with Terra, who, on the other hand, was a giggling mess. She had found everything absolutely hilarious—from her mother's stuck up friends to the way Tristian spoke differently to his father than he did to anyone else.

Worried they'd be found out, they snuck away from the party and back to Terra's room, where they sat laughing on her bed for over an hour about their parents' ridiculous expectations of them, about how Terra didn't even know if she wanted to be Priestess anymore, and how nothing really mattered because they were likely going to lose this war, anyway.

Then the laughing turned to flirting, and the flirting turned to light touches and wondering aloud to each other, yet again, why they hadn't yet. This had been happening more and more often with them—coming right up against the edge, only to shy away with some excuse. But after everything, after all the pressure her parents had been putting her under, she just couldn't bring herself to care anymore. They were both sober by that point, Terra knew it, but it felt easier for them to pretend this time they weren't. She thought that maybe this was what they needed.

"We've been at this for months, Terr," Tristian had whispered to her afterwards, gazing up at her from where he lay against her chest, those shocking icy blues hazed with what they had done. "We could make this work, you know." Kissing the dip where her neck met her shoulder, he told her, "We were always inevitable, you and I."

He had pressed his ear against where her heart drummed a mile a minute, as if committing its desperate song to memory. As if he wanted to keep it for himself. She had felt the warmth of his breath against her skin, a dragon warming its nest. Gazing at him, she had reveled in the rare moment of vulnerability he had given her, knowing in her gut it wasn't something she should ever come to expect from him. But that knowing made the moment all the more precious.

Now, only months later, as he sat perched on her bed, staring up at her as if she still held that fragile, long-lost moment in her hand, Terra ripped her gaze away from his. There was no use dragging up memories better left dead and buried. They were older. Wiser. And done.

"Tristian, there's nothing going on between Wil and I. For the love of the Magíck, leave it alone. Please." Terra rubbed at her brow as she stalked to the door. She was exhausted, and a headache had begun to bloom along her temples. Opening the door, she signaled for him to see himself out. Hennie '*who*'ed again in the corner, her wing feathers ruffling, evidently agitated at having been so inconsiderately disturbed.

"Screw convention, Terra." Tristian pushed off the bed, ignoring the open door. In less than a stride, he stood in front of her, pulling her into him as he swung his arm to slam the door shut. Before she could stop him, he bent down and pressed his lips hard against hers, pushing her against the bedroom wall.

Instinct told her to stop it, to remember who she was, who they were—and who they weren't anymore. But she shoved those thoughts back down.

Allowing herself to get lost in him, she put her arms around his shoulders, pulling him closer. He groaned in response, shoving against her harder, his fingers digging into her sides. He burned of desperation, more than she had ever seen from him, and his lips moved painfully against hers, as if trying to find some sense of purchase within them. As if grasping at life itself. As if wholly relying on this moment with her, relying on whatever was left of them, to stabilize his own crumbling world. His fingers played beneath the hem of her shirt, at the clasp of her jeans, ghosting along the sensitive skin there, almost in an asking, in a waiting.

Just one more time, she told herself, ignoring the tears beginning to well beneath her lids. But another part of her knew exactly how this would end.

Wilder's voice echoed in her head. *Sometimes you have to put your own gas mask on first.*

This moment had nothing to do with them. And it never had. For him, it had always been about escape—running to her when he couldn't handle everything else. But she couldn't be his saving grace anymore. Moving her hand to his chest, she shoved him away.

"No, Tristian. Just no." She quickly sidestepped around him as he stood there in shock. Striding clear across the room, she put as much distance as possible between them. Her gaze bore into the ground, her jaw tightening, determined to look anywhere but at him for a long moment, before she finally dared a glance up.

Tristian was glaring at her again, his breath coming in uneven heaves, his eyes on fire. "Okay," he said steadily, his tone a low snarl drenched in a chill so palpable it made her shiver. "So forget about you and me for a minute, then. Shouldn't be too hard for you, since it seems you already have."

Terra winced, his words slashing at her like freshly sharpened talons. He had no idea how wrong he was.

"Think about you, just you," Tristian argued. "When are you going to start making decisions for yourself, not just because mom and dad have a certain plan for you? You don't want the Priestess seat, and you know it. Damn it, Terra, we *all* know it. Just tell them."

"You're one to talk!" Terra shot at him, fuming again as heat rose to her cheeks and a dull but incessant throbbing pressed against her skull. "We both know the real reason you ended this Tristian—because Caolin told you to. Because you can't be seen entertaining the advances of a wyte.

So don't get on me for making decisions based on family duty. You did the same thing."

Tristian sucked in a breath, eyeing her skeptically, as if realizing something. "I want what I want because *I* want it, Terra. Not because my father tells me what to do," he hurled back, though his tone began to settle. "Yes, it's what he wants for me, but so do I, to my very core." He drew closer to her again, so close she could feel his warm breath as he spoke. But he held his arms pin-straight to his sides, his hands balled into fists as if fighting the urge to touch her. "Terra, you have no idea what you're doing or what you want. That's the problem here." Tristian's tone grew layered with an exasperated sorrow far too calm for her comfort.

"I know exactly what, and who, I want and don't want, Tristian." Terra mimicked his calm. "If you wanted us to end at your very core, then why are you here making some backwards excuse for amends, or whatever this is?" Terra asked coldly.

"I meant the Fae Army, Terra." His face went flat, but his tone grew suddenly vulnerable. *"That's* what I want, more than anything. And I know I have to sacrifice a lot to get there. I have to sacrifice other things I might want, too. I don't have a choice."

He stared at her again, his pained, wide eyes drinking her in, pleading for her to understand.

"But *you*," he went on, "you don't have a clue. You pretend. You think you know what you want, but you have no idea. The Council, the Coven, the Priestess seat…" he paused, as if there was something else he was going to add. "You keep trying to convince yourself what they want for you is what you want for yourself, when we both know that's not true. Not really. You keep talking yourself out of anything you could actually want, all for the sake of what's going to make your parents happy—what's finally going to make them proud of you. I just want to make sure that if you're giving up something you actually do want, like I have, it's for something else *you* want even more. Not what your mom and dad have decided for you."

He stared down at the ground, and Terra thought he suddenly looked so young. Like the broken ten-year-old boy she had first met all those years ago.

"Whatever that ends up being, Terra—I want that for you. What *you* want, *truly* want, at your core." He peered down at her one more time, his eyes unexpectedly regretful, before quickly kissing her forehead and leaving. Terra couldn't shake the feeling this was somehow his way of letting her go—of giving her some kind of…*permission.*

She stood in the center of her room, stunned and empty for what felt like a millennia, mulling over Tristian's words like they were gospel. He was right. And of course he would be; he knew her better than anyone. He had always been the one to tell her exactly what she needed to hear, even if it wasn't what she wanted to. That had always been what she loved most about him.

And it was true. She didn't know what she wanted. For herself. From her life. She didn't even think she knew how to. How to want something someone else didn't want for her first.

Something pricked at the edges of her mind, as if a gentle nudge sought to meet her, to finally whisper the answers she so longed for, but she pushed it away. A wave of fatigue overwhelmed her instead, her head encased in a dull ache, and Terra wandered to her bed without changing. She felt numb from the day, numb from Tristian, and she could barely see straight as she collapsed into the soft folds of her duvet. She fell asleep within minutes to an image in her mind of bright fae eyes shifting back and forth between icy blue and stormy gray.

CHAPTER TWENTY-TWO

By the start of the next week, Wilder and Terra had concocted a plan to locate the Book of Scales while avoiding overly curious eyes. They'd determined they'd each scour every nook and cranny of the abbey that could pass as a 'library'. Though Wilder made every excuse to help Terra with her own investigations.

He wanted to learn more about her, to dig into the reserved confidence she so carefully maintained around him. He wanted to understand the things that made her tick, to understand the fierce determination that seemed to drive her forward in everything she did.

"Terra," Wilder said, flipping through the pages of a heavy cookbook called *Cultural Eats of the Pacific Northwest* one morning while most everyone else was out. Terra had instructed him to pay attention to anything that seemed 'suspicious', but Wilder had no idea what that could mean, as the most suspect thing he found was a recipe for Native Alaskan Muktuk.

"Yes, Wil?" Terra's steady stare remained focused on the tome in her own hands.

"You said the other day you could only be with a mage." He hesitated, not trusting himself. She turned to look at him, puzzled. "I guess I'm just curious. Why? What's the hangup there?"

Terra searched his features, as if trying to determine why he was asking. For a moment, it looked as if she had stopped breathing, but before Wilder could think anything of it, her body relaxed, her expression replaced once again with a leveled confidence.

"I come from a long line of very well-known and powerful magem," Terra started, fingering the corner of a page. "My grandmother was a Priestess, as was her grandmother, and hers before her. Some believe our line goes back as far as the Fall. It's the greatest honor a wyte could be given, being chosen. And I've been molded since birth for this."

As Wilder stared at her, Terra's eyes seemed to soften, remembering. "My parents struggled to have me. For years. They thought the Sampson line had come to an end at my father." Terra swallowed. "It was their greatest shame—to not be able to keep the line going. To not have a chance at the seat that should, by right, go to their line first, if their child was qualified to take it.

"Because they remained childless, the Coven was forced to name an interim Priestess while they convened and decided what to do. But then I came into the picture. I was an answer to prayer, a blessing from the Magick. And no one came after." Terra paused, considering. "My future, before anything, is to be Priestess. After that, it's continuing the line. To have a child who will carry our magic into the next generation."

Terra snapped her book shut. Shelving it, she grabbed another with a shaky hand, but Wilder could tell she wasn't reading a word of it. "Obviously, that can only be done with another magem. The Myx curse doesn't allow for child-bearing between species. And even if a child were to survive, their magic would be unpredictable, like the Magi's. The Coven wouldn't allow it." Terra bit at her lip, fingering the inked script within the pages of the book. "It's not that I wouldn't *want* someone else," she said cautiously, her tone slow and measured. "It's that I know the reality of my situation. The duty I owe to my family, and to my Coven."

Wilder's gaze never left her face. She was trying hard to maintain an even expression, but there was so much turmoil shuddering beneath the surface, it made Wilder want to grab her and hold her. To assure her, just as she had done so many times for him, that it would all be alright. But he suppressed it. "I guess that's something I can understand," he said. Taking a step closer, he took the book from her hands and placed it on the shelf, relieving her of its burden.

"What?" Terra finally looked at him, her stare locking with his.

"Feeling like I have to meet impossible standards for someone's approval."

Terra sucked in a breath, and Wilder saw the pinch of tears along her lashes, her lips thinning. She blinked them away. "I do want it, though. The seat. I don't mean to imply that I don't. I know I could do so much good with it. Change so much. Be a better bridge between the Coven and the Magistrie. Right now, things are pretty tense. I could help."

"I believe that." Wilder smiled, admiring her resolve, but finding himself disappointed by it as well. "It's a shame, though."

"Why?"

Wilder shrugged, a smirk pulling at his lips. He handed her another book, the touch of his hand lingering on hers before he pulled away. "No reason."

Despite their concentrated efforts that week, they eventually came up short, forced to concede they had just as little chance of finding the book as anyone who had searched for it before.

Wilder spent the next few days in various training sessions, embracing any surge of emotion he felt. Just as he predicted, he saw the most progress with Tristian, who had a distinct and infuriating habit of always knowing which buttons to press. And those buttons had increasingly become more about Terra. The benefit was twofold: Wilder had not only begun to hold his own during combat, by which Tristian seemed to actually be impressed, but he could identify what he thought might be the Magíck—the same electric hum he felt each time he lost control of his powers.

Shifting and compelling continued to be a slog, and any growing confidence Wilder had from his improvements with Tristian were dashed in his work with Olivia and Harry. However, there were positive developments with each of them completely unrelated to Wilder's magic. Within a week of the dinner party, Olivia's interest in Wilder seemed to have waxed and waned, and she thankfully no longer looked at him any differently than any other of her friends. The change had been duly noted by Harry, whose overall disposition had markedly improved. While Harry had never been explicitly unfriendly toward Wilder, he seemed much more spirited and engaging, as if some potential threat had been extinguished.

Wilder also continued to study alongside Magi Maynestream. He had not only been tutoring him in the histories and extensive magic structures of the Eadar, but had been helping him tap into his subconscious mind to uncover any magic the Magi believed to be buried there. Through extreme relaxation and visualizations, Wilder sometimes felt a throbbing, buzzing energy lighting up every vein in his body. But each time Wilder felt the energy's intensity, a wave of debilitating fear struck him, and he immediately shut it off. Wilder never told the Magi about it, and shame gripped him each time. But as much as Wilder tried to keep it a secret, the deep blue discerning stare that followed each session confirmed the Magi was far more aware than he let on.

Chapter Twenty-Three

Wilder stumbled through the white, unsure of where he was, trying to ignore the gray eyes that watched him, though they were decidedly not his own. He had lost the silk blanket he had been found in, or it had been taken from him; he couldn't be sure. Gripped with distress, he searched, and searched, and searched, but to no avail. Wilder fell to the ground, and it began to shake. Suddenly, flames burst forth from widening cracks and fissures, surrounding him in walls of fire. The gray eyes transformed into luminous gold, piercing through to Wilder's soul. They saw, and they knew. Life breathed into his lungs, and his fears, even the ones he didn't know he had, all calmed. Peace, an all-encompassing peace, engulfed him, and he heard himself, and the earth, and the entire universe, sigh. Wilder's body grew light—alive in a way he had never allowed himself, magic sparking from the depths of his bones…

The sharp sound of birds in the garden snapped him from sleep, and Wilder's eyes flew open. In a daze, he stared at the ceiling, the wisps of his dream drifting far from his remembering as the world came into focus. Throwing back his covers, he placed his bare feet on the floor, trying to grasp at the unfurling vapor, trying to make sense of it. But with each passing moment, all thoughts of gray and gold eyes faded safely into the dark, untouched recesses of his mind, and he remembered nothing more.

***

Downstairs, Wilder found the group sitting in the living room watching the morning news. The newscaster, in her feigned concerned tones, stood recapping a distressing tale in front of a looming white building surrounded by tall black iron fencing.

"A recently kidnapped local woman has been located and placed into inpatient psychiatric care after unsuccessfully attempting to drown her newborn child, claiming it to be the devil's offspring. The child, the woman stated, was 'cursed' and 'needed to die'. Given the length of the woman's disappearance and her current state, investigators and mental health experts are looking into the possibility of drug use or serious mental health concerns, as well as searching for the next of kin for the child, who has made a miraculous recovery following the incident. There is no news yet as to whether the woman has any information about who her kidnappers might have been."

Olivia's whole body went rigid at the story, her lips drawn into a tight, thin line. Perched on the armrest next to her, Harry placed his hand on hers, not missing a beat. Her shoulders relaxed slightly, though her features remained grave.

"Well, that has all the makings of a Céad," Tristian said pragmatically, one ankle crossed over his thigh and his long, inked arms outstretched across the back of a sofa. He somehow managed to fill every inch of the love seat. He glanced at Terra standing behind Olivia, as if waiting for her to confirm his suspicions.

"It does," Terra agreed slowly. Crossing her arms, her eyes narrowed on the TV. She missed Tristian's attention entirely, her gaze flashing instead to Wilder as he entered the room.

"What should we do?" Harry asked. His stare was still fixed on the screen, his hand unmoving from its protection over Liv's.

"Do?" Terra's brows arched as she placed her hands on the back of the seat where he sat. "We can't really *do* anything. We aren't supposed to be getting caught up in this stuff, remember? Finding kids in schools is one thing. This is *wholly* different. I don't know how, but this has Markus written all over it. We should just tell the Council."

"We can't just leave it, Terra." Staring at the screen, Liv's expression teemed with resolve. "We don't know—we can't trust—that the Council will do anything about this." She fixed her insistence on Terra and gestured to the news story. "They might just write it all off as the ramblings of some crazy lady and wait for the kid to put on some magic show in ten years. It's what they always do. What they definitely *will* do is stop us from going." Standing, Olivia pointed to the screen. "I don't care who comes with me, but I'm going after that kid."

"Better to ask forgiveness than permission." Tristian shrugged as he sprang off the couch. "I'm in."

Harry nodded in agreement, and they all set their eyes on Terra, waiting. She looked pleadingly to Wilder, as if hoping he would act as some additional voice of reason.

He gave her a regretful smile. "All I know is, I would have wanted someone to come for me right off the bat. Instead of waiting to see what would happen, or what I could do. I would have given anything for that."

Terra's whole body slumped. Burying her face in her palms, she let out a low groan.

A wide grin spread across Harry's face. "Well, that settles it," he announced, jumping from the couch and grabbing his coat. "Let's go kidnap a baby!"

★★★

They arrived at the St. Dymphna Behavioral Health Sanitorium in a small town just outside of New Orleans within the hour. Tristian's driving had been almost as nauseating as the news story, and Wilder now found himself bent over double in the parking lot, holding himself up against the car and trying to keep his breakfast down. The rest of the group stood close by, discussing the plan for how they'd get in to talk to the baby's mother.

Terra, who had spent the entire trip silently sulking about being outvoted, seemed to have come to terms with the situation. She began assigning tasks to each of them to ensure the smoothest and quickest resolution, which Wilder found admirable—and rather cute. Harry, the only one of them able to compel, would make his way to whichever suite the mother was in, with Terra and Wilder as backup. Tristian and Olivia would run interference at the front desk, gleaning what information they could about the baby, all while pretending to be interested in volunteering.

They strode through two grand oak doors, chiseled with images of saints and angels. At the front desk, a homely, short woman with wavy peppered hair sat chatting on an old landline phone, twisting the coiling wire around her finger. As they approached, she gestured that she'd be with them in a moment, then proceeded to carry on with her conversation. A simple plastic name badge identified the woman as Helene.

"No, Veronica. I don't think he meant it at all! I'm telling you, you're better off leaving him." Helene's voice held a distinct southern drawl as she made her emphatic declarations to whomever Veronica was.

Terra frowned, indignation coloring her cheeks. "Excuse me, ma'am?"

"Oh goodness, Veronica. Give me a minute, hun." Helene did little to mask her annoyance. "What can I do for you, *dear*?" she asked Terra, her voice shifting to a mockingly sweet cadence, her mouth curling into a smiling snarl on the last word.

"I'm looking for a friend of mine. She might have come in yesterday. She just had a baby, you see, and we're all really worried about her."

Terra explained the phony situation with such bravado even Wilder was convinced of her desperate plight.

"Ah, yea, yea. We only had one little lady come in yesterday," Helene confirmed, holding a hand over the microphone. "Definitely a new mama, too. Poor girl. Just go on ahead and get you all signed in. Penny is in room 242." Helene threw five visitor badges onto the desk and went right back to her conversation.

The group exchanged fleeting looks before skilling their features into a practiced nonchalance. Tristian swiped the badges from the counter and they headed toward the main staircase.

Once out of earshot, Harry mumbled, "Here's to hoping Penny's just as willing to answer our questions."

They found the suite, and Harry, Wilder, and Terra slunk into the room. Tristian and Olivia meandered close enough outside to keep watch, but not close enough to give them away, busying themselves with perusing a corkboard pinned with layers of colorful flyers.

Penny appeared sound asleep, but the click of the door closing behind them jolted her awake. Her eyes flew open, and she surveyed them blearily before her attention settled directly on Wilder, her eyes going impossibly wide. Every drop of blood drained from her soft, round cheeks.

"Nurse! Nurse!" the woman shrieked, her voice cracking from the strain as a sob broke through her terror. "He's here! He's here! He's come to kill me!" Wrenching wildly, she tried to escape from the straps wrapping her wrists, holding her firmly to the bed.

Wilder panicked, lifting his hands to reassure her he meant no harm. Stumbling away, he tried to give Penny as much space as possible. Terra and Harry sprinted to Penny's side and attempted to calm her. Kneeling down next to her, Harry's jungle green eyes locked on hers and he whispered to her in a slow, soothing timbre while Terra traced subtle markings into the woman's palm. Penny eased, her shoulders relaxing against the pillows. Wilder peeked into the hallway to make sure no one had heard them. Tristian stood right outside, confirming all was clear, though the look he gave Wilder suggested he was less than pleased by the outburst, and probably blamed *him* for it.

Clicking the door shut, Wilder turned to glimpse Terra sitting on a medical stool next to the woman.

"Hey Penny." Terra's cadence came in a careful, soft song as she continued to trace markings into the woman's palm. The woman didn't seem to notice. "It's nice to meet you. I'm so sorry for that little scare. We're with the recovery program here. We wanted to ask you a few questions. Is that okay?"

Penny continued to stare at Wilder, her entire body still as stone, aside from her shallow breathing. She nodded, but her eyes never left his face.

"I was wondering if you could tell me about what happened yesterday," Terra said slowly.

Panic spread through Penny again, a tremble seeming to build from the marrow of her bones. Harry stepped in again to calm her, and she slumped against the pillows. Her eyes grew dreamy, and Wilder could tell how draining it was for Harry to continuously compel her, his lips thinning angrily each time she zoned out.

The woman finally began to speak. "I tried to kill her," she told them. "The demon. My poor baby. The devil cursed her. I...I know it's true. No one believes me, but...I promise it's true. She's a snake. She is! I swear it." A sob broke through her stream of words as she moved to face Terra. "I swear it to you. I do. She had scales and snake eyes and...and...*claws.*" Tears gathered in her eyes as Penny strained against the cuffs around her wrists. "My poor baby. She's dead."

Terra placed her hand on Penny's arm, giving the woman a small, consoling smile. "Your baby isn't dead, Penny. She's still alive. She's okay. She's being well taken care of."

Wilder knew Terra meant the words to be a comfort, but the woman's face shifted from immense anguish to a desperate fear. "No!" Penny shrieked, her teeth bared, her pupils dilated so considerably each eye turned black as pitch. Terra fell out of her seat, stumbling back. The woman remained resolute. "She's dead! She's a demon now! She's dead!" Her hysterical cries deflated into a muted keen. "Oh, my poor baby…"

Harry returned to the woman's side. "Penny," he asked, kneeling down. "Do you know who the devil was that cursed your baby? Did you know him? Did he have a name?"

The woman peered at Harry, as if seeing him for the first time, before glancing again at Wilder, a faint glow behind her stare, tears streaking her features. She didn't scream this time, but her eyes slitted as she studied Wilder. "He came out of nowhere and then took me with him. I was so scared. He had hair like fire and his eyes—they were the depths of hell itself. And that…that's where he took me. Into hell. He looked…so much like your friend." Penny gestured to Wilder with a bow of her head. "But that's not him."

The woman swallowed, sinking into her pillows and averting her gaze, as if trying to avoid the sight of Wilder. "He kept me in the dark. I don't know for how long. He…he *hurt* me. Over and over, until…her. It was cold there. And there was so much…*screaming*. Then, I just wasn't there anymore. I was back, and he left me. He went back to where he had come from. Back to the dead earth. Leaving me with *her*…" Penny whimpered. "He said he'd be back. But I knew she couldn't live. Shouldn't be allowed to. My poor baby." The woman dozed, whatever drugs in her system seizing her as she stared out the window, no longer acknowledging their presence.

"Can't you do something?" Wilder pleaded with Harry, his voice cracking. "Can't you compel her? Make her better? Get her to see reason? Convince her to take back her kid?"

Harry stood from Penny's side, sliding his hands into his pockets. Sweeping his hair from his brow, he gave Wilder a repentant smile. "I'm sorry, Wil. I can't. Her mind is an absolute mess. I wouldn't be surprised if whatever stone Markus supposedly has was used on her. I'd do more harm than good with the kind of compulsion needed to convince her to accept her kid. And besides that, what'll happen to the girl when she grows up and doesn't understand who she is? What if she becomes something unpredictable and ends up terrifying her mother all over again? It might send Penny into another episode like this. Humans aren't meant to see what she saw. To know what she knows. This is what happens. If she took back her baby, it might *actually* end up dead."

"I can compel her to calm. Or to forget. To *maybe* tell me everything she remembers about what happened. Only surface level stuff. But with the level of deterioration her mind has already undergone, I can't compel her to love a child she's so convinced isn't her baby at all. There's so much that could go wrong there."

Wilder's hands fisted, his knuckles peaking white against his freckled skin. He felt so incensed. But not at Harry. Penny had become nothing more than a shell of what might have once been a good and gentle mother, now wrecked by her unwilling involvement with magic. Creeping forward, Terra placed a blanket over Penny. She had begun to slumber as peacefully as could be expected, twitching at the hushed sounds of their conversation.

"The baby is a Céad, for sure," Terra whispered. Her familiar cadence quieted Wilder's fury. Moving to leaf through all the paperwork in the suite, Terra scanned the woman's medical charts and anything else that could help them find the baby.

"How do you know?" Wilder asked, tracking her movement across the room.

"Claws? Scales?" Terra said, reading through a sky blue file folder on a table next to Penny's bed. "I can't be certain, but that sounds like fae. I just don't know what kind."

"How do you know those aren't just the hallucinations of a disturbed woman?" Wilder eyed Penny warily as she hummed an off-key lullaby in her sleep.

"It's possible," Terra considered, "but unlikely. Especially given what we know about Markus and how he operates. We'll know more when we see the baby."

Wilder's throat felt dry. He swallowed to dislodge the disgust there. Scanning the bare room, he looked for anything that might help in the search. It was sterile and cold, everything in it an off-kilter shade of gray. Even the view of the yard beyond the window appeared stark and unfeeling. An off-white business card lay on a table near the door, and Wilder picked it up. The bold lettering across the top read 'Child Protective Services'. He could just make out the name and number for a Henrietta Carmichael scribbled hastily across the back.

"This might help." Wilder handed the card to Harry, and Terra came to check it out.

"We'll have to call her." Taking the card, Terra inspected the tight script. "She'll know where the baby is." She flashed a grin at Harry. "Harry, I think we might need you to do a little more persuading, if you're up for it."

The corners of Harry's mouth lifted to meet his excited gaze. "Well, well, well. Look who's suddenly into breaking all the rules." He threw Terra a puckish wink. "Welcome to the dark side, Terr. It's a lot more fun here."

CHAPTER TWENTY-FOUR

A brief phone exchange with Henrietta Carmichael had the case-worker effectively persuaded Terra was Penny Livingston's first cousin. The group made their way to 1506 Pumpernickel Way, where the baby had been placed with an emergency foster family. Henrietta would meet them at the house. Wilder tried to quiet the discomfort the situation arose in him. On the way, Harry filled Tristian and Olivia in on what the woman had told them, and how she had mistakenly identified Wilder as her attacker. Tristian listened carefully, his features frozen and unflinching as he navigated the empty midday roads.

When they arrived at the house, Wilder, Tristian, and Olivia stayed in the car. Tristian rolled the windows down to eavesdrop on the conversation, ready to step-in if needed. Striding up to the front door, Terra and Harry eyed the lawn and vacant street warily. The door swung wide, and a slight woman with blonde hair shocked through with wiry white greeted them with a relieved smile. She handed the sleeping babe to Terra, and a large pink bag of supplies to Harry, without a moment of hesitation. A hint of faint unease on her otherwise kind face, Wilder overheard just how relieved the woman was the child's family had been found. To Wilder, it sounded far more like relief to be parting with the child herself. Harry evidently had the same suspicion.

"I'm sorry," Harry said, inclining toward the woman, "I hope you don't mind me asking, but…is there something wrong with the baby? You seem…bothered."

"Wrong? Oh no. Um, no. I don't think so," the woman backpedaled. "Only, we've had some strange happenings since she arrived yesterday. It's nothing, I'm sure. My little boys were just saying they saw things around her crib. Just such big imaginations, those little ones! And the door to her room kept sticking shut. Just really odd things. But I'm sure there's nothing to it!" The woman feigned a hearty laugh, though she sounded as if she was reassuring herself more than anything. "Just the wild imaginations of a couple of toddlers, right? Nothing to it at all!"

Terra and Harry glanced at each other, and Terra clutched the little girl closer to her chest. "Of course." Harry smiled, his eyes flashing at the woman. "I'm sure it was nothing at all." The woman's stare dazed for a moment.

The two toddlers in question began yelping and tussling in the background. Shaking her head free of her momentary trance, the woman excused herself and retreated into the house. Tristian's eyes narrowed as he studied the baby, his stare flashing between the infant and Harry, who appeared to be thumbing a quick text at the door while the woman remained distracted. A message pinged on Tristian's phone. Glancing down, he took a deep breath before muttering, "She's fae."

At the front door, Harry's attention fell on the foster mother, who had rejoined them at the threshold. Frazzled, she seemed more than ready for the visit to be well and over.

"How do you know?" Wilder asked Tristian.

"Harry. Some Céad have unique…skills," Tristian explained, eyeing the conversation on the doorstep. "It's always random, and rare to begin with. Harry can sometimes sense them, sometimes distinguish between the different types. But it's hit or miss. Subjective."

"That's how he knew about the rogues in the alleyway?" Wilder asked.

"Exactly." Tristian's fingers thrummed against the steering wheel.

Wilder stared at the baby sound asleep in Terra's arms, willing himself to feel anything about the child, but to no avail. The foster mother retreated into her home once more, just as a turquoise blue sedan parked along the road in front of the residence. A dark-skinned woman in jeans and a fitted blazer stepped from the car, a Child Protective Services badge swinging from her neck. Sweeping across the lawn, Henrietta Carmichael greeted Harry and Terra in the driveway.

"I'm sorry I'm late," Ms. Carmichael told them, her accent kind but firm. "I'm afraid there's been a bit of a hiccup with the background checks. We weren't able to find your information in our records for Ms. Livingston's next of kin. Given her current state, I'm sure she simply forgot to mention you." She waved an errant hand as if to reassure them these things happened all the time. "No worries at all. But, if you two don't mind coming back to the office, I'm sure we can get everything sorted out." Her smile didn't reach her eyes.

Harry and Terra glanced at each other again, and everyone in the car tensed. Terra shifted the sleeping baby in her arms. Stepping forward casually, Harry threw the woman a bright, winning smile before placing a hand on Ms. Carmichael's elbow. He spoke to her in a whisper Wilder couldn't hear, and he saw her eyes twinkle and fog. A moment later, Henrietta cocked her head and smiled sweetly. Shaking Harry's hand with genuine warmth, she wished him and his family all the best as they struggled through "such a difficult time." Without another word, she returned to her car and left.

Terra stared up at the clouds, as if collecting herself, before approaching their vehicle. After carefully passing the little girl to Liv in the backseat, Terra climbed in next to her. "I was really hoping we wouldn't have to do that," Terra said, massaging her temples. "Her people might start snooping and asking questions."

"We'll be long gone by then," Harry assured her from the front. "We didn't have any other options."

"Yeah…I guess." Terra's tone was flat as she stared out the window.

Wilder, sitting on Olivia's other side, peered down at the infant. Everything about the child bordered colorless. The soft ringlets of her hair grew in a peculiar, stark silvery white, and even her ashen skin lacked any noticeable vigor. Wilder touched her cheek with the back of his hand, almost to assure himself she was actually alive. Her face felt warm to the touch. She opened her dusty, gray eyes, the same color as his own, in response to the unwelcome disturbance. After briefly glaring up at Wilder, she squirmed resolutely away and back to sleep in Olivia's arms, letting out the tiniest tuft of a contented sigh.

"Isn't she beautiful?" Olivia crooned, stroking the minute white ringlets as the baby snuggled further into her chest. "She needs a name, I think. Jeselle. That was my grandma's name. I always thought it was so pretty."

"Don't get too attached, Liv," Tristian warned. Rotating the wheel, he veered onto the highway. "We're taking her to the Council as soon as we get back."

"What!? Why?" Olivia protested. The baby squirmed in her arms, agitated by the sharp pitch of her cry.

"Well, first off, because they're going to find out anyway. What were you going to do, Liv? Hide her in your dresser drawer?" Tristian asked, a chuckle warming his mocking tone.

"Well, no…" Liv admitted. "I hadn't even thought that far ahead."

"I didn't think so," Tristian said. "Aside from that, she might be just another Céad to you, but if my suspicions are correct, that right there is Markus's daughter."

★★★

The Council, as the group had predicted, was less than pleased with their little adventure and the miniature creature they had brought home with them. Raiya and Sofia even threatened to anonymously return the child to the state, though they weren't at all serious about it. But as they gathered in the parlor, all castigations came to a halt when Tristian shared his theory about who the child might be.

"What makes you so sure?" Caolin asked his son. Crossing his burly arms, he lifted his strong chin. A tinge of calculation, met with a subtle layer of pride, emanated from him as he regarded the way Tristian recounted their investigation.

Tristian stood at attention in front of the Council, pressing his hands roughly into the small of his back as he relayed the new information with militaristic efficiency, though his words sounded far less confident than they usually did. Wilder wondered if the change had to do with his father's presence there.

"The first indication was how the woman responded to Wil. Markus is a Summer, after all. They would share at least a slight resemblance." Tristian's eyes flashed to Caolin, as if waiting for his approval. "And since we know Markus has a reputation for impregnating random humans and fae for his own sick means—" his words held a distinct layer of disgust. "The possibility isn't unlikely."

"She also said," Terra added, "that he hurt her. Repeatedly. And that she remembers *screaming* wherever she was. She said her attacker returned to the 'dead earth' when he left her. Everything points to her being in Lus Halla, or what's left of it, anyway. She could have been there for a long time. Long enough to conceive and give birth."

Rickard rubbed his thumb along his chin. "That would mean Markus would have not only brought her to Daoine itself, but also returned her to the human realm after the baby was born. Her time restrained in the Eadar, the trauma I'm sure she endured there, and her likely exposure to the stone, would certainly explain her disturbed mental state," he ventured. "If that is indeed the case, this situation would be quite unprecedented. Markus usually limits attacks of this sort to wherever his targets currently are, or else never lets them leave Lus Halla. Certainly not alive. I don't even know of a human able to withstand being in the Eadar for that long. As far as we know, he's never brought anyone into Lus Halla as a victim, only to release them later. It doesn't make any sense."

"Unless, of course," Magi Maynestream added, gesturing toward the little girl still sleeping soundly in Olivia's arms, "the child was conceived, born, and returned with decided intention. *Left behind* with decided intention. And the mother left alive for the purpose of caring for her. For what purpose, I cannot endeavor to guess."

The rest of the Council grew pensive, their gazes considering as they studied the baby. Olivia held the little girl close to her chest, as if terrified they would decide on some evil scheme to take Jeselle away from her.

"It may be best if we consult with the Watern," Tremaine suggested. "They have capabilities far beyond our own, and could garner further insight into the child's origins or abilities. We can't be certain of Markus's intentions in creating this child, or in leaving her and her mother alone to fend for themselves. If that was his intention at all. There's no knowing whether he's even aware of what's currently happening with the two of them. We're sitting ducks if he returns and discovers we have her. And not knowing what she's capable of, what kind of magic he's wrought on her, there's every chance he intends to use her as some kind of weapon."

"It is possible," Rickard said, running a hand through his red-brown hair. "But that isn't to say she couldn't also become a key asset to ending this war. A weapon of our own."

"Either way, she would be far safer, I think, in Eaigan, than she would be here," Raiya said. Peering at Olivia, she gave her a loving, apologetic look.

Olivia, who sat feeding a freshly awoken and apparently famished Jeselle from a bottle she found in the supply bag, remained silent, her gaze never leaving the little girl. But Wilder could see a single tear betraying her calm as it glided down her cheek. Throat bobbing, she peered up at the Council, resolution hardening her caramel eyes. "Whatever's best for Jes."

"It's settled then," Sofia said softly, striding over to rest a consoling hand on Olivia's shoulder. "She'll be taken to the Glass City first thing tomorrow morning."

Chapter Twenty-Five

After a somber dinner at which most of the Council and her friends attempted to comfort a withdrawn Olivia, Wilder left to get some air in the garden. The woman's panicked expression when they had first locked eyes haunted his churning thoughts, and he desperately wanted to be alone with them. The stars were out, lighting the magnificent sky and garden below. Wilder stared at the expanse of night, marveling at how so many of the twinkling lights remained visible this close to the city's heart.

Ambling about the garden, Wilder was only half aware of the path he followed as he ducked through the trees. The sound of the rustling wind and the gentle trickle of the fountain followed his steps, but his attention was instead on the multitudes of questions that had arisen since leaving the sanatorium. Above all, he contemplated his apparent resemblance to Markus. It made sense they would look similar. From what he understood, they were both from the same Season. But the fear that had darkened the eyes of that young mother had been more than alarming. Would she have reacted so intensely to only a slight resemblance?

The subtle echoes of an argument floated through the cool night air, and Wilder's curiosity once again got the better of him. Practicing his 'lightness of foot', as Barrett liked to call it, he edged *somewhat* soundlessly across the garden, eyeing a series of windows left open to let in the evening breeze—and which now did little to block the raised voices of the

Council from Wilder's fully engaged ears. The way the room over-looked the garden suggested this was Magi Maynestream's office.

"You're being ridiculous, Caolin," Wilder heard Sofia say in a firm snap. Wilder could only imagine the cutting glare she was throwing at him. "You're letting a past petty feud with Markus and the rest of the Summers color your judgment. As the Fae representative here, you have a responsibility to put whatever previously held grudges and biases you still hold aside for the sake of this Council, and the members of this House, of which *he* is included."

"Don't you speak to me about Council loyalty, Sofia. We all know your allegiances continue to lie with the Magem, regardless of your own role here," Caolin rebutted, his own tone scathing.

"I hardly see how *our* role within this Council is relevant to the current discussion, Caolin," Tremaine added, his deep voice flat, but no less agitated.

"I second that," Wilder heard Rickard admit, though in a much more respectful manner than the other three exhibited. "The boy might possess some surface level similarities to Markus. We agree on that. But that, by no means, suggests he might be as much of a close relation as you're suggesting, Caolin. It's possible, of course, but I question whether your theory is founded more in prejudice than in fact."

Wait. Are they talking about me? Wilder swallowed hard, growing worried about the direction of this conversation.

"Consider it, all of you," Caolin reasoned. "We know Markus is capable of doing exactly what I'm suggesting already. The proof is sleeping right down the hall in our own Olivia's bedroom. Why *wouldn't* he, *couldn't* he, have done this before? He's a mastermind. He has means available to him that even we do not know the ends of. What would have stopped him from raising a son in the human world with the sole purpose of infiltrating the Council and the Magistrie. I certainly wouldn't put it past him."

"I wouldn't put it past him, no," Magi Maynestream's voice agreed, "but I have also spent some time with the boy…"

"As have I," Rickard added, his tone sharp and defensive.

"And while I have my own hesitations regarding his origins," the Magi went on, "I do not believe the boy to be manipulative or conniving in any sense of the words. I hardly think him capable of being the spy you suggest him to be, Snow."

"It is possible he is who we believe him to be, and does not yet know it," Raiya added thoughtfully. "You yourself have mentioned your own misgivings about the visions you've had regarding the boy, Magi."

Wilder started, peering upward as if he'd somehow hear them better. *Maynestream's been having visions—about me?*

"What visions?" Sofia's voice cracked. "This is the first I'm hearing of this." Wilder felt slightly relieved he hadn't been the only one not aware of these visions until now.

"They are by no means definitive, Sofia," the Magi confessed. "They are as unclear as the entire situation with the infant. Raiya and Caolin were informed of the visions prior to now simply to help identify possible relatives of the boy, for which they have determined there could be none. Other than whom we have only *speculated* and not at all *proven*."

"But what is it you *saw*, Magi?" Tremaine asked, his tone impatient.

"Upon meeting him, I saw a royal lineage, and power with origins as ancient as the Tuatha de Danann," the Magi explained. "I have no doubt power far greater than what he has yet displayed is present in his blood, which could make him a valuable ally to have in this war." The Magi paused, and Wilder thought he might be looking at Caolin with the same knowing disapproval the Magi sometimes gave Wilder.

"Also in the vision," the Magi went on, "his eyes, particularly their gray hue, were a most prevalent theme, if not *the* most prevalent. It could be only a coincidence that the baby found today also bears the same color. Springs, of course, are known for the shade. But not knowing as much as we should about Maluum, and since neither the boy nor the baby possess the fullest presentation of any particular Season, it is possible the color may indicate an origin in some kind of blood magic. There's no way to be sure."

Wilder leaned in closer, not wanting to miss a single word.

"What we do know is that by the time Wilder would have been conceived, Markus was already working closely with Haman. There is every possibility his conception, if Markus is at all involved, could have been influenced by her."

Wilder heard a collective gasp.

"You don't believe her to be the mother, do you?" Tremaine asked, his voice edged in shock.

"Oh, that is not at all possible. No. The first thing blood magic takes from any wyte is her ability to reproduce. Haman's role, if she's had one at all, would have been by influence alone," Maynestream assured him. "And from what I can tell, the boy is full Fae, not a Myx. So his mother could only be fae or human."

Wilder had heard enough. His whole body quaked as he clutched at the ground, abnormally detached from himself and the voices that continued somewhere in the background, delving ever deeper into his identity. Without knowing exactly why, he started sprinting to his room, as far away from the unnerving discussion as he could get. But the suspicions of the Council, and their speculations about his parentage, trailed him the whole way back.

Chapter
Twenty-Six

Wilder didn't even try to sleep. What was the point?

After digging through his bag, searching for the only comfort he knew, he held his red blanket in his hands. Running the smooth fabric between his fingertips, he pressed the gold embroidery along the corners.

Was Markus really his father? And if he was, had he ever really wanted him to begin with? Did he have a heart enough to? And what about his mother? Where was she? Maybe he had murdered her. Or she had gone crazy after his birth, just as Penny had, and this cloth was all he'd ever have of her.

Then realization struck him—the way Rickard had looked at him the other night. When Master Lyre had said there hadn't been any other reason for Markus to break in. Rickard hadn't truly believed that. What if he had known, even then, what the other reason might have been?

What if Markus had tried to get in because *of him?* After tonight, it was clear enough the Council, save for Rickard and Magi Maynestream, distrusted Wilder. And they clearly believed Markus had some connection to him.

What if they're right? Wilder considered. *Why shouldn't they distrust me? Even if I'm not working with him, if Markus really is my father, who knows what he might do to get to me? And who knows what else I'm capable of?*

Wilder thought of all the awful things he'd ever done in his life, of the people he'd hurt. Suddenly, he knew in his gut it must have all been because of his blood, because of who he was at his core: the son of a murderer. Kyle broke into his thoughts, broken and burned after Wilder's fit of rage. He thought of the little girl he had once played with as a boy. She had stolen his toy and wouldn't give it back. He remembered how angry he had gotten, and how the ground wrenched beneath her in response. Trying to run away, she had tripped as the earth buckled, breaking her ankle. Her terrified face faded into Penny Livingston's, and he now felt convinced she had every reason to be as afraid of him as she was.

Wilder bartered with himself about whether he should stay at the abbey. He couldn't imagine leaving his new friends. Couldn't imagine leaving Terra, and whatever had been growing between them these last weeks. But in the end, he knew what needed to be done. To keep them safe—to keep *her* safe. Resigning himself to the situation, Wilder packed up what few things he had, determined to quit the Council House. Maybe Terra had been right. Maybe there really was something to giving yourself up for the people you cared about. If he truly was Markus's son, he knew Markus could be after him—might want him for some awful purpose. He might try to use Wilder against the Council, and Wilder couldn't let that happen.

After scribbling a short, hastily written note for Terra, Wilder hurried from the room, finding no one wandering the halls to hinder his exit. The moonless night had grown colder. Turning the collar of his jacket up around his neck to block the humid breeze, he crept down the cobbled streets toward the French Quarter. There was a bus stop near one of the main roads he could wait at until the morning. From there, he didn't know where he'd go, but he knew it would be best to get out of the city. He needed to get as far from Terra and the others as possible. Maybe he'd find a small family in some rural town and disappear into the human world as an insignificant farmhand.

As he trudged along, Wilder had the distinct feeling he was being watched. Glancing over his shoulder, all he saw were empty, cobblestoned streets, dimly lit by stretches of lamplight. Ahead of him appeared the same. He could almost make out the raucous illumination of some nearby restaurants and bars less than a quarter mile away, and decided he'd take refuge there. Stepping up his pace, he pushed his hands into his jacket pockets, but still couldn't shake the itch that someone lingered closer than he felt comfortable with.

As he passed a set of multistory apartments, ivy wrapping their painted iron verandas, Wilder noticed two shadows slink out of the alley between the buildings. The shadows moved with an eerie ominous grace, their only discernible features the glistening shine of their bright eyes.

Rogues.

Wilder scanned the street for a place to hide, madly hoping the two shadows either didn't see him, or if they had, wanted nothing to do with him. But the rogues stalked closer, and there was no way they weren't headed right for him. He had no other choice. Reaching into his bag, he pulled out a wooden shortsword Barrett had gifted him. Wilder had hoped the younger boy could've trained him how to use it, but that time had passed, so Wilder would just have to wing it.

The rogues closed in, and Wilder realized they were identical twins. Both women had stick straight, jet black hair that tumbled down their shoulders and back, almost reaching their waists. They each wore full body form–fitting black uniforms lined with pockets and sheaths that held an innumerable number of lethal weapons. And they probably knew far better than Wilder how to use them.

Wilder balked. They were identical to the woman with the knife he had seen in the woods the day he had first come to the Council House.

"How lovely to see you again, Wil," one of the sisters drawled. Her sinister, sweet voice did nothing to encourage Wilder's trust of them. "Out for an evening jaunt, darling?"

"Uhh, yeah. And sorry, I don't mean to be rude, but I've got other plans, so if you two don't mind, I'll be off now." Wilder feigned a casual air, but his heart threatened to beat out of his chest. Taking a step away, he turned to run, but a swift whoosh sounded overhead. One of the twins landed with unearthly ease only a foot in front of him, a short blade playing in her hand. Wilder froze. She snaked closer and gave him a disarming smile. Wheeling around, Wilder found the other twin had drawn even closer still, and his false confidence deflated.

"What's the rush, sweetheart?" the first twin crooned, running the pad of her index finger under his chin. She smiled seductively before joining her sister's side. "We only wanted to introduce ourselves." At this proximity, Wilder noticed the only difference between the twins—each had one jet black iris and one magnificent silver iris, though the placement appeared opposite on each sister.

"I'm Kyra," the first twin said, "and this is Lynx." She motioned to her sister.

"Right. I wish I could say it's nice to meet you both, but…" Wilder shrugged noncommittally, occupying himself with finding an escape route. His racing heart beat heavy and he couldn't think straight.

"We were wondering if you wouldn't mind assisting us in a *teensy* little task." Kyra's voice rang bright and melodic, like rain hammering silver.

"Insignificant, really," Lynx added.

"Mmm, yeah. Afraid not…sorry ladies." Wilder tried again to cut around them.

"You see," Kyra cut him off, stepping deftly in front of him as she brought the edge of her blade up to his throat. Wilder sucked in a breath at the feel of the cold steel pressed against his skin. "A friend of ours with whom you've recently become acquainted was blessed with a little bundle of joy." Wilder swallowed.

"We were so disappointed to find out the little ray of sunshine had been taken away before we could check in on her," Lynx explained in her honeyed lilt.

Kyra slinked closer, her movements feline, wrapping her free arm around Wilder's neck. She pressed the dagger in her other hand even more firmly against his jugular. "And it seems," she whispered in his ear, "that you are one of the few who not only know where the little one is, but have access to her." She released her grip around his neck, tapping his nose with each word. "Just…as… we…speak."

Wilder felt his heart skip a beat. She stood so close now he could smell the sweet mix of jasmine and teak emanating from her. She drew closer again, and he couldn't be sure if she was getting ready to kiss him or knife him. "How lucky for us, don't you think, sister?"

She removed the knife from his throat, and Wilder stumbled away, raising the wooden sword and glaring. "I'm not helping you get to Jeselle, or anywhere near the Council House."

"Cute," Kyra said, winking at him, though her tone held considerably less charm than before. Flicking a glance at her twin, she sheathed the blade in her hand.

"What damage do you think you're going to do with that, little fae baby?" Lynx mocked, eyeing the wood in his hand.

"Be nice, Lynx. He needs him willing," Kyra muttered to her sister.

They both took a step back, and Wilder hoped they might be retreating. But a moment later, they each touched one hand to that of the other, motioning into the air with their freed palms. Wilder watched in horror as shadows—corporeal, solid shadows—formed at their fingertips, creating a black net as dark streamed from the depths of the surrounding alleyways and night sky.

With another wave of their wrists, the dark mass shot straight for him. Dropping to the ground and rolling, Wilder narrowly avoided the blast. He heard the shadow wrap itself around the building before it blew a massive chunk from one of the apartments. Dust and debris filled the air. Through the tumult, Wilder sprung to his feet and maneuvered around the twins, bashing one of them in the head with the shortsword and knocking her to the ground. The other swiveled to continue the assault.

"Don't…you…dare…touch…my…sister," Kyra said, each word a verbal blow between strikes. His blood thrummed, his focus sharpening. Surprising himself, he blocked each of the punches with languid agility before flipping the second twin onto her back. A steady rhythm of electric energy, which hadn't been there before, pulsed through his body. Too fast, Kyra was on her feet, and Wilder tried to swipe his foot behind hers, but he lost focus on blocking her strikes in the process. Punching him squarely in the chest with more force than he was prepared for, she sent Wilder crumpling to the ground.

Lynx rose, and identical expressions of rage seared across the sisters' faces. Wilder considered the irony of his finally getting somewhat of a handle on magic before he went and died. "Maybe we'll have to do with just one of the two, Kyr," Lynx said. She stepped forward and booted Wilder in the ribs, forcing him down as he tried, and failed, to defend himself. He heard several distinct cracks as his chest exploded in pain.

"We'll come back for the other one. Don't worry," Kyra assured her. Her eyes glinted as she drank in the crumpled heap in front of her. "He'll be happy enough with this one."

As they bent to grab a hold of Wilder, another dark shadow dropped from a terrace above, landing steadily between Wilder and the twins. The shadow rose, a dragon uncoiling from its slumber, and Wilder glimpsed the glow of white blond hair as the streetlights lit the figure.

"Get up, Summer," Tristian ordered, glaring ruthlessly at the twins. Wilder didn't need to be told twice. Holding his chest and wincing, he struggled to his feet. Breathing was agonizingly difficult, each rush of cold air coming in uneven gasps, searing the cracks along his ribcage.

"Ah, baby Snowflake…What a pleasure," Lynx said, eyeing Tristian up and down. All murderous advances stilled, a tinge of fear marked her flirtatious tone as the twins slowly withdrew from the hulking figure. "I see the handsome apple doesn't fall far from the gorgeous tree. *Do* tell your dear old dad we said hello."

"You have approximately thirty seconds to return to whatever hell hole you two slithered from before I start snapping necks," Tristian growled. The twins smiled demurely before wheeling and sprinting with inhuman speed toward the alley from where they first came. As they rounded the corner, Wilder saw a dim flash of light, and then the night went silent again.

"Why didn't you go after them?" Wilder choked out angrily, holding his chest. Tristian spun on Wilder.

"They're more trouble than they're worth," Tristian snapped. "And what the hell are you doing out here alone?! Are you daft, or do you actually have a death wish?!"

"I was just trying to catch a bus out of here…" Wilder explained weakly, still gripping his chest and struggling to catch his breath between words. "The Council thinks Markus might be my father. And if he is, I can't let him use that to get to you all."

"Ah. So both then…" Tristian mocked before smacking Wilder upside the head. "No one likes a martyr, Summer. Now get inside before *I* end up killing you." Wilder conceded, too broken to fight him. He tailed Tristian the short distance back.

Rickard and Caolin waited for them in the foyer. Looking around to see if any of the other Council were waiting, Wilder was relieved to find the rest of the downstairs empty. He took one look at Rickard's concerned face and felt instantly guilty. Caolin maintained his usual unbothered disposition. His son must have learned that from him.

"What happened?" Rickard asked, placing his hands on Wilder's shoulders. Wilder held his chest and tried not to breathe too deep.

"I found this dimwit running away with some sorry excuse about saving us all from Markus. He made a few friends on the way," Tristian snarled, glaring at Wilder.

"Rogues?" Rickard asked, stepping away to study the extent of any injuries.

Tristian paused as he peered at his father, before finally announcing, "The twins." The measure of finality to his tone sounded as if those two words explained everything they needed to. Caolin's collected demeanor imploded within moments, his glacial eyes lighting to a crackling crystal. He gave Tristian a curt nod before sprinting through the front door of the Council House. Tristian's knowing gaze followed him.

Rickard grew panicked, but Tristian assured him his father wouldn't find them. "They're gone. Took a portal back, I assume." Tristian's timbre sounded forlorn; defeated. It struck Wilder as odd, given that the twins had run away from *him*.

"Oh, gods," Rickard sighed, scrubbing at his face. "You're both lucky you're not dead. Do you know what they wanted?"

"They wanted the baby," Wilder voiced through clenched teeth, wincing as each word tumbled from his mouth. "And me."

Rickard's eyes went wide, his lips thinning, but he bowed his head in a slow, understanding nod. "I see. We'll have to inform the Magistrie. It's apparent now that he's targeting the abbey. As for you," he looked at Wilder, "that was foolish, Wil. As admirable as I'm sure you intended it to be, it was foolish. What on earth drove you to make such a decision without consulting any of us?"

Wilder sat down on a bench and rested against the wall, gasping for air. "I overheard you and the rest of the Council." Closing his eyes, he struggled for breath, wheezing. "I heard you talking about me. And Markus. And who you think I am. If I am his son, if he wants me, I can't let you all get hurt keeping me from him. Or if I end up doing something to hurt all of you."

Wilder felt a hand wrap around his upper arm. "We need to get you to the infirmary," Rickard said. "You likely broke some ribs. Maybe even punctured a lung from the sounds of it. Sofia needs to see to you." Tristian grabbed Wilder by the other arm and helped him to his feet.

"As for your assertions," Rickard's tone grew gentler as they led Wilder through the building, "while your actions were noble, they were unnecessary. The Council *as a whole* does not and will not hold your *suspected* parentage against you, or use it as a means of defining your character. That, my friend, we expect you to do yourself. And while your attempt to leave and spare us from some future attack was quite unneeded, I hope you can see how much it shows exactly what kind of character we *are* to expect from you." Wilder could almost hear the beam of pride in Rickard's words, but doubt continued to gnaw at him. How could he ever be sure he wouldn't become an echo, a mirror, of who his father supposedly was?

They reached the darkened infirmary. Tristian supported Wilder as he laid down on one of the hospital beds.

"Now," Rickard added, "I can assure you we are all just as safe with you present as we would be if you were to leave. Though, if tonight is any indication, the same cannot be said for you. I genuinely hope you will not let the conversation you heard earlier discolor any intentions you had of staying. And while we cannot stop you, if you do choose to leave, I will warn you that at this point, doing so would be against your own best interest. If Markus wants you, he will find you. You are far safer here, with us, than you would be on your own."

Wilder's vision blurred, dark spots obscuring the edges. Pain cascaded through him, and the only words he could muster were a shallow, gasped, "Yes sir," before he passed out onto the pillows.

Chapter Twenty-Seven

The sound of large wings beat against Wilder's eardrums and ruffling black feathers filled his vision. A pair of dark, beady eyes turned to look at him, and within its stare, Wilder met with the heart of darkness itself. The sound of wings morphed into a rumbling purr, and the pressure of a vibrating weight across his chest called him back from oblivion.

Opening his bleary eyes, he saw a black tail flicking lazily from side to side atop his blankets. Blinking at the too bright light rushing in from the windows above him, it took Wilder longer than he would have liked to remember where he had fallen asleep, and what had happened the night before.

"Good morning, sunshine," a pleasant voice tuned from next to him. "I see you've met Bean." Wilder blinked again to find Sofia standing over him, dressed head-to-toe in a simple white ensemble and wrapped in a white nurse's apron. She poured a glass of water on the nightstand next to his bed. From this close, Wilder could see thin lines winging each of her emerald eyes, and mousy gray speckling strands of the chestnut hair she wore in a tight bun.

"What happened?" Wilder asked. "What did you give me?" He rose slowly, bracing himself with his forearms, and pressed himself up against the headboard. At his sudden movement, Bean shot off his chest and scuttled away dramatically. Wilder took a steady, measured breath, unsure of how quickly he should allow himself to move. He checked his body for any trace of the pain he had felt the night before, but besides a slight tightness in his chest, he could move freely and breathe deeply. Sofia handed him the glass.

"Drink. You've had quite the evening. You ended up here last night with no less than four broken ribs and a punctured lung. And from what I understand, you were lucky. The twins are nothing to trifle with. As for your current state, that was all you." She beamed at him, but he peered up at her, confused. He took a sip of water before she answered his unasked question. "After observing your little altercation last night, your friend Tristian thought you might have a bit more magic in your bones than you thought. He challenged me to let you heal naturally."

Water sputtered across Wilder's blankets. "He did *what?!*"

"Now, I know it sounds drastic." Lifting her hands, she motioned for him to keep calm. "But believe you me, I would have stepped in to intervene if I had even an inkling of him being mistaken."

"That's reassuring…" Wilder told her with the slightest edge of sarcasm. He slouched into his pillow. Smiling at him again, Sofia took his glass and placed it on the nightstand. His head spun, and he couldn't be sure if exhaustion, dehydration, or shock was the culprit. Just then, the double wooden doors at the end of the infirmary burst open, and an irate Terra stormed in. Every muscle in Wilder's body tensed, but it had nothing to do with fear.

"Are you an actual idiot?!" Terra yelled, her voice reverberating off every inch of the room. His bedposts rang and the medical tools in a nearby cabinet shuddered and tinkled, matching her pitch. Wilder could have sworn he felt his mattress vibrate. Had her voice somehow been magically projected, or was she just that loud?

"Terra…" Sofia softly warned her daughter before gathering her things and heading toward the infirmary offices at the far end of the ward.

"Sorry, mom," Terra called after her, flustered. She wheeled on Wilder. "But really! What on earth were you thinking?"

Wilder stared up at her, drinking in the way her fury lit her eyes and warmed her cheeks. "Well, I guess I had some noble aspirations of saving the world," he said, sinking into the bed as her temper subsided. "They were apparently unrealistic, or so I've been told."

"Yeah. They were." Terra let out a deep sigh of exasperation, dropping into a seat next to his bed. "Please never do it again." Placing a hand on his arm, she looked at him with such insistence he couldn't help but agree to whatever she wanted.

"As you wish," Wilder said, smiling weakly up at her. He felt drained, like he had just been hit by a freight train. His entire chest felt achy and tight. But as he studied Terra, he found himself far happier than he had been a few minutes ago, convinced he'd never seen anything more exquisite—temper and all.

Any trace of whatever filter normally kept him from openly admiring her was lost to his exhaustion. Her hair shone gold in the sunlight streaming in from the windows, and her tawny skin glowed over the lines of her high cheekbones, as if she'd spent the morning sitting in the sun. He found himself jealous he couldn't be the very sunlight that had kissed her skin. He considered how stupid he had been to think he should leave her—leave whatever was building between them. Even if he could never have it for himself, even if she'd never allow it.

"What're you staring at?" Terra asked. She quickly removed her hand from his arm, but Wilder saw a faint blush creep across her cheeks.

"Nothing," Wilder shrugged, breaking from her stare. He'd have to be careful with this from now on. Careful with them. He didn't want to scare her away. But he knew he was about to. "Terra, I have to tell you something."

Terra stilled, worry crossing her features. "What?"

"Last night, after dinner, I overheard the Council talking. About me. They think—" he paused, still coming to terms with the possibility himself. "They think Markus is my father. And last night, when I met the twins in the alleyway, I think they might have confirmed it."

Wilder stared at the cabinet of medical supplies across the room, looking anywhere but at Terra. She didn't say anything for a long moment, and Wilder was worried what he'd find in her gaze when he finally looked back at her. But when he did, there was nothing but sympathy there. Her whole body had relaxed, as if Wilder hadn't told her anything more than that he'd decided to get a dog.

Terra sighed. "I figured it was something like that. Wil, you didn't need to risk your life because of who your father might be. You didn't know. You can't control your parentage."

"I didn't do it for me, Terra. I did it to protect you. All of you."

Terra stared at his sheets, biting her bottom lip. He needed her to understand. Needed her to know why he did it, and that he'd do it again in a heartbeat, if it meant keeping her safe.

"So you think Markus might be your dad," Terra finally said, her lips drawn.

"Yeah," Wilder confirmed, his voice heavy.

Terra put her hand on his arm, and his skin warmed beneath her touch. Her mouth relaxed into a smile. "We'll deal with it."

Wilder nodded. It was a better reaction than he could have hoped for. It was then that he remembered everything else that had happened the day before. "Wait. How's the baby? And Liv?"

Terra welcomed the change of conversation. "They're both great," she said, but her smile seemed strained. Lowering his chin, he raised a single eyebrow at her, giving her a knowing look.

"Okay… Liv, not as much. She's still pretty upset, but I think she's come to terms with what needs to happen. Especially after last night. We're actually headed to Eaigan in the next hour or so. I went down to breakfast thinking you'd be joining us, but then Tristian told me what you got yourself into."

"Yeah. Not my brightest moment," Wilder said, eyeing Terra apologetically. "But I could probably still go. I'd like to, anyway."

Eaigan—the Glass City. He knew the chance of seeing an actual Fae city would be well worth whatever discomfort he might endure. He also couldn't deny wanting to spend every waking moment next to Terra from now on. If he couldn't keep her safe by leaving, he'd do it by never leaving her side.

"Are you sure? Don't you have to rest and heal?" Terra asked. She peered down at the tightened bandages wrapped around his bare torso.

"Uh," Wilder started. But Sofia strode back into the room with a firm determination that reminded Wilder distinctly of her daughter.

She answered for him. "Not at all! He's good to go. You'll likely experience some soreness, and you'll need to take it easy for the next few days. At this point, you're just taking up space." Sofia fussed over him, ushering him from the bed. Standing quickly, Wilder's body hummed with energy, and despite the creaking pain between each of his ribs, he felt more alive than he ever had before.

"He's healed?" Terra asked, two lines appearing between her brows. She stood from her seat and her mother threw Wilder's pillow from the bed. "How's that possible? Even with potions, he'd at least have another few days."

"He didn't need any potions, honey," Sofia explained, pulling off the sheets while Wilder strained to pull his shirt on over his bandages. Terra took pity on him and gave the hem a helpful tug. "He healed all by himself. Give your friend a little more credit. He's much more powerful than you all seem to think."

Terra cocked her head at Wilder, astonished. "Wow, that was quick. How come you didn't tell me you could access your magic?"

"I didn't really know I could," Wilder shrugged. "I thought I felt it last night, and a few times the past week, but I didn't know I could heal."

"Maybe *you're* the one that needs to be giving the Magick a little more credit," Sofia chastised, brandishing a finger at him. "Now out—out. I need to get cleaned up in here," and Sofia shepherded them hastily from the infirmary.

CHAPTER
TWENTY-EIGHT

"So how far away exactly is this Glass City?" Wilder asked. The group had been driving for well over an hour, and the baby had become fussy. Wilder could tell she would either soon start wailing or start pooping, and he didn't care to be locked in close quarters for either of those eventualities.

"There's no exact distance," Terra explained. "We could have gotten there from the city just as well as from where we're going."

Wilder started, looking down at Jeselle, who now had a look of concerted determination on her face, her tiny hands balled into fists. "Then why, might I ask, are we risking the health of our nostrils by driving so far to get there?"

"Because, dimwit. You got attacked last night and someone wants that baby," Tristian said. "Markus is going to be watching all the Waterways near the city. He knows we're trying to figure out what to do with her. Without knowing whether the Watern will let us in, let alone take her, we can't risk him knowing where we're going. We're driving as far from the city as possible so we're not tracked and attacked when we leave. From here on out, we have to be a lot more careful whenever we leave the abbey."

"How do we know he won't be watching this one?" Wilder asked.

"We don't." His matter-of-fact tone lacked the coldness Wilder expected from him. "But the probability is significantly less, so we're going with it."

"Ah." Wilder felt slightly guilty that his decision to leave last night was the catalyst for these new precautions. Jeselle cooed beside him, and he noticed the infant had become remarkably flatulent. She stared up at Olivia with a massive grin spread across her face and let out a giggle. "Then might I suggest we take a quick breather?" Wilder rolled the window all the way down, sticking his face out.

"There's no need. We're here." Tristian pulled onto a nondescript one lane dirt road. They followed it for another quarter-mile before coming to an empty campsite settled at the edge of an enormous lake. Copses of trees bordered the water on all sides, shielding them from view. They truly were in the middle of nowhere. Wilder got out of the car as fast as he could, almost gagging.

"Oh, don't be such a baby, Wil." Olivia laughed at him while she started to change Jeselle on the empty seats. "She can't help it."

"Doesn't mean I don't wish she could," Wilder combated, glancing at Jeselle. Staring up at him with her big gray eyes, she smiled incandescent-ly. What a difference a day made. She let out a tiny giggle at his attention on her, and he halfheartedly admitted to himself she was *kind of* cute. In that moment, it dawned on him that this little girl might be his sister, the only family he'd ever known.

"Come on!" Tristian called out, already feet ahead as he strode onto a worn wooden dock built out onto the surface of the lake. "This might take a while and I'd rather be back before dark."

Come where? Wilder inspected their surroundings. No boats were roped to the dock, and no other paths led out of the campsite other than the one they had come in on. But as Wilder walked onto the dock with Harry, Liv, and Terra, he saw Tristian toss a small jewel into its depths. It created a perfect ripple across the surface as it sunk to the bottom.

They sat there waiting, staring at the spot where the gem had sunk. Wilder almost asked what they were waiting *for* when he saw the jewel floating up toward the surface—faster and faster. Except it wasn't the jewel at all… A woman rose from the depths, her entire scaled flesh appearing set with precious stones. The scales of her tail shimmered in gorgeous rivulets as the sunlight streamed through the rippling water.

Her *tail…*

Wilder's eyes grew wide, and he felt his jaw drop open at the fins he saw beneath the water. "That's a mermaid…" he whispered to no one in particular.

Terra walked up next to him and chuckled. "Of course it is. What did you think it was going to be? A beluga whale? Mere are some of the most common watern, and they're the keepers of the gates of Eaigan."

Wilder stared at the lake woman holding the lost jewel in her hand. Her gaze glowed an ethereal midnight blue, scattered with the sea, stars, and whirling galaxies. Her stare fixed on his own, and he found himself getting unendingly lost in those constellations. The world shifted beneath his feet, and he felt his own planet spinning on its axis. His whole body grew light, absorbing the night sky within her stare. He melted into it, wrapped and floating in the twinkling liquid starlight. Nothing else existed beyond her. She was the most enchanting creature he had ever laid eyes on, and he knew he would do anything for her—be anything for her. Smiling at him, she beckoned him into the deep. Taking a step forward, he sat on the edge of the dock, preparing to jump into the waters to meet her call. But before he could, a pair of powerful arms wrapped around his, yanking him back onto the dock.

Wilder struggled against the arms now pinning his own to his sides, his still healing ribs groaning from the abrupt movement. Whipping his head back and forth, he rose from his daze, trying to figure out how he had ended up on the damp wood. Distantly, he could hear Terra and Olivia laughing from somewhere close by. Wilder looked up to see a wholly entertained Harry beaming down at him, a flush of delight coloring his pale cheeks. His arms stayed wrapped around Wilder's shoulders, barricading him from any more attempted jaunts into the lake.

"What happened?" Wilder shook his head, trying to dislodge whatever might be left of the trance.

"She compelled you." Harry's eyes glistened with mirth as he released Wilder. "For her own amusement, too. She's got a sense of humor." Wilder peered up to see the mere giggling just as heartily as the rest of them. The sound spoke of twinkling stars and the rising moon.

"Yeah, yeah. Very funny," Wilder grumbled, getting to his feet. Lake water sloshed onto the deck from his soaked sneakers.

"My sincerest apologies, Summerson," the woman said. Wilder couldn't place the otherworldly accent she spoke to him with, but it sounded like a strange mix of Irish and Scandinavian. "It is not often we happen across fae lacking the wherewithal to withstand our persuasion. Twas far too amusing an opportunity to let pass."

Wilder glowered at her.

"As for the rest of ye, you've come bearing a gift, and I thank ye for it. How canna be of service, my young ones?" The mere surveyed the group, her midnight eyes refracting the lake's reflected sunlight.

Tristian took a knee on the dock and bent over the edge, bringing his face only inches from hers. "We've come to request entrance to your magnificent Glass City, lovely jewel of the lake." Tristian gave her his best smolder, and she gave him a coy smile in return.

"Ah. That is no small request, son of Winter. For what purpose would ye be making such an application, I wonder?" She peered up at him from where the lake rippled around her bare shoulders, trickles of it streaming from her hair down her neck and arms. She wore an ancient, discerning gaze as she studied Tristian. Wilder got the distinct feeling she already knew why they were there.

Straightening his shoulders, as if made uncomfortable by her stare, he averted his eyes from the mere's. "We've come across an infant. We believe her born of fae and human, and influenced by blood magic. But we're not sure. She is sought after by the rebel Markus, and we believe he desires to use her as a weapon. We seek a conference with the Synod to discuss these concerns and request their superior guidance on the matter." Tristian did his best to flatter while remaining as diplomatic as possible, and Wilder found himself impressed by the attempt.

"Curious," the mere whispered. Moving to observe Jeselle, she lifted her arms from the lake. "May I see the babe?" Tristian looked at Olivia. Her lips tightened, but she bowed her head and carried Jeselle to the water, resting her with the greatest of care into the outstretched arms of the water fae.

Tucking a curl away from Jeselle's face, the mere studied the little girl's features, gazing into the depths of the infant's pale eyes. "Mmm. Indeed." The lake rolled and rippled around Jeselle, leaving her dry and untouched by the cold water. When she had finished her consideration, the mere peered up again at the group. She handed Jeselle to Olivia as they waited for her verdict.

"Ye will be permitted entrance into the Glass City." Her lilting cadence sounded of strings across water. "Should the Synod deem ye a threat to our people, ye shall be slain forthwith. We welcome ye and yer kin to Eaigan." Waving her hand over the surface of the lake, a series of earthen steps descended from beside the dock, guiding them into the depths. Without another word, she disappeared beneath the surface with a flick of two tail-fins.

Chapter Twenty-Nine

Wilder stood stock-still, the gears in his brain working overtime. How exactly did someone keep themselves from coming across as a threat to the Watern?

"Don't worry," Terra told him, patting his arm encouragingly. "They have to say that. It's the safest place in the world. Or, well, in general…" Terra squinted, thinking hard about her wording. "All that to say, there's a reason why it is. You'll be fine."

Wilder nodded, staring blankly at the steps, but her explanation did little to calm his reservations.

Tristian turned to address them, his tone firm. "Remember. Do not eat or drink *anything* while you are down there. It'll mess with your mind. Stay close. Don't lose sight of any of us, and don't get distracted. We're their guests, and they'll treat us as such. But they *will* take prisoners if they believe for a second you can't be trusted. And they'll find a reason to keep any one of us if they get too curious. Stay as unassuming as possible. Everyone got it?"

Wilder gulped, but everyone else nodded in understanding.

"Okay. Let's go." Tristian led the group down the steps, and Wilder followed. He thought the hems of his jeans would be immediately drenched, but the water pooled around his ankles without so much as touching him. Wilder continued to wade into the lake, but before he had time to prepare himself, he felt a rush of cold press into him. A moment later, he landed, completely dry, on solid ground—no lake in sight. All around him, the others had joined, gazing up at their new surroundings with wide eyes, and Wilder trailed their stares.

Standing still as stone, his feet rested on a pathway made of fluid silver starlight. He couldn't tell if they were inside, outside, or still on Earth at all. A massive ocean of jet black cosmos reached from one unending expanse of the world to the other, filling the space both above and beneath the pathway. Pillars and swirls of dancing multicolor aurora raged overhead, illuminating the dark sky of the realm, glowing as bright as the sun itself. Beyond the glorious lights, radiant planets and stars sat so precariously close to the city beneath, Wilder thought he could have touched them from the top of one of the many purely glass buildings lining either side of the starlit path.

Wilder threw a glance behind him to inspect the passage where they had come in, but found only a milky waterfall twinkling with stars rushing from nothingness far above into nothingness far below. This place sang of unreality; ocean and cosmos intertwined. A glowing opal moon jelly floated across Wilder's peripheral, its tendrils brushing along his neck as it chased a shooting star moving across the world of its own volition.

"Come," the midnight fae beckoned as she swam along the starlit path, the scales of her tail mirroring the aurora above. "The Synod awaits."

As Wilder took a careful step forward onto the liquid silver stars, the glowing light swelled and flowed beneath his feet like a river. "The path is called Loinnír," Terra told him as he stared down at it. "It, and all of Eaigan, is said to have been gifted to the Watern by the first dragons, who bent all of time and space to create it. It's been called the dragon's most magnificent love song."

As they strode after the water fae, Terra gestured to the buildings on either side of the path and beyond. Their solid foundations seemed to have been built on open air. Some appeared to be businesses, libraries, or infirmaries, while others looked to be homes, places of worship, or shrines. Each building had been crafted of translucent, unmarked glass. Wilder surveyed the city, stunned to find that everything happening within each establishment was entirely visible to whoever glimpsed inside.

"There are no secrets here," Tristian whispered, taking note of Wilder's expression.

As they passed through the city, Wilder noticed the majority of the populous had stopped to stare in their direction. Wingless fae-like creatures, both with and without tails, watched their advance across the city. Unintelligible whispers encircled them, but Wilder didn't know if he could actually hear them or if it was all happening in his head. Gazing at the Watern, he couldn't help but feel like every person in this unreal place knew everything about each of them.

Outside the main stretch of Eaigan, at the very end of Loinnír, a colossal cathedral towered over it all, reaching so far into the midnight sky it could be seen from any place within the city. While the structure was also made primarily of glass, the crafter had incorporated both wrought iron and polished ash wood. It spoke in angles and artistry, and appeared reminiscent of two churches of a similar style Wilder had visited on a field trip to Arkansas when he was younger. Wilder remembered what Magi Maynestream had said about the Fae taking pride in building things for humans, and he considered whether those churches had been influenced by Eaigan itself.

Tristian slid close to Wilder again. "They might say things to you the rest of us can't hear. They might try to get inside your head. Do your best to not let them. I'll handle most of the conversation." Wilder started, but before he could ask Tristian how exactly one was supposed to keep someone out of one's own head, they arrived at the entrance to the cathedral.

The thick ash wood doors were carved with depictions of slumbering dragons on one side, and giant, soaring eagles on the other. Both sets of creatures were encircled by two globes, inset into the wood and inlaid with veins of multicolor precious stones; emerald, sapphire, ruby, beryl, onyx, amethyst, opal, and even more that Wilder had no names for. Between the two globes stood a giant tree, holding the globes within its branches. The tree's roots reached beyond the bottom of the doors, its branches reaching into the heavens.

The doors opened of their own accord as they approached, as if manned by phantom hands. A simply constructed chamber lay on the other side, a short series of stone steps leading them from the threshold of the cathedral down into its heart. The walls and roof were crafted of the same luminous glass as the rest of the city, held together by thick, arching pillars of iron and wood. Starlight and aurora danced above their heads, brightening the chamber to a multi-hued glow.

At the end of the cathedral, mounted on a lifted dais of glass and marble, stood six elegant silver thrones, each simply but matchlessly constructed unlike any of their brethren. Behind the thrones, on another higher dais almost hidden by shadows, stood a seventh, its seat empty. Perched on each of the first set of thrones were six remarkably ancient creatures, all appearing to be fae. Despite the deep wrinkles set into their skin, they maintained the ethereal beauty and allure for which the Watern were known. Wilder couldn't help but be entranced once again. Thankfully, this time, none of them made any endeavor to compel him. At least as far as he knew.

"Welcome, Daughter of the Earth, Daughter of the Moon, Son of the Night, Son of Summer, and Son of Winter. We hope yer finding yer visit to our illustrious Glass City to yer liking," a fae woman on the far right greeted them. Rising from her throne, she sauntered forward to where they stood.

Various other fae erected on the sidelines of the cathedral drew closer as well, offering the group a medley of delectable assorted teas, fruits, cheeses, crackers, and meats. Wilder's stomach rumbled audibly at the sight of the multiple trays and platters, and he reached to pluck an olive off one of them. He felt Terra's hand on his arm, subtly pulling his own down and holding it tight around his wrist. Peering at her, he saw her mouth a distinct '*No!*', a panicked expression crossing her features before she trained her face into a neutral visage. He remembered then what Tristian had said about not accepting any of the food.

"Our visit has been most pleasant, gracious Lady Lysella." Tristian bowed to the advancing fae, ignoring Wilder's misstep. "I trust you've been informed of the reason for our call upon you this day?"

"Indeed, we have been informed," Lysella answered with a brisk bite. She peered past Tristian and directly at Wilder, before angling to further study each one of the group.

"Ah, the minds of these ones are so… *thrilling.*" She sauntered along their line. "So much love. So much heartbreak. So like the humans they are." She spoke as if they were not there at all, and Wilder wondered who she was speaking to. As if hearing his internal question, Lysella flashed her yellow eyes at him and sneered. "This one," she strolled over to him, pushing his red hair from his forehead, the tresses running through her clawed fingers in a gentle and troubling caress. "This one doesn't even know who he is…what he possesses."

Wilder stared into her catlike gaze, struggling to understand what she could mean by that. It was vagueness drenched in a deep knowing that could mean anything at all, but really only meant anything to her and the rest of the Synod. A whisper breathed through his mind like wind chimes. *Do ye know who ye are, Summerson? Do ye know who ye will be?*

Tristian betrayed his forced calm with a swift menacing glare at Lysella, as if warning her she came close to overreaching. Chuckling, she removed her hand from Wilder, her eyes flashing between them as she studied them both. Tristian whispered to Wilder, "Don't let her get in your head," before regaining his stoic composure. He sliced another glare at Lysella before announcing to the entire Synod, "Our immediate concerns are in regard to the infant, my Lords. We are not here about the boy."

"Shouldn't ye be, though?" Wilder heard Lysella whisper, just loud enough for only Wilder and Tristian to hear. Tristian continued to ignore her.

Shuddering, Wilder shoved Lysella's earlier croon from his mind, instead scowling at Tristian's choice of the word 'boy'. He was hardly that much younger than Tristian himself. But Lysella continued to inspect Wilder, as if he were a toy she was deciding how to best play with. He had let his guard down when he had glared at Tristian, and he felt her feline claws break farther into his mind. He shoved at the feeling of them and they retreated, but it had been long enough. Wilder saw her lips rise into a perceptible smirk. She sliced a glance at Tristian, and then at Terra, before her intrusive eyes settled squarely back on Wilder, smirking again at her new found pet.

As Tristian continued to address the Synod, Wilder scanned the room, diverting his gaze to anywhere, anything, but her. Wracking his brain for the most random thing he could think of, he decided hastily on umbrellas. He thought of every kind of umbrella he had ever seen; every color, every fashion, every imaginable use for one. He felt her eyes on him as she chuckled again. She must have grown bored, because she shifted her attention to Tristian before arcing into a graceful glide back to her throne. Settling her lithe forearms along the armrests, her clawed fingers lightly scraped at the brushed silver.

Another of the seated fae came forward, swimming across the short distance. He took the baby from Olivia, who had been cradling her in her arms. The watern had eyes like pearls and a blood scarlet tail, its scales glinting heavenly gold in the light of large living orbs floating indiscriminately around the room. Wilder swore he could hear the orbs whispering to each other.

The finned fae held Jeselle in his arms, staring down at her as if inspecting the mind of his charge. The room sat in complete silence as the moments passed, save for the trickling of a few small waterfalls encircling the room. Five full minutes lapsed before he announced, "She is neither water nor fair, nor any other. She is like dust. Ash. We canna know as of yet what she will become. But she will be safe here. Should ye agree, the child will stay in the Glass City to be grown and instructed by our people, raised as one of our own. This is the surest way of determining what she is, and what she will become."

"Thank you, Moarlin," Tristian answered, gracing him with a deep bow. "Yes. As representative for the New Orleans Council, her current guardians, we do believe a relocation to Eaigan would be in her best interest." Wilder heard Olivia release a small sniff, but otherwise remained silent. "The Council, as conduits for the Magistrie, would like to request, if it is within my Lord's goodness, frequent updates regarding her well-being, as well as any discoveries concerning her origins or powers as they present themselves."

"I do not foresee that being an issue, young Snow. We will keep you apprised of Jeselle's development. Now, will that be all?" Moarlin fixed his gaze on Wilder, his eyes shifting between his face and his bright red hair.

"*Yes*, my Lord. That will indeed be all." Tristian stepped in front of Wilder to block him from the view of the Synod. "We thank you again for your venerated hospitality and for honoring us with your incomparable guidance." He bowed again, aiming to disarm and distract while shielding Wilder from their prying eyes and minds.

"Indeed." Moarlin continued to study the situation with intrigue. "Viviayne will lead ye to the waterway. It has been our most *particular* pleasure." Moarlin gave Tristian a subtle bow of his head, and the group moved with careful steps to exit the cathedral. As they followed the night touched fae who had first escorted them, every eye in the chamber shadowed Wilder. The orbs continued to whisper.

A small, wispy, entirely green fae girl clothed in lily pads and petals, her hair like thin spun gold, held the door ajar for them. "Hello, Tristian." The smile painted on her lips appeared demure and inviting, and her lilt belled like the first spring rains.

"Cassandria." Tristian gave her an impassive nod as he passed, not even deigning to meet her gaze.

Harry smirked, amused by the interaction, and Wilder thought he saw Terra roll her eyes before she moved to latch the door behind them with more force than necessary. The hint of a smirk played across Tristian's features.

As their feet made contact with Loinnír, Wilder exhaled the bated breath he had been holding, unsure of whether the Synod would choose to release them; to release *him*. He contemplated whether every guest that visited with the eerie throned creatures felt like a prisoner being weighed and measured. In the relief of Eaigan's main stretch, Wilder inhaled the faint smell of salt on the breezeless air, and they journeyed in wordless trepidation back to the milky falls, ignoring the continued whispers of the Watern and their curious Glass City.

PART THREE

Chapter Thirty

A month had passed since Wilder and his friends had left Jeselle with the Watern, and his training sessions had progressed with some marked improvements. His body could access his inbuilt magic well enough. He could heal quickly, protect himself from Harry's compulsion, and his strength and agility had reached well beyond a basic human level. But it wasn't enough for Wilder to be wholly satisfied. He still couldn't use his magic at will—on his own terms.

As his lack of significant breakthrough persisted, the readily repeated adage of 'It'll all come with time' wore on him. Given the Council's matched exasperation with his development, he knew they probably didn't agree with the statement either. Though Markus had made no further attempts to abduct Wilder or attack the Council House since the incident with the twins, he knew it was only a matter of time before they were threatened again. And Wilder refused to be a liability when the inevitable assault ensued.

A warm, late April morning found Wilder in the Magi's office working on two of the three basic tenants of elemental magic: movement and manifestation. A long table laden with candles, baubles and trinkets, small cups of water, nuggets of gold, colorful gems, dead flowers, and vials of foul smelling syrups had been placed in the center of the Magi's office. Wilder faced the collection from one side of the table as the Magi observed his work opposite him. The table, its contents, and the abilities at which Wilder now engaged, were the same he had been practicing for weeks now.

Wilder squinted at a small, gold-plated pocket watch laid among the clutter.

"Concentrate. Magíck first, then the work," the Magi reminded him.

Wilder shut his eyes and probed inward, locating the rhythmic hum of quiet energy coursing through his veins. Nudging the hum with his mind, he willed it to wake, and felt the hum quicken and expand, lighting his bloodstream. Opening his eyes, he focused on the pocket watch again.

"Corraí." Wilder willed the magic to unclasp the latch holding it closed. Nothing happened. Wilder scowled, frustrated by his incessant battle with what should be such simple magic.

"Remember, we do not *will* things to be done. We partner *with* the Magíck with confidence, but we do not control it. Again." The Magi gestured for him to retry, stepping away from the table.

But Wilder wasn't sure he wanted to partner with anything, let alone some invisible and debatably non-existent force. Either way, he closed his eyes again, prodded at the rippling energy, and instead intentioned to *ask* the magic in his veins to unclasp the latch. A faint pulse echoed through his body and the uneven trickle increased to an unwavering flow, brimming with power. Directing the flow toward the watch, Wilder focused on the metal brass of the latch, imagining it unlocking in his mind's eye. "Corraí." The watch unlatched and the cap sprung open, revealing the clock-face and a faded inscription inside.

What good is it to see if one does not do? Though purpose be a gift, to live it is by choice. – For my dearest one. Mother.

Before he could ask what the inscription meant, the Magi snatched up the watch and closed it with a snap. "Good," he said, giving Wilder a curt, approving nod. "I want you to continue practicing your Corraí, even when you are not here. Now that you have a better handle on magic, I expect you to be exercising it as often as feasible. As it becomes second nature, you will lose the need to speak it into happening. The muscles of your mind will bring it to fruition on its own, without the words."

Instructing Wilder through another course of Corraí, the Magi guided him through the mental weightlifting of relocating each object in front of him across the table with varying degrees of force. Wilder completed the tasks with mediocre skill, each object tottering slowly through the air, but he still found himself delighted by the headway he made. While a flying gold nugget would do nothing to combat a mutinous fae and an all-powerful maniacal wyte, he was on the precipice of being able to defend himself. And that, for today, felt like enough.

Magi Maynestream transitioned him to Léiriú, the deep blue and stark white of his gaze patient as he prompted Wilder to light a candle and fill an empty glass with water. Again and again, nothing happened, and no amount of asking the Magíck to step-in made any difference. In his frustration, Wilder slammed his fist onto the table. The baubles and trinkets clinked and rolled, and the viscous liquids in their beakers and flasks sloshed. Aggravation flared wildly through his veins, spurred on by his utter exhaustion at working at this for what had felt like hours.

Wilder glanced up at the Magi. "What am I doing wrong? I've done everything you've told me to."

"Léiriú is tricky. It is by far the most difficult of the three roads. You are attempting to produce an element seemingly out of nowhere. It is not easily done."

"Clearly," Wilder grumbled, his fingers clenched around the edges of the table, glaring at the unlit candle.

"However, when you allow your awareness to widen, you will see that it does indeed come from somewhere after all." Wilder looked up at the Magi in confusion. The Magi grinned and moved a few steps over to reveal the fireplace behind him, which had not been lit when Wilder had begun his practice.

It now burned steady, roaring with life and alight with a scorching, crackling blaze.

***

Lunch was a quiet affair. Harry and Barrett were investigating potential unfound Céad at schools out in Baton Rouge, Terra had left to spend the afternoon with her Coven, Tristian was in meetings all day as he trained with Council leadership, and Olivia had disappeared elsewhere, though Wilder had no idea where she could have gone off to. It felt strange to be the only one not engaged in some meaningful task, so Wilder just stared at the last dregs of his minestrone soup, wishing he had found out about all of this earlier than seventeen. He felt like a ten-year-old just learning how to crawl.

Trudging to his room, he spent the next two hours staring at himself, yet again, in the bathroom mirror—but this time it was part of his homework. Olivia, Barrett, and Rickard had decided that Wilder had attained enough rudimentary knowledge of shapeshifting to accomplish the most basic elements on his own. They all believed, at this point, it was his own fear and subconscious obstinacy sabotaging his progress. Unfortunately, Olivia and Barrett couldn't help him with that, so he was left to his own devices—though he'd still check-in with Rickard at the end of each week to discuss any improvement, or lack thereof.

Wilder pressed his hair back and inspected his ears in the mirror. They looked exactly how any normal human ear should: rounded helix, attached lobes and all. Wilder, however, reminded himself that, in reality, they weren't supposed to be human. Rickard had explained acknowledging the truth of the situation might help, and Wilder would try anything to get past whatever held him back.

"You have pointy ears," he said to himself. "They're not supposed to look like this. You have pointy ears."

Wilder continued to stare at himself in the mirror, but his ears remained as steadfast in their roundness as ever. He tried again, this time using the method Olivia had taught him. Reaching inside to wherever his true self was supposed to be, he willed it to come forward, all while simultaneously imagining his human ears melting away. Still, no luck, though he could swear he felt some inner part of himself swat away the unwelcome intrusion.

Wilder inclined over the counter and inspected himself more closely. Without warning or preamble, a voice he didn't recognize echoed through the silent bathroom.

"Corraí. Tras-Athrú."

The voice sounded firm, laden with deep authority. Wilder stumbled away from the mirror, his back hitting the wall, and scanned the room in bewilderment. "Who's that?" he said stupidly into the air. Peeking behind his shower curtain, he realized he couldn't even be sure the voice had been audible.

No one answered. He looked back at the mirror and studied his ears again. Corraí and Tras-Athrú. The first road he had practiced that morning, but the second he knew only in theory—transmutation. Tras-Athrú was the practice of turning an element in one state into another, associated state, like water into ice. Unfortunately, he was about as acquainted with Tras-Athrú as he was with shapeshifting itself, though he considered the two might be intrinsically related.

"Sorry, random voice in my head," Wilder whispered tentatively into the emptiness. "Not sure that one's going to work out."

He eyed himself in the mirror again, and despite his hesitation, Wilder figured there couldn't be any harm in giving Corraí a shot. Closing his eyes, he pricked at the magic flowing through his veins. He found it rushing with more life and vigor than it had been when he had first touched it that morning. Allowing himself to rest in it, he asked the Magick for use of Corraí. His magic sung through him, reaching through his skin and settling like glowing embers within the folds of his ears. He held his hair back again, studying himself.

"Corraí." His timbre sounded far more confident than he felt. Reaching into some place deep within his core, he imagined the false presentation in front of him melting away, the natural display moving into place instead. He had barely spoken the words before his ears warmed against his fingertips. Wilder watched, stunned, as his ears softened and dematerialized before his eyes. His rounded helix sharpened to a distinct point. His stomach flipped and Wilder gripped the edge of the counter to assure himself he remained in his body. As the magic faded, he was left with what he instinctively knew was at least one genuine attribute of his truest form, and the first physical confirmation of his fae origins.

A giddy grin replaced Wilder's shock. Ripping off his shirt, he twisted around to inspect his porcelain back, his shoulder muscles rippling beneath his skin. He pulled his arms into his chest to get a better view of his shoulder blades. Wilder noted with vague acknowledgment how much more fit he'd become since he first started training with Tristian. But that subtle thrill felt negligible at the prospect of shapeshifting. Wilder closed his eyes again and concentrated, following the same process as before, imagining his long-lost wings moving through him and into place. But the magic did not come. In confusion, Wilder nudged at the steady hum of energy within him, asking the Magíck again for help. The disembodied voice pressed at his mind.

Tras-Athrú.

"But I don't know Tras-Athrú," Wilder said to no one. The voice didn't answer.

He looked over his shoulder and down at his back again. Taking a deep breath, Wilder humbled his ask and nudged at the magic in his veins, this time asking it to partner in the way he knew he should have before. His blood stirred in delight and expectation. Closing his eyes, he let his concentration travel along his spine as he ruminated on the concept of Tras-Athrú.

Images of shifting elements flashed through his mind, courtesy he knew of the incorporeal presence continuing to press upon him—a dead flower reversing into its full bloom, water shifting into cloud form before flooding the earth with rain, a rock dematerializing into sand, and forming again into a beautiful glass chalice. He racked his brain as to what his undetectable wings had to do with the images the voice showed him; how wings could shift from one state to another.

His skin tingled as the magic flooded the flesh along his back. Opening his eyes, he peered over his shoulder again. In the mirror, he saw subtle sparks of light, almost indiscernible, travel in arcs down his lower back and up along his shoulders. The sparks wrapped around his upper arms, the white-blue speckled light spreading across his bare skin. He studied his back closer, tracing what faint glowing lines he could reach with the pad of his index finger. Perhaps his wings weren't hidden at all… What if they had been transformed? Had become a part of his very skin?

"Tras-Athrú." Wilder's words grew saturated with a confidence he knew was not his own. The sparks pulsed, sending a shock through him. Wilder threw his hands onto the wall across from the mirror, steadying himself. Looking over his shoulder, he saw the jagged outline of wings pulsing again with a steadier glow, arcing bolts of miniature lightning shooting across them. Swaths of his skin brightened into a luminous white light, flaring with incandescence as they peeled themselves from the folds of his body, spreading wide behind him. The room lit so bright Wilder's eyes struggled to adjust.

Blinking at himself in the mirror, he saw that the blades were formless, made entirely of crackling white light laced with shots of blue veins and venules. The span of the wings themselves were his arm's length wide, and rose three heads higher than his shoulders.

Wilder's heart leapt. "Whoa." Wholly mesmerized by the sheaths engulfing him, he reached out and touched the hindwing with his fingers, expecting a shock, but feeling only pulsing power matching that of the magic bursting through his blood. Despite their lack of substance, Wilder felt the tentative touch of his own fingers along the bolts of light. The experience felt both foreign and yet somehow familiar, as if he knew they had been there from the start, as if the light were a part of Wilder himself. He instinctively stretched and maneuvered the muscles where the wings connected to his spine, and they folded themselves in and out as naturally as crossing his arms, the shadows in the room shifting and cowering in response.

Nearly blinded by exhilaration, Wilder turned to stare at himself in the mirror, struggling to comprehend that the eerily familiar creature standing before him was himself. Inclining closer to the mirror, he studied his stormy gray eyes, remembering the comments made by Terra and the Council about the oddity of them. Though they were without a doubt his favorite of his human attributes, if they had been shifted, he was determined to shift them back.

Ignoring a slight pang in the back of his mind, he began the same Corraí process as before, thrilled to see what color they would become. "Corraí," Wilder commanded, his hands gripping the countertop as zeal flooded him. He drew closer to the Magíck, to the now familiar rush, but the magic in his blood hesitated—warning him away from the endeavor.

Wilder rolled his shoulders, unperturbed. "Corraí," he repeated with more authority. The pulse in his blood faltered again, burning his veins. But with another push from Wilder, the magic cascaded into his irises. The stormy gray dissipated like smoke, lightening and revealing the glowing amber of a setting sun. Just as realization dawned on him that these, these were his true eyes—a deluge of grief so intense he gasped out loud consumed him. He collapsed onto the cold ground, overcome by wracking tears and immense panic.

He couldn't breathe. Loneliness inundated him. Desperation clung to his soul as he lamented the loss of something dear ripped away without warning. Though he had no idea what it could have been. "No," he gasped through choking sobs, staring at the white tile floor and pushing himself up on all fours, a confusion of unbidden tears blinding him. "No. NO. Corraí...CORRAI." He screamed into the silence, yelling the word like a prayer.

Wilder felt the weight of his wings disappear as the light went out from the room and his grief dispelled. The pressure in his chest lifted, allowing him breath again. He sucked in heavy drags of clean air. Numb and detached, he lifted himself off the ground and left the bathroom, avoiding any glimpse of himself in the mirror, though he knew without question that the amber eyes were gone, replaced once again by the comforting color of slate, silver, smoke, and ash.

In a weary haze, Wilder collapsed into a spent heap onto his bed. He wrestled with sleep, staring at his blank wall for hours and ignoring each knock at his door calling him to dinner, friendship, and a route to peace. The child in him, long ago buried, cried out for him to hold fast to whatever was left of the anguish his amber eyes had triggered—to hold fast to the stone and steely gray of his adopted eyes. They were all he had left of whatever he had lost, and he would never change them again. Not for anything. When sleep finally took him, his mind grew fitful, disrupted by the disturbing musings of his nightmares.

He stood in an unending white room, lit by nothing, and yet bright to a disorienting degree. Gold eyes watched him, attempting to break through the melancholia that held him stifled in a straitjacket, unmoving and unable to defend himself or anyone else. A swath of crimson silk fabric ran through his mouth, drying his tongue and throat, making it impossible to speak or scream. A bronze framed mirror stood in front of him, the frame carved of the sky and sea. In it, he saw the echo of a beautiful gray-eyed woman reaching out beyond what the mirror displayed, arms outstretched, her elegant face wrought with despair. She knelt onto the ground and wept, her head hung low and her shoulders quaking with each sob, though no sound of the scene escaped the mirror.

Wilder wanted to reach out to her, to comfort her, to protect her from whatever had broken her, but he couldn't move or speak. Cursed to only watch, tears gathered in his own eyes. Through the blur, Wilder noticed the ghostly gold eyes blink with sympathy. The room filled with a thick, white smoke, obscuring the woman from his vision.

He woke in a cold sweat, his dream fading into muted memory, before sleep took him once more.

Chapter Thirty-One

Wilder woke in the dead of night. Glancing at his clock, he found it nearing 4:00am. Wide awake, rearing with unsettled energy, and with little interest in attempting to sleep again, he got up and dressed in under a minute. All he wanted, all he *needed*, was to blow off some steam. Wilder made a beeline for the training room, heartened to find the punching bag hung in place and ready for him.

His magic vibrated through his veins, singing to him, calling him to move. To fight. It was as if his experience earlier that night had left a crack in the wall between him and his magic, and the energy on the other side was leaking through, brighter now than ever before. He let it take control. It felt so much easier than working out everything rushing through his mind.

The next few minutes were a violent blur. The bag swung with unnatural momentum as Wilder punched, kicked, and did anything and everything short of destroying the plastic covered sack of sand. The lamps above flickered on and off while white light danced around him, casting shadows across the rafters and reflecting off the glinting silver blades lining the walls.

A hearty laugh sounded from the doorway, and Wilder swiveled around. At the threshold, Harry stood with his arms crossed, watching the display with amusement.

"Oh, don't let me stop you. Looks like you're making progress. Two or three more and it'll definitely be dead." His laugh lit his fatigued eyes, shadows clung to the hollows above his cheekbones, and his voice sounded edged with weariness. "Nice wings, by the way. Lightning. That's fitting."

Between his rage and frustration, Wilder hadn't bothered to wonder why his wings seemed to appear so effortlessly now. As if the wall no longer held them at bay.

"Sorry I woke you up," Wilder said, guilt rushing to his cheeks as his wings sputtered out. He hadn't realized how much noise he had been making.

"You didn't," Harry said, shrugging. "I've been up for a while."

Wilder nodded and slumped onto the floor, spent but somehow still raging. Shutting his eyes, he breathed deep, stilling his heart and trying to quell the firestorm of anger and pain that had been ravaging him for hours.

"Not so fast, Summer," Harry said, kneeling next to him and punching him in the shoulder.

"Ow!" Wilder's eyes snapped open, and he glared up at Harry.

"Stop covering it," Harry told him. "It won't go away if you don't let it out. If you don't address it. This is where you need to be if you're going to find balance." Standing up, he held out his hand. "Let's go. Right now. You and me. Get it out."

"What?" Wilder peered up at him in confusion, ignoring Harry's outstretched palm. His thoughts muddled with the drop in adrenaline, but despite his exhaustion, the raging continued beneath his skin.

"Talk it out. Fight it out. Whatever it is, you clearly need somebody. It's 4:30 in the morning and you've spent the last half hour waking up half the abbey, taking whatever this is out on a punching bag. Has it worked?"

"No." Wilder admitted, groaning into his core.

"So, back to the drawing board. Either fight with real life flesh and blood," Harry patted his own chest, "or talk. What's eating you alive?"

Wilder stared up at the rafters, panic edging along his periphery, but he stopped pushing it down. "I don't…I don't want to become…Tristian," Wilder said, stumbling through the thoughts as they collided out of his mouth. Guilt coursed through him again, and he wondered whether he should be discussing this particular fear with Tristian's best friend.

"Okay…" Harry said slowly, his tone betraying his bewilderment as he sat down across from Wilder. Laughing, he reclined on his outstretched arms. "Lucky for you, and really for all of us, you're not. Problem solved?"

"Sure. Yeah," Wilder agreed, shaking his head and pushing himself off the ground to leave. He knew he shouldn't have said anything.

"Wait, Wil. Forget I said that." Harry put a hand up to stop him. His face was gaunt with exhaustion, but his half smile continued to brighten his eyes. "Explain what you mean."

Slumping back to the padded floor, Wilder paused to gather his thoughts. "I mean…he's all emotion. Right? Literally raw, uncontrolled emotion, all the freaking time. It's terrifying and intimidating. Rickard and the Magi say the root of my abilities, the root of my control over my magic, lies within my connection to everything I'm feeling. But I *don't want* to feel the things I'm feeling. And I definitely don't want to become Tristian. He just seems completely ruled by it."

Harry studied the pads beneath them, before saying, "I get it, I do. But I don't think you're seeing the situation clearly. You don't need to become Tristian. I can assure you of that, at least. Tristian is a product of his upbringing, of who his dad raised him to be. His tendency towards…*indelicacy*…and open displays of aggression might help him to some degree. But I wouldn't mistake his tactlessness as something you need to aspire to just to control your magic. It might be helpful, I guess, but not necessary. If anything, his brashness is holding him back just as much as your refusal to acknowledge certain things holds *you* back. He needs to learn some temperance just as much as you need to learn to let yourself feel, and feel without exploding. Without letting it get the better of you."

Wilder nodded, considering Harry's observation. His eyes burned, his knuckles were beginning to bruise, and his brain felt cloudy and numb. But the truth, however uncomfortable, sank in. "Yeah, right. Thanks Harry."

"Anytime." Harry ran a hand through his dark, disheveled hair, bringing out the stark white of his skin. He looked even more pale than he usually did.

"So what kept *you* up so late, then?" Wilder asked. "You look like you haven't slept in weeks."

"Worry," Harry answered, shrugging. "I haven't seen Olivia in days. I'm sure she's been in, but not often. Rickard's at his wit's end. He's worried about her, too. Have you seen her? Or heard from her? Has Terra said anything?" A shadow of weary hope clung to his features, adding a deeper tone to the purple half moons under his eyes.

"No. Not at all. I mean, I've noticed she hasn't been around as much, but I figured she was off doing something for the Council, so I didn't think anything of it. I take it this isn't like her?"

"Not really. I mean, she's always been a bit rebellious, but she's never been so careless to not let us know where she is or if she's even okay," Harry said. Wilder could see Harry's panicked exhaustion settling over him, moving through his weakened body as if he struggled to keep himself upright.

"I'll keep an eye out for her. Maybe try to get through to her if I see her around," Wilder reassured him. "Harry, are you sure you're okay? Have you been eating?"

Harry averted his gaze. "Some," he brushed away Wilder's question with an irreverent nod. "But yeah, thanks. I really do appreciate that."

Wilder nodded, continuing to eye how rough his friend looked. He had been so preoccupied with his own stuff, he hadn't realized how serious things had been getting with Olivia.

"Anyway," Harry pushed himself up off the floor, "you should probably get some sleep. You look drained. But I'm here if you need to talk, need a distraction, whatever." He paused, considering his next words. "You don't have to carry it all on your own. That's what we're here for. You're family now." Harry moved to leave.

Wilder peered up at him. "Hey. Same goes for you."

Harry paused at the doorway, his head hung, but he nodded in thanks and waved goodnight, exiting the room. His final three words clung to Wilder as he ambled to his own quarters, finally exhausted enough for sleep, and hoping Harry would find his own as well.

Chapter Thirty-Two

Wilder opened his eyes to the morning light with an eagerness he knew better than to allow himself. He was scheduled to spend the day with Terra in the Apotéca, and he'd be lying to say his anticipation had more to do with learning the differences between magem and fae magic than with spending prolonged time with her—alone.

Recalling how annoyed he had been with her when they first met, he chuckled. The last thing he had expected all those months ago was how taken he'd become with her, and he had even less of an idea how to handle it. The only person he'd consider talking to might be Harry, especially given his own ongoing experiences with unrequited feelings. But since Harry's best friend was Tristian, who still seemed to hold some flame for Terra, that was decidedly not an option.

Part of Wilder knew Terra was a profound distraction to his learning. When he should've been listening to her lessons on the precise way to grind jojoba seeds, he'd instead be watching her, or otherwise reveling in the feel of her skin whenever she'd correct the movement of his hand at the mortar and pestle. Often, he'd purposely do something wrong just so she'd draw closer and fix his moment of ineptitude. But he couldn't help himself. He was so far gone at this point, he'd use any excuse to spend time with her. Though he did reprove himself regularly for allowing the distraction. Plus, he knew his infatuation was futile. Terra had hinted to as much during so many of their interactions, as if she knew what was on his mind, and knew neither of them should entertain the idea.

In his gut, he knew he'd have to do better about focusing if he was going to make any headway with his magic, and also knew it was for the best he not waste his time with the whole endeavor. But he just couldn't help the thrill that shot through him whenever her emerald eyes locked on his, or the way his bones sang when she got close.

It was those very bones that told him something about today would be different.

Wilder leapt out of bed and dressed in a sprint, tearing off his sleep clothes and settling on jeans and a charcoal shirt Terra had once said brought out his eyes. Sprinting downstairs, he grabbed a banana, an orange, two Poptarts, and two mugs of fresh steaming black coffee—just how she liked it—from the kitchen. Once his arms were piled precariously high, he padded down the narrow stone staircase to the Apotéca, balancing his bounty with careful concentration.

Even with his improved footing, Terra started as he made a ceremonious entrance, stumbling on the last step and dropping the banana and the orange. The latter bounced and rolled toward Terra's feet. Her laugh echoed through the chamber. It had become his new favorite sound. She retrieved the orange from beneath her table and wandered over to give him a hand.

"You know, you don't need to bring me breakfast *every* time you come see me. I've been able to feed myself for a few years now." She took a careful sip from the mug he handed her, a playful twinkle in her eye. His gut did a somersault, as if forgetting, once again, that he was there to focus on his lesson. "Though it's always appreciated. Thank you."

"I know," he said. "I just figure if I keep you well fed, you're more likely to forgive me when I accidentally blow something up." Wilder's forced chuckle failed to veil how serious he was. Two weeks ago, he had unintentionally added oak-bark instead of ash wood to a potion they had been working on, and they spent the next thirty minutes waiting for the Apotéca to air out all the smoke.

"I've already told you, you're not going to blow anything up. And even if you do, I'll *valiantly* step in and shield you from harm." She flipped her hair onto her back dramatically before sitting down on a barstool with her coffee, returning to the book she had been perusing. Wilder sucked in a breath as the scent of sage, lemon, and lilac suffused the air, garnering control of his senses in a way he'd never experienced. His stomach flipped and tightened, and he realized he never noticed the scent before, but now he couldn't pay attention to anything else.

Wilder strode over to her, some no longer repressed part of him commandeering his body and actions. As he inclined beside her at the table, she looked up at him in surprise, and he locked his stormy stare with hers. "I'm not so sure about that. Isn't that *my* job?"

Confusion lit her widening gaze at the distinct change in his demeanor and tone. He reached down to tuck a loose strand of her soft hair behind her ear, his hand resting along her neck as he slowly rotated the seat of her barstool to face him head-on. She didn't move. And she didn't seem to be breathing, either.

He didn't know what he was doing. Didn't know what he was thinking. But he kept going. *Good. This is good,* his bones seemed to sing out to him, ignoring his gut's protestations that he was walking headfirst into dangerous territory.

Wilder drew his hand slowly down her neck, shoulder, and arm before it came to a rest in a light grip around her wrist. Never breaking from her stare, he took a careful step closer to her, so they were only inches apart. A buzzing energy pulsed between them, and Wilder was sure it had never been there before, either. Or maybe he just hadn't been as aware of it as he was in this moment. Terra gazed up at him with the intrinsic curiosity she had for everything in life, as if in a trance and unsure of how to react. The hairs on the back of his neck stood on end.

Wilder knew her better now. He knew she had been uncertain about him at the start, but he had gleaned enough from their interactions over the last few months that regardless of how she felt about him being fae, and whatever future they might have, the attraction between them was decidedly mutual. Even if she forced herself to ignore it. But now, some innate part of him was determined to bring this thing to a head. To whatever end.

Terra's crushing green eyes stared wide and steady as his blood drew him closer. Closer.

The sound of something loud dropping onto the ceiling above shattered through the thinning air, and Terra coughed, swallowing hard and breaking her gaze from Wilder's. Releasing her wrist, he took a step away, cursing the clumsiness of whoever was right above them.

Terra shook her head, as if clearing her mind. Rising from the barstool, her voice trembling, she finished his earlier thought. "Um. Well. Not if you're busy blowing everything up." She assumed an effortlessly bright smile, patted his chest, and ambled away with a feigned nonchalance.

Wilder chuckled at her reaction, and at his own brashness. This burgeoning side of him felt both characteristically unlike him, and entirely natural at the same time. Reclining against the heavy marble table covered in books and jars of pleasantly scented salves, he watched her retreat.

"You make a good point," he called after her, taking a bite from his Poptart. Wilder could just make out the hint of a blush on her cheeks, and the way she now tried to hide her grip on a new table far across the room as she struggled for breath. He could almost feel her heart racing from where he stood. *Good.* The loud, innate magic coursing through his bones wanted her to be uncomfortable, wanted to push her, to break the two of them out of this ridiculous status quo. Whatever it took for her to admit what was happening between them. At this point, he didn't even care if it came to anything. He just wanted her to be honest—with herself and with him.

But she pressed the conversation forward, and decidedly away from where he had been hoping it would go. "I didn't see you at all yesterday.

How were your lessons with the Magi?" Terra asked, trying to mask her cracking voice with an easy confidence. She began prepping ingredients in front of her, leafing through the pages of an open book while she measured.

"Oh..." Wilder's mind went blank. He retraced his night to yesterday, floored that in his thrill to see her, he had forgotten everything that had happened in his bathroom, and the tumultuous evening that had followed. He felt the color drain from his face. When he didn't finish his response, Terra glanced up at him.

"Hey, are you okay?" Her brow narrowed in concern. Leaving the book, she padded back over to him, as if forgetting everything that had just happened between them, and placed her palms on his forearms to steady him. A spark shot through Wilder like lightning. "Did I say something wrong?" she asked.

"Uh, no. No. Not at all." Wilder shook his head as he tried to dispel the fog from his mind, and all-together failing to quiet the dramatic gymnastics his stomach was engaged in. "Yesterday was...unexpected, I think. I'm making a lot of progress, though." He made a half-hearted attempt at a smile.

Terra stared up at him for another moment, her eyes slitting, before trouping to her station and shutting her book with a snap. "What do you say we take a break from magic today, okay?"

Wilder's heart sank. *Shit.* He knew he shouldn't have come on so strong. He had been looking forward to spending the day with her. "Hey, look, I promise, I really am—" he started.

"We'll go on a field trip instead, just you and me. Let's get out of here," Terra added, her winsome smile reaching her eyes. Her irises twinkled between light and shadow, echoing the flickering of the candles and torchlight in the room.

Wilder's heart pounded heavy in his chest, and he prayed to whatever Magíck might be out there that she couldn't hear the sound bouncing off the walls. "Okay. Sure. That sounds great."

***

Terra took Wilder to Café Du Monde in City Park. It felt oddly unnerving to revisit a part of his human life knowing he could no longer claim to be one, and that Terra wasn't one either. Studying the other visitors at the park, he checked to see if the old woman he had once played chess with would show up again. He then wondered if any of the other people here were secretly Céad, and figured that the majority had no idea who, or what, stood only feet away from them.

After ordering their food, they rested outside beneath a swooping oak, the warm glow of the late morning sun kissing their skin as they settled across a small patch of green lawn. Watching Terra, he worked through his fourth beignet, more than content listening to the memories she shared of climbing the sprawling oaks when she was little, and how she and Liv would frequent the spot when they needed an escape from Council life.

"It's normal, you know. Getting overwhelmed by everything that happens there. Especially when you're first starting off," Terra said.

Wilder knew she meant to open the conversation for him to explain what had happened the night before, but he couldn't bring himself to go there yet. He was still recovering from whatever had happened, or almost happened, in the Apotéca. He internally kicked himself for getting so close and not kissing her when he had had the chance.

"Do you think that's why Olivia hasn't been around as much?" Wilder asked, wrapping his arms around his knees. "I think Harry's worried about her. I saw him in the training room last night. He couldn't sleep either."

Terra stared into the black depths of her coffee, and her slowly narrowing brow told him she hadn't been expecting this question. Wilder watched her as she seemed to consider what to say.

"I don't know what's going on with Liv, but I'm worried, too." Peering at him, Terra's expression grew strained behind a subtle glisten. "I know she's seeing someone, but her distance is out of character. I'm just as confused as Harry is. And for the first time in my life, I don't really know what to do. She's my best friend, and I don't know what to do…" Tears brimmed beneath her lashes as she stared back into her mug.

On instinct, Wilder put his arm around her. He knew he couldn't fix this for her, though every part of him wanted to. But he could at least be what she needed in that moment, *anything* she needed. And she let him. Resting her head on his shoulder, he held her, her silent sobs muffled by his shirt. With each one, her trembling frame grew more and more relaxed, and a tinge of pride swelled in Wilder's chest at her finally showing this side to him.

After a moment, she heaved a sigh, hastily wiped at her face, and lifted her gaze to his, almost in thanks. Pulling away, she asked, "You saw Harry in the training room last night?"

"Um, yeah. We…talked through some things, I guess. About what happened yesterday, mostly…" Hesitating, he peered at Terra. Instinctively, he knew her curiosity had nothing to do with any self-serving expectation or personal agenda. She genuinely cared.

He started to tell her about some of the night before, his intention to only give her a brief summary. He could do that, at least. But whether it was his exhaustion or just Terra's calming effect on him, he couldn't stop, or at least he didn't bother to, and instead told her everything. He detailed his shift in his bathroom: the voice, his ears, his wings, his eyes; and the numbing shroud that cloaked him afterwards; what he could remember about the woman in his dream, the gold eyes that had been haunting his sleep, and about his crippling fear of not being able to control his emotions, or his magic—though he left his concerns about Tristian out of the commentary.

She sat and listened, never offering anything more than a gentle nod. As he grew more and more comfortable, he began to uncover everything he had been holding onto; all the things he hadn't even known he was upset about. He told her how angry he was with the Magíck, if it was real at all, for the life he had been forced to live until that point. For taking his parents from him, for leaving him alone to fend for himself, and for keeping him in the human world his whole life, when the whole time he had belonged somewhere else. He wrestled with why such an all-powerful being would allow such terrible things to happen, to him or to anyone else, and how he could possibly bring himself to connect with something that betrayed him long before he had been old enough to defend himself. He told her about his fear that everything pointed to him being Markus's son, that so much of the Council believed it to be true, and his dread they might be right. Finally finished, he drew in a sharp breath, laid down on the grass beneath him, and stared up at the flawless sky, stunned by himself for the second time that day.

"Wow. When you talked about blowing something up this morning, I didn't realize you were talking about yourself," Terra said, chuckling. Wilder stared at her, his brows lifting in surprise that she didn't seem the least bit fazed by his rant.

"Listen," she said, "without getting into a philosophical debate about hope or the nature of good and evil, what I can tell you is that everything you're upset about is fair and valid. I can't begin to imagine what you went through growing up. And you're right. You belonged with your people. But—and I know this might be hard to hear—*but*…as crap as it is that you dealt with all of that, I want you to consider that the Magíck might not have played the role you're thinking in what happened to you."

"You can't seriously tell me this all-powerful creator thing didn't have control over what was happening to me, Terra," Wilder argued. Drawing himself up, he stared at her in shock. "That seems pretty contradictory. Why should I bother believing in its supposed endless power, if that's the case?"

"I'm not saying it didn't have control, Wil. I'd actually argue it worked through everything happening to you to bring you to us. Obviously, I'm not all-knowing, so I have no idea why any of it happened, or why any of what we experience every single day happens. But there is more at work in this world than what all of us tend to believe, or what we tend to blame."

"What do you mean?" Wilder asked.

Terra paused, tilting her head as she studied him. "What do you know about the Dahrk?"

"Only what Rickard mentioned. Which was very little. Something about its connection to Maluum. But not much more than that."

Nodding, Terra fell silent and looked down at her hands. "The Dahrk is another part of our legends people have trouble believing. It's easier to blame people, or the Magíck, for the things that piss us off, than to consider there might be greater forces at work. The Dahrk is the antithesis of the Magíck. It's more than just something that goes bump in the night, scaring little kids into behaving. I know it's still as good as a nursery rhyme to you, but if you dug deeper into the histories of our people, into our ancient writings, you'd realize it's so much more than that. The Dahrk's greatest ability lies in distracting and embittering people of the Magíck from the call of their blood. The call to create, and to do good, with the gifts we've been given. It *wants* us to blame the Magíck for *its* role in the suffering we go through."

"That's all fine and good, Terra. But in that case, I'm having a really hard time understanding how something can be all-powerful and still allow this Dahrk, or whatever it is you'd rather I blame, to have the hold it does on the world, or on our lives," Wilder said, his voice a low grumble.

"That's just it. It's so much bigger than us, Wil. So much bigger than we'll ever be able to understand. We're not the first of the Magíck's creation, nor will we be the last. The Dahrk itself was created by the Magíck before it became the Dahrk, and the old stories tell us the Magíck granted free will to *each* of its creations, however unfortunate the outcome of that decision has become. We're in the middle of a far greater battle than just what we can see with our own eyes, and we're only pawns in that game." Terra's lips thinned, her jaw tightening. "At the end of the day, your perception of the situation is something you need to settle within yourself. I'd just hate for you to struggle with the source of your control over your powers out of misplaced frustration."

Wilder stared at her, her green eyes blazing. Something he had never seen in her had sparked there, waiting for him to understand. He placed his hand on hers, and she let him. He didn't know what else to say, or what to believe. His mind had grown numb, yet again, and it wasn't even noon yet.

Clearing her throat, she took her hand from his. "As for your dreams, and especially your hearing a voice telling you how to shift, I'm curious about that. Most people have dreams, obviously, but yours seem to have a different quality to them. They could be pointing to more ancient magic than you might yet know about. Prophecy and dreaming like that is more common in the Magem and the Watern than it is in the Fairn, but definitely not unheard of. The whole hearing a voice thing though, *that* I've just straight up never heard of in any of my own studies."

She considered for a moment, tapping her index finger against the tip of her nose. "In either case, I think I'd like to take you somewhere new—if you're up for it. I know someone that could…*help*."

Standing, she held out her palm, peering down at him with the same eager hope he had seen in her when he first arrived at the abbey. Grabbing her hand, Wilder pulled himself up slightly too hard, just enough that she lost her balance and collided into him. She shoved him back, rolling her eyes but still rewarding him with an amused grin and a shake of her head.

"Where to?" he finally asked, just as intrigued by the prospect as Terra was with his unexplained abilities.

Terra released a deep breath, as if coming to terms with the inevitable. "Time to go meet the Coven."

Chapter Thirty-Three

The New Orleans Coven was a motley mix of old-school witchcraft hidden conspicuously alongside a rustic, new age bar and restaurant, where throngs of tourists and locals were enjoying an early lunch. Chipped, painted signs guided curious visitors in the direction of tarot and palm readings, and gemstone-powered energy healing. Whatever Wilder had been expecting when Terra brought him here, this certainly hadn't been it.

"Don't let the front fool you," Terra said, indicating the signs. A wrinkled old woman in a patterned hair wrap, bejeweled with tarnished metal coins, sat facing away from them in the room's corner, plopped cozily on a cushy-looking ottoman. She peered down at the palms of an expectant young blonde woman who kept asking her questions about her dog and 'the one'.

"Some of the older ones have fun making a little money off the tourists, but none of what we do for them is legitimate. It's just a distraction. The best place to hide is in plain sight, after all." She led Wilder through a doorway strung with hanging beads and stones, along a narrow hallway, and then down a staircase far from the bar.

The staircase opened to a large living space dug within the earth itself, the room decorated in a similar style to the Apotéca at the Council House, though with far more personality. Scattered along the far side of the room, patterned and embroidered divans circled a tarnished wood table. Atop it sat a collection of mismatched mugs and a stone Kintsugi teapot.

Hand-woven twill and canvas rugs covered every inch of the floor, just as books upon books, far greater than the Council House contained, paneled every inch of available wall space. Where there weren't bookshelves, there were narrow doorways leading to at least a dozen adjacent rooms, each threshold hung with either colorful, patterned fabric or more strings of beads, gems, coins, or shells.

Wilder surveyed the room just as the squat fortune-telling woman from the bar strolled into the Apotéca, followed shortly after by a statuesque, serious-faced woman in a heather-gray suit. Wilder's eyes went wide. The old woman looked so much like the woman he had played chess with in the park. All except for her eyes, which glowed hazel rather than a raging blue. She didn't seem to recognize Wilder at all.

As the women entered, he tried not to laugh at the stark contrast between them. The hair of the serious-faced one had been pulled into so tight of a bun, Wilder wondered how her hair didn't tear out from its roots. Everything about her polished persona felt entirely out of place in the patch-worked hubbub of the Apotéca. The older woman, however, seemed right at home.

"Ah, Terra m'dear, I'd hoped you'd be stopping by. I have that book about sleep remedies you were asking for." Throwing a gnarled finger in the air, the old woman retreated through one of the doorways before bustling back out, holding a tattered leather book with worn and peeling bronze lettering.

"Oh right, thank you Madam Malia." Terra managed a half-hearted smile as she took the book, but the arrival of the two women had unnerved her. Her usual bright and cheery demeanor had been replaced with one of serious propriety, her eyes flashing at the tight haired woman before glancing back at Madam Malia. "This is my friend—Wil. The one I was telling you about." Tilting her head toward him, Terra eyed Madam Malia with a distinct expression Wilder couldn't quite place.

"Ah, yes. The Council's new fae child. A pleasure, boy. Wonderful to meet you." Madam Malia grabbed Wilder's hand, warming it between both of her own, and beamed up at him with a knowing grin that made Wilder feel overexposed.

He couldn't help himself—she looked so much like the woman in the park. "I'm sorry. Have we met before?" he asked her.

"Not yet in this life, my boy. But here we are now," the small woman sputtered, utter delight ringing through her. Wilder had no idea how to respond to that.

The tight haired woman offered little more than a jeer at Wilder before turning to Terra. "Ms. Sampson, I'm so happy you've come in today. I wonder if I might have a word?" Her voice sounded of silk pressed with spoiled butter.

"Of course, Priestess." Terra nodded, but her shoulders noticeably tensed. Looking at Wilder, she sent her signature reassuring smile his way. "Don't worry, Madam Malia will take good care of you. I'll be back in a little bit." She followed the Priestess from the room, the woman's two-inch heels echoing like the distant blows of steel swords as they retreated through another hallway.

Wilder peered down at Madam Malia, who continued to stare up at him with an eerie perceptivity that reminded him distinctly of Magi Maynestream.

"Mm, sweet summer boy. Welcome again unto the fold of the Eadar." She bustled back through the same sage green veil emblazoned with a gold Celtic cross she had disappeared behind before. Tarnished copper coins hung from the frayed edges along the bottom, weighing it down.

"Um, thanks?" Wilder called after her.

Popping her head through the cloth, her eyes narrowed on him with suspicious accusation. Wilder started at the abruptness of her re-entrance.

"Why do you wait there so befuddled, boy? Come! In, in." She shooed him through the veil and into another cozy room decorated like the chamber outside, though far smaller, with only enough space to fit four or five people. She motioned him to take a seat, and Wilder reclined on a burgundy chaise lounge laden with overstuffed throw pillows. The woman began readying a pot of tea on the other side of the room. Humming an indistinguishable tune, she shuffled along to her own music. Squatting next to a short wooden table, she threw a medley of herbs from a spice rack into a steaming kettle hanging over a fire within a small earthen hearth. Wilder's eyes widened in shock as he studied the wall space, realizing there wasn't a discernable chimney in the room. Before he could say anything, the smoke from the fire evaporated into thin air, hitting the edges of an invisible sphere.

"I always find a spot of tea to be just the thing, don't you?" the old woman announced. "Always good for calming the nerves and helping us see things more clearly. Yes, yes." She stirred the mixture with a long wooden spoon before ladling it into a mug.

"Sure…" But the only thing Wilder *was* sure of was that he had no idea what she was talking about.

Madam Malia handed him the mug, and he inhaled a deep breath of the steaming vapor. A potpourri of fragrances enveloped him, saturating the small room. He could make out hints of lavender, orange, and sage, though there were a number of others he couldn't place. The scent was tranquilizing as it drifted into his nostrils, and after a careful sip, he found the taste even more so. Taking another larger gulp, calm permeated every inch of his body.

"My dear Terra tells me you are struggling with your magic, my boy. With your future, your past, the whole gamut indeed."

"Oh, um, yeah, I think so." Wilder nodded, his mind suffusing with a soft, dreamy haze.

"Yes, yes. Fear can be such a fickle friend, my boy. Protector and connivance alike. And we don't often get to choose which role he will play, do we?"

"No, we don't." Wilder's heavy head lolled, and he was only half aware of what the woman was saying as cotton padded his ears and a dense fog engulfed him.

Blocking his eyes, bright beams of sunlight blinded him. He tried to make sense of his surroundings, and where the old woman had gone, but he couldn't. He didn't know where he was, or who he was, or if he was a who at all. The world had become soft and flashing, each bright white flare accompanied by a deafening and disorienting ringing. Nothing he perceived connected or made much sense.

A glade beside a cerulean river. Music from a nearby celebration floating through the breeze. A willow covered in Spanish moss. And beneath it, a young man with wild red hair kissing a girl in a short jade dress, his hands hidden beneath the drapery of chestnut brown. A flash.

A young man with platinum blond hair kneels down, determination crossing his icy blue eyes as he stares at the ground, the blade of an elegant silver sword kissing his shoulder and neck. A flash.

A beautiful, dark-skinned girl lay on the ground in racking sobs, a young man with jet black hair holding her, tears falling in waterfall streams from his jungle green eyes. A flash.

The green eyes shift to piercing, luminous gold, and the ringing grows louder until it thunders. A flash.

A skeletal man in a darkened room, cloaked in drab rags, lays unmoving on blood soaked cobbled floors. Rusted shackles wrap his thin wrists and ankles. A flash. A thousand naked, graceless bodies dance around a cold fire, their skin painted glowing red, their hollowed eyes brimming with tears, a thousand thorned whips dancing across their flesh. Next to them, a pile of unmoving bodies, all pale as death and drained of blood.

A flash, another crash of thunder, and the room lights as if struck by lightning. The lightning wraps around a blond man's body before he collapses at the foot of a tree, its roots reaching into the heart of darkness, its branches into the heavens.

A familiar voice called to him in the distance, a golden thread leading him back. The thunder subsided, and the flashes dimmed to a steady pulsing, the velvet touch of the chaise lounge coming slowly into focus, along with a pair of startling green eyes.

"Earth to Wil." Her crystal voice shattered through the fog, and Wilder noticed the distinct silhouette of a woman fading along with it, a part of his soul reaching for her, as if it knew exactly who she was. "Hello? Anyone home?"

"Terra?" Wilder lifted his heavy head from the throw pillow he had fallen onto. "I think there was something in the tea..." He peered at Madam Malia through one eye, the room far too bright and moving too quickly. Chuckling, she took an unbothered sip from her own burnt orange teacup.

"Lightweight, darling," the Madam said, a mischievous glint in her eye. "But I do hope you were able to find what you were looking for."

"I don't think I'd know it if I did," Wilder said, rubbing his forehead. He felt like he teetered beneath a veil between realities, trying to gain some kind of footing. The room continued to pulse. "There was a woman, at the end. In the fog..."

"Ah! Brigit! Lovely girl. A crackerjack at cards, that one," Madam Malia exclaimed, her voice far too cheery given what Wilder had just experienced.

"What?" Wilder asked, his mind still muddled.

"Ignore her. She says things," Terra said, pressing back Wilder's hair and checking his pupils. "Dream tea is heady stuff, *especially* for someone who already tends towards prophetic dreaming." A guilty blush colored her cheeks as she whirled to glare at the Madam with marked vexation. "I had *hoped* Madam Malia would take it easy on you."

The Madam just laughed again. "In my defense, *you* didn't tell me he was a dreamer, dear," she shrugged. "And really, I did take it easy on him. That was half the dose! But you and I both know that boy needed to see whatever it was the Magick called him to. You'd think you'd be more grateful." Shaking her head ruefully, she clicked her tongue. "Now, pip, pip. It's best you be off. I've got a standing appointment with my crochet needle."

Without much more than a few waves of her wrinkled fingers, Madam Malia ushered Terra and a still disoriented Wilder from her room.

CHAPTER
THIRTY-FOUR

After arriving back at the Council House, Wilder and Terra went their separate ways, neither of them asking much about what the other had been up to at the coven. Wilder could tell whatever Terra had discussed with the Priestess wasn't something she wanted to talk about, and she could likely tell the same about him and the tea. Bidding him a quick goodbye, she disappeared down the hall toward her father's office.

Now alone, Wilder had no idea how to make sense of what he'd seen. He wandered through the abbey, replaying the flashing scenes through his mind, confounded by all of them. Were they real? Was all of it going to happen? He thought of the kiss—the girl had unmistakably been Terra, but besides the red hair, the man she had been with looked nothing like Wilder. His heart sank. He thought of the other scenes; the blade against the blond man's neck, the dancing bodies covered in blood, the man in chains, the man at the foot of the tree. He had never seen the last two men before.

Could I just have imagined everything? Could it have all been a metaphor?

But the younger blond man he had known. It had been, without a doubt, Tristian. Remembering each piercing inch of the blade lying against his shoulder, its sharp edge kissing the rough skin of Tristian's neck…Wilder shook his head, dispelling the vision. Maybe they *were* all metaphors. That had to be it.

His thoughts led him to the training room where he found Tristian, Barrett, and Harry sparring. Standing at the doorway, his eyes fell on

Tristian. Rocking back and forth where he stood, a look of ecstatic liberation painted Tristian's features, an expression Wilder rarely saw on him. He was in hand-to-hand combat with his younger brother, and unquestionably winning. Harry was settled on the sidelines, leaning cool-ly against the wall, his arms crossed, offering *whoops* of encouragement to either side of the scuffle. Tristian's wide, gregarious grin brightened the icy blue of his determined features. Harry called time, and Tristian released his brother from a chokehold before raising his arms in triumph. For the briefest of moments, Wilder saw the side of him Terra and Harry had come to know and love.

"Care to join, Summer?" Tristian called out to him, striding confidently backwards, his arms open in an invitation. His drawl seeped a smug haughtiness that made Wilder reconsider whether Tristian might not be half bad.

"I'm not sure if your pride could handle the defeat I'd feed you, Snowflake," Wilder told him, striding over to the group. Tristian glow-ered at the moniker.

"I'm sure his pride could use the ego check," Harry said, smiling at Wilder.

A bright voice called out from the doorway. "If someone needs an ego check, count me in!" Wilder spun to see Liv skipping into the room, her wired eyes fixed on Tristian. "Care to play, Winter?"

"A dance with a wolf?" Tristian chuckled. "It's been ages. Let's go, little girl."

Harry's eyes, alight at first at seeing Olivia, narrowed as he inspected the scene. Wilder knew Harry could tell something was off about her, but seeming unable to discern what, he stepped forward to count off the fight. "On my mark…GO!"

The brawl began, and Olivia quickly got a leg up on Tristian, speedily moving from side to side to confuse him as he attempted to grab her. Her movements seemed jerky, so unlike her usual grace, but fierce and unrelenting, nonetheless. As Tristian circled around again, Liv sprinted forward, pummeling him in the chest with her entire weight and throwing him off-balance. He spun and fell to the ground, and she jumped onto his back, each of them vying for control over the fray. In a flash, Tristian flipped himself over, maneuvering Liv beneath him and securing her into an unbreakable hold.

"Give up yet, wolfie?" Tristian taunted, the gibe tinged in a brother's affection as he grinned down at her.

But under his weight, a wild panic took control of Liv. Her eyes perceptibly darkened, her mouth drawing into a bared snarl. Her canines descended, her eyes flashed yellow, and she ripped herself out of Tristian's arms, throwing him to the ground. Just as he righted himself on his feet, she advanced—an untamed beast set free. In one sudden move, she extended her nails and swiped, swift and sure, across Tristian's chest, leaving behind three shallow, bloody gashes.

"What the hell, Liv!" Tristian stumbled away, holding his chest. Liv made to go at him again, but not before two bodies hurled themselves at her, knocking her to the ground. In less than a second, Harry had maneuvered on top of her, holding her arms as she continued to lash out, snarling like some caged feral animal. Once he could tell Liv was handled, Barrett hurtled over to Tristian to make sure he wasn't seriously injured.

Harry screamed at her, his eyes locking down on hers. "Liv! Liv! Stop! What are you doing?! Stop!" Wilder could see panic and hurt move unspoken between them.

Liv evidently saw it too, because she shuddered. Her shoulders slumped, her fangs retreated, and her breath caught as she forced it to even. Her eyes, brimming with tears, shifted back to their warm caramel. As Liv's body went limp, Harry leapt off her and helped her sit up. Glancing over at Tristian, horror crossed her now fully aware features as she took in the silver painting his fingertips. "Tristian, I'm so sorry...I didn't mean—"

"It's fine, Liv," Tristian said, holding up his bloodied hand; cutting her off while surveying the damage. He still appeared in shock. The gashes on his chest had already begun to stitch themselves together. "Really, it'll heal. It's fine."

Liv's eyes flashed down at his chest, her eyes widening. Her breathing amped up again, coming in shorter, shallow gasps. "I've…gotta go," she said, pushing herself off the pads and making a beeline for the door with unimaginable speed.

"Liv, wait! You shouldn't be—" Harry started, but Liv had already disappeared. "…alone."

CHAPTER
THIRTY-FIVE
Harry

Harry paced around his room, the sound of his frantic footsteps distant in his own ears, but they remained the only thing grounding him to his body. This Olivia was not his Olivia. His Olivia was luminous and shining like the sun. *This* Olivia had been darkened—tampered with.

Harry knew she had her struggles, but they had never mattered to him, not really. From the first day he had found her until now, he always knew he'd walk with her through anything. And he knew she knew that. Or at least he thought she did. But something was happening to her now he didn't understand, and it wasn't something she was letting him into. When she had bolted from the training room, Harry had chased her down, determined to stop her. To reason with her. But she had been too fast. By the time he had crossed through the front door of the Council House, she was gone, leaving behind only a subtle scent for him to follow.

And damn, her scent… Harry didn't know how his strange ability had found him. It had all started shortly after he had been turned. One minute he was struggling to control his insatiable hunger, the next he could scent the essence of people on them, even from miles away. The blossoming power had played a huge role in stifling his desire to feed, at least on fresh blood. It was kind of hard to do that when you could sense someone's soul.

As Harry continued to pace, he knew he didn't need to follow Liv's scent. He knew where she had ended up. Just as he knew he couldn't go there alone. It would be as good as suicide. A knock sounded at his door and he sprinted to it. Harry found Tristian and Wilder waiting on the other side, both armed with an astounding assortment of armaments. Inhaling a deep breath, he refocused on the situation.

"Have you considered you're being a bit excessive, Tristian?" Harry asked, eyeing the menagerie of weaponry.

"No way in hell am I going into a wolf den empty handed," Tristian grumbled, a darkness in his words, his icy gaze ablaze. He had changed out of his ruined, bloodied shirt and into a plain black tee, bringing to stark attention the menacing black marks wrapping around his arms. Everything Tristian did was calculated and intentional, this display no less so. Only fae warriors chose to ink themselves so overtly, and walking into a clan of wolves with his tattoos blatantly visible was a fierce warning to others against engaging, if not a war-cry in itself.

Harry looked at Wilder, a heavy metal club in his hands, a machete and a ruby-hilted dagger sheathed at his sides. Tristian turned to assess Wilder as well. "I figured this one could use all the help he can get." Wilder glared at him.

"You sure about this, Wil?" Harry asked. "We're not about to go make any friends."

Wilder shrugged. "Not a problem. I've already got some."

Harry groaned and nodded. And Tristian had a point. The New Orleans Lycan clan was dangerous at best, and they weren't exactly the biggest fans of the Council or their progeny. Harry had been astounded to hear they were so welcoming of Liv when she had first told him she was hanging out there. He had warned her they might not have the best of intentions because of who she was, but she ignored him, claiming they were 'perfectly good and lovely people'. But the changes she had been exhibiting recently—the temper, the dark edge—had led him to believe that wasn't at all the case.

They left the Council House through a back alleyway, careful to avoid anyone in the hallways. Tristian had let Terra know where they were going just in case something happened to them, but swore her to secrecy for the time being. After hearing about Olivia's outburst in the training room, she had readily agreed, giving them a few irids to hide their movement and protect them on the way. She only fought Tristian on his adamant refusal to let her go with them.

They drove in silence through the city, Tristian at the wheel. The sky darkened and the streetlights blurred as they rushed past. Harry didn't care how fast they were going. Strangers strode the sidewalks as the dinner rush began, their unbothered smiles so foreign to him as they sidled in and out of restaurants and shops. He couldn't feel anything other than panic. What if he never saw her again? Never again felt the warmth of her smile? Harry took another deep breath, steeling his mind. No. He wouldn't let himself think like that. He prayed to the Magick, for whatever it was worth, that he would find her alive.

After what felt like a lifetime, Tristian steered onto a long gravel drive-way leading to a large two-story house on the edge of town. Motorcycles, sports cars, and beat down jeeps were scattered across a massive lawn lit by four individual bonfires and the lights from the house itself. Groups of men and women, all lycan, surrounded the fires and hung on the porch railing—hooting, drinking, and ignoring the newcomers. Rock music blared from inside.

Harry, Tristian, and Wilder stepped out of the vehicle and edged up to the house, their weapons deftly hidden within the folds of their clothes. Harry's awareness suffused with the scent of wolf. Sometimes the scent wasn't half bad, but these weren't pleasant in the least.

The partiers sneered at them as they walked up to the house, but continued with whatever they were doing, as of yet unbothered by the newcomers. Though a few yellow stares eyed Tristian watchfully. Harry figured they had no idea who they were, or else they'd already be beaten to a pulp. He had been counting on the clan's ignorance of their Council affiliation to get the trio through the front door. But the way out would be a different matter entirely.

"Stay close. Talk to no one. Let's find Liv and get out of here," Tristian instructed them. Harry and Wilder nodded, and Harry internally chuckled. It was funny to hear Tristian, who had always been up for a fight, now advising against it. Either he was maturing in his political understanding, or was scared shitless by the situation. Harry hoped to the Magick it was the former. If Tristian was scared, that meant something.

Walking through the front door, Tristian grabbed three beers from an icebox sitting at the entrance. "Blend in," he said, handing one to each of them. They twisted off the caps, but none of them took a sip. They needed to have clear heads to get out of here unscathed.

Lycan were strewn across couches or hunched over tables, playing card games, drinking, smoking, or engaged in some other form of debauchery. The echoes of distant whoops and yells drifted in from the backyard. Harry made eye contact with a burly man, forged of muscle and tattoo, idling against a counter-top in the kitchen. Watching their entrance into the party with marked interest, the man sloshed a sip from his own drink. Someone inclined to say something to him, and the man guffawed, his rumbling laugh filling the house. But his stare followed them as the three slipped deeper into the den.

Harry surveyed the rest of the house. Tristian watched him, waiting.

As Harry breathed in, all he could scent was wolf—and not his own. Somewhere in this house, though, he knew he'd find a subtly different scent; one he knew better than any in the world. One he had grown to love. Harry often found himself leaning closer to her, just to breathe that scent more deeply. She had never questioned it. He knew she wanted his closeness as much as he did, he could feel that much in his bones, even if she'd never openly admit it. And while her scent had always been distinctly wolf, it had hints of citrus and summer, an intoxicating aroma all her own. It reminded him of home; of her. He would know it anywhere. And he knew, in his gut, it was close by.

Trailing the sound of bawdy laughter, they maneuvered through the bustling crowd and sidled onto the back porch. A group of younger lycan were playing drinking games in the wraparound's corner. Farther into the backyard, a giant pool sunk into the ground, littered with foam noodles and plastic tubes, some holding wholly bare-skinned female lycan afloat in the water. Harry hastily averted his gaze just as another loud yelp sounded from above. A blond teenage boy clad in black boxers flew from the roof and through the air, managing an impressive back-flip and landing with a loud splash into the pool below. The crowd cheered, and Harry heard a group of the celebrators upstairs.

The trio rushed down the steps to peer over the edge of the rooftop. Another boy with shaggy brown hair crawled through an open window, preparing to shadow his friend's descent. Harry arced a glance at Tristian and Wilder, who were both eyeing the scene speculatively, as if sensing something amiss. Harry tuned his hearing to a distinct rush of voices arguing on the other side of the window.

"Ugh! Just get rid of her, Pieter. She's such a bore. Why do you even bring her here?" a female voice complained.

Pieter. He knew that name.

As a male voice drawled a response, the wind picked-up. A familiar scent, coming from the suites upstairs, saturated Harry's awareness.

Liv.

But the citrus and summer was layered with something bitter and rotten. The same scent that had been on her when she had assaulted Tristian. Harry didn't waste another moment. He sprinted back up the porch steps, through the screen door, and to the front of the house. Dashing up the stairs leading to the second story, he was barely aware of Tristian and Wilder trailing his heels, or of the numerous sets of eyes glaring at him from the party below.

Harry scanned the second-floor hallway, looking for the room the boys had been vaulting from. Smoke drifted from one of the cracked doors, and he crashed through it, splintering the wood as it smashed into the wall behind. The lights were dimmed and loud, beating music bumped through the space. A scattering of wolves, all looking to be in their early twenties, sat crossed-legged on the carpeted floor and spread across a fourposter bed, taking hits from hand-rolled cigarettes and a garish glass bong being passed around. Each of their eyes glowed a bright yellow. Harry hissed at the sight and the rotten scent, knowing it instantly.

Wolfsbane.

Scowling, Harry shoved further into the room, pressing past the crowd of bleary-eyed lycan, tailing the call that always led him to Olivia. All his senses could tell she was close, and he knew in his gut she wasn't safe. His eyes fell on a half-closed door at the far end of the room.

An imposing boy with hazy yellow eyes stepped in front of Harry, blocking his path and stupidly depositing his hand on Harry's chest. "Hey, man, what're you—"

Harry didn't wait for him to finish. His fist connected with the boy's jaw, sending him reeling into the circle of the other lycan onlookers. Fangs descending, Harry wheeled around to snarl and slice a menacing glare at the group. Some stared at him in stunned fascination, while others bolted clear out of the room.

Tristian and Wilder, their hands at their weapons, charted every movement around them, ready to engage if the need arose. But the rest of the young wolves didn't move. Harry figured it was more likely because they were stoned out of their minds, and had no clue how to react, than because they were actually scared—but he'd take it.

Harry pivoted back toward the door, which led to another adjacent space. Rushing through, his eyes adjusted quickly to the darkness. A desk and a bookshelf lined one wall, while the others were plastered with posters and ripped magazine pages. The room was wholly empty of people, aside from a petite, spritely girl in black leggings and a white crop top laying unconscious on another fourposter bed. Her tight, dark curls spiraled down her face, obscuring her features. Darting to her, Harry prayed she was only asleep.

CHAPTER THIRTY-SIX
Harry

Olivia's face had gone colorless. Pushing back her hair, Harry touched her skin, expecting its usual warmth. But it had grown cold, now covered in a thin sheen of sweat.

"Shit," he whispered, his breath hitching as panic coursed through him. "Liv! Liv!" Harry called to her, trying to shake her awake. She didn't move.

He bent close, his ear hovering above her lips, straining to hear a breath, a heartbeat, anything. After the longest silence Harry had ever known, a barely audible fluttering thump sounded from Olivia's chest. Harry released the breath he had been holding, and he swore he could have cried.

A scuffle sounded behind him, and Harry spun to see a thin but broad-shouldered lycan with a shot of chocolate brown hair pinned against the wall, held aloft by his collar at the hand of a familiar irate blond. The lycan was clad entirely in black, his left arm marked by a sleeve of interlacing tattoos, a layer of facial scruff darkening his jaw. He couldn't be much older than nineteen or twenty. Harry knew him immediately.

Pieter. His name rang through Harry's mind like a curse.

"What the hell did you do to her?!" Tristian shoved the wolf against the wall, hard, and Pieter winced. Speckles of paint from the wood panels dislodged, falling in chips beneath his flailing feet.

"Nothing! She was smoking with us and she couldn't hang!" Pieter begged. "She did it to herself, man, I swear!"

Harry's blood boiled, but before he could so much as move, Tristian threw the wolf into the empty room and surged atop him, smashing his fist into Pieter's face before standing and punting him squarely in the ribs. A streak of red colored Tristian's hand, and Pieter's own came away from his face painted in blood. His nose bloomed a bright purple, no longer the same shape it had been moments ago. Pieter moved to sit up.

Harry leapt from the bed and shoved Pieter back down with the sole of his combat boot, pressing into the lycan's neck. "You will live. For today. But if you *ever* come near her again, I swear to the Magíck, I will end you. Slowly. And in the most savage and inhumane ways you can imagine." Harry's flat, firm growl did little to disguise his seething inner chaos. Flashing his fangs at the wolf, Pieter flinched under Harry's foot. Harry pressed down on his throat harder.

"Did she take anything other than the wolfsbane?" Harry shot at him, watching the wolf's eyes pop as he fought to breathe. "Tell me!"

Pieter struggled to gasp out a response through the pressure on his neck. Harry let up slightly enough for him to answer. "No! No. Just the bane, I swear."

Harry removed his foot and sent a second crippling strike into the wolf's ribs. He heard a distinct crack fill the space. Stalking back to the bed, he put his arms under Liv's still motionless body and lifted her, holding her close to the warmth of his own. He prayed some of his life, whatever he could claim as still his, would sink through his skin and into hers. That somehow his closeness would keep her alive long enough for them to fix this—fix her.

Side stepping Pieter, still scrunched and whimpering on the bed-room floor, Harry left him there.

"These guys are out of it," Wilder said, cocking a perturbed eyebrow at the stone-still lycan. He had kept watch over them, most of which had remained in complete confusion, the drug continuing to slow their senses. Wilder eyed Liv in Harry's arms, and Harry could tell he was fighting to keep his reaction at bay, if only for Harry's sake. "Is she okay?"

"No," Harry told him, his tone flat. All he could focus on was making sure he felt every slight movement of her body, anything to confirm she was alive.

"But she will be," Tristian quickly added, looking at his friend and giving his shoulder a brief, reassuring squeeze.

Wilder nodded, before telling them, "Some of these guys left when they heard what was going on next door. I'm sure the rest of the house knows what's happening by now." He gestured downstairs.

"Then I'd say we've overstayed our welcome. Let's get out of here." Ignoring the still stunned lycan warily watching them, Tristian guided Harry and Wilder out of the room and down the stairs.

Liv remained motionless in Harry's arms, her own hanging limp across her chest and down her side. Harry blessedly heard her strained breathing from time to time, but the shallow gasps were too far apart for his comfort. At the base of the stairs, they stopped short, met there by the tattooed man Harry had seen in the kitchen. He positioned himself squarely before them, his muscular arms crossed and a smug grin on his wide, tanned face, blocking their path to freedom.

"Council babies!" Raising his arms in a mock welcome, he greeted them loudly, announcing to the whole house exactly who they were. Harry saw the color drain from Tristian's face. Wilder stopped in his tracks, standing motionless, his eyes darting around the room, likely scanning for a way out.

"We're not here to start any trouble, Kane," Tristian said, straining to keep his cool. Training with the Council leadership had evidently been paying off.

"Ah, but you already have, boy!" Kane laughed. No one else did though. All around Kane, Harry saw lycan fists clench, their bodies inching closer to the staircase. Countless eyes, many of them a bright, unearthly yellow, watched them.

"We've dealt with the individual wolf who wronged us, Alpha," Tristian responded, his tone measured and edged with the deep respect he knew Kane entitled to as leader of the clan. Harry blinked, stunned but wholly impressed by his friend's tactfulness. A year ago, this would have been a head-to-head dogfight. "Your pup is upstairs, and still alive," Tristian clarified. "He'll recover. And we have no qualms with the rest of the clan."

"Of course he will!" Kane answered with a mocking laugh, putting his large hands on his hips. A few of the other clan members joined in hesitantly. "But why, might I ask, was it necessary in the first place? *Hmm?* I certainly didn't invite any Council brats to crash my party. And yet, here you are." He waved a hand at them. "Drinking my beer and starting fights with my cubs. And I thought the Council could be *trusted,*" Kane scoffed, raising his brow and waiting for their explanation. But Harry didn't trust that any explanation would be good enough to justify their presence. As Kane stared at them, his eyes slowly shifted from a murky brown to a rich bronze. The color of alpha eyes preparing to command his clan.

"One of us *was* invited." Harry heard himself say, his voice cracking. Taking the last few steps down to Kane, he showed him Olivia's motionless body.

Kane inspected her, his hard eyes widening, shifting from instigative to shocked. "I was not made aware she was under the Council's care," Kane said, his previous jibes replaced by what seemed to be sincerity. But something about the way he held himself straighter made Harry question just how unaware he had actually been.

"I understand she's a wolf, but she was raised as one of us. And we came to bring her home. That's all," Tristian said. "When one of your wolves, the one who invited her here, tried to stop us, we were forced to intervene."

Harry nodded, confirming Tristian's claims, but vaguely thought to himself they weren't *necessarily* forced, and they did enjoy beating the crap out of the creep immensely. But he kept *that* part of the story to himself.

"She'll need immediate attention, Alpha," Tristian added, and Harry could hear a pleading in his tone. Harry couldn't tell if the plea had been genuine, or if Tristian understood exactly what the display of desperation would require of Kane. Tristian's voice rose, as if to make sure everyone in the room could hear. "She has wolfsbane poisoning," Tristian continued. "We found her unconscious and alone. We don't know how long she's been in this state. A few more hours and she won't make it."

Jackpot. Harry knew Kane couldn't object, otherwise he'd risk showing his clan he didn't care about the lives of his wolves. It was an old, lesser known tenet of Lycan law—that regardless of clan of origin, an Alpha must treat the life of each wolf as sacred. The Alpha of any clan was expected to lead by this truth. The precept was only overlooked in times of explicitly declared war between clans, but this instance was far from that. Tristian was counting on Kane to believe that as well.

Hesitating for a moment, Kane's bronze gaze narrowed on Tristian. He likely hadn't been expecting Tristian to be so well versed in their code. Releasing a sigh, his eyes shifted again from bronze back to a murky brown, before giving them a curt nod and stepping away, allowing them to pass. On cue, the rest of the pack released any shifts they had summoned, retreating to carry on with their evening.

As the trio made to pass, Kane threw out his arm to block Tristian's advance. His voice was a harsh whisper. "You're either very brave, or very stupid, to come looking for her here, Snow." So Kane *did* know who Tristian was, and who his parents were. "For what it's worth, I do apologize on behalf of my clan. The pup in question will be dealt with. However," Kane inched closer to Tristian, his distinct gravel now threatening. "I better not see *any* of you on my lands again, or you won't live to see the sunrise." His eyes fell on Harry, and on Olivia in his arms.

Tristian glared at Kane, his glacial eyes a bright cold. "At least *she* will today. No thanks to any of you." He gestured to Liv. "So much for watching out for your own, Kane. And by the way, the same goes for you *and your clan.* If *any* of you come near her again, we won't hesitate to finish what we started this evening. And next time, it won't be something your *pup* can recover from so easily."

Kane shrugged, took another step back, and gestured toward the door. They staggered in silence across the front porch and darkened lawn. Yellow eyes reflecting the fires trailed their retreat, as if each lycan had somehow already been silently made aware of what had happened inside the house.

When they finally arrived at the car, Wilder quickly opened the door for Harry. He laid Olivia gently across the back seat and got in after her, lifting her head to rest in his lap. Wilder and Tristian took the front. Tears threatened the corners of Harry's lids as his hand brushed through Olivia's curls of its own accord. The other lay steady against the curve of her neck, his fingers in constant vigil for the presence of her weakening heartbeat.

"Well, now we know why Liv's been acting so weird," Tristian remarked, anger tinging his voice. Harry caught his eye in the rearview mirror as they drove. "She's going to be okay, Harry. Most of that was for show. We'll get there in time. Don't worry."

Harry nodded, slumping against the headrest, the adrenaline that had been coursing through his veins over the last half hour finally starting to settle.

Wolfsbane. Never in his life would he have thought Liv would be that stupid; that desperate. He swept her hair from her face. Her breathing remained uneven, and Harry noticed his own breath struggling alongside hers. "You know, we're going to be in pretty deep once the Council finds out about this," Harry said, watching the streetlights flash past. "The Magistrie won't be happy about it either."

"I know." He heard Tristian's cautious voice from the front. "But we didn't have a choice."

"Why?" Wilder turned in his seat to look at Harry. "What does the Magistrie care?"

Harry stared down at Olivia, running his hand through her dark curls, tucking them behind her ear. "Things are tense between the tribes of Céad outside of Teír and the Magistrie right now. If we weren't at war with that clan before, I wouldn't be surprised if we are now."

CHAPTER THIRTY-SEVEN
Olivia

Olivia's mind pressed in on itself. All she could see was black—black blacker than the night. It was the black of void, from which all starlight and moonlight had been sucked clean, like the way someone pretentious might suck the marrow from the shell of an oyster. She was alone here. And scared. So scared. Heckling laughter diffused through the dark; from somewhere beyond the dark. So the dark had an end, then? She tried to move toward it, but she realized she didn't have a body anymore. Were they laughing at her? She cried out, but no one could hear her. She was going to die. She knew it.

Her life replayed itself—the uninvited scenes projected onto the choking black walls. She watched the images as they flashed, one after another. Sparking alight with mounting torment as she laid there, her mind forced her to relive the darkness of a not so distant past, and the memories she had tried so hard to forget.

A four-year-old girl was being beaten by her momma, her momma's eyes bloodshot from the drugs she was always using.

The scene changed. Her momma was being beaten by faceless men, all different, but all the same. She watched as they did unspeakable things to momma, before the little girl ran away, hiding where she hoped the faceless men wouldn't find her, too. Cowering in a corner, she begged the air, begged anybody, for help. Bright pillars of light filled the room, as tall as the ceiling, making a shield around her. No one came into her room that night. But she didn't sleep. When light finally crept in from the rising sun outside, she found her momma bloody and bruised on the living room floor. She cried over her, but her momma pushed her away. The little girl made a grilled cheese sandwich for momma, anyway. That always made the little girl feel better, so maybe momma would want some too.

The scene changed. Momma walked down a church aisle lined with flowers and leaves, next to a man in a suit with happy eyes. He seemed nice enough. He bought the little girl candy and read her stories sometimes. Her momma stopped taking the drugs that made her sad and angry, and stopped bringing the scary men over. The little girl clung to a real hope now. Hope that momma might have the space to love her, like how mommas on the TV shows loved their own kids. Maybe she would make her cookies, paint with her, and take her to the zoo to look at the tigers. But the hope didn't help, and momma still didn't look at her or play with her. She was always sent to her room to play alone.

The scene changed. The little girl's auntie came to visit. She was six now and had a brand new sister. Baby girl was small and wriggly and cute as a button. Baby's big brown eyes looked at the little girl like she was her whole world, and the little girl would have moved all the heavens for her. The little girl noticed momma and new poppa felt the same way, loving on the baby like they never did with her. They held baby when she cried, smiled big smiles at her, and talked to her while they played. The little girl asked her auntie why momma couldn't love her like she loved the baby. Taking a sip from a yellow can, her auntie's words slurred a little. She told the little girl her momma never wanted her. That she came from a bad night in momma's life, and the little girl would always remind momma of that. The little girl cried into her pillow. She wanted to run away. Her momma wouldn't miss her. But she knew her baby sister would, and she couldn't leave her. So she stayed.

The scene changed. Her sister was crawling and holding herself up on tables. And the girl, not so little anymore, was angry. Angrier than she had ever been. But not at her sister and not at anything at all. She was just angry. The girl felt something moving inside her. She clawed at her stomach as it gurgled and burned. Her legs and arms and back hurt so much, and she just kept getting angrier. The girl ran outside and into the woods behind their house, as far as she could go. She didn't want to be so angry so close to baby sister. She was scared she'd do something awful to her. The girl kept running, and running, and running—until the whole world went black.

The girl woke up the next morning covered in dirt and blood, her clothes ratted and falling apart. Her shoes were gone. She ran home, crying and scared. Her momma yelled at her for being so dirty and told her to go clean up. She hadn't even noticed the girl had been gone for so long. She didn't notice the blood.

The scene changed. It was a month later. Looking up at the full moon through her bedroom window, the girl felt it call out to her, and she remembered nothing else. When the daylight came, she was chained to a tree in her backyard, her momma screaming at her and her poppa staring at her through the kitchen window, a phone pressed against his ear. The girl cried and screamed, begging her momma for help. Her momma just yelled, telling her she wasn't her daughter, and she should have gotten rid of her a long time ago. The girl couldn't see through the tears in her eyes, but she could hear her little sister crying for her inside the house, her little voice screaming, "Wiv! Wiv!"

Strength she didn't know she had pushed through her body from deep in her bones, and she broke the chains that held her to the tree. She ran inside, past her poppa who tried to stop her, and into the living room where her baby sister stood in a play pen, reaching for her. The girl cried, knowing she had to leave, and knowing she couldn't take her sister with her. "I love you with my whole big heart," the girl said to her as momma and poppa bounded into the room, screaming at her to get away. Baby started crying again, and the girl took one last look at her sister before taking off through the front door—never looking back.

The scene changed one last time. The girl was covered in dust and dirt, her clothes hanging off of her too thin, tiny frame. She slept in the corners of alleyways, avoiding everyone. Her only friends were the stray kittens that slept in the cardboard boxes close by. The girl dug through trash cans and dumpsters for scraps of food. The strangers she saw worked hard to not look at her. They had better things to do. Fearing the day when the moon would call to her again, the girl watched in terror every night, its freckled white face looming larger and larger.

She was digging through yet another trash can when she felt a warm hand on her shoulder. Wheeling around, she found a boy with wild black hair watching her—seeing her. He had the most beautiful green eyes she thought she'd ever know. He smiled at her and asked if he and his dad could get her some lunch. Half of her wanted to run away. Why was he being so nice to her? But she felt something else, almost like a thin invisible thread snapping into place between them, and Olivia smiled for the first time in a long time.

The scenes stopped, but she could still feel his warmth next to her. She could almost smell him now—like pewter, earth, and rain. Somewhere in a far off distant place, she heard the laughter die and felt her body, so far from her, moving through empty space. The heat of him surrounded her, as if life itself was seeping into the dark to hold her until it all finally ended, and she thought that if she was dying, she wanted to go like this—wrapped in his warmth and his smell and him.

Chapter Thirty-Eight
Olivia

Olivia awoke to light streaming through too many windows. Grumbling, she strained away from the intrusion. Her stomach burned, her muscles ached, and her throat felt parched. Her tongue puffed like cotton and her head throbbed. She fought against the fatigue slowing her mind, but to no avail. While it took her far longer than it should to figure out where she was, she had no trouble recognizing who had fallen asleep in the armchair next to her. Harry's sleek black hair swept across his forehead, his expression relaxed in the throes of deep sleep. He was still the most beautiful thing she'd ever seen.

"Harry?" Olivia's voice cracked from lack of use. How long had she been asleep? She needed water. "Harry?"

Eyes snapping open, Harry started, his hands wrapping around his armrests to steady himself. He looked around blearily, as if trying to figure out who had spoken to him. At seeing Olivia, her smile weak but wide, he jolted from his seat.

"Liv!" Harry grabbed her hand, using the backside of his other to check her skin for fever. "Are you okay? Do you need anything?" A sheen of tears brightened his eyes, their green in sharp contrast to the dark purple beneath them, but he didn't let himself cry.

Olivia sucked in a breath, but it tasted stale. Seeing how panicked he was, her heart broke with the guilt that she had done this to him. "Just water," Olivia whispered, smiling up at him, though tears pricked behind her gaze. As he moved to grab the pitcher and a glass on the nightstand, she took the opportunity to scrub at her face. She didn't get to be sad about what she'd done. This was her fault, and Harry was the one dealing with the consequences. He deserved so much better than that. Better than her.

"How long was I out?" she asked, training her question into a bright, emotionless lilt. She didn't want him feeling like he needed to console her. Shame washed over her again. *She* should be the one consoling *him*.

He eyed her warily, knowing exactly what she was doing. He always did. "Three days," he said, ignoring her obvious attempts at distraction and handing her the glass. She forced herself to take a sip while he roamed over her masked expression with a careful discernment. "Sofia worked her magic, as usual. But she said it might take a while for you to fully recover. The wolfsbane did a number on you." Brushing her curls from her face, he tucked a few strands behind her ear.

Shutting her eyes, she rested into the warmth of his palm, her body betraying her as she felt the cool of a single tear on her cheek. Harry wiped it away with his thumb. Opening her eyes, she found a sea of green locked on her, more love in them than any one person had ever shown her. More than she deserved.

He wouldn't ask her why she had started using the wolfsbane. But she knew he wanted to know—and why she hadn't gone to him first. She knew she owed that to him, at the very least.

"I just wanted to feel in control, Harry," Olivia began. "I felt like if I could bring my wolf side out, get it to take charge, maybe I wouldn't be so scared all the time. Maybe I could be brave enough to forget about everything that's happened. Brave enough to feel worth being a part of something bigger than myself." Harry stared at her, his eyes pleading, silently telling her for the hundredth time that he knew she was more than worth all of that already. But he said nothing.

"I know it's silly. But giving up Jeselle. Leaving her in Eaigan. It felt like losing Elodie all over again. I thought Pieter understood. He said it would help. He said people rarely smoked too much, that the bane only hurts when it's concentrated. He said people change and go full wolf before it gets too bad, so I figured I'd be okay." Olivia let out a sob as she collapsed in on herself.

"I felt something telling me no, Harry. And I ignored it. I kept going. I just wanted to feel better. And the rest of them seemed fine. Like they could handle it. But it just got worse, and by then I had had too much and no one cared. They just kept laughing and left me alone, telling me I'd sleep it off. But I knew something was so wrong. I kept hearing howling through me, like my wolf was dying—like *I* was dying. But every time I tried to reach out, I couldn't get to it. I was so scared and I couldn't get to it."

Harry quickly moved to her side, putting his arms around her.

"I just wanted to belong somewhere, Harry. I thought they understood." As Olivia's body wracked with sobs, Harry pressed a kiss against her curls, letting her come undone against his chest.

"You belong *here,* Liv. With us. With *me.*" Harry's voice had grown taut, as if willing her to hear him, agree with him.

But Harry didn't deserve this. He didn't deserve everything she put him through, how she pulled him in and pushed him away. And she knew she'd never be good enough for him. Worthy enough to deserve how much he believed in her. So she'd never keep him from finding someone better. She had promised herself that a long time ago.

Olivia pulled away from him. "Harry, you should probably go." Sniffling and wiping her eyes, she sucked in a steeling breath and gave him as genuine of a smile as she could muster. "I promise I'm okay."

But from the stonebound look on his face, she knew he didn't buy it for a second. Moving off the bed, Harry knelt next to her. "No." His lips set into a hard line.

Brow knitting, she peered up at him in confusion. He never told her no. Not when it came to this. "What—?" Liv started.

"You're not allowed to send me away anymore. I'm not letting you," he said. "You've gotta stop, Liv. I'm done with this." His gaze on her had gone cold. Olivia felt the invisible tug at her heart again, the thread between them thrumming to life. She just stared at him, still confused.

He's done with this? He's done with me…

Realization was a dragon. It sheathed its taloned claws into her core, keeping her from moving while it devoured her whole. The tip of one of those talons pricked at Olivia's heart now, its flesh hardening and shattering into a thousand edges, each one shredding the inside of her chest. He wouldn't let her push him away because he'd just leave altogether. He had finally had enough. This had been the last straw.

Sucking in another breath, she nodded, tears gathering once more. But she pushed them back and broke from his stare. *This* was what she deserved, and she'd live with the consequences. "Then you *should* go, Harry. It's for the best." Olivia tried not to let her voice crack.

"Liv…" she heard his own soften. "Liv, that's not what I meant." Taking her hands in his, Harry pressed a finger against her chin and turned her gaze back to him. Understanding bloomed in his stare as he seemed to realize how she must have misunderstood.

"I'm not leaving you, you dummy." He laughed, but each of his words were an oath. A promise. "But I *am* done letting you leave. I'm done with you not letting me in when you need me the most. I don't care how hard you fight it or try to run away. I'll always come after you, and I'll always be the place you know you can come home to." He brushed away more of her tears, resolve hardening his expression. "And I will wait however long it takes for you to realize that. I just need you to stop pushing me away."

Choking out another sob, the words burst from Olivia before she could stop herself. "Stop doing that, Harry. You can't wait for me. You're too good for me, in every possible way. I don't deserve someone like you, and I can't bear to lose you when you finally realize that." It was everything she had never let herself say in all the years they had known each other.

Harry smiled, his brows lifting in amusement, but was otherwise unfazed by her miniature rant. "I know." He winked, and her eyes widened in shock. Placing his hand on hers, he amended, "What I mean…is that I know you've always believed that. And it's my fault for letting you. I didn't know how to make things clear without making you feel forced into something I didn't know you even wanted. I was waiting for you to decide, and it backfired. I was so stupid, Liv. I'll live every second of my life from here on out making that up to you. Proving to you how wrong you are about yourself. How good *you* are. How worthy you are. How much you belong here, with me. And how much I love you. Liv, you know that, and you've known that for years. I'm just not going to be quiet about it anymore."

Olivia's head spun, and the thread between them thrummed again. Gazing into his jungle green eyes, she didn't believe a word of what he had said. Not because he had said it, but because she knew he was wrong about her. But she also knew, without a doubt, that his promise to stay, at least, was true. Knowing exactly what she was thinking, as he usually did, he leaned forward, and finally, after years of waiting, kissed her. Her whole world shifted into place, and for a moment, time stood still.

Chapter
Thirty-Nine

Wilder navigated the shelves of the fully restored library, perusing the dusty titles and tomes, many in languages he couldn't decipher. Magi Maynestream had him working on a particularly ridiculous assignment about the importance of staying hydrated during extended magic use.

Wilder had scoffed during their previous lesson, putting his foot down and asserting his need to train more rigorously. The Council still didn't know about their altercation with the wolf clan the week before. And none of them were in any particular rush to tell them about it. But the evening had been a stark reminder just how dangerous this new world could be.

During combat training with Tristian, Wilder had transitioned from using wooden swords to steel blunted with magic. While he was still nowhere near as agile or strong as Tristian or Barrett, he was decent enough to hold his own, at least for the first three to five minutes of the melee. And thankfully, it was taking him less and less time to heal from the bruises and aching muscles left behind after each skirmish. As for magic, he could now move it through his body using each of the three roads at a basic level, and could comfortably shift into and out of each of his hidden fae traits, save for his eyes, which he had unwaveringly decided would stay the same stormy gray. Each time he did shift, he became more and more aware of a still, small nudge at the back of his mind—an ever present living force he still struggled to understand.

None of that seemed to matter to the Magi, though. Despite his progress, Magi Maynestream remained resolute, explaining that Wilder's overzealous pride in the manner of his tutelage was proof enough Wilder wasn't as ready as he believed. And so, as instructed, Wilder would spend the next several days on what the Magi called 'nutritional theory'.

A collection of books Wilder assumed would be useful for this inane project rested on a scrappy unburnished table at the end of the book-shelves. Wilder placed a worn, navy blue hardback, entitled *Waters of the West – The History of Lakes and Rivers in North American Water Magic*, atop his mounting stack. As he trudged back to the bookshelf, he became aware of the already quiet library growing immensely more still and silent, as if thickened with a layer of dust and frozen in time. His footsteps, which had before caused the aged wooden planks beneath his feet to creak and bend, were now muted, and he could no longer hear the distant rumble of voices and doors opening and closing in the hallway beyond.

A faint phantom tug clawed at him, the air around his chest tightening, as if an invisible thread pulled him to the exact same spot where he had removed the last book from the shelves. Instinct bade him to follow the tug to the empty space, only to find it no longer empty. A new book had taken its place. Wilder's eyes narrowed on the book before glancing around to investigate the scene. Surely someone else in the library was playing tricks on him.

"Harry! I know it's you. Are you really that bored?" he yelled into the empty space, but his voice didn't echo the way it usually would. Wilder rubbed at his ears, perplexed. He checked behind each of the neighboring shelves, but the library remained just as deserted as when he had arrived.

Retracing his steps to the book, he found nothing particularly extraordinary about it. A thin layer of age coated the book's burgundy cover, its gold-leaf lettering peeling along the edges. Propped unassumingly against the book next to it, it seemed as if the book had been there the entire time. Wilder removed the tome from the shelf, turning it over in his hands. Its cover felt warm against his palms; like the greeting of an old friend. At first, Wilder could have sworn the title was written in yet another language he couldn't translate, but as he inspected it closer, the letters bent and blended in a rush of inky sand. He blinked. Staring down at the book, the words *Stone and Scale* materialized across the spine.

Opening the cover, he leafed through the pages, surprised to find nothing inside other than blank, crinkling aged parchment. He flipped back to the front, finding a small handwritten inscription on the inside cover.

Child born of bloom and rain
Left alone in wooded plain
Grown among the sight unseen
Lost unto the olde summer leaves
Return will he when dragons reborn
Return will we 'fore throne restored
Come will she when darkness descends
First of her kind to ride again
Books and bindings come undone
When beheld by rightful son
Until true, humankind remains
In gravest peril by reddest fae
Should stone and scale be left unturned
Dark will rise and Earth will burn

As if sensing Wilder had finished the verse, the book shuddered in his hands, warming until the cover felt ablaze with molten heat. Wilder dropped the book, more from shock than from pain. Inspecting his hands, he found them unscathed. Peering down at the book on the ground, he watched the cover begin to disintegrate, the edges alight with flame, as if the cover were crafted of charred coals crumbling to dust from the heat. When the burning had subsided, Wilder retrieved the altogether new book laying at his feet.

The rich brown leather now felt cool to the touch, just as any other tome might. The cover and its stitching were unmarked and otherwise perfect, as if it had just been bound yesterday. Wilder leafed through the pages again, finding they now held troves of information in a flowing, tight script he couldn't decipher. The text was all aligned beside exquisitely drawn illustrations of flying beasts, various creatures he had no names for, and glowing colored orbs so beautiful the heavens could have sketched them. Everything in him refused to believe this could be what he instantly thought it was, but he knew enough about magic at this point to know this was no ordinary book. It pulsed with life, and clearly had not wanted to be found.

At least until now.

Leaving his stack of volumes behind, Wilder raced to Magi Maynestream's office, the book in hand, ignoring the shouts and waves from those he passed on the way. Rounding a corner at blinding speed, he ran headfirst into Master Lyre, knocking him to the ground. Wilder paused long enough to help the librarian regain his balance, his glasses still askew, before taking off again, calling out behind him, "Sorry!"

He heard Master Lyre tatter a quick "I never!" as he disappeared from view.

Wilder burst through the Magi's doors and found him meeting with Terra. They each glanced up in alarm at his sudden entrance.

"Wil, are you alright?" Terra asked. Her brown waves had been pulled into a high ponytail, loose strands curling around the nape of her neck. The linen fabric of a white summer dress grazed the skin of her shoulders, bringing out the bronze glow of her skin, recently touched by the scorching late spring sun. The scent of sunbathed sage and lemons barreled off of her, nearly incapacitating him as he bounded into the office. "You look like you just ran a marathon," she said, continuing to eye him with confusion.

Tearing his gaze away from her, he forced himself to focus on the task at hand. "The book!" Wilder insisted, piecing his thoughts, and breath, back together—an effort he found increasingly more difficult with Terra in the room. "I found it. The Book of Scales. I think, anyway."

He paused to take a heavy gulp of air before crossing the room and handing the book to Magi Maynestream, perplexed when he noticed the cover fade into an aged burgundy again. The Magi opened the book, but from where Wilder stood, he saw the previously filled pages were once again blank, the only script visible the same inked prophetic words Wilder had come across when he first found it.

After reading through the verse, the Magi peered up at Wilder, bewildered. "Mr. Ansley, while I admit this is quite an interesting verse, to be sure, and likely worth a study, I don't understand your surety in this being the Book of Scales. Seems to me just an old journal."

Wilder's brow knit as he looked down at the book. Why had it transformed itself again? Was it trying to hide from the curious onlookers? As Wilder stared at the book, its presence seemed to pull him forward. A familiar hum coursed through his veins, imploring him to take hold of the book once more. Sidestepping around the desk, he took the book from the surprised Magi's hands and it shuddered with an approving purr. They all watched as the book burned, charred, and peeled apart, just as it had for Wilder in the library, though the heat it radiated now had receded to a comfortable, dull warmth.

"My word..." the Magi whispered as Wilder held the book out for him to scour the now full pages. "This is...a development." He continued to scan the book in Wilder's hands, evidently not as baffled by the incomprehensible language as Wilder was. "Most of this is written in Old Daoine," the Magi shared. At the look of confusion on Wilder's face, he added, "It's a language derived from the gods, the Tuatha De Danann. Daoine, the great Fae city where Lus Halla resides, was named for them."

As he continued to examine the pages, his grizzled features lit with astonishment, and he cleared his throat. "Well, as I am sure you have heard from Master Lyre, the legends surrounding the true Book of Scales speak of a magem with close ties to the fae. The mage had supposedly been instructed to study and record everything he knew of the dragonstones and the dragons themselves, including how each stone could be used and influenced by either the Magíck or the Dahrk. Not many believed the book to actually exist, and if I am to be honest, I included myself in that number. But…" he paused, continuing to stare at the pages. "If I am not mistaken, from what I can tell thus far, this might just be that same book."

"I'm sorry," Terra interjected, her eyes fixed on the Magi as she stared at him skeptically. "Do you mean to tell me that not only can you read Old Daoine, but that *this* book, here…*in this room…*was possibly written *before* the fall, might also be one of the oldest books in the Eadar, and could likely confirm the actual existence of the dragons and the dragonstones?" Terra's eyes widened, blazing with an indescribable fire. Wilder could see her history-loving gears revolving at breakneck speed, and his chest tightened. "Could I look closer?" Terra asked as she sidled next to Wilder, the bare skin of her shoulder grazing his arm, and he involuntarily leaned into the touch.

"Of course." Wilder placed the book on the Magi's desk and stepped away, just to see what would happen. The book shifted to its blank state. As he touched it, the glamour once again peeled away. Wilder glanced at Terra, locking eyes with her. Reading the unasked question on his face, she voiced to the Magi what Wilder could not.

"Magi, why would the book only show itself for Wil?"

"Your guess is as good as mine, Ms. Sampson," the Magi said, bowing so close to the book, his nose ghosted barely an inch above the text. He perused the page with a miniature pair of spectacles hanging on a thin chain around his neck. "Though I wonder whether the writer of this verse could perhaps have something to do with it." He studied the lines again, whispering to himself, "*Books and bindings come undone.* Hmm. Indeed."

Terra's lips drew into a thin line. Looking away from Wilder, she joined the Magi in his study of the curious book. As they scoured the pages, Wilder noticed the Magi's chameleon pacing along a log, seemingly bothered. Wilder removed his hand from the book again, ignoring Terra's huff of annoyance, and padded over to the gold-rimmed tank. Clearly unsettled, the chameleon appeared to be trying to gain freedom from the confines of his glass box, clawing at its invisible walls and glancing fervently at the window across from them. Wilder's eyes flashed to the window just in time to see a shadow move across the sill. Stepping around the tank to gain a better vantage, he pulled back the rush of curtain blocking his view of the garden, but found nothing to be amiss—observing only the fading light of the oncoming night and a pitch black raven flying across the ramparts.

The door opened behind him, and Wilder wheeled to see James arriving to announce that dinner would be ready soon. Thanking him, the Magi assured they would join shortly. James nodded, but hesitated as he caught sight of the book. Terra and the Magi continued to converse in hushed tones, too preoccupied to notice James's widening brown eyes. But Wilder could have sworn a hungry, desperate fire, markedly different from Terra's, had lit behind James's stare. Realizing too late that Wilder was watching him, James diverted his gaze from the book, gave Wilder a kind, unassuming smile, and exited the room.

The Magi, who seemed to have grown more and more troubled over the past several minutes, courteously dismissed Wilder and Terra from his study, indicating he would need to meet with the Council to discuss how to proceed. Before they left, he instructed them to keep the matter under wraps until he told them otherwise. Nodding, they left him and the book behind.

CHAPTER FORTY

Quiet enveloped their brief trek to the dining room, Wilder and Terra both so deep in thought they had barely noticed members of the Council hastening toward the Magi's office. Wilder, in his defense, had found himself too absorbed with the waning phantom tug on his heart, faintly drawing him back toward the study, to say anything at all.

Dinnertime was in full swing when they arrived, Harry and Tristian hooting as they threw buttered bread rolls at Barrett. Agiley swiping them away, Barrett remained focused on his mashed potatoes and meat loaf, glowering at the two from beneath his lashes. James was fully engaged in telling the duo off, threatening them with one form of punishment or another, none of which seemed to faze the two miscreants. Wilder eyed James warily, but the man resolutely avoided his gaze.

It was a welcome relief to see Harry smiling after the ordeal with the wolf clan, and its terrifying aftermath. It had been hours before they had known Olivia would survive the nightmare. Olivia, though finally awake, was still in the infirmary, her recovery progressing slower than they all had hoped. Despite that, Harry was unmistakably happier than Wilder had ever seen him before. He had been spending every waking moment with Liv, helping her heal and training under Sofia's guidance.

The dinner party barely noticed Wilder and Terra join them as they claimed two seats at the end of the table, far from the jesting. Terra inclined as close to Wilder as she could without drawing suspicion.

"So, are you going to tell me how on earth you found the Book of Scales?" she teased in a hushed whisper that sounded half accusatory, half in awe. "What? You just decide to go looking without me?"

"Terra, I don't even know," Wilder admitted, his voice barely audible over the ruckus across the table. "I don't know how to explain it. It just sort-of…*showed up*. I swear." Peering down at her in a plea, he knew she saw his panic building. Her teasing smile faltered, her features growing concerned. Wilder continued, "And what's even weirder—right now I can still *feel* it. Like it wants me to come back to it." Wilder glanced over his shoulder at the entrance to the hallway.

"Okay. That *is* weird…" Terra agreed. Studying her empty plate, she pressed her tongue against her teeth, absentmindedly rolling her cutlery in her hand. "Maybe just ignore that? Ignore *it*. We don't know enough about this book; about what it might want."

"What it might *want?*" Wilder gaped, edging closer to her, his voice straining to keep their conversation from the multiple other keen ears at the table. "Terra, it's a freaking *book*. You're talking like that thing is *alive*." Even as he said it, the reality of the situation slowly dawned on him. However odd it might be, living books were no longer in the realm of impossibility.

Terra gave him the same gentle look, her eyes glowing with sympathy, as when he had first arrived at the Council House. When he had first learned about magic, and had been terrified out of his mind. He hadn't told her that's what he had been feeling, hadn't even really known it himself in that moment. But she had known, even then. Just as she had known exactly what he had needed to hear.

"I felt its presence, Wilder. And I know the Magi did, too. For all we know, it might be. Alive, I mean. Aware. Trying to get to you. Trying to communicate with you." Terra placed a comforting hand on his forearm, meeting his gaze once more. Goosebumps shot across his skin and his stomach tightened, as it usually did in these too brief of moments with her.

Sensing eyes on them, Wilder glanced across the table. Tristian watched them from between Harry and Barrett, now engrossed in their own argument, debating the best choice of weaponry against a Faed—whatever that was. Tristian's expression was unreadable, his icy blues flashing between Terra and Wilder, and on Terra's palm meeting Wilder's skin.

Lifting her hand, Terra settled it into her lap as she, too, noticed him. A flash of something crossed Tristian's features before his usual nonchalance adeptly replaced it. Tristian's gaze flew to the doorway just as his father strode into the room, Caolin stopping abruptly at the threshold.

"Wilder. Terra. Tristian." The cold man tucked his icy blond chin, his callous face as unreadable as his son's. "Please follow me to Magi Maynestream's study. We have a matter to discuss."

Terra gave Wilder a reassuring nod before rising from the table. Silently following, Tristian moved to hover close to Terra. Wilder joined them, ignoring Tristian's subtle display of what he assumed must be dominance. He didn't care, and he honestly didn't have time for it. All Wilder could feel was the pounding of his heart, so loud he was sure everyone could hear it, and that same adamant tug, pulling at him with renewed fervor from down the hall—as if the book knew he was coming back. His blood thrummed in his ears, and Wilder felt both in the room and altogether elsewhere.

★★★

The three crowded around Magi Maynestream's desk while Caolin took his place beside the rest of the Council. Wearing expressions of solemn contemplation, the Council assessed the trio, but Caolin's stare never left Wilder.

"Welcome back," Magi Maynestream said brightly, smiling at Wilder and Terra, but a somber air that hadn't been there earlier ached through his tone. "The Council has been in some discussion regarding the events of this evening, as well as some new developments we have become privy to."

"New developments?" Terra asked, a sardonic edge to her words. "You mean besides our friend lying bedridden in the infirmary and a long-lost book that only responds to Wilder randomly showing up in our library?"

Tristian shot a confused and rather taken aback glance at Wilder and Terra. It was a novel look for him.

"Yes, Terra," her mother said. A knowing, amused smile played on her lips despite the demeanor of the room. "Besides all of that."

Tristian spoke up, his curiosity evidently getting the better of him. "What do you mean—developments?"

Rickard resumed the report. "As Wilder and Terra are already aware, Wil has come across a book we have reason to believe is indeed the Book of Scales. The Magi has confirmed the presence of a deep magic within the tome, making it quite impossible for this to be any kind of forgery." Rickard side-eyed Caolin, whose stare had narrowed on Wilder, but said nothing.

Of course Caolin would believe Wilder had somehow made this up. Wilder glared right back.

Rickard went on. "We have also received word from Eaigan about the child, Jeselle."

Wilder started, his stare falling back on Rickard. After everything they had been through the last few weeks, he had almost forgotten about the colorless child with eyes so like his own. His sister, if the Council's suspicions were correct.

"The child's wet nurse alerted the Synod of some peculiar happenings," Rickard said. "Apparently, she has been growing and developing at an astronomical rate. Already she is walking on her own. She has also said her first words and communicates quite effectively with those around her. If she cannot verbally ask for what she wants, she sends images to communicate her needs. While such abilities are not unheard of in some Watern children, Jeselle is not of their blood, so there is some confusion as to how she possesses such abilities."

"Okay. But what's that to do with the Council?" Tristian asked, shrugging. "Children with different abilities, while rare, are nothing new. Given her origins, and her possible connection to blood magic, it shouldn't be that surprising."

"That is not all," Rickard shared. The expressions on the rest of the Council grew even more withdrawn, a few shuffling on their feet. "Last night, her wet nurse heard the child…*singing.* Concerned, she entered her room to find a pillar of light standing next to her crib. It disappeared as soon as the wet nurse walked in. But when she went to check on Jeselle, she found her laying beside…" he paused, as if trying to believe it himself. "Well…a dragon egg."

Wilder heard a sharp intake of breath, and glanced over to see Terra's mouth agape in stunned silence.

Tristian rolled his eyes. "So they found her with a giant rock? The Watern are a strange people. I wouldn't be surprised if they gave her one. Maybe they think she's some special gift to the world. Odd, but okay…"

"I take it that kind of thing isn't exactly normal…" Wilder asked, ignoring Tristian as he looked at Rickard.

"Not in the least," Rickard said, his mouth tight. "And, not exactly, Tristian. The egg in question was not made of stone—at first. They questioned the wet nurse extensively. She tried to remove the egg from the crib, but as soon as the child was no longer within its proximity, the egg *then* shifted to stone. When it was restored to the child, it transitioned again to its unbound form. The Synod has confirmed the phenomena themselves. We know the Watern do not lie. We have no reason to believe they aren't being truthful about what they've seen."

Tristian's mouth popped slightly open, stunned into silence.

"Sounds like a lot of magically shifting things have been showing up lately…" Terra interjected, rubbing at her temples. "Okay. If this is all actually happening, I guess it's worth asking—do you think the egg could be one of the supposed stonebound from Teír?"

A few of the Council shrugged, at a loss for words.

"We've sent word to our counterparts within the Magistrie to investigate," Raiya explained. "But as it takes significant time to bypass the wards protecting the 'eggs', we may not know for several more days. And given this discovery, the likelihood that the eggs in question may *actually* be eggs, after all—" Raiya blinked, as if struggling to comprehend her own words. "We've also recommended the Magistrie increase protections around the vault. There are dozens of eggs safeguarded there. If they truly are dragon eggs, we can't afford for a single one of them to fall into the wrong hands."

Dragons. Real dragons. Wilder's gut flipped at the prospect, and a low rumble thundered against his soul. "So what does this all have to do with us?" Wilder asked, astounded, but still unsure what it all meant.

The Council regarded one another before Rickard stepped around the desk to stand in front of Wilder. Placing his hands on his shoulders, a deep gravity betrayed what Wilder was sure should have been a comforting stare. "Wil. We think it would be best for you to go to Teír."

A loud buzzing filled Wilder's ears, and the earth seemed to buckle beneath him. He must have misheard. He wanted to ask Rickard to repeat himself, but he felt like a frog had gotten stuck in his throat and was now beating against his jugular, trying to escape.

Rickard must have read the trepidation on his face, because he quickly added, "You wouldn't be going alone." He glanced at Tristian and Terra. "Tristian, Terra, Barrett, and myself would accompany you."

The other two appeared taken aback by the news, looking at their parents for confirmation.

Caolin moved to stand in front of them. "You are both adults now, old enough to take on more responsibility within the Council, and you've had enough training to begin more serious instruction within the Magistrie. You're intelligent, understand the Council's mission, and have shown enough promise for this challenge." A paternal warmth Wilder had never heard from him saturated his tone. Tristian and Terra stared in stunned silence, but each eventually nodded in resignation.

"As for you, Mr. Ansley." A cool chill had returned to Caolin's words. "I'm sure you're well aware the question of your own origins has been a topic of increased discussion. Markus's interest in you, as well as your discovery of the Book of Scales, has given us little choice for how to proceed. Your safety here will continue to be compromised, and your abilities have reached a plateau. The depth of training we can provide has surpassed what your education now requires. In full transparency, we believe you have far greater power than what we can cultivate, and you'll be in more adept hands, and far safer, within the wards of Teír." His cold eyes bore into Wilder's, as if waiting for him to fight the decision, or his claims.

The earth continued to sway, and Wilder thought he might fall into the fissures surely opening beneath his feet. He didn't understand. He felt like he was right at the edge of accessing the full scope of his magic. Even the Magi had suggested as much. Was this block, whatever was still stopping him up from time to time, just more than what the Magi could help him with? Or was there something else to this decision? Something to do with the visions the Magi had had about him? The thrumming of the book on the Magi's desk vibrated against his soul, dragging him from his thoughts. No one else seemed to notice it.

"In addition," Tremaine added, his voice as grave as the others, "both Jeselle and the book must be taken to Teír. While the child remains safe in Eaigan, the Watern are also at their limit for what they can do. She'll need to be studied by the Magistrie, and the egg returned to Teír along with her. And since Markus knows the child has been removed from her mother, it'll only be a matter of time before he comes to retrieve her. We're shocked he hasn't tried since your encounter with the Kerdasa twins, but we're sure another attempt will be made soon. As for the book, which we now suspect he must have been trying to access when the library was destroyed, it cannot be here when he decides to return. There's no knowing how the information in this book could strengthen his position in this war."

Tristian and Terra revolted in unison.

"Wait. You can't just send us away knowing you're going to be attacked!" Terra shouted at them, unmasked fear darkening her features as she pleaded with her parents.

"Why aren't you coming with us if you're so sure he's about to strike?" Tristian hurled in just as much protest. "I should stay here to help protect you all!"

Raiya gave him a soft, motherly smile that brightened her cheeks, and for a moment, Wilder found himself slightly jealous of Tristian. Striding to him, Raiya placed her hands on Tristian's shoulders. "We're calling in reinforcements from the surrounding regions, so the Council House will be well guarded. Olivia is in no condition to be moved, and it's in her best interest Harry remains with her, though we'll allow him to make that decision for himself. All of us should be in Teír by summer's end, but we'll have to prepare the Council House for our departure. Our absence cannot be an invitation for Markus to raid whatever is left behind."

Raiya paused, giving Tristian a deep, knowing look. "And you'll all need Seasuír representation when you arrive in Teír, as both your father and I will remain here. You will need to lead in your father's stead, Tristian." Wilder peered at Caolin, who was mirroring Raiya's intense inspection of their son.

Tristian continued to fume, his fists gripped at his sides, but seemed to accept the reasonability of the explanation. He nodded, but the lines of his jaw did not ease.

"Well, that settles it," Rickard announced, though nothing felt settled for Wilder. "All we have left is to retrieve Jeselle from Eaigan, and she'll travel with us to Teír. Plane tickets have already been purchased and reinforcements are on their way. We'll depart as early as possible tomorrow. Prepare yourselves this evening—it'll be a long journey."

Wilder's head spun at an uncomfortable speed. Plane tickets? He didn't even know where Teír *was.* And why were they traveling by plane? With all the magic in the Eadar, was there not some faster way to get there? He thought of the water that transported them into Eaigan and wondered why something like that wasn't an option.

"Tomorrow is…so soon," Terra whispered, looking up at her parents. "I haven't said goodbye to Liv. And what about the Coven?"

"The Coven is aware of the circumstances and understands the need for your leave," Sofia assured her. "They've already agreed to be part of the resistance we're developing." Terra nodded, and Sofia added softly, "I suggest you say your goodbyes this evening, Terra. You may not see Liv for some time. But I promise, as soon as she's better, and the House warded adequately, we'll *all* be joining you in Teír."

"Yes, ma'am," Terra said faintly, staring at the ground. Her mother left her position among the Council to place a kiss on her head. Noticing a tear sliding down Terra's cheek, Wilder fought himself to not lean over and wipe it away.

The Magi released a heavy sigh. "Let's get some sleep, everyone. We have an arduous day ahead of us." He turned to Rickard. "I expect you will share this information with Harry and Olivia?"

Rickard nodded, his face grave but composed as ever.

"Good, good," the Magi added, exhaustion evident beneath his mismatched eyes. "I will share it with the rest of the household. I'm sure

Master Lyre will be happy to hear he was indeed correct about The Book of Scales. Though I'll likely never hear the end of it." Sighing again, the rest of the Council laughed lightly, and the heavy weight in the room alleviated an infinitesimal degree.

Chapter Forty-One

Wilder wandered the abbey, committing each turn and alcove to memory. It was with concerted effort he didn't leave the abbey altogether, if only to witness the city's vibrant lights and laughter just one last time. Having arrived at the Council House only a few short months ago, it had already felt like a lifetime. Somehow, this place had come to feel just as much like home as the city surrounding it. As he walked, his thoughts roiled, and the fear of leaving the only home he had ever known churned to a bitter fire, burning him from the inside out. Moving around far too much as a kid, this city had been his one constant. Through every change, it had been the backdrop, steady and alive and *his*. Its radiant life had tethered his soul, keeping him from losing himself when the world asked too much of him.

Wilder found Terra in the gardens, a delicate shadow hidden among the stars and citrus blooms. Wilder caught the scent of lemon and sage as he strode to where she was perched on a framed wooden bench, its curling iron encircled by the early summer blossoms. He couldn't tell if the scent was coming from her or the gardens, but he let it soothe him, nonetheless. Settling only a hairsbreadth away, Wilder tracked Terra's gaze to the massive expanse of cloudless starlit sky above.

"It's the same sky in Teír," she said breathlessly. She sounded distant, and he didn't know if she was speaking to him, or affirming the truth of it for herself. Her gaze bounced from star to star, as if weaving the constellations with an invisible thread. Without thinking, Wilder placed his hand on hers. Never diverting her gaze from the sky, but as if just realizing he had joined her, Terra intertwined her fingers with his.

"What's on your mind?" she asked.

Wilder turned his attention to the lines of her profile, a corner of his lips pulling into the hint of a smirk. "That if I wasn't positive you'd hit me, I'd probably kiss you." Wilder had intended for the statement to sound playful, but he didn't say it without some seriousness.

Terra scoffed, removing her hand from his and punching him in the shoulder.

Flinching away, he threw her a wide grin. "See what I mean?" he said, swatting at her hand.

Laughing, she asked, "Okay, but really. How are you feeling about leaving?"

Wilder lifted his eyes back to the night sky. He hadn't wanted to think about it, but he could hardly think of anything else. Continuing to stare into the speckled void, he told her exactly what he thought about leaving New Orleans; about what this city meant to him, and how saying goodbye felt like losing a part of himself. Like another change, another decision, had been made for him, without his consent. Part of him knew it needed to happen, but it didn't curb the anger or the hurt.

Terra studied him, saying nothing. A moment later, she leaned forward and kissed his cheek. Wilder stiffened in shock. But before she could pull away, he turned his head to face her. His lips hovered so close to hers, he could actually do it if he wanted to, could actually kiss her. She froze, her breath catching. Surprise lit her star speckled gaze. But she didn't move. As if daring him to.

"Probably best I don't push my luck, huh?" Wilder asked, his stare searching hers. There was a hesitant fear within it, and as much as he wanted to, today was not the day to toy with the fragile beginnings they were building. He had time.

Terra swallowed, as if her mouth had gone dry and was continuing to struggle with the way her heart pulled her back and forth. "Yeah. Probably."

Sighing, Wilder pressed his lips to her forehead, and felt her whole body relax at the touch. "I can wait."

Chapter Forty-Two

Back in his room, a heavy blanket of exhaustion covered Wilder, his mind tripping over itself as it muddled through the onslaught of the day. Terra and Wilder had stayed in the garden for only a few more minutes before she had left to say goodbye to Olivia and Harry. Despite his weariness, his mind buzzed with frantic energy. His fingers itched to draw—to sketch Terra. It was something he hadn't done in months, not since before he had come to the Council House. But the image of her face, her emerald eyes lit by the moon and the stars, wouldn't leave him. He grabbed his sketchbook and pencils and flipped to a blank page.

As he drew, he thought of New Orleans, its raucous energy, and of his life here. And he thought of Terra, the warmth of her skin, her lips so close to his, and the scent she had left on him—of lemon and lilacs brushed with the end of spring. The same threads, the nostalgic ache of home, the ache for her, laced the two.

Vision blurring, Wilder's fingers slipped along the shadowy smudges of her neck. His mind was so exhausted from everything else happening, he couldn't even begin to make sense of what was happening *with her.* With them. She was torn. He knew it. And he knew why. Choosing him would mean risking something she had built her life on. Something her parents had built their lives on. As badly as he wanted her, it wasn't a choice he'd ever force her to make.

Wilder's eyelids slipped closed, his pencil falling from his hand, his sketchbook resting on the comforter. As sleep gentled his mind, the hum of the Book of Scales tugged at him once again. He tried to ignore the sensation that something of his own heart called to him from where the book waited across the abbey. Wilder curled his pillow around his head, as if it might block out the hum. Turning toward the window, he watched the reflections of the streetlights paint the panes of glass in green, yellow, and red. As his eyelids drooped, Wilder vaguely acknowledged the play of dancing shadows, light creeping and fluttering onto his walls as clouds swept over the moon outside.

A sleepy, dense fog soothed and lulled him into a numbing slumber. Veined with deep throbbing purple light, the fog seeped into his brain and dreams, muting everything with slow-moving tendrils, wrapping around him in a loving embrace. Whispering, the fog caressed him into a restful, white peace. But far in the distance, in a whimper he could barely hear, Wilder felt a faint nudge, warning him to stay alert. Something oddly sinister seeped through the fog, surrounding him in a sedating poison.

"Wil," a female voice whispered to him, singing sweet and lovely in all the wrong ways, sending chills down his arms and spine. The voice was the poison, and the poison was the voice, and it all wrapped around him in the dense fog. *"Good boy. You found it. I'm so proud of you,"* the voice preened, its tendrils stroking his cheek. He could almost feel the throbbing venules slinking across his skin, coiling around his neck. If he could have quivered, he would have.

Wilder's mind clunked and shuddered, the poison slowing his thoughts. Something hummed in his veins, telling him to fight the voice, to get away from it, but it was too late. He couldn't move. Couldn't think. Couldn't speak. All he could do was lay there, formless in the white, listening to that voice.

A male tenor cut through the fog, the steel swipe of a sword. In its air of regal command, Wilder felt a tug of familiarity. *"Bring us the book, my son. Join us. Your people need you. Bring us the book."*

Shots of pain, grief, and longing stabbed through him as that one word rang again and again through his mind. *Son.* Hope blossomed from the echoes of that longing, the first blooms of spring after the last snowfall of winter. Scraping at the recesses of his memories, Wilder searched for where he knew that voice. But in the dense haze, he either found nothing, or simply lacked the wherewithal to know where to look. In his searching, he felt another nudge. A gentle roar strained through the pulsing purple fog, fighting to get through to him.

The male voice said his name, and Wilder desperately tried to place the voice again, but the tendrils of venom numbed him even further, crippling him from the inside out. It didn't want him looking. A distant terror brewed in what remained of Wilder's awareness, but that part felt so disjointed from him. All he could think about was being called son, and who this voice might belong to.

Images he had no recollection of began to flash through his mind, as if someone else's memories were breaking through. Images of a path he had never followed. A path leading from the Magi's office—where the Book of Scales was being held and protected by magic wards—into rooms he had never been in, and through doors he had no inkling of having been doors at all. The path trailed unlit hallways to the far side of the abbey, near where he had sat with Terra what felt like only an hour ago. The images slowed to a halt, finally leaving him in a simple chamber. It contained little more than a bookshelf, a desk, and a metal bed frame covered by a thin, threadbare cloth mattress. Long, jagged cuts covered the walls, as if massive claws had slashed into the stone, tearing entire chunks from some sections. A thin layer of dust and cobwebs coated the chamber, as if not a soul had entered it in over a century. Something drew Wilder's attention to the bookshelf, and he saw himself placing the Book of Scales on the empty shelving.

"Bring the book, my son. Leave it here."

A rumbling growl broke through his consciousness, and he tore his stare from the shelf. The roar, no longer distant, ripped through his awareness, severing the fogged tendrils still wrapping around him. Releasing their grip on him, the venules sputtered their poison into the void. His mind clunked faster, steadily increasing speed. He felt, rather than heard, the male and female voices shouting in anger at the disturbance. But what they said–what they knew— stopped his blood in its tracks.

"She'll burn for you."

Suddenly, a wall of bright white surrounded Wilder, and molten gold eyes edged with illuminating life glared at him—willing him, *commanding* him to wake. And to run.

Whipping himself out of bed, Wilder tripped on to the cold floor as his sweaty sheets tangled his ankles, their final words, their final threat, echoing through his mind. He glanced at his clock. Three thirty in the morning. The dawn remained hidden beyond the horizon, but Wilder didn't care how early it was. This couldn't wait. He bounded through the abbey, his legs taking him faster than he would have been capable of months ago, before stopping and pounding on the first and only door he could think of.

"Terra! Wake up! Terra!" He shouted into the closed barrier, trying the locked handle. The condensation from the warmth of his breath pooled on the surface of the glazed wood.

Wilder heard the sound of a lock unlatching, and Terra eased open the door, blurry eyed and bewildered. She wore a set of midnight blue pajamas freckled with stars, and he wondered distantly if their time in the gardens had inspired the choice.

Blinking into the hallway light, she surveyed the sweat drenching Wilder's bare torso and the red strands clinging to his forehead. "Wil, what happ—"

"Markus. He knows about us, Terra. And he wants the book. I need to see the Council. Anyone. *Now.*" He released a wracking gasp, knowing it had nothing to do with his sprint across the abbey and everything to do with the utter fear of what he had just experienced. Markus and Haman had somehow broken into his mind, and they knew about Terra. Markus really was his father, and he was trying to get to him—manipulate him. Trying to get to *her*.

Terra nodded, her perplexed expression shifting to serious as she understood the gravity in his tone. Grabbing his hand, she pulled him down a set of halls before opening a door identical to her own. They entered a cozy living suite, complete with an ample kitchen and buffet area, dining table, plush padded couches, and a fireplace. More doors surrounded the living room, which was warmly decorated in jeweled blues and greens. Terra left Wilder at the dining table, retreating beyond one of the doors.

Inhaling a deep breath, Wilder surveyed the room. Pictures of a young girl littered the walls and fireplace mantle. In one, the little girl swung from a tall oak's branches in City Park, her father gazing up at her with a radiant smile, pride gleaming behind his russet eyes. In another, she fed birdseed to a tiny puff of white feathers, her green eyes alight as she crooned at the baby owl. And in another—the girl must have been close to eleven or twelve—she stood beside her mother in the same Apotéca only two flights of stairs below them. The two mixed the elements of some kind of potion, endless books scattered around them. But the little girl only had eyes for her mother, peering up at her with endless admiration.

This was Terra's family. This place was her home, too.

Wilder tried not to think about how his presence, his arrival in her life, was now the primary reason her family would be torn apart in less than twelve hours, forced into a separation likely thousands of miles away. The guilt settled in his gut like a weighted stone.

Before he had any more time to berate himself, Terra reappeared, her mother in tow. Sofia had wrapped herself in a sensible white robe, the cotton fabric covering the length of a periwinkle nightdress. Her hair was disheveled from sleep, but her green gaze appeared bright and alert. So much like her daughters.

"Wil, what's wrong?" Sofia asked, placing a hand on his shoulder. Her gentle features displayed nothing but concern as her eyes flashed across his features. He tried to ignore how nice that felt—to be cared for by a mother, even if it wasn't his own.

"Markus," Wilder said in a plea. "He's coming for the book. Soon."

The color drained from Sofia's cheeks. She took a step back. "How do you know?" she asked, her tone shifting. Her question hadn't been inked with even an ounce of suspicion. Sofia now was nothing more than a well-trained member of the Council, investigating all the facts before deciding on the best course of action. So much like Terra.

"And he knows about," Wilder paused, glancing at Terra, whose lips tightened, but she nodded. "About Terra. About how I—" Wilder couldn't bring himself to finish. What would he say? How he felt about her? How he had almost kissed her less than four hours ago? He couldn't bring himself to speak into existence the danger he had unwittingly put her in, simply by being who he was. Because of who his father was. The truth stole the air from his lungs.

Sofia gripped his shoulder, as if assuring him he could go on. Wilder explained what he remembered about the dream. He told her about the voices, and how he knew the male had been Markus. How Markus had called Wilder 'son', and how he had tried to convince him to bring the Book of Scales to the darkened chamber. Wilder then described the place and the path.

"I didn't bring him the book. I swear," he added fervently, shaking his head.

"I know, Wil." Sofia said, releasing a defeated sigh. She placed her hands back on his shoulders. But her encouraging smile didn't reach her eyes. Turning from him to Terra, her tone shifted again to an earnest urgency. "Wake your father. Tell him about the dream. I'm taking Wilder to the Magi."

Terra nodded before her gaze fixed on Wilder, the gentle crinkle in her eyes a consolation that everything would be okay. The stone in his gut lightened, though only a little.

***

In the Magi's office, Sofia stood at Wilder's side, her hand a present comfort on his shoulder. The Magi stood behind his desk, robed in red velvet pajamas trimmed with gold and green, and Wilder was vaguely reminded of Father Christmas. Wearing nothing but a pair of shorts and the sheen of drying sweat himself, Wilder squirmed at the cold hitting his bare skin. Exhaustion ripped through him, and he swayed on his feet.

At Sofia's instruction, Wilder repeated the dream to the Magi, just as he remembered it. But just as before, he left out the constant presence of the gold eyes that had been trailing him for weeks—and had ultimately rescued him. He didn't want to answer questions about those. He didn't know where he'd even start.

Never diverting his attention from Wilder and his tale, the Magi hung on every word. As Wilder described the room across the gardens, the Magi circled to the window and peered across the grounds. He stared out, as if he could see past the dark still shadowing the far end of the abbey, and the stone walls beyond.

Behind them, the door clicked open. James strode into the room, as if called there by some silent behest, wearing what appeared to be fighting leathers. "Yes, Magi?" James asked, his eyes fixed on the Magister, his hands clasped firmly behind him. Suddenly, Wilder saw him like he never had before; a soldier and a protector—of this place and its people. Wilder's heart warmed, remembering what Terra had said about James's past and his deep connection to the abbey.

"I have reason to believe the abbey has been infiltrated. I need you and Caolin to investigate. Particularly the shifting rooms," the Magi instructed.

James's eyes darkened, and Wilder couldn't be sure what now settled there, but the rest of James's features remained expressionless. Giving the Magi a deep bow, he left the room. Rickard, Tremaine, and Terra arrived on the heels of his departure, all three fully clothed in the same kind of fighting leathers, and each strapped with weapons of varying degrees of lethality. The dark brown leather clung to every curve of Terra's body, accenting the golden highlights in her serious eyes and braided hair. Wilder fought to tear his stare from her, to look at anything else. Withdrawing, the Magi began to converse quietly with Rickard and Tremaine near the fireplace.

Hearing footsteps in the hallway, Wilder glanced back. Tristian and Barrett strode in, each wearing the same leathers as the others. Watching the scene unfold, guilt bit at Wilder again as he realized he was the reason they were all gathered here now, a small army of troops preparing for battle. Barrett sidled to Terra and yawned. Placing an affectionate arm around his shoulders, she rested her cheek against his white blond hair, and Barrett inclined into her sisterly warmth. Despite the hellish morning, Wilder couldn't help but smile at the display.

Tristian padded to Wilder, carrying a bundle in his arms. "Let's go, Summer," he said, his voice a weary gruff beside him. He grasped Wilder by the shoulder, but there wasn't an ounce of aggression to these summons, his tone only the low, slow timbre of resignation. "We leave within the hour."

Twenty minutes later, Wilder had showered, packed, and dressed in the extra leathers Tristian had brought him. The leathers had once been Tristian's, and to Wilder's surprise, they fit him perfectly. They were warm, yet breathable; firm and durable, yet flexible. As he threw a brief glance at himself in the mirror on the way out, he idly wondered what everyone expected to happen today that required being armored in these.

Wilder followed Tristian down the stairs, his pack in hand. They met Terra, Rickard, and Barrett in the foyer, each donning their own packs of clothing and belongings—the Book of Scales among them. A somber air stifled the group, their movements slow and methodical. Rickard handed out several heavy, rounded stones, each as blue as sapphire, explaining they had been protectively spelled the night before. The five of them would walk to a local park twenty minutes away, where they would travel to Eaigan through a small millpond. It was the closest entrance, and they didn't have time to attempt the crossing elsewhere. As they wouldn't be returning, the risk of being attacked afterward would be low. The irids would keep them hidden along the way, deterring anyone with ill intent from getting too close. After retrieving Jeselle and her egg, they'd use the Waterways in Eaigan to travel to Florida, mostly to confuse anyone watching. From there, they'd board a plane to Brazil, where they would travel by ship to Teír.

Wilder nodded, devoid of any questions. His mind had gone an uncomfortable shade of numb. Wilder pocketed his stone in an unassuming leather satchel strapped across his waist, alongside the machete and ruby-hilted dagger Tristian had gifted him. The others did the same, and without another word, they left the Council House behind.

CHAPTER
FORTY-THREE
Terra

It was too early in the morning for anyone in their right mind to be out and about, so Terra and the group traveled in an easy silence along the empty cobbled streets, the first rays of dawn peeking over the horizon. Rickard, Tristian, and Barrett had taken the lead, Terra and Wilder trailing and watching from behind, a short distance gathering between the two groups.

The irids in their pockets would keep them safe for the short trek to the park, the magic within making the group effectively invisible and silent to anyone looking for them. The magic wouldn't last long, half a day at most, but it was long enough to get them to Eaigan.

Ever the gentleman, Wilder had offered to take Terra's bag. Too tired to insist she could handle it on her own, she let him. Terra was still struggling to wrap her mind around everything that had happened in the last twenty-four hours. And struggling even more so to imagine what might happen within the next week. Her best friend had almost died, Wilder had somehow uncovered a legendary book confirming the existence of both the dragons and the dragonstones, Markus had somehow infiltrated not only the Council House, but Wilder's mind, and an egg, an actual, *unbound* dragon egg, had just shown up in the crib of a child with inexplicable abilities. To top it off, Markus now knew exactly who she was, and what she apparently meant to Wilder.

Hell, *she* didn't even know what she meant to Wilder.

And now they were all being shipped off to the safety of Teír.

Rubbing at her temples, Terra couldn't help but feel like there were so many more pieces of this intricate puzzle still missing. But she also didn't want to think about any of it. Not yet.

She didn't want to think about the danger they were in, or the gnaw of the ever-present Priestess seat looming on her horizon, closer with each step toward Teír, where the seat held its claim within the Magistrie's High Council. She didn't want to think about whether she wanted it, and what that meant for her place within the Coven or the Council.

She didn't want to think about how quickly all their lives were changing—unraveling.

As they walked, Terra watched Wilder: the way he moved, the way he slowed his steps to stay close, the way his hand gravitated just slightly towards hers. *He* was all she wanted to think about. Studying the perfect, angular lines of his face, she could almost feel the distance between them, could cut the tension there with the daggers she had strapped across every inch of her. Even before Wilder had come to her room last night, she had struggled to sleep, his words echoing through her head.

If I wasn't positive you'd hit me, I'd probably kiss you.

And then he almost did. And she had wanted him to. And then, she hadn't. She didn't know what it was he actually wanted from her. She didn't even know what she wanted from him. Could she *allow* herself to want something? Want whatever was happening between them?

Before she could stop herself, before she could tell herself no, just as she had so many times before, she reached for his hand. Wilder's breath caught, stirring him from the thoughts commanding his attention. *This* was what she wanted. Just this once. Even if her opinions on everything else about the trajectory of her life, her future, were irrelevant. Even if all she could have were these brief glimpses of contentment, at least she could have them for a time. At least she could take this moment as her own, regardless of what it cost.

Wilder hesitated before she finally felt the heat of his fingers intertwine with her own. Never turning to look at her, his brows rose in confused surprise, his focus still fastened ahead, as if making sure the attention of the rest of the group remained occupied.

Terra heard Wilder sigh before moving to idle behind her, as if trying to hide the encounter from any prying eyes that might chance a look back. But he never once lost grip of her hand. He traced hesitant circles along her wrist while she stared blankly ahead, pretending nothing was amiss. It took everything in her to not crumble completely as he leaned forward, his breath tickling her neck. "What's going on, Terr?"

And she realized she had no clue whatsoever. She didn't know if it was the early morning, the lack of sleep, the way those stormy gray eyes had crippled her last night in the garden, or her fear of leaving everything behind, but something had driven her to act far more rashly than she would have in the past. What was she thinking? Was she starting something she shouldn't?

All she knew for sure was he had never once called her 'Terr', and she had liked the sound of it.

They entered the park's lawn, the branches of towering oak trees sweeping the ground, their immense canopies shielding the group from the rising sun, the shadows from their leaves dancing along their footpaths. The birds sang, welcoming the morning and guarding their conversation, and the wind blew a light breeze from the north, whipping the unbound wisps of Terra's braid behind her. Wilder tensed at the breeze, at whatever blew his way, but he said nothing, still waiting for her response. Slowing, he pulled at her hand, as if trying to put more distance, more privacy, between them and the group ahead without causing too much concern.

Terra stopped in her tracks, and Wilder bumped into her as she whipped around to look at him, ripping her hand from his. Gray eyes blazed down at her, flashing across her own in curiosity. It was always a wonder to her that he never met her tenacity with fear or annoyance.

"I don't know," she finally told him, her voice a snapping whisper. "I never know what I'm doing with you. What to do with you. I don't know what you want from me, or what I want, or what I'm even allowed to want. Maybe I just haven't had any coffee yet, so I'm not thinking straight. Maybe just…forget it. We don't have time for this, Wil."

Terra moved to step past him, but she felt Wilder's hand circle her wrist, spinning her back around to face him. "Oh, no you don't." He took a step forward, filling the space between them. She felt his hand at her waist, keeping her from pulling away again. His stare bore into hers.

"No more running away, Terra. *I think* you're finally thinking more clearly than you have in months. This'll only take two minutes. We'll catch up. But I need you to tell me what's actually happening with us. We can't keep doing this. I can't keep doing this. I just need clarity."

A moment later, he was pulling her into a dense tangle of oak branches, shielding them from the sight of the group ahead. After dropping their bags and making sure they hadn't been seen, he took a measured step closer, pushing her against the oak's gnarled trunk. The air between them thinned until nothing but their leathers and an impossible tension remained a blockade. Slowly, as if second guessing himself in each moment, he rested his forehead against hers. Knotting his hands into the hair below her braid, he gripped the strands, as if holding onto her would somehow keep him from moving too fast too soon. As if she'd break into pieces if he came any closer. He pulled his head away from her, and she dared a look into his gray eyes, only to find a storm gathering there. Neither of them was breathing as he broke from her gaze just long enough to glance at her lips, before his eyes rested again on hers.

"Tell me what you want me to do, Terra. I need you to decide, because I won't force this. But you know me, and you know I've already decided. I know what I want. This is on you." The deep rumble of his voice was a hunger edged in fear. She could tell he didn't want to mess this up. Didn't want to make the wrong move. But she didn't know what the right one was either.

Before she could respond, before she could decide, before she could assure him they'd figure it out, the sound of unsheathing metal pierced the air, where the birds no longer sang, and a twin set of blades flew to rest across each of their throats.

CHAPTER FORTY-FOUR

"What's this? Has baby Summer gotten himself a girlfriend?" Wilder heard a familiar voice croon in his ear, and went rigid. "Whatever *will* Papa think of your *interesting* tastes, I wonder?"

Behind Terra, Kyra Kerdasa held a dagger across her throat, the blade shining a silverish-purple in the morning light. Terra's skin puckered where the blade sat against it. Staring into her green eyes, Wilder saw them shift to a rageful calm. He could see Terra investigating every avenue of distraction, assessing which weapons she might be able to utilize against the duo.

As if sensing her intentions, Kyra's mouth quirked into a bitter smirk before she began unsheathing the various daggers strapped across her, Kyra's other hand remaining motionless at Terra's neck. "Not a single word or spell from you, little wyteling," Kyra purred in Terra's ear. "Got it?" She pressed the blade harder against her throat. Terra managed a small nod, her lips pulling into a tight line. Rotating the blade against Terra's skin, Kyra said, "It's a shame you're not human. I would have *loved* to add your traitor blood to the offering."

"What do you want, Lynx?" Wilder growled, his hands lifted in surrender to keep the twins from making any rash decisions with Terra. Lynx and Kyra were so close, he was sure he could burn them if he tried, but he couldn't risk hurting Terra in the process.

"Thank you for asking so politely. How considerate of you," Lynx hummed. "The same thing we wanted the last time we chatted, if it's not *too* much trouble. Your dear papa is missing you, and we've come to take you home. Though it's unfortunate baby sister can't come along too." Wilder tensed and glared at Kyra, who had finished disarming Terra and now stood smirking at him, playing with another blade in her free hand.

"Oh, and that little book up ahead, if you don't mind," Lynx added, "though I believe a friend of ours is handling that." As she spoke, Wilder heard shouts in the not far off distance as Rickard, Barrett, and Tristian engaged with whatever unnamed force Lynx and Kyra had brought with them.

"You really made this all too easy, Wil," Lynx whispered in his ear, the hiss of her breath cool and uncomfortable. Her hair fell over his shoulder as she ran a finger along his neck. "We're going to have *so* much fun together. You'll forget all about your little friend in no time."

Terra stiffened in front of them, glaring at the twin, dark resolve blossoming. Before Wilder could stop her, the corner of Terra's mouth twitched, and the blades at both of their necks flew to the ground. The twins hesitated a split-second too long, and Wilder elbowed Lynx in the ribs, the blow sending her reeling. But before Wilder could make another move, Kyra's second blade glistened along Terra's neck, this one piercing her skin. Lynx returned a heartbeat later, her dagger pressed to the small of Wilder's back, where she could sever his spine with the easiest of twists.

"Did I not make myself clear, girl?" Kyra hissed, pushing the blade harder into Terra's larynx. Sucking in a breath, Terra tried to keep herself from making any sound, but a whimper escaped her as the edge of the purpled blade split her skin.

Another shout in the distance demanded their attention.

"Let's join them, why don't we?" Lynx unhitched the blades at Wilder's sides, adding them to her own repertoire, before poking him with the tip of her dagger through his leathers. A wet feeling rubbed against his skin, suggesting she had drawn blood.

He trudged forward, and Kyra clicked her tongue at Terra to get her moving alongside them, her knife never leaving Terra's throat. They reached a small clearing and found Tristian brawling with a fae rogue, the rogue now struggling against a blinding chokehold. A pale blue tint painted the rogue's handsome features, his moonlit eyes bulging at the pressure around his neck, his feet flailing feebly as he danced on the precipice of unconsciousness. But when Tristian glanced up to see Terra with the blade against her neck, and who held her captive, he dropped the rogue onto the ground before lifting his hands in surrender. Icy cold crossed his features, and he looked nowhere but at Terra, and at the crimson blood now pooling along the blade. Red beads trickled down her throat, staining the neckline of her leathers.

Wilder's own throat bobbed, as if the blade was held against his own, and he stared at the cut along Terra's neck, unable to do anything to save her. It was his fault she was in this position. If something happened to her, he'd never forgive himself. And if he didn't do anything to save her, and she somehow survived this, he'd never let *her* forgive *him*.

His mind turned over itself, running faster than he could keep up with. Something Terra had once told him beat like an unmistakable drum against his soul, its rhythm breaking through the chokehold of fear trying to freeze him in place. That she usually felt the Magíck most when she admitted to herself she needed it. *We weren't made to be apart from it*, she had told him.

Help, Wilder voiced through the chaotic tumult of his thoughts, sending the word out into the ether—out to the Magíck, to whatever was supposedly out there.

But nothing happened.

"Now, we're not here to cause any trouble," Lynx announced daintily to the group, her sweet cadence mocking. "We just want the book, and the boy, and we'll be on our way. No harm done." She shrugged, as if her request were the simplest thing in the world.

Wilder flashed a look at Tristian and Rickard, silently pleading to let the twins have him, if only to keep Terra from them. They shook their heads, suspecting what he was trying to do. But he remained resolute.

"Okay," Wilder said, his voice clear as it echoed through the glade. "I'll go with you."

He glanced at Terra, her eyes pleading for him to try anything else as she struggled against Kyra's hold. Tearing his eyes from hers, he stared instead at Tristian, willing him to protect her at all costs. Tristian's jaw tightened at Wilder's apparent surrender, and Tristian and Rickard began arguing with him across the clearing.

But Wilder couldn't hear them. Silence had fallen, a phantom voice whispering through his mind. *Léiriú.* Roiling thunder reverberated against his bones. His blood, which hadn't stopped surging since Kyra and Lynx had discovered them, now pulsed with a new but familiar presence. A steady electricity flowed clearer and brighter than he had ever felt it before, asking him, once again, to allow it in. To let it help.

He stared at the ground, realizing what was happening, and what he needed to do. It was the only way to save her, and he knew it. Closing his eyes, Wilder submitted his entire self over to it, over to the will of the Magíck, over to the pulsing energy seeking to control his body. Wilder thought this moment—this connection he had been fighting for months—would rip him apart, cleaving him in two and leaving his soul bloody and defenseless. But instead, every cell in his body seemed to *rest* in its presence. The weightless feeling of safety, of calm, of home, met him there.

Wilder opened his eyes and stared at the scene unfolding with an awareness that was not his own. The sound of the world returned, the thrumming presence in his blood suppressed only enough to keep him from shifting, to keep him from giving away what was about to happen. But Wilder knew each step he needed to take. Beyond the canopy of the trees, beyond the edge of the awareness of the twins, storm clouds mustered, Wilder's soul drawing them closer.

"Oh, goodie! Road trip! We're going to have the best time, won't we, Kyra?" Lynx cheered at Wilder's apparent surrender.

Sneering, Kyra kept her eye on the others and on the blade at Terra's throat. "So glad we've finally reached an agreement. See? That wasn't too hard." She brushed a gentle hand along the top of Terra's head. Terra flinched at the touch. "Now hand over the book and we'll all be on our way."

Wilder peered at Tristian, who had braved a glance up at the sky and was now watching the clouds moving in. The corner of Tristian's mouth lifted into a perceptible smirk as he realized what Wilder had planned. Looking to Rickard, Tristian nodded at him, prompting him to give the twins the book. Rickard's eyes widened in confusion, but he seemed to trust whatever exchange had happened between him and Wilder. Flipping his bag to his front, he dug through it slowly, as if to buy them time. The wind picked up around them, the leaves stirring and the branches bending and moaning against the rush. Birds flittered about, looking for refuge from the oncoming tempest.

"Lynx…" Kyra called, her hand at Terra's neck trembling as she eyed the skies above, which had morphed into a menacing gray.

Lynx had the decency to appear concerned as she yelled at Rickard, any semblance of sweetness dissolved, her sharp voice cracking. "Well, get on with it! Where's the book?"

Léiriú, the whisper said again, ringing across Wilder's skin. Each inch vibrated with the power of the presence held just beneath it.

Lightning cracked through the air in the distance, and thunder trembled the earth in response. The twins simultaneously jolted, and Kyra dropped her blade from Terra's throat, her hand smeared with her blood. The skin where the blade had cut Terra bloomed a deep purple. After sprinting across the field to join the other three, Terra shot a glance at the sky that told Wilder she also knew exactly what was about to happen. Retreating, the twins gaped up between the trees as the sky steadily devolved into a dark, tumultuous black.

"There's no way he's that strong already," Wilder distantly heard Kyra mutter to Lynx as they stumbled further away. He could barely hear them over the sound of thunder rumbling back to back.

Léiriú. Wilder wasn't sure if it was the phantom voice or his own he heard in his ears, but he felt the power beneath his skin direct his hand, reaching into the sky itself.

He pulled, and a single bolt of lightning cracked, splitting a tree nearby clear in half. The fae rogue, who had been watching the prior exchange with amused interest, now bounded across the field, cowering behind the twins.

Wilder's body grew strained, focused on the storm and the placement of the strikes, but he knew, even with the Magíck calling the shots, he didn't have the control to truly end this—to burn each of their worthless bodies to the bloody crisp they deserved. Especially not without endangering his friends if the strikes got too close—too unwieldy. Stepping forward, he placed himself between them and the twins. He let the pulsing energy lead, releasing each rush in a mental swipe toward the terrified rogues. They stumbled away, their eyes shifting between the building storm, Wilder, and the bag holding the book. Another glorious strike pierced the ground at the twin's feet, leaving a small patch of charred earth, smoke rising from its remnants. The force of the strike threw the trio against a copse of trees.

But in the flash of the next bolt, before Rickard, Tristian, and Barrett could join the attack, before the accompanying thunder could shake the earth again, the rogue and the twins had disappeared into thin air.

All at once, Wilder's body slackened, releasing his hold on the storm, and on the presence beneath his skin. The rush that had coursed through his veins dimmed, and the burnout barreled through him a second later.

As the thunder above them settled, moving farther away, Wilder collapsed, disoriented and empty. Likely sensing he was spent, but otherwise okay, Rickard and Barrett moved to search the trees and shrubbery, but found no signs of the twins or the rogue.

Wilder peered across the clearing, where Tristian was trying in vain to get a good look at the cut on Terra's neck, the blood still trickling into a dark pool along her collarbone.

But it wasn't clotting.

"Tristian, I'm fine, I swear!" She pushed him away, thrashing in protest. But her behavior, her resistance, was so unlike her that Tristian looked at Wilder, pleading, as if he would somehow know what to do, could somehow make her see reason. But as Terra fought him off, sweat beaded on her forehead and the color drained from her face. Her movements grew jerkier and more awkward. Dark purplish veins, so like the ones from his dream, spread lazily across her neck, up her jaw, and down her shoulder.

Wilder's heart wrenched. *Poison.*

"Terra?" Tristian reached out for her, but she collapsed onto the ground, barely breathing.

And Wilder felt the earth beneath him buckle again.

Chapter Forty-Five

Wilder stared up at the parlor ceiling, unseeing. He couldn't think. Couldn't breathe. His lungs were slowly shrink-wrapping his heart, which he was sure had stopped beating altogether.

All thoughts of Eaigan and their move to Teír had been postponed. Tristian had brought Terra back to the Council House, the rest of them tracking quickly behind, retrieving their bags and joining Tristian at the abbey only minutes later.

He had done what he could to heal her, but the poison had fought against his magic.

The spread had slowed, though. At least they had that.

Wilder hadn't been there when Sofia took Terra to the infirmary. And now, no one was allowed in the room while she worked on her. While she tried to save her life.

Rickard paced in wide circles around the parlor—the same parlor where Terra had first told Wilder who he was all those months ago. Collapsed on the same couch she had sat on that night, drained beyond all belief, Wilder tried desperately to breathe in whatever scent remained of her on that couch...on him. He had been so stupid. And she was all he could think about now. How she had looked at him right before they had been attacked. The little gasp she had let out when he had gotten close enough to finally kiss her. The warmth of her fingers intertwined with his. Her scent. *Her damn scent.*

Wilder hid his face in his palms, letting out a low groan. This was his fault. He had gotten them caught. He hadn't been paying attention. He hadn't protected her. Worse even, he had distracted her at the worst possible time. And now she hovered on the precipice of death, poison leaking into her blood, into her heart. *His* heart. His fault. Terra would die, and it would always be his fault.

Raiya entered the room and surveyed the scene: Tristian brooding in an armchair in the corner, his forehead pressed against the whites of his knuckles, Rickard wearing a ring into the aged wood beneath him, and Wilder staring at the ceiling, numb and all but dead to the world.

"Rickard?" she asked lightly, and Wilder glanced up at her. "You called for me?"

Ceasing his pacing, Rickard joined Raiya at the threshold, his eyes dark with a wild anger Wilder had never seen on him before. "The irids didn't work, Raiya. They still found us." He held out the blue sapphire orb to her. "Why didn't they work?"

Taking the stone, Raiya wrapped her hand around it, closing her eyes and concentrating. A whole minute passed before her eyes snapped open and she glared at the stone, the blood draining from her face. "They didn't work because they weren't spelled to," she finally whispered.

Rickard's own face paled beyond his already bone white pallor. "What do you mean they *weren't spelled to?* We all watched as you spelled them, and we *all* triple-checked them last night. We *all* confirmed they were ready to go!" His voice teetered on the edge of a savage darkness only a centuries old vampyr could be capable of.

"I *know* this, Rickard. I was *there,*" Raiya snapped, her nostrils flaring. "The irids must have been intentionally emptied or replaced without our knowing." Betrayal crossed both of their features.

Wilder could see it took everything Rickard had left in him to not take the small stone from her hand and throw it clear across the room, but he wouldn't be surprised if the stone wasn't now dust in his tightened fist.

Just then, a bell tolled through the abbey.

"Terra?" Wilder and Tristian said in unison, both snapping to attention at the sound.

"No…" Rickard said slowly. Hesitating, he sniffed at the air. And then the scent hit all of them at once.

Fire.

***

The bell continued to sound across the abbey as they sprinted through the kitchens and into the gardens, meeting with the rest of the Council on their way. Colossal plumes of smoke rose from the pillars of fire now engulfing the back half of the cathedral, exactly where Markus had told Wilder to leave the book only hours ago.

What the hell… Wilder stared in shock as the blaze gathered strength.

Caolin stood at the base of the flames. Jagged, pure white wings etched with venules of crisp morning blue wrapped around him, the display he normally kept hidden now serving as protection from the overbearing heat. He sent rushes of ice into the heart of the flames, but the fire continued to flare. Following his father's lead, Tristian joined him, though the ice in his own blood seemed weaker than his fathers. Magi Maynestream began to manipulate a steady stream of water from a nearby fountain, whipping it in arcs over the garden and toward the fire, but it didn't do much to douse the flames.

"Now would be a great time for a little rain, Summer!" Tristian yelled back at Wilder as they attempted, with little success, to calm the ravaging blaze.

Wilder blinked, still struggling to understand what was happening. His gaze flashed between the burning building, the Council trying to save their crumbling home, and the sky above. Exhaustion gripped him. His bones hurt, his muscles spasmed, and his brain felt like it had been flayed over an open stove top. The little time they had had between their encounter with the twins and now hadn't been nearly enough to heal and recharge for what this situation required of him.

With what meager little Wilder had left, he closed his eyes and opened himself to the magic thrumming in his veins. The pulse weak but steady, he asked the Magick to give him enough for this—this last thing. Grasping onto the electric hum in his blood, Wilder willed the droplets in the sky to gather and build, willed the clouds to move and coalesce, willed himself to open to the power he knew lay on the other side of himself. Opening his eyes, his vision blurred, and he could just make out the dark storm rolling in, could feel the tiny droplets begin to fall in a light shower, cooling his feverish cheeks. With one last push, he willed a deluge, an absolute torrential downpour, over the abbey. At the sound of the instant rush of rain, the world went black. Wilder fell into the void—molten gold eyes watching him, and the leathery folds of luminous gold wings engulfed him.

Chapter Forty-Six

Wilder awoke in the parlor, staring bleary eyed at the ornamental ceiling. Someone had wrapped him in a blanket, the smell of a cup of steaming chicken broth and a fresh slice of bread wafting over from the coffee table beside him.

"Eat, Wil. It'll make you feel better," he heard Sofia offer from somewhere next to him.

Sofia.

Wilder snapped off the couch. "How is she?!" he sputtered, but the sudden movement did nothing to help the raging headache that had taken hold of his brain. Head spinning, he collapsed again, his whole body trembling as if it had been burned and blistered from the inside out.

"Eat," Sofia said more firmly. "Terra will live. I've made sure of it." Wilder met her eyes, their familiar green heavy and clouded. "Harry's in there taking good care of both her and Olivia now."

Wilder noticed the dark circles creating hollows on her drawn features; her tear-stained cheeks rubbed raw from wiping them away. He couldn't imagine what it had been like for her, having to save her own daughter from the clutches of death itself. But if anyone could have done it, it was her. Guilt ate at him again, but her assurance of Terra's survival was all Wilder needed. Through the rage that wracked his body, he forced himself up, this time more slowly. Wincing at the movement, he dunked the bread in the soup and took a bite, but refused to savor even a morsel.

Rickard reappeared, followed by the rest of the Council, their faces gaunt and troubled.

Tristian peered up from where he had been bent over in the armchair, dark bruising circles forming beneath his own eyes from the magic he had spent that morning. "By Dagda, what's wrong now? Besides everything else that's happened in this godsforsaken day."

"James is missing," Tremaine announced with no preamble. "Caolin believes he may have been the one to start the fire. The Book of Scales has disappeared as well."

"James?" Tristian's gaze narrowed in confusion, his mouth slightly agape. "That doesn't make any sense. The Council House is his. He's sworn to it. He wouldn't set the damn thing on fire. He's been here practically his entire life."

"It makes no sense to any of us either, but it is all we've been able to gather from the day's events. We will begin a citywide search as soon as we have more bodies on the ground." Magi Maynestream told them, his voice tinged with an ancient sadness. He had surely known James for more years than Wilder had even been alive.

"You can't believe he hasn't found a way to get out of the city by now." Tristian countered. "If he's smart enough to betray us without getting caught, he's smart enough to hightail out of here."

"Perhaps. Perhaps not," Raiya added. "We're watching the Waterways, as are the rest of the Council Houses in bordering regions. If he uses them to get anywhere, we'll be alerted. He, of course, knows that."

Tristian nodded, adding in barely a whisper, "He'll probably stay close. Especially after what happened with Terra. He'd want to know she's okay."

"In spite of everything, I'd venture to agree," Rickard said. "Either way, reinforcements will be arriving shortly. As soon as they're here, we'll set off for Eaigan again. We cannot wait any longer."

"Without Terra," Wilder said, though he didn't intend it as a question.

"Yes," Rickard confirmed regretfully. "She'll be staying here to rest and recover alongside Liv. As soon as they are both better, they'll join us in Teír."

Wilder nodded, resigned but understanding. Nothing should keep her from healing. And his continued presence here would do nothing but endanger her. He needed to leave, needed to leave her, and as soon as possible. But something in the back of his mind was bugging him, something the twins had said.

"Rickard." Wilder looked at him as the man turned to leave the parlor, the rest of the Council already disappearing from view.

"Yes?" Rickard paused, glancing over his shoulder.

"When Terra and I got attacked, one of the twins said something. At first I didn't think anything of it, but it just sounded so strange… She said something about it being a shame Terra wasn't human, because she couldn't add her blood to 'the offering'."

Rickard stiffened so completely Wilder thought Caolin may have frozen him from behind. Slowly, as if realization were dawning on him, his eyes widened. "An…*offering?*"

Wilder followed his stare as Rickard's gaze flashed to Tristian, who had gone stock-still as well, his mouth set tight, his pupils flitting back and forth as if trying to remember something.

Crossing the room to the bookshelves, Rickard pulled a large tome from the middle, the words *Tales of Sea and Sky* inscribed along the spine. A small tuft dusted the air as Rickard cracked it open. The volume appeared to be a book of old fairytales, the front cover displaying a winged man on the back of a dragon.

"What—" Wilder started, but Rickard held up a finger to silence him as he flipped through the pages. "I don't think you've ever heard the full story, and it might be helpful if you did."

"Rickard, it's a *nursery rhyme,*" Tristian tried to argue, but Rickard silenced him as well before beginning to read.

"*In the beginning, the gods, the first of the Magick's creation, and the Magick Himself, created the humans and the Fae to live upon the Earth. The humans and the Fae lived in peace and partnership for a great many years, learning from each other, tending well to the Earth they had been given, and walking with the gods and the Magick upon its ground.*

The gods, bright as the stars, adored the Fae. They gifted the Fae with abilities greater than that of the humans. But in their love for the Magick as well, they also decreed the Fae the protectors of the humans, and a covenant of blood was established between them. The Fae were beautiful, powerful, and good—and they treated the humans with love and compassion, using their magic to ensure humankind's wellbeing.

As a reward to the Fae, and in their curiosity to see what the Fae might make of them, the gods gifted the Fae the dragonstones—granting their bearers enhanced abilities far beyond what the Fae could do. Along with the stones, they also gifted the Fae the fierce and mighty dragon. The power each stone possessed was unique unto the stone, and served as an elemental bridge between the Earth and the Heavens. Only those wielding a dragonstone were permitted to partner the power of the dragon, linking them intimately with the Magick Himself.

Peering into the Magick in a way no other creature could—the dragon saw into time and space at will, altering and bending it. The stones, and the dragon, were a reminder to the Fae, and to the humans—and to the beings that would follow—of the greatness and authority of the Magick they worshiped.

For a time, the Dragoned Fae ruled the earth, protecting and serving humankind. Peace reigned. And with the Magick's support, after a time, the gods created the Lycan and the Magem, drawing from the powers of the Earth herself.

But one of the oldest of the gods became tired of what he perceived to be the Magick's tyrannical authority. He wanted to influence the creations he had a hand in making without the oversight of the Magick. And so, to spite the Magick, the deviant god, now known only as the Dahrk, secretly began to seep into all of creation, growing in them like a poison.

Pride swelled in the hearts of the Fae, and they sought to command the humans, pressing them to worship and revere the Fae as the truest representation of the Magick on Earth. All the while, the Fae became jealous and uneasy of the powers possessed by these newer creations—speed and strength that rivaled their own—and of their growing partnership with the humans.

In their learning and their progress, power sprung from all the earthly beings. Eventually, the Vampyrs came to be, though through and by the hand of man, alongside the power of the Dahrk.

Fearing their reign threatened by so many new beings with powers different than their own, the Fae declared war on the Magem, Vampyrs, and Lycan.

Only some disagreed with the conflict. The Dragoned fae, who maintained a deep connection with the Magick and knew the role the deviant god had in the strife that had befallen the world, would take no part. The Dragoned continued to live by the covenant created between the Fae and the gods, which commanded them to protect all of humanity. The Dragoned were supported by a small Council of humans, magem, vampyrs, lycan, and fae, who sought to create a rule made by all, for all.

But despite their efforts, and despite the Dragoneds' refusal to side with the Fae in their warring, the stones—which had been intended by the Magick to represent His goodness—instead began to symbolize the Fae's authority and rule. The rest of creation, in turn, grew weary of the control wielded by the Fae, coveting their power for themselves.

The humans, the weakest of the creation, fell victim in the crossfires of the Great Wars, no longer protected by those who had once been sworn to them. In fear for their lives, the humans hunted down members of the other species as a means of protecting their own people.

And the deviant god delighted in the havoc he had created on the Earth.

Forced by the Dahrk's decisions and the suffering of His people, the Magick punished all of creation for their foolishness and arrogance, all while attempting to remedy what had befallen humanity. A veil settled across the Earth, a Shroud to cast all of magic, and all but the humans, behind—exiling the Fae, Magem,

Vampyrs, and Lycan to an existence outside of the knowledge and awareness of humankind. He took back the dragon, bound their remnant in stone, and scattered the dragonstones to where only the worthy could ever hope to one day recover them."

Rickard paused, his eyes widening as he scanned the script. He began again.

"The Dahrk remained, his presence on the Earth spreading and rooting into the Earth and Sea. Even now, it calls for the death of the Magick's people—each human life taken by the hand of a Céad, an offering of blood made out of malice and another soul claimed by the Dahrk, thereby making him, his presence, and his rule over the Earth even more complete.

But we know there will come a time when the forgiveness of the Magick will restore the dragonstones to their rightful people. There will come a time when the dragon will return, preventing the Dahrk from its claim upon another soul. And we know a semblance of the first Council remains to this day, instilling peace and order across the now broken lands, in partnership with the Magick's will for His world."

Rickard stopped reading, but he didn't look up from the book. It lay open in his hands, both of which appeared to be shaking.

"That's a nursery rhyme?" Wilder balked.

Tristian glared at him. "Yes. And that's all it is. A nursery rhyme," Tristian said, shaking his head. "A kid's story to keep us from getting too full of ourselves… to keep us from treating the humans badly." But the tremble in his voice suggested he might believe otherwise. He had gone ghastly pale.

"That's what we thought about the dragonstones, Tristian," Rickard combatted, finally looking up at them. "But how much of this story has already proven to be true?"

Wilder looked at each of them, his own voice growing heavy. "That…that last bit. About the offering." He swallowed hard. "The kidnappings. What if they aren't revenge? What if they're some kind of…payment?"

CHAPTER FORTY-SEVEN

Sofia gave Wilder and Tristian each a tonic to revive their bodies enough for extended movement, though their magic would need more time to rest. Wilder downed the tonic in one gulp, and the throbbing pain in his head and bones lessened to a dull ache. Staring into the empty bottle, he realized so many things all at once.

Whatever blocks had kept him from controlling his powers were effectively gone, the hum of a constant powerful presence lighting his bloodstream without any effort from him. And even though Wilder couldn't see them, the presence of the gold eyes remained, hiding within the folds of his mind, waiting for him should he decide he needed them. Guilt still gnawed at him, but resolve had joined it, the two standing hand in hand. He'd find a way to end this. To get back at Markus for what he'd done to Terra. To all of them. Even if he had to use his connection to him to do it.

As the others left the room to prepare for their leave, Wilder grabbed his bag and wandered to the parlor desk. Penning a thorough letter, he failed to stifle his shaking hands with each word he wrote. Finishing, he reached into his bag and pulled out his sketchpad, ripping the last page from it. Folding the two sheets together, he placed them in his pocket, running his thumb over the smooth paper as he joined the others in the foyer.

After respelling the irids, Raiya had double and triple checked their effectiveness. She handed them directly to Rickard, Tristian, Barrett, and

Wilder. They placed the stones in their satchels before proceeding to the infirmary for another round of final goodbyes to Harry and Olivia.

And Terra.

Olivia seemed in good spirits when she saw them, her bed pushed next to Terra's, who remained sound asleep. Olivia was now walking entirely on her own, though it did cause her some shortness of breath from time to time. She told them she had been about ready to leave the infirmary, but then Terra arrived, so she felt she'd be of better use staying close to encourage her recovery. Harry, of course, would stay wherever Liv was.

Through the gloom shadowing Wilder's thoughts, he found himself thankful for them, relieved that even though he'd be gone, Terra would have others looking out for her. Watching Terra's breathing, his heart eased at the sight of her even, deep sighs. The threading purple veins had retreated from her jaw and shoulder, and had lightened to a sickly lavender. A thin layer of sweat still coated her forehead and neck, where wisps of her chestnut hair clung to her skin, though it appeared mercifully less pale than before.

A fresh wave of resolve coursed through Wilder. As Tristian and Barrett said their goodbyes to their friends, Wilder stood back, refusing to allow himself to get close to Terra. His presence, their relationship, whatever it could have been, meant nothing but danger for her now. He wouldn't risk putting her in that kind of situation again. Nodding his thanks to Olivia and Harry, they all shared their hope they'd see each other in just a few short months.

"You'll love Teír," Harry told him, giving his shoulder a reassuring squeeze. "There's no place like it."

"Hmph," Wilder grunted, the sound a jagged scratch against his raw throat. He felt so utterly removed from the room, he couldn't even imagine what Teír might be like, other than a chance to train and take down Markus. As his stare fell back on Terra's sleeping frame, he realized he didn't even want to consider what the next few hours might be like, either. Not without her.

"Harry. When she wakes up, will you just give her this?" Wilder handed the folded notes to Harry, the weight of them leaving his hand settling on his shoulders. In that moment, he knew even if he ever saw her again, they wouldn't be the same. For her sake, he'd have to learn to be okay with that.

"She'll be okay, Wil," Harry added in a low voice only he could hear. Wilder met his gaze and had to stop himself from crumbling right there in the infirmary. He held his jaw tight and nodded before leaving the room.

★★★

Their trek back to the park and to Eaigan remained silent and uneventful, the irids finally working as they had intended them to the first time, though the company and conversation was resoundingly more reserved. The Synod welcomed their return to Eaigan, or whatever passed as welcoming for the Watern. The quiet unreality of the realm, the stifling salt air, and the curious magic that whispered through the night, poking and prodding at Wilder, were all a bit more than he could handle. He was thankful they wouldn't be staying there long.

While Lysella inspected Wilder closely, a cat ascertaining how successful she'd be in cornering and devouring a panicked mouse, Moarlin proceeded to explain what they knew about Jeselle, her budding powers, and her dragon egg companion. Jeselle's progressive aging, and the appearance of the egg, had led the Synod to believe she had been influenced by dragon magic, as the dragons were known to have the ability to bend and manipulate time.

The matter-of-factness with which they shared the information with the group made Wilder shift uncomfortably, and he wondered if the

Watern had also grown up with the belief that the dragons had never been real, or if their understanding of the origin story had been different than the rest of the Eadar's.

Lysella's cat-eyes narrowed, and she tilted her ethereal head at him, her long fingers coming up to curl a strand of her thin navy hair around an elongated nail. *Catching up, are ye?,* a whisper slithered through his thoughts. *Ye is not far off, truth be told.* Wilder's brow furrowed, and he instinctively slung up a black shade around his mind to block her out. Her mouth fell open in shock, but she recovered her misstep a moment later, eyeing Wilder skeptically but turning her attention back to Rickard.

"Well, when might we expect to see her?" Rickard asked Moarlin a bit too harshly. The morning had clearly taken a toll on his tactfulness, and Wilder could tell he was just as anxious to leave the Glass City as Wilder was.

Moarlin gestured to the front of the hall, and the doors behind them opened wide on a phantom wind. A statuesque fae, more human looking than any of the other Watern Wilder had seen, strolled through the doors, her hand clutching that of a small girl, who appeared no older than two. Another fae, dressed in some kind of uniform, trailed faithfully behind them, carrying a black velvet pillow in his hands as he traipsed carefully into the hall. Atop the pillow rested a large, gray dragon egg, made entirely of scaled stone. Jeselle looked behind her and up at the uniformed fae, as if making sure her egg didn't stray too far.

As she had grown, the little girl's features had not changed. She remained colorless, with hair and eyes the neutral shade of ash. But Wilder could see an unmistakable knowing in her eyes, as if her tiny body, despite how quickly it had advanced, had not yet caught up with her discerning mind. As the woman and the girl established their places beside them, Wilder peered down to see the little girl staring up at him, her gaze intent and unreadable.

"Sendaeya, of course, will proceed with you to Teír," Moarlin added, indicating the little girl's wet nurse with an irreverent flip of his hand. Sendaeya nodded at The Synod, and Rickard threw her a thorny glance.

"Of course," Rickard agreed, nodding once. But a flat stillness lay across his voice as he continued to assess the reserved Watern woman beside them. This hadn't necessarily been part of the plan, but Wilder could tell Rickard knew there was little he could do about the situation now.

"A Waterway has been prepared for you. It will release you within an airport in the southernmost tip of the Americas." Moarlin's voice had grown bored. "Do let us know how your travels fare." But Wilder thought he sounded as though he had little interest in hearing anything about their voyage.

Chapter Forty-Eight

Jeselle sat between Wilder and Sendaeya on the plane, her petite hands laced in her lap and her short legs kicking up and down energetically as they waited for takeoff. Her egg had been locked safely away in a chest in the compartment above. A light snoring was already coming from where Tristian, Barrett, and Rickard sat just behind them.

The little girl had been given a small stone, made of ruby, spelled to glamour her features to appear more human, as each of the fae had naturally done. It seemed the little girl had a mind of her own, and had a tendency of refusing to shift as she was told.

"A fine spirit she has," Sendaeya had told them before they left Eaigan, looking down at the little girl with complete love in her eyes.

"Sure. As long as it doesn't get us killed…" Rickard had responded, handing her the stone and eyeing the little girl warily.

The glamour hadn't been so much to hide them from the eyes of the humans—the Shroud took well enough care of that. At least it was supposed to. They instead hoped to stay hidden from the sight of any Céad, quite possibly rogues, who might be lurking too close for comfort.

Now on the plane, the little girl was handling the takeoff far better than Wilder. As Wilder clutched at the armrests, his gut churning and his jaw clenching at the vertigo-inducing shift in speed and direction, Jeselle just watched him, her gray eyes wondering quite loudly what on earth was possibly wrong with him. The expression felt so familiar, Wilder almost saw Terra's green eyes staring back at him. He shook his head, freeing her from his mind.

"So judgmental," Wilder muttered at the little girl when the plane finally leveled off. He hadn't expected a response from the two-year-old, but Jeselle locked eyes with him, that same intelligent knowing shining through, and smirked.

Smirked.

Wilder grumbled, too tired and testy to deal with her antics. "Brat," he said, mussing her silver curls as he readjusted in his seat. "Go to sleep."

The sun had already set, and Wilder needed the sweet reprieve of sleep more than anything. Not only to recuperate his magic, but to shield his mind from the recurring memories of Terra that continued to hound and haunt him. Settling into her seat as well, the little girl turned to face him, continuing her inspection with an unearthly discernment. Finally, she set her tiny hand on his wrist. Her skin felt warm—warmer than what he expected from this miniature sprite of a girl.

Wilder started, images suddenly flashing through his mind at high speed, all of Terra, though she appeared healthy and spirited. These were the girls' memories of when she had last seen her, and she had somehow known he needed them.

An intense calm soaked into his soul, in no way connected to anything he'd be able to achieve himself. Staring down at her, Wilder whispered to the girl, "Thank you." His lids began to grow heavy. From beneath his lashes, he saw the little girl smile and close her eyes, before sleep finally took him. Her tiny, delicate fingers stayed wrapped around his wrist, and he didn't dream at all.

★★★

The sun blistered down on Wilder as they journeyed from the Fortaleza Airport to the coast of Ceara, where massive ships were being readied to withdraw from shore with everything from excitable tourists to precious cargo. Gulls cried and shrieked overhead, and the smell of the ocean, its salt and brine, clung to the air and his burning skin.

Tristian held Jeselle's hand, a novel sight for anyone who knew him. The girl had taken off running haphazard around the worn, wooden docks twice, giggling like a banshee, so the gesture was more one of necessity than anything else. Jeselle now watched the surface of the water as a school of pink dolphins bobbed in and out of the rippling currents, eyeing her with just as much curiosity as she showed them. Even though the group was on the farthest side of the port, far from prying eyes, Rickard had instructed them to maintain their shifts until he told them otherwise.

As Rickard and Sendaeya left to speak with the captain of their ship, the crew hauled what little belongings they had brought onboard. They would buy whatever else they needed when they made port in Teír. Drinking in the flurry of movement, Wilder listened to the shouts of the sailors as they prepared the ship for departure. Various Céad worked the mast and sails, rigging and pinning as the first mate called out their orders. None of them had shifted to appear human, but the few humans that walked the docks didn't spare them a second glance.

Wilder's attention ran along the railing before his stare fell on a shock of furry red. At the ship's edge, an eerily familiar fox met his gaze, its beady black eyes steady on him. Wilder squinted up at it. Surely his mind was playing tricks on him. There was no way the same creature from all those months ago was now here, thousands of miles away from its original home. Just like him. A flash of light moved past the fox, probably just a glare from the sun, and then the fox was gone, as if it had never even been there. But Wilder could have sworn there had been something within the light itself.

A loud splash drew his attention from the ship, echoing from between where two catamarans had been tied-off and berthed, the boats bobbing indiscriminately as miniature waves bumped against their sides. Wilder looked around, but there wasn't another soul in sight. He heard another splash, closer now, and it sounded oddly like a tail slapping the surface of the water. Thinking a dolphin must have gotten caught in some ropes beneath the docks, Wilder padded to the dock's edge to investigate. As he stooped on the damp wooden paneling to survey the waters below, midnight eyes suffused in starlight greeted him, vivid galaxies dancing only inches from his face.

"Crap!" He stumbled as far back as he could without falling off the other end of the dock, but Viviayne reached out with a single scaled hand, her gentle smile reassuring.

"Do no be afraid, son of Summer. I come bearing ye no ill-will. I only wish to speak with ye." The ring of her voice misted through the salty air like midnight rain.

"That's unfortunate, because I don't really want to speak with any of you," Wilder said, but his curiosity was piqued. Inching a single step closer, he maintained his distance. "Why are you here?" he asked, despite himself. His gaze narrowing on her with intense suspicion. "What do you want?"

"I come to ye with a warning, Summerson. I could no tell ye in the city of night, where the faces watch and know. But ye needed to be told, 'fore yer feet touch the many sands of the land of Teír."

Wilder eyed her warily, reminding himself to keep whatever kind of shield he could up while in her presence. "What do I need to know?" he asked, edging closer. Glancing over his shoulder, he saw Rickard still chatting with the captain, and Jeselle and the others still playing with the dolphins, all entirely unaware of the conversation happening just a few feet away.

"Ye are not who they think ye are, Summerson. Ye are not who *ye* think ye are. But they will use it against ye all the same. Keep your wits about ye. This story, yer story, is far larger than time can hold."

Her words were as vague as the Synod's had been when he had first met them, and it did nothing to help his mounting confusion. She drew her eyes to Jeselle, who looked to be feeding the dolphins tiny minnows Barrett had bought her from a street market just outside the docks. "Look out for the little one, though she willna remain so small for long. We have delved into her mind. She will become much more, she is capable of much more, than any of us could even dream. The magic in her is dark, light, and powerful beyond measure. It knows no bounds. She hath been kissed by opposite sides of the same coin, and that coin remains tossed. Beware of how and when it may land."

"What does any of that even *mean?*" Wilder begged as he bent further down, his knees hitting the dock in front of her.

Viviayne only gave him her characteristic coy smile before blowing Wilder a demure kiss. His cheeks flushing, she dove back into the depths of the sea, the scales of her jeweled tail glistening in the sunlight as she sank beneath the waves.

EPILOGUE
Adria

Laughter filled the stone hall as Adria gazed out onto the Seasuír Court, her mind slightly hazy from the wine she was cautious to only sip. Harps and flutes and lilting voices like bells floated through the chamber as fae danced, arcing and bowing with each crescendo and diminuendo—all in celebration of the long-awaited Summer Solstice. The chamber radiated with the power the solstice had on their land, each fae glowing with its magic. Adria looked up at the night sky, spread wide and fully visible through the glass ceiling, opening the chamber to heaven's pale moonlight.

Josiah drew closer to her, his own amber eyes bright with the honeyed mead from his glass. "Careful, love," he said, his mouth a teasing grin as he placed his palm across her stomach. "Your people might actually think you're having fun."

"Oh hush." She swatted his hand away. "Madam Maire gave me permission, and you know I won't drink too much."

Chuckling, Josiah peered across the ornate head table draped in the flora and foliage of another radiant summer. The band began a new number, more spirited than the last. Cheering, each fae took a drink from their own glasses before stomping the ground to the rhythm of the music. The earth thrummed in response, joining their song.

Without warning, the music was jarringly cut off. The dancing ceased. Murmurs filled the chamber, the entire court turning to eye the musicians in confusion. In the silence, Adria thought she could hear her heart drumming in her chest. From somewhere beyond the crowd, a blood-curling scream echoed through the room, followed by another stab of silence. Adria's grip tightened around her goblet, and she rose to get a better view.

Someone near the band shouted. "Dagda defend us—he's dead! His throat's been slit!"

A heartbeat later, a horn blasted from outside the hall and screams erupted, raining down on the crowd like daggers. The room fell into a mind-bending panic, and the drumming in Adria's chest grew louder, before she realized it wasn't coming from her at all. Within moments, Lus Halla began to reverberate instead with the oncoming tremble of hammers on stone, and the thunderous barrage of war drums.

Adria turned to Josiah, cold sweeping her bones. "What's happening?" Her voice cracked in the rush, but he didn't answer. From where she stood, Adria saw men she didn't recognize barrel into the chamber, their moonlit eyes searching the crowd before settling on her and Josiah. Then the bloodbath began.

If Adria had thought she knew the sweeping paralysis of debilitating fear before that moment, she had been dismally wrong—though it now took only moments for her and the dark, deafening plunge called terror to finally become most irrevocably acquainted.

Josiah ripped Adria from her seat, but not before she saw the swinging flash of swords in the lamplight, and the shining silver blood of her people painting the cobbled floors. Ignoring Josiah's pull on her gown, Adria continued to stare as body after body collapsed. She stood, frozen in time, as her people's cold and empty gazes stared back up at her, praying for a rescue that wouldn't come.

Adria barely registered an attendant hurrying to Josiah's side and whispering in his ear. At the sound of the name on his lips, she tore her gaze from the ravages unfolding in front of her. Josiah's panicked expression disappeared so quickly, Adria thought she might not have seen it at all. His features betraying nothing but fierce resolution, he grabbed Adria's hand, kissed it, and pulled her through a curtain of thick vines. Within moments, she was squinting into the dark of a dank tunnel she hadn't even known had been there to begin with.

Adria stood rooted, struggling to make sense of each moment. Tugging on her hand, Josiah hastened her forward. "Come, Adria. We must go *now*."

She nodded, her breath coming in short bursts as she ran faster than she ever thought possible. The screams of those they had left behind followed them, haunting their path to salvation. The hot, metallic reek of wet blood filled her nostrils, and it was with concerted effort she did not double over and vomit at the stench. Josiah remained next to her, hurrying her along as she stole a glimpse back toward their ravaged home.

Who would be attacking? Who could have reason to? They had only just signed a treaty with the Lycan last week; a truce both sides had been hard pressed to achieve. The Vampyrs would never attack with such impetuous stride. If they had reason to at all, they tended towards subtlety in their dealings. And the Magem; the Magem were the Fae's own dearest friends. They would never betray the Seasuír Court.

The stones along the tunnel glistened in the torchlight, casting ominous shadows in strange places. The attackers were closing in on them. She was sure of it. They would never make it out alive.

As the two weaved further down the dark tunnel with seemingly no end, Adria stole a sidelong glance at Josiah. She jolted, taken aback by his expression. His face was contracted in a way she had never seen on him. Anger had settled there, and deeper still—betrayal. She knew that expression, had seen it before, though not on him. Her beloved's characteristically handsome features were now eerily reminiscent of that of his older brother, Markus.

Once Adria's oldest and closest friend, Markus had been absent from Court for over two seasons, but she recalled the night he had left. She remembered Markus's rage at Josiah and their father, Samael. Adria's heart had broken into pieces for him, witnessing the disbelief he had endured at the hands of his family, the Court, and the Magistrie. At the decision they had made, though she had known, even then, it needed to be done. Markus would not be King.

Adria's enduring love for her friend had etched that hurt into her heart like chiseled stone, a wound deepened by his tears of jilted betrayal two years before. When she had first told him of her decision to marry Josiah. She would never forget what that news had done to him. And she knew she would never forgive herself for the aftermath, for the ruin of the broken trust between them.

The mouth of the tunnel suddenly widened into the open air of rolling dark green plains and ferocious wind; the night sky towering above them. They were on the coast of Daoine now, tempest waves crashing against the rocky shore with untamed violence. Lus Halla was far behind them, though a distant red glow continued to light a small portion of the horizon. As a storm gathered strength in the north, an entourage of trusted attendants readied a ship along the shore.

The screaming had stopped, or perhaps had been drowned out by the steady campaign of drumming continuing with such offense Adria believed her heart would never know another rhythm. She'd be imprisoned reliving this day with every breath she took, until she breathed her last.

Josiah hurried her onto Luas, the Fairn's renowned sea vessel christened for its unmatched speed on open water. It would now be relied upon to be their ultimate saving grace. To Adria's great relief, several more fae had managed the dauntless escape and had already boarded the ship. More continued to join them, their pitiful cries for their lost city, and the screams of their terrified children, piercing the night.

"All is ready, Your Majesty," the ship's captain called out to Josiah. "The sooner we leave, the better. We'll be having a rough time if we don't outrun this storm."

"As you will, Captain." Giving the captain a curt nod, Josiah surveyed the green plain around the dock, searching for any other stragglers; any other survivors.

There were none.

The sailors hoisted the ship's enchanted white sails into the night sky, the emblazoned crest of an eagle embraced in the rays of a shining sun gleaming luminous in what remained of the half-moon—its light peeking imperiously through the clouds of the oncoming storm. With a final call from the crewmen, the ship lurched forward, tearing away from the shore with reckless abandon. The crew failed to mind the surrounding rocks as they drove into the cruel waters. Luas would undoubtedly need repairs when they arrived, but Adria couldn't say when, or where, that might be.

Wresting a hold of the stern, Adria feared what would happen should she ever decide to let go. Josiah appeared beside her, placing one steadying palm on her hip and the other with tender care across her belly.

"What's happened? Where are we going?" she asked him, succumbing to a numb displacement from everything that had occurred within the last half-hour. Despite their distance from shore now, the steady beat of war drums continued to course through her veins.

Josiah released her, taking a place at her side, diligent not to turn toward the others behind them. Staring into the ominous deep, his haunted eyes brimmed with a grief so profound he refused to allow his people, or whatever was now left of them, to see. Gripping the ship's railing with his outstretched hands, he sighed, a single tear sliding down his carefully controlled features. He uttered what Adria already knew, and in desperation, wished wouldn't be his answer.

"We course for Teír."

Reviews

Did you love Red Summer? Can't wait for book two?
The best way to support indie authors (and to make sure the next book makes it to the finish line!) is to leave a review.
I (Ana) personally read and am eternally grateful for each and every review, and will try my best to respond! I write for my readers, and always want to hear how these stories impact you.
You can leave a review for Red Summer on GoodReads or Amazon.

Coming Soon

Sneak Peek of Stone and Scale Book Two
Summer of Dust and Ash

―――◆○◆―――

Tristian had always loved the sea. One of his first memories had been playing on the shores of Daoine, the blinding summer sun shining over the Atlantic as the waves taunted and chased him in and out of their foaming maw. Gripping the railing in front of him, he breathed the salt air, the ocean wind wrapping Tristian's skin in the briny film of the deep abyss below. Standing on the deck of Luas for the first time in years, he let himself believe nothing but the endless hope of open ocean lay ahead.

Rickard strode up from behind, joining him at the bow, his russet eyes fixing on the horizon. "You've been distant these last few days," he said, turning to search Tristian's features. Tristian knew he wouldn't find anything revelatory in them.

Maintaining his grip on the railing, Tristian stared into the brackish depths. "Did you know, when I was younger, I wanted to captain this ship?" His voice was low, almost lost beneath the sound of the waves crashing against the bow.

Peering at Rickard, Tristian saw a slight smirk inch across the vampyr's features. "Somehow that doesn't surprise me," Rickard said, his tone amused. The man closed his eyes and lifted his chin, as if to feel the sea breeze brush his cheeks. Tristian waited for him to say more. But he didn't.

"I was five. Maybe six. It was right after the kidnappings had started. When they shut down the Ways," Tristian told him.

Rickard nodded, lifting his gaze to the cloudless sky. "I remember."

"Before then, I had never been on a ship." Tristian paused, smiling as he recalled the first time he had come aboard. "I thought it was the greatest thing in the world. The smell of the salt, the gulls crying out. The way the crew worked together, so in sync. I had wanted to feel that same rush of open sea every day of my life. That same sense of brotherhood. Obviously, I didn't know exactly how to explain it back then, but it was enough that I told my dad one day I'd captain this ship."

Rickard smirked again, pride lighting his features. "I'm sure Caolin had something to say about that."

"Doesn't he always." Tristian returned Rickard's grin, but he could feel something bitter biting through. "He just laughed at the idea. 'Don't think so little of yourself,' he told me. 'No son of mine would be destined for so menial a role as a ship captain.'" Tristian felt Rickard tense. "But back then, I thought nothing could be more noble than captaining Luas. Nothing more important than helping our people get back to Teír in the only safe way left."

Rickard stared out over the sea, nodding into the silence between them. The rest of the Council knew how Caolin could be; his tendency toward stubborn pride and control. Rickard himself had gone head-to-head with Caolin from time to time. Though as of recent, it had been happening more and more often. Tristian knew Rickard wouldn't speak an ill-word against Tristian's father, at least not to Tristian. But the strained look dimming Rickard's expression made it clear he wholly disagreed with Caolin's opinion of his son's supposed 'destiny'.

"I think you are your own man, Tristian," Rickard said, and Tristian didn't miss the acidity beneath his words.

Tristian watched the ocean swell as the ship moved onward, nothing ahead for as far as the eye could see. "I was young then, though. Naïve. Maybe my dad was right. I didn't know—couldn't understand—the bigger picture. What really mattered." Tristian's timbre had grown stiff.

"What do you mean?" Rickard turned to him, his eyes squinting against the spray of sea mist, but Tristian thought he saw a whisper of protectiveness cross them.

"As the war went on, as Markus gained more and more power, we stopped taking Luas as often. I'm sure you remember it better than I do. When the Magistrie told everyone, especially the Fae, to limit travel and remain hidden and warded. When we all started to realize how serious the war was getting."

"Of course." Rickard nodded. "Your family had been assigned to the Council House around that same time." A hesitant weight settled over Rickard's tone, as if he was being careful to not mention an integral part of the story. But Tristian knew what had crossed his mind. It was the same thing that had been consuming his own since the moment Tristian stepped onto the enchanted ship.

Tristian didn't like talking about it. And those closest to him, like Rickard, knew better than to bring it up. Even Terra had only mentioned it once, and had regretted it within moments of seeing his reaction. Tristian felt a familiar, unwelcome pressure build behind his eyes. Blinking, he pushed it down, skilling his features back into the cool bearing he usually maintained. He let go of the railing. Adjusting his jacket, damp with salt and spray, Tristian shoved his hands into his pockets before turning to Rickard.

"Then you'll remember what happened next. I learned pretty quickly that my father was right. Nothing is more important than family; than duty. And there's nothing quite like the torture and murder of the person a little boy loves the most to remind him of that fact." Tristian's tone bordered on indifference as he searched Rickard's condoling stare, daring him to disagree.

Rickard's shoulders slumped, as if disappointed by the outcome of Tristian's story. "Tristian, what happened to your brother—" Rickard started, shaking his head, but Tristian lifted a hand to stop him. Letting his statement falter, Rickard sighed.

Tristian didn't want to hear anymore. Now all this ship represented was what his life could have been, what Aydrian's life could have been, if not for Markus. If not for the twins. If not for this entire world going to complete shit.

GLOSSARY OF TERMS

The Shroud

A magical veil that separates the Céad from human awareness and knowledge. The Shroud conceals the existence of the Céad and their magic from humans, effectively exiling them to live outside human perception. Though Céad can still interact with them, humans cannot see the Céad for what they are. The Shroud, however, has been thinning, leading to increasing incidents of Céad detection.

—◦✦◦—

Maluum

A dangerous and illegal form of blood magic that taps into the power of the Dahrk. A distortion of the Magíck, it brings irreversible harm to those who practice it. The Dahrk grants its practitioners an inordinate level of power, far beyond typical magical abilities, but at a cost.

—◦✦◦—

Waterway (The Ways)

A highway of interconnecting tunnels maintained and guarded by the Watern.

—◦✦◦—

Irid

A magically imbued stone used to store magic, either in its raw form, or as a specific spell. After use, the magic is depleted from the stone.

Dragonstones

Nine magical stones (similar to irids) created by The Magíck itself, and bestowed to the Fae by the gods. Each stone grants the bearer unique enhanced abilities, and serves as a bridge between the Earth and the Heavens, though each stone can be used with ill-intent. The Dragonstones were originally believed to be symbolic, referring only to increased magical powers once held by the Fae before the Fall.

The Dragoned

A group of Fae uniquely gifted by the gods with the ability to partner with the Magíck, enhancing their magical abilities beyond typical Fae capabilities. The Dragoned were tasked with protecting humanity, adhering to a covenant established by the Magíck and the gods, and they refused to participate in the Fae's war against other Céad species, choosing instead to uphold their duty to safeguard all of humanity. The Dragoned are remembered in legends and stories, symbolizing a lost era of harmony and power. However, some believe the Dragoned did not just have enhanced abilities, but were the first riders, partnering with actual dragons to do the will of the Magíck. Most of the Eadar, however, does not believe the dragons themselves ever existed.

The Three Roads

The fundamental branches of elemental magic, used to focus the movement of magic.

- **Corraí** (Movement) – Involves manipulating objects or elements by moving them through space without physical contact. It's about directing energy to shift things.

- **Tras-Athrú** (Transmutation) – Involves transforming one element or state into another, such as turning water into ice. Altering essence or form.

- **Léiriú** (Manifestation) – The creation or summoning of elements seemingly from nothing, such as producing fire, water, or other substances. The most challenging road, it requires a deep connection to a source.

The Book of Scales

A legendary compendium of knowledge, the Book of Scales is rumored to have been compiled by an ancient Magem who worked closely with dragons and their riders before the Fall. It is believed to contain invaluable information about the dragons and the dragonstones. Many question the book's existence, just as they question the existence of the dragons and dragonstones themselves.

People To Know

The Magíck

The divine Great Creator of all things; humans, gods, and Céad included. The true access point of each Céad's powers.

The Dahrk

The antithesis of the Magíck. A powerful presence that seeks to kill and destroy all of creation. The Dahrk can influence a Céad's powers if they are not careful, or if they seek to use its influence.

Céad

A being that is not entirely human, but may appear so. A Céad could be any of various species that possess magical abilities and are concealed from humans due to their nature and powers. These species include the Fae, Magem, Vampyrs, and Lycan, who were separated from humanity by a magical veil called the Shroud, enacted by the Magíck to protect humans.

Fae

- Fairn – Seasuír (Court) – A type of fae, distinguished by their use of external elemental magic and shapeshifting. The Fairn are comprised of four Seasons of fae, each with a unique coloring; Summers, Winters, Autumns, and Springs. However, the appearance of a Fairn's wings is directly connected to the type of elemental magic they are strongest in. Powerful and historically revered, it was Fairn pride that led to conflicts with other races, and the eventual Fall. The Fairn are regarded by most as the highest of the fae, and are led by the Seasuír Court, a governance of Fairn nobles that oversee their people. The Fairn are in close partnership with the Magistrie, and many fae nobles choose to serve within both governments.

- Watern – A type of fae, distinguished by their use of internal mind magic and shapeshifting. The Watern are comprised of more ethereal fae, including the water-based *mere*, and are more often depicted with a cosmic or water-based appearance, as influenced by their home—Eaigan. The Watern do not hold to the belief that the Fairn are the head of all fae, and do not opt to serve the Magistrie. They maintain a small governance within themselves, led by a group of Watern elders; the Synod.

- Natuine – Include 'the people in the trees' (miniature winged fae with more spritely/nature-bound personalities) and the animals (Faed) that have followed Wilder most of his life.

  ○ The Faed – Wise and eerily aware animals, many of which partner with the Magem as familiars.

Lycan *(Clan)*

Shape-shifters capable of transforming into wolf-like forms, Lycan possess enhanced strength, speed, and senses, as well as the ability to shift in and out of their wolf-based traits. Newer Lycan shifts are controlled by the moon, but with training, they can learn to shift at will. Lycans are tribal, and live within clans led by an Alpha. A stubborn and hot-headed people, they are known for not liking or respecting the Magistrie. Lycan are made weaker by wolfsbane, though in certain preparations, some Lycan have been known to use the herb to strengthen their control over their ability to shift.

—◦✦◦—

Magem *(Coven)*

A magical being akin to a witch that derives their power from the Earth, rather than directly from the Magíck.

- Wyte (Madam) – A female magem. Elder wytes with consider-able ability can earn the title of Madam.

- Mage (Magi) – A male magem. Elder mages with considerable ability can earn the title of Magi.

- Priestess – The head of the Eadar's magem, the Priestess works closely with each Coven to ensure the progress and success of their people, and partners closely with the Magistrie, sitting as a member of the High Council.

—◦✦◦—

Vampyr

Vampyrs are characterized by their enhanced physical abilities, such as speed, strength, and heightened senses, as well as their need to feed on blood, ability to compel humans, and ability to heal others with their blood. Most Vampyrs learn to manage their need for blood through non-lethal means. Vampyrs were created through the influence of the Dahrk on human actions, and were created specifically to take human life.

Vampyrs face prejudice from other races due to the origin of their creation, and their individual struggles to maintain their humanity after becoming vampyrs.

—◦✦◦—

The Magistrie *(The Council)*

The authoritative body within the Eadar, the Magistrie is responsible for overseeing the Céad, maintaining order across the Eadar, and maintaining the protection of the humans. Within the Magistrie are multiple Council Houses, dispersed throughout the world to ensure peace and secrecy. The Magistrie is based in Teír, the central hub of the Eadar. It holds significant influence over the everyday lives of its people, and is tasked with critical responsibilities like mediating interspecies tensions. The head of the Magistrie is the First Magister, who sits on a High Council comprised of the leaders of each species of Céad (aside from the Watern).

The Tuatha De Danann

A collection of gods worshipped by many in the Eadar, particularly the Fae. They created and gifted Lus Halla to the Fae people.

Places To Know

The Eadar

The hidden, magical world of the Céad that exists parallel to the human
world, but is concealed from it by the Shroud.

Teír

The distant, hidden homeland of the Céad, far from human populations.
It serves as one of the last strongholds where Fae, Magem, Vampyrs,
Lycan, and other magical beings can live openly without the need to
conceal their nature from humans.

Daoine (Lus Halla)

The ancestral homeland of the Fae, Daoine is a sacred place created by
the Tuatha De Danann specifically for their kind. Lus Halla is the seat of
the throne of Daoine, the beating heart of the Fae people.
Both Daoine and Lus Halla traditionally move to one of four predeter-
mined locations when a new Season of Fae ascends the throne.
In Markus's theft and corruption of Lus Halla, he has moved it to a new,
unknown location—making it inaccessible to the Fae and the Magistrie.

Apotéca

A specialized, underground chamber used by Magem and their covens
for practicing their most potent magic.

Eaigan

A realm within the Eadar, Eaigan is the domain of the Watern. A city made entirely of glass, it is known for bearing no secrets, and can be accessed only by use of the Waterways.

PLAYLIST

Theme
Game of Survival – Ruelle

Chapter One
Embers – Just Jack

Chapter Five
Secrets (Cellar Door) – Radical Face

Chapter Nine
If I Were The Devil – Colby Acuff

Chapter Ten
Illicit Affairs – Taylor Swift

Chapter Twenty
Always Gold – Radical Face

Chapter Twenty-One
Exile – Taylor Swift and Bon Iver
That's Us – Anson Seabra

Chapter Twenty-Six
Earth – Sleeping At Last

Chapter Thirty-Two
I Found — Amber Run
Fallen — Gert Taberner

Chapter Thirty-Six & Thirty-Seven
Hold On — Chord Overstreet

Chapter Thirty-Seven & Thirty-Eight
Carry You — Ruelle and Fleurie

Chapter Forty One
In Need — Gert Taberner

Chapter Forty-Three
War of Hearts — Ruelle

Chapter Forty-Four & Forty-Five
Pluto — Sleeping At Last

Chapter Forty Seven
Ran Away — Hollow Coves

Chapter Forty-Eight
The Ship In Port — Radical Face

Listen on Spotify

ACKNOWLEDGEMENTS

First and foremost, to every single person who encouraged me, prayed for me, donated funds, or spoke invaluable wisdom and guidance into my life as I struggled through all the things writing a first novel comes with—from the bottom of my heart, thank you. You knew nothing about this book, but you knew me, and that was enough for you.

To all my Beta Readers, the very first to read Wilder's story and journey with me through it. Thank you for helping me see the Eadar through your eyes. Your belief in this world got me to the finish line. Danica, thank you for being the first. You saw the earliest version, and despite its struggles, you still loved it. I can't wait to finally show you book two. Becca, the words I have for you are wildly insufficient. My biggest cheerleader and #1 fan. Your encouragement was everything I needed. Thank you for loving and investing in these characters, these people, as much as I have. And thank you for realizing the power behind this story and the true hope for it. 'Wilderra forever.' Savannah, I'm so grateful for the way this story brought us together, and for your love for these characters, and your endless encouragement of me. You were so integral in this story making it this far.

To my momma, who gave me life and taught me how to live it, thank you for teaching me hope and resilience. I love you.

Last, but above all most important: to my Addison. My rock, my best friend, and my greatest supporter. You saw me through the worst parts of this process, and celebrated with me through all the best. I couldn't have picked a better husband and partner to share this joy with. 'I love you' doesn't cover it. Not even close.

ABOUT THE AUTHOR

A lifelong reader and writer, Ana Lee lives in North Carolina with her husband and three hilarious pups. During a trip traveling the US in 2022, Ana was enchanted by the vibrant culture of New Orleans, and the Eadar sprang to life in her head.

Three years later, her first novel, Red Summer was finally ready to see the light of day, with an entire series planned and ready to follow.

A lover of all things fantastical and romantic, while also enjoying a deep dive into the gritty and dark depths of reality, Ana has been most influenced by the work of J.K. Rowling, C.S. Lewis, J.R.R. Tolkien, Cassandra Clare, Sarah J. Maas, and Leigh Bardugo. Red Summer was written as an ode to each of their worlds, and as a thank you for instilling the love of magic, fantasy, romance, biblical allegory, and divine influence in her heart.

For the most up-to-date news on the series, follow Ana on Instagram, Facebook, and Substack.

Insta: instagram.com/analeewrites
Facebook: facebook.com/author.analeewrites
Substack: substack.com/@analeewrites